Praise for Mike Blakely

"A fine spinner of tales, Mike Blakely is
a poet and musician at heart."
—Elmer Kelton

"Blakely writes with a beauty that rivals
the Big Bend country."
—Terry C. Johnston

"Blakely brings a fresh and wonderful
new voice to the Western."
—Norman Zollinger

"A gifted storyteller . . . a remarkable eye
and feel for physical action."
—*Texas Books in Review*

"Blakely's writing is crisp, enticing,
and underscored with depth."
—*American Cowboy*

"An almighty narrative talent."
—*Booklist*

BY MIKE BLAKELY
FROM TOM DOHERTY ASSOCIATES

DEAD RECKONING

AND

THE LAST CHANCE

MIKE BLAKELY

A TOM DOHERTY ASSOCIATES BOOK | NEW YORK

This is a work of fiction. All of the characters, organizations, and events portrayed in these novels are either products of the author's imagination or are used fictitiously.

DEAD RECKONING AND THE LAST CHANCE

Dead Reckoning copyright © 1996 by Mike Blakely

The Last Chance copyright © 1994 by Mike Blakely

All rights reserved.

A Forge Book
Published by Tom Doherty Associates
175 Fifth Avenue
New York, NY 10010

www.tor-forge.com

Forge® is a registered trademark of Macmillan Publishing Group, LLC.

ISBN 978-0-7653-9353-1

Our books may be purchased in bulk for promotional, educational, or business use. Please contact your local bookseller or the Macmillan Corporate and Premium Sales Department at 1-800-221-7945, extension 5442, or by e-mail at MacmillanSpecialMarkets@macmillan.com.

First Edition: February 2018

Printed in the United States of America

0 9 8 7 6 5 4 3 2 1

CONTENTS

DEAD
RECKONING

ONE

Dee Hassard shifted his rear end across the wagon bed, trying to avoid the splinters that angled from the rough boards. The cuffs behind his back held him to the steel springs of the buckboard seat, and the back of the seat bounced down on his shoulders every time the wheels hit a rough spot in the road. He sat backward in the wagon box, looking over the tailgate at the road winding snake-like through South Park.

"People are just so damned gullible," he said.

Frank Moncrief glanced over his right shoulder at his prisoner. "Plain stupid to fall for what you tried to pull," he replied. He looked beyond the two-mule team, scanning a timbered ridge a half mile ahead. This prisoner didn't have any partners coming to rescue him as far as Moncrief knew, but it didn't hurt to be watchful.

Hassard's leg irons rattled across the wagon bed as he squirmed for comfort. "You'd be surprised," he said. "It's the smart ones that're most gullible. They're easier to get intrigued. They're ambitious. They're not necessarily greedy, but they'll risk a small fortune if they think there's profit in it."

Moncrief's eyes swept the horizon for smoke, dust,

buzzards—anything that might warn or inform him. He saw only the snow-capped peaks of the distant ranges, the hacklelike timber on the high rolls, the great verdant grasslands guiding the South Platte through its undulations.

Crisp air cooled his nostrils, his throat, his lungs, charging him with something close to rapture. This place was big and simple, the way Frank Moncrief liked to live. It was primary, right down to the broad swaths of color— the bracing blue sky, the succulent green slopes, the icy whites of clouds and mountaintops—flecks of it all reflected in the blackness of the lucid river.

It galled him to be here on this wagon. He would much prefer a saddle. After he delivered Dee Hassard to the state penitentiary in Cañon City, he was going to trade his old buckboard and mule team for a good horse. He would take his time riding back to Fairplay, straying off this beaten trace to look over the hills when the notion struck him. He could almost feel the rhythm of the lope now.

"You can soak any ol' half-wit for a couple of greenbacks," Hassard continued, "but if you want to run a high-dollar confidence game, you have to go after somebody rich. And how do you think they got rich away out here in Colorado Territory? Well, not by bein' stupid. But not by playin' it safe, either."

"Still," Moncrief said. "Diamonds in South Park? I don't see how you pulled it off as long as you did."

"Hard work," Hassard said. "I know you think that's a line of bull—a confidence man workin' hard at anything— but it's true. You can't make it look too simple or too easy, or the mark will catch on. You've got to make it look complicated, like any other kind of business.

"Now, with the South Park Diamond Field, what I did was, I let my victims come to me. After I brought that first diamond into town and let the word slip out, I made myself scarce. I'd sneak out of town at night and give the slip to anybody tried to follow me. Mystery, Sheriff Moncrief, that's what got 'em. When the report came back from that jeweler in Denver that I had sure 'nough found a raw diamond, then all I had to do was wait."

Moncrief glanced down at the cuffs around the seat springs. He wasn't taking any chances with this flimflam artist. Hassard was built scrawny, but he had a tricky look about him. He stood only about five-seven, weighed maybe a hundred fifty with the cuffs and leg irons. But little men often knew how to equalize.

Moncrief had been on the trail of some road agents and hadn't taken part in Hassard's arrest or trial, but his deputy had briefed him. Hassard had been cooperative. He hadn't put up a fight during the arrest. Hadn't tried to escape. Pleaded guilty. But he was too damn sure of himself. Too casual. The man was going to prison with higher spirits than most men took into whorehouses.

"Was that diamond real," Moncrief asked, "or was the report from Denver faked?"

"The diamond was real."

"Where'd you get a real diamond, uncut like that?"

Hassard chuckled. "This ain't my first game, Sheriff. I got it and a dozen more like it off a jeweler back east on another job. Fenced the rest of 'em and kept the one for this swindle."

Moncrief hissed. "'Swindle,' my foot. Plain ol' stealin' is what it was."

"Now, I resent that, Sheriff. A regular thief would have just broke into Sam Cornelius's saloon and robbed the till. My way of takin' his money was slicker, more daring. And I got more money than any sneak thief ever could have. But you gotta work hard at it. When Cornelius offered to buy the diamond field from me, I could have took him up on it right away and lit out with the money. But I strung him along. I wouldn't have nothin' to do with him at first. Didn't want to look too anxious. After his price got high enough, I agreed."

Moncrief snorted his amusement. Sam Cornelius was one hell of a saloon operator, but what did he know about diamonds? "You mean he handed over all that gold dust? Just like that?"

"Hell, no. He was too smart for that. He wanted to see the diamond field first. So I blindfolded him and took him to it. I had salted it with a bunch of worthless pieces of agate, but he didn't know one rock from another. When we got back to town, I showed him all sorts of forged documents and contracts from the gemstone companies in New York. That hooked him. He paid me the gold dust then, and I got the hell out of Fairplay."

Moncrief could not hold back the chuckle. "Diamonds in South Park!"

"Why not? They got diamonds in Arkansas, don't they? I'm tellin' you, it was the slickest piece of work I ever did."

"Then how come you got caught?"

Hassard spat over the side of the wagon. "Because that tricky bastard Cornelius stole one of my fake diamonds from the diamond field. I found out later that he had a hole in the sole of his boot, and he stepped on top of one of those agates I had showed him and pushed it up in the toe of his boot. He knew that if he'd have tried just pickin' it up, I'd have seen him. Anyway, he tried to sell it in Denver, and a jeweler told him it wasn't worth a damn. They tracked me down before I could board the train to San Francisco. If Sam Cornelius hadn't been a thief, I'd have gotten away with it all. But there went three months of hard work in Fairplay wasted."

Frank Moncrief grunted. "Well, you won't have to do any more of that hard work for a spell," he said, turning to locate a hawk he had heard scream in the sky. "You can take it easy, bustin' rocks in Cañon City for the next five years."

The wheels of the buckboard hit a washed-out place in the road, slamming the spring seat down on Hassard's shoulder. "Ain't that a hell of a deal?" he said, grimacing through the pain. "It ain't like I murdered somebody. Hell, I never hurt nobody in my life. I met fellas in Fairplay who have shot and killed men over cards, and they're still walkin' free. And me, I pull a little swindle and get five years, hard labor."

Frank Moncrief drove the wagon around an easy bend in the road and saw the campground come into view. There the road veered away from the river, over the dry prairie toward Cañon City. It was early in the afternoon yet, but the mules had been pulling since dawn and needed rest. Anyway, this was the recognized campground on the Fairplay to Cañon City road, and Frank Moncrief liked it. Sleeping by the river would beat making a dry camp out in the open park. The stars would come out tonight like gems in Dee Hassard's fake field of diamonds.

"Maybe if you'd have given the money back, you might have gotten off a little lighter," Moncrief said.

"I tried to explain to 'em that I lost the money to a gambler in Denver. He cheated me blind, Sheriff Moncrief. I swear, there are so many crooks in this territory a man can't earn a living. When I get out of prison, I'm goin' back east."

"You'll stay out of those confidence games if you know what's good for you," Moncrief warned.

Hassard shook his head. "I'm too set in my ways."

"You're a young man yet."

"Yeah, but I've been workin' angles since I was a kid. People don't change, Sheriff. You ought to know that in your line of work."

Moncrief drove the wagon down next to the river and pulled the reins back. The bank wasn't steep here in the level park; the river looked like a manicured irrigation canal except for its aimless meanderings. "My brother sure did," he said, setting the brake. "I once drove him on this same route, cuffed to the wagon, just the way you are. And this is where we camped together the day before I put him in prison."

Hassard craned his neck and looked Moncrief in the eye for the first time that day. "Your own brother?"

"That's right." He grabbed his bedroll from the wagon box and threw it down on a patch of soft grass. "He was a hired gun for the Bayou Salado Ranch years ago. Wild as a drunken buck back then. Killed a few rustlers here and there."

Out of habit, the law man began walking a broad circle around the campground, looking for tracks coming or going. Had someone been here today? Yesterday? Could somebody have concealed a gun for Hassard to use on him in the night? Hassard didn't have a partner in the territory that he knew of, but confidence men often worked in pairs or in teams. He wasn't taking any chances. Satisfied that the camp had not been used in a week, Moncrief returned to the wagon, took the hobbles from the bed, and went to fix them on the mules.

"Killed a few rustlers, huh?" the prisoner said. "So, you jailed your own brother for murder."

"Naw, nobody cared about a few dead rustlers," the lawman answered. "But he stayed drunk too often, got fired, and went to rustlin' the ranch's cattle himself. I figured I better arrest him and get him tried before he wound up lynched."

"Your own brother . . ." Hassard lay on his side behind the buckboard seat. It felt good to stop here, get the weight off his hind end for a change.

"Best thing ever happened to him. He got religion down there in prison. Made a preacher. Maybe you've heard of him. Name's Carrol."

Hassard's chains rattled as he squirmed to a sitting position. "Carrol Moncrief, the fightin' parson? He's your brother?"

"Full blood."

"Well, I'll be damned. Wasn't he in on some big fight this spring?"

"He shot a couple of hard cases who tried to steal some horses from a camp meetin' he was preachin' outside of Pueblo. Just winged 'em."

Hassard chuckled. "Don't sound like he's settled down much to me."

"Oh, he's changed. Before he got religion, he'd just as soon kill you as look at you, and he'd do about anything for a dollar. He was a sight worse than you, Hassard. You said yourself you never hurt nobody in your life. Carrol's done worse than hurt folks. That's why I say you can mend your ways. If Carrol Moncrief did, you can, too."

Hassard shrugged and lay back down on his side. "What's he doin' with hisself these days?"

Moncrief slipped the bit from a mule's mouth and let the beast wander off to graze. "He rides a circuit all through the territory. Preaches at weddings and funerals and camp meetings. Picks up a dollar here, dollar there. Got a letter from him last week. Said he hired on to guide some bunch of religious fanatics from Clear Creek over to the Western slopes."

"Religious fanatics?"

"Yeah, the Church of the Weeping Virgin, or some such name as that. From the states. They want to build their own town out in the wilderness. Be lucky if the Indians don't slaughter 'em all. Anyway, Carrol is supposed to meet 'em on Clear Creek and guide 'em over the mountains."

Hassard lay on his side in silence. He could just see the fighting parson taking a band of fanatics over the divide. Odd things happened out here. That's why this was such fertile ground. People here would fall for things like diamonds lying around on the ground in South Park. "Hey, Sheriff," he said suddenly. "You gonna let me loose so I can accomplish my toilet?"

The lawman dropped the wagon tongue and reached into his coat pocket for the keys. "Never heard it said that way."

"You have to learn to talk like that if you want to bamboozle those rich Easterners. You'd never know it to look at me now, but I can clean up like the starchiest dandy you ever seen," Hassard claimed.

Moncrief unlocked the cuffs. "Get out," he ordered. He looked the swindler over as he watched him rub his wrists and climb out of the wagon bed. The reddish-blond stubble on the man's face, the tattered wool suit, and the moth-eaten hat made it difficult indeed to see him as an Eastern dude. "Hold your hands out," he said.

Hassard put his wrists together in front of him and let Moncrief fasten the cuffs again. "I'll only be a couple of minutes, then I'll help you set up camp."

"I'll do it myself. You'll stay cuffed to the wagon."

Hassard shrugged and turned toward the river. He ambled toward a patch of cattails downstream and downwind, the chain straightening between his ankles with every stride. He followed a narrow path into the cattails, the obvious latrine location for the campsite. He knew it well. He had memorized every step of this trail before he ever set foot in Fairplay. The South Park Diamond Field scam really was the slickest piece of work Dee Hassard had ever pulled off, and it wasn't over yet.

He found the rock he had planted there before and stopped beside it. He looked back toward the wagon, saw Moncrief watching him over the back of the second mule. He unbuttoned his pants, letting them drop to his ankles. He squatted, and Deputy Frank Moncrief disappeared behind the veil of cattails.

The stone between his feet rolled over easily, revealing the bundle of oilcloth pressed into the soft ground. He picked it up, trying to keep the cuffs from rattling as he pulled back the folds, revealing the .36-caliber Smith & Wesson revolver. A few specks of rust had appeared on the blue gunmetal, but otherwise the pistol seemed no worse for the wait.

When Hassard came out of the cattails, Frank Moncrief was throwing firewood out of the wagon bed. The lawman had stopped to gather the wood in the timber on one of the high rolls. "You want to sit on the seat, or on the ground?" the sheriff asked.

"The ground, I guess," Hassard said, approaching. He saw the deputy reach into his pocket for the keys. "You'll never guess what I found over there," he said.

"A diamond?" Moncrief answered.

"Somethin' more valuable than that." Hassard reached into his coat and put his hand on the revolver stuck in his waistband. He saw the key drop from Moncrief's hand. He pulled the weapon out, grasping it in both hands.

Moncrief froze with his hand on his sidearm. He heard the wind moaning among the wheel spokes. That hawk screamed down on him again. "You're makin' a mistake, Hassard," he said.

The confidence man showed his straight white teeth and chuckled. "Take off your gun belt and throw it over here."

"No." He saw his mistake now. He had stopped to camp at a recognized campground. He should have chosen some random site.

"I'll kill you if you don't."

"You're liable to try killin' me if I do, but you better think hard about it. That gun's been out there in the cattails a while from the looks of it. It might misfire."

"It might. You a gamblin' man?"

"If it shoots, you think one shot from a thirty-six cal will kill me?"

Hassard's eyes twinkled. "It's been known to happen."

"All right, say it does happen. Say you kill me. You'll just make things worse. You're not a murderer, Hassard, you're just a two-bit confidence artist."

Hassard sighed. "I think I better clear somethin' up with you, Moncrief. You remember before, when I said I had never hurt nobody in my life?"

"I remember."

"I lied." He tightened his finger on the trigger.

The mules leaped when the pistol fired, one of them almost throwing itself down, its front legs hobbled together as they were. Moncrief fell back against the wagon and slumped to the ground, blood gushing from his head wound.

Hassard cocked the pistol and watched. The lawman kept breathing for a couple of minutes, but Hassard just waited. Another shot might alert somebody, he thought. Probably not, but it didn't hurt to be careful. When he was sure Moncrief was dead, he put the pistol in the wagon bed and reached into the lawman's pocket for the keys.

The gun belt was hard to drag out from under the dead weight of the body, and when he strapped it on, he found that it needed a new hole for the buckle, his waist being much thinner than Moncrief's. He fished a pocketknife from Moncrief's pants and sat down to bore the new hole.

He looked at the dead body and shook his head. "It's a wonder what some people won't fall for," he said.

TWO

Sister Petra knelt at the altar of the tiny adobe chapel, her fingers moving methodically from one rosary bead to the next. She whispered the prayers unconsciously, her eyelids quivering. Her neck ached from bowing to the crucifix on the rude wall. Her knees throbbed with pain, even on the goose-down pillow she had brought from her room. But she felt little of this world, heard her own whispers only as an echo of something far distant.

Suddenly she fell still and silent, no one watching her, no world existing for her beyond the adobe walls. "Amen," she said, her voice snapping the trance. She had prayed alone, from dawn to dusk, for nine straight days. Now it was in the hands of God.

The sun had fallen behind the Sangre de Cristos, and light had grown dim in the chapel. Sister Petra opened her eyes and stared at the gray shadows. After nine days, her mind had become as a clock, able to sense sundown as if she had watched it happen.

She pushed herself up from the altar, rubbing her sore knees. Hunger growled in her stomach, and she smiled. She hadn't felt this carefree in weeks. Now the answer would come. If the village of Guajolote died and blew away with the dust, it was God's will.

The Ojo de los Brazos land grant had been acquired by American land speculators in Santa Fe. Guajolote and almost forty-five hundred acres surrounding it were for sale. The sage plains where the villagers grazed their herds and flocks: for sale. The mountain slopes where they hunted and gathered wood: for sale. The beautiful springs in the foothills, pouring twin arms into the Mora River: all for sale. Even the earthen homes of the villagers were for sale, and Sister Petra had learned that a prospective buyer was on his way from the states to view the grant.

"How can they do that?" José Villareal had demanded of her. "You are an Anglo. You know what they are doing." He was the village alcalde, and the news had quite understandably enraged him.

"But I don't know," Sister Petra had answered. "I don't understand it any more than you do."

"What are we going to do?"

"I will go to Santa Fe and find out."

So she had gone. She had found the speculator, an immaculate little American lawyer called Lefty Harless whose office stood near the Palace of the Governors.

"It's very simple, Sister," Harless had said matter-of-factly. "The county taxes were delinquent on the Ojo de los Brazos grant. I paid the taxes, thereby acquiring the land."

"But we've been paying the taxes regularly," Petra argued. "There must have been a mistake in the records."

"No mistake. The taxes went up in your county. You didn't pay at the new level."

"No one told us," she complained.

The lawyer shrugged. "It was published in the newspapers."

Petra gasped in frustration. "Mr. Harless, we are a remote village. Few of our people even read. We hardly ever see a newspaper."

"That's very unfortunate."

"How did you, in Santa Fe, manage to find out that our taxes were delinquent before we did in our own county?"

Harless picked at something between his teeth with his thumbnail. "I have friends in the county government up there."

Petra fumed. "I can see that you do." She pursed her lips and glared at the little cheat. "We'll pay you back. What did the tax increase amount to?"

Harless spread a smug smile across his face. "The taxes have gone back down to their original level, but that's hardly the point, Sister. I own the land now, and I intend to sell it to the first buyer who will pay my price."

"But what about the people?" Sister Petra snapped. "Do you think you've bought their souls? Have you sold your own?"

The speculator shifted his bloodshot eyes. "What do you mean by that?"

"What about the homes of the people, their village, their lives?"

Harless answered coolly. "It's a free market. Buy the grant yourself if you're so concerned about the village."

"How much?" she asked.

"A dollar twenty-five an acre."

Sister Petra had squinted her bright green eyes at the speculator. "But that's over five thousand dollars!"

"Fifty-six even," he had said.

That number had burdened her like a cross on the long walk around the mountains back to Guajolote. Fifty-six even! He had said it so casually, as if it were nothing! But by the time she returned to Guajolote, she knew what she would do. It was all very simple. Give it over to God. She would devote nine days of prayer to the matter—a novena.

And now the final day of her novena had passed, and she was free of the responsibility she had taken on for the village and its people. She picked up her pillow, walked to the door, looked down on the adobes perched along the bank of the generous Mora.

A rooster strutted in front of her. She lunged at it suddenly, hissing and waving her pillow. She laughed as the bird went cackling down the street.

The dry summer evening caressed her as she walked through the village, arching the stiffness from her back. It was a blessing to live here; one she too seldom gave thanks for. She would have to remember to thank God first thing tomorrow, but right now she was all prayed out. Kentucky would be in a muggy nighttime swelter, she mused. Dusk in New Mexico was Sister Petra's heaven.

She missed Kentucky sometimes: the greenery, the long cadence of rainfall on the shake roof, the lush aromas of moldering timber. But never did she regret leaving. Her purpose was here.

She had lived in Guajolote five years now, and was loved by everyone—even that old politician José Villareal, who resented the people seeking the advice of Sister Petra above his.

She had done everything she knew to save the village from the speculators. If the grant sold, and the villagers lost their homes, it would be the will of God.

She had started her first day of prayer asking only that the will of God be done. But now she realized, as she followed the frightened rooster down into the village, that she had asked for something very different on this ninth day of prayer. It was just a vague recollection now, in this world of earthly toil, but she had been praying all day for a number.

She didn't care to speak to anyone as she made her way through the village. She was too exhausted to even seek a greeting. She wanted only a meal and a long night's sleep.

"Is it nine days now, Sister?" the voice said.

She saw José Villareal sitting against the wall of his house. "Yes," she said. "God is making up his mind what to do with your village now. I hope you will be ready."

The alcalde chuckled. "Bless you, Sister Petra. I don't think all your praying will do any good, but I will remember that you tried."

"Only good comes of prayer. It may not seem good to us, but we cannot see as much as God."

"Go get some rest," the alcalde said, waving her away. "You are not making any sense."

She was starving when she reached her door. How long had it been since she ate well? How much sleep had she gotten over the past nine days? It had been fitful sleep, reciting Hail Marys and Our Fathers in her dreams. What was that number she had prayed for all day? Her mind was numb. She couldn't remember.

When she opened her door, she smelled the aromas of tortillas and *queso* in the tiny room, and it made her smile. Some kind woman had made something for her. She lit the candle, found a flask of wine beside a basket of food.

She filled a cup. The wine would strengthen her, give her energy to stay awake long enough to eat. The first sip was like a balm, and she recalled, suddenly, the number:

"fifty-six even." Just as the land speculator in Santa Fe had said it. Had she been wise to pray so for money?

"You should be careful what you pray for," she said to herself in English. That was strange. She hadn't spoken a word of English aloud since Santa Fe.

The wineglass slipped from Petra's hand, and she faintly heard it shattering. A blinding white light had burst into the room, consuming her. And as she floated, she felt the warm voice of God surging through her flesh, rattling her very bones:

"The cross awaits you on the mountainside."

THREE

He stood on a high roll of the grassy plains, his arms folded across his chest, cradling his Remington rolling-block hunting rifle. The sky was pink in the west, purple above him, charcoal gray in the east. He simply stared at it with his mouth open, his eyes sweeping ceaselessly across it.

Clarence Philbrick had been brought up in Vermont, where the sky was a patch of benevolent ether hemmed in overhead by treetops. But here the great void had beaten back everything and swelled to the point that Clarence felt as if he were standing naked on a liberty dime.

He stared silently, mentally composing an entry for his diary as he tried to soak in the infinity of it all. Back east, he mused, my view of the sky was like that of a trout searching the surface of his dark pool for mayflies. But here I am as a wild soaring goose, enveloped in tideless reaches of oxygen.

Clarence couldn't help thinking of things in terms of fish and game.

A ladle clanged against an iron pot down the slope, and he turned toward camp. He had built up a powerful hunger skinning buffalo all day, and now he was ready for some hump stew and that delicacy of the plains—boiled tongue. He saw the line of hunters forming at the cook's cauldron and hoped they would leave some cornbread for him.

It was getting cooler now with the night coming on, and Clarence was glad. It was hard to wear his oilskin hunting coat when the sun got high, and if he didn't wear it, he had to keep it rolled under his arm when he walked, tied behind his saddle when he rode, or pinned under his knee while he skinned buffalo. The idea was to prevent anyone from picking up his coat for whatever reason and feeling its heft. Clarence had twenty-one pounds of gold sewn into his coat, and he would just as soon nobody knew about it.

He had gotten the idea from his father, Herbert Philbrick, who had gone to California back in '49 and struck a rich placer load near Mariposa. Herbert had melted his gold dust into bars and sewn them into his coat before returning to Vermont. He had hired on as a deckhand for the homeward voyage, so no one would suspect the wealth he carried.

Clarence's father had put quite a sum of money away for him in a trust fund, which he wasn't to touch until he was thirty-five years old. "Nobody has any sense until they're thirty-five years old," Herbert had said. "And damned little then."

But more so than the gold, Clarence treasured the stories his father had brought back from California. He made his father repeat often how he had fought off claim-jumpers and thieves; made a fortune with a pick, a pan, and sweat; survived two trips around the Horn. The stories made Clarence anxious to go west himself, to have his own adventures, but the adventures he had in mind would require capital.

"Go on if you want to," his father had said. "I'm not stopping you. It'll be good for you. Make a man of you."

Clarence was twenty-five and considered himself a man already. "But I need the money," he tried to explain.

The old forty-niner smiled and puffed on his pipe. "I left for California with three dollars and fifty-seven cents in my pocket. I'll stake you to the same amount."

Clarence had thrown his arms in the air and flung himself against the bookshelf in his father's study. "But you've said yourself there will never be another gold strike like California. It's cattle now, and a man needs capital to buy his first spread. The panic has driven land prices lower than they've been in years. Now is the time to invest."

He had left it there, exasperated, and stormed out of his father's study. Weeks later, his father called him back in to show him something.

"Look what Senator White gave me today, son. It's a photograph. Have you ever seen anything like it?"

Clarence had taken the large print and looked at it—like looking out through a window across the continent. Every grain was like a living atom, and the scene swept him back through all the lost moments since the shutter opened, casting him out through the very lens of the photographer's camera.

He found himself standing on high ground, the rocky grades around him devoid of life, windswept, streaked with snow. But it was the cross that made him shiver. Etched in new-fallen snow, it spanned one whole side of the highest peak in view, settling comfortably into natural time-carved crevices.

"What is this place?" Clarence had asked.

"It's a mountain peak out west. Colorado, I think. The chief photographer of the Hayden Survey made the picture. Senator White gave me his copy."

"You see, that's why I need the money!" Clarence blurted. "I'm missing these sights! I'm missing everything!"

He had persisted, day after day, week after week, until finally his father had agreed to a compromise.

"All right, Clarence," the elder Philbrick said, "I'll let you have five thousand dollars to get you started in the cattle business. If you lose it, that's tough. I will not, on my life, let you have one cent more until you are thirty-five."

Herbert Philbrick fully expected his son to lose every penny of that five thousand. The boy had no business sense and no aptitude for anything besides fishing and hunting. But he thought of it as an investment in his son's education. Once the boy went broke, he would have to learn fast out there—or die.

Clarence was so thrilled the day his father offered the compromise that he ran down to Lake Champlain and went swimming, though it was April and the water was frigid. He began writing letters before he had even dried off, and within two months had found a ranch in his price range in the Territory of New Mexico. The brochure sent to him by a land speculator named Lefty Harless described the spread:

"The legendary Ojo de los Brazos League . . . granted by the government of Spain in 1814 . . . confirmed by act of Congress of the United States . . . nestled among the foothills of the Sangre de Cristos Mountains, flanking five miles of the Mora River . . . It encompasses 4,480 acres of prime grazing land, hundreds of which might be brought into a high degree of cultivation. . . . Surrounding the grant are hundreds of thousands of acres of free government range. . . . The Ojo de los Brazos League includes a Mexican village called Guajolote, which might be exploited for its peasant workforce or removed from the ranch."

The price was six hundred dollars over the five thousand Clarence's father had promised him, so he had to sell his collection of fowling guns and fly rods to raise the remainder. The only gun he kept was his Remington rolling-block hunting rifle. To pay for the trip west, he had to sell his favorite Morgan stallion and all his riding tack. He understood that the English saddle would be frowned upon out west, anyway.

By the end of June, he still didn't have train and stagecoach fare to get him all the way to New Mexico, but Clarence could wait no longer. He wanted to be in possession of the Ojo de los Brazos well before autumn. Lefty Harless insisted on being paid in gold coin, fearing the panic would lessen the value of paper money. As there were no banks or railroads in New Mexico, Clarence had to make his own arrangements for getting the gold to Sante Fe.

"Do what I did," his father suggested. "Sew it into your jacket."

So Clarence converted his fifty-six hundred to twenty-dollar gold pieces—280 double eagles weighing almost twenty-one pounds. These his mother quilted into the lining of his favorite oilskin hunting jacket. She paired the coins, sewing four rows down the front, two rows in each sleeve, and six rows across the back.

"Dress like a common workman, and travel cheap," his father advised. "Don't let that jacket get beyond your grasp, and above all, do not let anybody pick it up."

The young Vermonter headed west on the rails in early July. He stretched his spending money as far as it would go, but arrived in Denver broke, save for the gold sewn into his coat. He met some sportsmen heading out onto the plains to hunt buffalo and hired on with them as a skinner. He had field-dressed a lot of deer back east and figured skinning a buffalo would be no more difficult.

It turned out to be a good deal more difficult owing to the size of the animals and the humps on their backs, but Clarence worked hard and learned fast. The third day of the hunt, some of the sportsmen accidentally stampeded a small herd of bison past their skinner, and Clarence killed a big cow with his Remington.

So it was that Clarence Philbrick strolled down to the camp cook's kettle now feeling like a seasoned plainsman. His clothes were bloodstained, his hands tanned on the backs and blistered on the palms. He swaggered to the end of the grub line and left his Remington leaning against a wagon box.

"See anything up there?" asked one of the hunters, a man from Illinois.

Clarence shook his head. "Sky and grass."

The hunting guide stepped up beside Clarence holding a tin plate of stew. He wore his hair and mustaches long. "Better turn in early tonight. We leave for Denver before dawn."

"Yes, sir," Clarence answered.

"I'm goin' right back out with another party if you want to hire on again. You can double your wages."

Clarence fought back a prideful smile. "Thanks, but I need to be getting on to New Mexico. I've got a job waiting down there on a ranch."

The plainsman nodded. "I'll pay you when we get to town. You'll have about fifteen dollars comin'."

Clarence grinned and picked up a plate. "Been a long time since I had that much money in my pocket," he said. He held his plate out to the cook and glanced across the tailgate of the chuck wagon. "Any cornbread left?" he asked.

The cook sneered. "Some of them greedy bastards took two," he said under his breath.

Clarence shrugged, poured himself a cup of black coffee, and went to sit on the bed of the wagon where he had left his Remington. He ran the journal entry through his mind again so he wouldn't forget it: . . . a trout in his dark pool . . . searching for mayflies . . . a wild soaring goose . . . tideless reaches of oxygen.

When he got back to Denver in a couple of days, he

would have a bath and buy a train ticket as far south as the tracks went. Pueblo, he had been told. But before he boarded the train, there was something he wanted to do. It wasn't the sort of thing he would want to enter into his diary, but he was on his own out here. Who would know? Who would care? He was going to visit one of those fancy Denver whorehouses.

He remembered something the family gardener had once told him as they shared a bottle of port Clarence had smuggled out of the house: "It ain't how deep you fish, son, it's how you wiggle your worm." He smiled. Yes, Clarence thought, angling can be made to serve as a metaphor for almost anything.

FOUR

The old mule was sore-footed from the long ride, but Dee Hassard awarded her no sympathy. He kept a switch busy across her rump and cussed her every time she slowed her walk. He had traded Frank Moncrief's other mule for an old saddle at Tarryall and had ridden down the South Platte toward Denver.

Now Denver was in sight below, and he was riding up to the rocky outcropping over Clear Creek where he had hidden the gold from the sale of the South Park Diamond Field. After he recovered Sam Cornelius's Fairplay dust, he would board an eastbound and live it up for a couple of months before his earnings played out.

He wondered if anybody had found Frank Moncrief's

body yet. He had made a hearse of the sheriff's buckboard and left it over a hill, out of sight of the road. Even if somebody had found Moncrief by now, there was still plenty of time to get away. The news could travel no faster than a gallop.

He stood in the stirrups and stretched his neck, for the gold was close and he was looking for the place. It was just over the ridge here somewhere, he recalled. As he approached the summit and spotted the rocky point, his eyes bulged. He shifted his reins to his left hand as he pulled back on them, putting his right palm on the grip of Frank Moncrief's Colt.

A man was seated on the outcropping, his foot just inches from the hole in which the Fairplay gold lay hidden. The man had his hands inside some sort of box on a portable table. Nearby stood a fine white mule wearing a saddle. Between them and the man stood a tripod holding a black cube with a cloth hanging from it.

The man looked up, tossed his head, smiled. "Howdy," he said, leaving his hands inside the box. His build was compact, like Hassard's. He had sad eyes, wavy brown hair, and a full beard, well trimmed.

"Howdy, yourself," Hassard said. He glanced down into the creek valley as he heard a faint line of song. A chorus was singing some hymn down there. He spotted the tents and wagons of a campground below, then glared at the stranger with his hands in the box. "What you got in there?"

"I'm washing a photographic plate," the man said. "I just made a view of Clear Creek with Denver and the prairies beyond."

Hassard nodded and took his hand off his gun grip. "What for?"

"It's my job," the man said, his beard revealing a smile. "I'm W. H. Jackson, head of the photographic division of the Hayden Survey. I'd get up and shake your hand if I could."

"That's all right," Hassard said, getting down from his mule. He rubbed his rear end. "I saw you down below and got curious. Thought you were some kind of prospector or somethin'."

The confidence man looked down on the campground of the hymn singers again, lingering over it this time. He recognized the tune: "Will the Circle Be Unbroken." "Never saw a photograph bein' made before," he said.

"This is just the plate," Jackson explained. "I'll have to take it down to the studio to print photographs."

Hassard shot a quick glance at the hole under the rock where he had stashed his gold. "What the hell is the Hayden Survey?"

"Government geological explorations," the photographer said, "headed by Dr. Ferdinand Vandeveer Hayden."

"And you go around and make photographs of everything they explore?"

"Not everything. Just the points of interest." Jackson removed his hands from the box. "Maybe you've seen some of my photographs from Colter's Hell in the Yellowstone country."

Hassard put his hand on his chin. "You mean the geysers and hot springs and all?"

"Yes." He had opened the box and was removing a developed plate of glass.

Hassard stuck his thumbs under his gun belt and approached the photographer. "Now, tell me the truth, Jackson. Is that Yellowstone country for real? I can spot a hoax, you know, and them geysers don't set right with me."

"It's real, all right," Jackson said. "I brought the photographic evidence back to Congress. Why do you think they established the national park?" He put the exposed glass in a pan of fluid on a rock and wiped his fingers on his shirt.

"I figured it was some kind of government scam. What the hell do we need a national park for, anyhow?" He looked into the pan at the plate of glass, unable to see a picture in it. "I believe I've heard of this Hayden Survey before," he said. "Were you all in Fairplay last summer?"

"We were," Jackson said.

"I thought so. I was just there a few days ago. Folks are still talkin' about you-all down there. Said you was on some wild-goose chase to photograph some mountain cross, or holy snowy cross, or some such thing."

Jackson's sad eyes twinkled as he looked up from his work. "We found it," he said. "I was the first to photograph it."

"But what is it?" Hassard demanded.

Jackson stood erect, pointed west. "It was just a legend until we located it. I had talked to a lot of people who knew of it, but none who had ever seen it. Then, as luck would have it, we ran into an old prospector up in the Sawatch who claimed he had seen it once. He was lost when he stumbled across it, then he found his way, like magic."

"Stumbled across what?"

"The Mount of the Snowy Cross. The old man told us

it was visible only from a few places above timberline. He said the best place to see it from was Notch Mountain, an easy landmark to recognize because of the notch in its summit. So I took the photographic division over the Great Divide at Tennessee Pass. There's an old Indian trail that leads from there past the base of Notch Mountain. We had to leave the mules below and carry the camera and chemicals and plates on our backs. A couple of miles above timberline, we finally came over the summit of Notch Mountain, and there it was, standing across a high mountain basin."

"There what was?" Hassard said.

"The snowy cross."

"But what the hell is it?"

Jackson put his feet together, stood straight, and spread his arms. "It's a huge cross formed by snow packed into natural crevices in the slope of a mountain peak. It stands a thousand feet tall." He let his palms rise above his shoulders. "The arms lift upward to heaven like this, hundreds of feet wide. The top of the cross reaches the very peak of the Mount of the Snowy Cross. I just got a glimpse of it before clouds moved in and obliterated it."

"I thought you said you got photographs of it."

"We had to camp on Notch Mountain overnight," Jackson said, letting his arms fall. "The next morning the clouds cleared long enough for me to make eight exposures. One of them was excellent. It was an extraordinary experience."

Silence surrounded the rocky outcropping over the creek, and Hassard found the image of the snowy cross on his mind now even clearer than that of the gold hidden at the photographer's feet. "I guess everybody knows about it now," he said. "Like them geysers up in Colter's Hell."

Jackson shrugged as he moved his glass plate to another pan of fluid. "The photograph circulated fairly well in certain circles back east, but oddly enough, the Snowy Cross is still thought of as a legend out here."

Hassard recognized a new tune in the valley below: "The Old Rugged Cross." "Funny they should start singin' that," he said.

"Not really," Jackson replied. "They do a lot of singing, and that's one of their favorites. We're camped not far down the creek from them, and I hear them singing several times a day."

"Who are they?"

"Some bunch of religious fanatics who call themselves the Church of the Weeping Virgin." Jackson took the glass plate from the pan of fluid and carried it to a box on the ground beside his pack mule. "Mind opening that lid for me?"

Hassard took the cover from the sturdy wooden box to reveal padded slots inside, most of them holding plates of glass. He held the lid as the photographer slid his negative into one of the empty slots. "The Church of the Weeping what?" The swindler's interest rose. Hadn't Frank Moncrief mentioned something about this?

Jackson motioned for Hassard to replace the lid on the box and took a fresh plate of treated glass from a holder near the camera. "Weeping Virgin. They seem like simple Christian folks, but their late founder was an eccentric who claimed the angel of the Virgin Mary spoke to him in dreams."

Hassard chuckled. "What did the ol' girl say?"

The photographer was installing the plate of glass in his boxlike camera. "According to this prophet—his name was Wyckoff—she instructed all faithful Christians to renounce materialism and give all their money to the church, which seems awful convenient for Wyckoff, since he controlled the church finances. Also, he claimed the Virgin Mary said to shun outsiders but embrace anybody who accepted their religion. Well, that's what got them into trouble."

"How's that?"

"Wyckoff told his people they were going west to establish a new community in the wilderness. But before they did, they made a sweep across the southern states preaching and looking for converts. They let some black folks join."

"Alongside of white folks?" Hassard said.

Jackson nodded. "And worse. One of the white ladies from up north decided she wanted to marry one of the black men from down south. This Reverend Wyckoff said the Virgin Mary had told him that one day all the races would be as one, and so he married this couple in their camp somewhere in Arkansas. They were mobbed by some local thugs, the newlywed couple and Wyckoff lynched."

Hassard's eyebrows raised. "Who's leadin' 'em now?"

"They're waiting on a guide to take them into the mountains. A Reverend Carrol Moncrief. Maybe you've heard of him." Jackson put his head under the black cloth hanging from his camera.

"Sure," Hassard said, grinning. "He rides a circuit big as the territory. I met his brother down in Fairplay." He turned to look again at the hole under the rocky outcropping where his gold lay hidden. "You gonna make some more pictures?"

"Yes," Jackson said, coming out from under the hood. "The sun's good right now. Say, how would you like to get into one of them?"

"A photograph?" The swindler's smile broadened. It was something akin to becoming immortal, getting one's picture made. "It won't really steal my soul, will it?"

"Not unless your soul is very loose. Stand there on that boulder." The photographer glanced up to judge the light. "Quick, before that cloud covers the sun."

Hassard felt giddy as he stepped onto the boulder, the vast grasslands behind him. He held his coat back to reveal Frank Moncrief's gun belt and Colt revolver, his own rust-speckled Smith & Wesson tucked under the cartridge belt.

"Look at the camera," Jackson said.

Hassard raised one eyebrow. This was a little risky, he realized. He had heard of detectives using photographs to track people down. But Hassard made it a policy to change his appearance after every job, anyway. In that way, the photograph might actually help cover his trail. He heard the shutter open and close, felt the cloud shade him.

"What did you say your name was?" Jackson asked. "I try to identify my subjects when possible."

"Hassard. Dee Hassard." He heard the pilgrims strike up a new hymn in the valley below.

"And what is your profession?"

"Investments."

Jackson left it at that. "You're welcome to come down to the studio tomorrow and see a print."

"Thanks all the same," Hassard said, turning for his mule. "But I've got places to go. Good luck on your survey this summer."

"We're going down to the San Juans by way of Fairplay. Want me to pass anything along to anybody down there?"

Dee Hassard put his foot in the stirrup and climbed onto the weary mule. "I don't have any friends there," he said, smiling. "I was just passin' through." He touched his hat brim and reined his mount down the slope toward Denver.

He would have to come back later for the gold, but that didn't matter right now. The money didn't sway Dee Hassard the way the plotting did—all the risky conniving and the feeling of power he got when he made a slick escape, or even when he rescued a botched job like he had done in South Park.

And right now, he could feel an idea coming on. All those gullible Weeping Virgin idiots waiting for a new prophet down there in camp. He had never heard of the late Reverend Wyckoff, but he would have bet his entire diamond field haul that the good reverend was more confidence man than prophet.

FIVE

May Tremaine's new shoes were not meant for walking. She had blisters on her feet the size of dimes—about two dollars' worth, judging by the sharp pains that stabbed her with every step.

Most of the stores and shops had shut down, late afternoon filling the streets of Denver with shadow. She felt tired and dirty. If she didn't find some work now, it would mean another night in the wagon yard, and that man there was going to expect reimbursement tonight. He had told her as much when she left this morning.

She saw a door ajar down the street and quickened her step, though it felt like walking barefoot over sharp rocks. The sign simply said HARDWARE, a commodity about which she knew nothing. She reached for the door, but it opened before she could grab the brass handle, and a man stepped onto the street.

"Sorry," he said. "Closed for the day."

"No, I'm looking for a job," May replied.

The man turned his key in the lock. "Well, we're not hiring." He turned to walk away.

"Wait!" May cried. "Please, wait."

The man stopped in the street and turned.

"I have no money. I have no place to stay. I'll work for room and board. Just until I find something else. Please. I'll do anything." She gestured toward the store, but she knew the man would take it the wrong way.

He smiled with one side of his mouth as his eyes traveled

down her skirt and slowly back to her face. "My wife wouldn't approve of that sort of arrangement. Good luck." And he left, shaking his head as he walked away.

May thought about that man back in the wagon yard. It wouldn't be so bad. He had bathed last night, and had made sure she knew about it this morning, having worn oil in his hair and a clean shirt. But where would it get her? A restless night on a bed of straw? She would be better off hiring herself out as just a regular whore. At least then she would get paid.

Up until a couple of days ago, May thought she had made it in Denver. She had landed a job in a shoe shop, and the cobbler had advanced her a pair of shoes, as hers was pretty much worn out. The job had gone well for a week. Then, two days ago, while cleaning up after hours, the cobbler had followed her into the back room. When she reached up to put a pair of shoes on a high shelf, he grabbed her from behind, squeezing her breasts with both hands, pressing himself against her.

She had gasped and wrenched violently away, elbowing him in the mouth as she stumbled and fell to the ground. She sprang and ran, made it to the door, and bolted out to the street.

"Hey!" was all the cobbler said as she ran away.

She had made just enough money that week to earn the shoes that were giving her blisters now. She walked on. She wasn't going to sleep on that wagon yard straw again tonight.

May didn't know what she did to make men come after her like that. When she looked in the mirror, she didn't see a pretty woman. She thought her eyes and her lips were too large. Her face was too wide, her chin too weak. She had always wanted to be tall and skinny and able to run like a deer. But she was of medium height, too curvaceous to be considered skinny, even though she carried no extra weight. She didn't see herself as pretty, but men had been groping for her since she was fifteen.

It had started with her uncle, the husband of her mother's sister, an army captain back in Iowa. He was quite a dashing character, having done battle with Indians on the plains. It was true that May had flirted with him in a girlish way, but it never even remotely occurred to her that she might summon the monster in him. She was visiting on the army post for the summer, and her aunt had gone to town one day, leaving her alone in the captain's quarters. The captain came home in the middle of the morning, asked her to come into the bedroom, and pushed her onto the bed, falling on top of her.

"If you scream again, I'll hit you," he said, pressing his hand hard over her mouth. "You've been wanting this and now you're gonna get it." He felt like he weighed five hundred pounds on top of her. And though she cried the entire time, he seemed not to notice, and even told her how good she made him feel.

There were others who tried—men and boys—and she let the more persistent ones succeed. May came to believe that this was a terror all girls just suffered because men were bigger and stronger, and because they harbored that monster in their hearts. When she told her best friend about it, her friend never spoke to her again. Then she knew her life was different. It wasn't all girls; it was just she. She honestly did not know why. She never purposefully sent signals to any men, but they swooped down on her like birds of prey when she was in any way alone or vulnerable.

When she met Charlie Holt, he seemed different. He was from Kansas and had come back to Iowa to visit family. He was far from refined, but impressed her with his honest talk. Built solid from toil, he nevertheless seemed gentle. He courted her like no man had ever done, taking her to church services, sitting with her on the porch. At twenty-three, he was four years older than May. He had been farming for five years in Kansas and had a sod house built there. He described the country in simple words that made her want to see it. Two weeks after she met him, they were married.

Kansas wasn't as beautiful as May had hoped, but she made a home there. About the time she started to like it, her husband went to town one night and got drunk. Over the next few months he started drinking more frequently, turning ugly when he came home.

"I don't know why I married you," he said one night. "God, if I'd known you was barren, I never would have."

May didn't understand these things, but she didn't see how she could be barren when she had been pregnant before. When she was eighteen she had suffered six weeks of sheer mortification when she became pregnant by a friend of her older brother. She never told anyone about the pregnancy or the miscarriage, adding the memories to the other ghosts that trailed her.

"Another thing," Charlie Holt added. "You tried to make me think you was a virgin, didn't you? I knowed the first night we was married you was a far sight from a virgin."

The next time Charlie came home drunk, he hit her in

the face with his fist for no reason, then passed out on the bed. May had been pinned down and shoved around a couple of times, but she had never been hit. It hurt bad when Charlie hit her and made her feel like some kind of scared varmint animal in a trap.

Weeds grew up in the cornfield, and Charlie lost his draft horse in a card game. May kept a fine garden that helped to feed them, but one night Charlie poured kerosene down each row and burned it. "Teach you to mock me, goddammit, woman!" he cried, a whiskey slur stringing his words together.

May tried to stop him, but he grabbed a barrel stave and hit her with it until she was curled up on the ground whimpering.

That was all May Tremaine intended to endure. After Charlie finished his bottle and passed out, she made sure he wouldn't wake up by ringing a frying pan on the top of his head. She then packed everything she could carry and left in the middle of the night for Denver. She took her maiden name back and tried to forget she had ever been married to Charlie Holt.

She had heard that men out beyond the frontier held a higher view of the fairer sex, as women were scarce out there. Well, maybe it was true for other women, but not May. The cobbler and that man at the wagon yard had convinced her. She was doing something to provoke them. She would stop it if she knew what it was, but she didn't know. Now she was hungry and starting to think that she should use it to her advantage—whatever it was. They were going to keep coming after her, anyway. She might as well get paid for it.

Limping, she came to the house of red curtains she had seen earlier in the day. How did one apply for a job as a whore? Walk in? Maybe she should use the back door. She sat down on the front steps of the place and squinted back the tears. Maybe this was all she was good for. She had heard stories of whores marrying wealthy men out west. Maybe this was where her fortunes would change. Things couldn't get worse.

As she took off her shoes to soothe her feet, the door flew open and a cowboy staggered out, yelling as if he had a herd before him. A trail boss followed the cowboy and pushed him so hard that the cowboy tripped down the steps past May. He rolled when he hit the street and came up with his fists in front of him. Then he saw May, opened his hands, and adjusted his hat.

"Well, howdy," he said as the trail boss stepped off the stairs to the street.

May just looked away from the cowboy as she rubbed her feet gingerly.

"Where was you thirty minutes ago?" the cowboy said.

The trail boss laughed. "You mean thirty seconds."

"Hey," the young drover said, squatting in front of May, "you comin' off work or goin' on?" He grinned and put his hand on her knee.

She drew away, glancing at the boss for help, but the older man just stood staring. "I don't work here," she said. "I was just resting."

"Come on with us," the cowboy said, grabbing her wrist. "We'll go dancin' or somethin'." He stood and pulled her toward the dirt street.

She tried to wrench free, but his grip twisted her skin. "My feet hurt," she said. "I can't go."

He jerked her toward him, clamping an arm around her waist, lifting her from the steps. "I'll carry you, then. You don't even have to step on them sore feet."

The trail boss sighed. "Now, you better leave her be."

"We're dancin'," the cowboy answered.

May tried to push herself away, but the cowboy squeezed her as if he would break her back. She twisted her face away from his whiskey breath, and as she writhed in his grasp, she caught sight of a man trotting toward her on the street. A good-looking young man, well built, wearing an oilskin hunting coat.

SIX

Put her down!" Clarence Philbrick said.

The cowboy looked at Clarence but kept his hold on May. "Mind your own business, son," he said, though he was not even twenty.

"I'd hate to have to whip you right here in the street," the Vermonter said, "but I will if you don't let her go." He looked at the trail boss, and the older man simply backed away a couple steps and leaned on the rail of the whorehouse porch.

The cowboy let May slide out of his grasp, and she sprang to the steps. "Stranger," the cowboy said, "if you was to try whippin' me, and I ever found out about it, I'd kick your ass all over the prairie."

Clarence cocked his arms and showed his fists. "I'll risk you finding out."

The cowboy put his hands on his hips and sized up his opponent. He looked at the trail boss.

"What are you waitin' on?" the older man said. "You been wantin' a fight all day."

The young cowboy grinned and took his coat off, throwing it aside. "Ain't you gonna get ready?"

"I believe I am ready," Clarence replied. The gold coins sewed into his sleeves were going to slow his punches somewhat, but he didn't dare take the coat off here.

"All right," the cowboy said. He raked his boot in the dirt like a bull, got wild eyed, and rushed the Vermonter, growling to the tune of ringing spurs.

Clarence stepped gracefully to one side to avoid the rush and jabbed the cowboy in the side of the jaw as he tried to swerve. The cowboy stumbled to one side and plowed headlong into the dirt.

The trail boss laughed. "Lovin' or fightin', you don't last long, do you, boy?"

The cowboy scrambled to his feet. "Stand still this time!" he ordered. He set his smarting jaw and came at Clarence again, more carefully now. Just as he drew within striking distance, he took one big step and swung the pointed toe of a boot at the Vermonter's groin.

The kick was not well disguised, but it still took Clarence off guard, and he had to hump his spine and spring backward to evade the worst. The boot caught him in the stomach, and the cowboy's fist clobbered him over the back of the head, but Clarence latched onto the leg and yanked upward with everything he had, throwing the cowboy so hard that dust flew out from under him when he hit.

The trail boss whistled a laugh up his throat and slapped his thigh.

Clarence circled and went back to his kind of fight, his fists waiting. When the cowboy sprang, he ran hard at the Vermonter, the whites of eyes and teeth showing his anger. This time Clarence used the momentum. He stood his ground, leaned into the attack, and snapped a jab into the cowboy's nose. Blood spurted as the drover stood up, and Clarence followed with a hard right that made the cowboy's knees buckle.

"All right, stranger," the trail boss said, stepping between the two. "That's enough."

Clarence stepped away and let the older man help the cowboy to his feet.

"Somebody was gonna have to do that sooner or later today," the boss said, looping the bloody cowboy's arm over his shoulder. "I'm just glad it wasn't me." He winked at Clarence, ignored May, and took the young drover away.

May buckled her shoe and stood on the steps. "Thanks," she said, looking at the ground, avoiding Clarence's eyes. She was grateful, but for all she knew, this man might treat her rougher than the cowboy.

"Don't mention it," he replied.

They stood awkwardly in silence as a steam whistle wailed far away at the depot. "My name's Clarence Philbrick," he said, thrusting his hand toward her.

"May Tremaine." She briefly touched his hand.

He took a good look at her for the first time. Her face was doll-like, blushing about the cheeks, brown eyes matching swirls of hair. He had kept in his mind, since leaving Vermont, a vague notion of courting Western women, though he knew they were few. It just went to prove his instincts. Yes, things were going to pan out here.

"Well, you can go on in now," May said, feeling uneasy under his stare.

Clarence looked at the whorehouse door and the red curtains in the window. "In there?" he said, trying to sound astounded. "You don't think . . . I was just walking back to town from camp. Just passing through this way."

"Well, so was I," she said. "My feet hurt, so I sat down here for a minute. I didn't know . . ." She made a remote gesture toward the door.

Clarence took his hat off and raked his hair back. "I was going to have some supper," he said. "Would you think me too forward if I asked you to join me? My treat. I just got paid." He cringed inwardly. Yes, of course she'll think you're too forward. You just met her, you idiot.

May started to decline, but a hunger pang stabbed her stomach, and she got practical. "I'd like that," she said. "I don't know anybody here." She stepped down from the stairs, smiling through the torture of each stride.

They walked to a seemlier quarter of town, May trying her best to hide the limp.

"Did you get hurt back there?" Clarence asked.

"I'm wearing new shoes," she said.

In the café, they talked about where they were from, but neither cared to volunteer a reason for coming west.

May tried to remember her manners as she ate, though she was starving. "Where did you learn to fight like that?" she asked, moving her plate to cover some gravy she had slung onto the checkered tablecloth.

"I was on the boxing team in college." He chuckled. "Some of those tactics that cowboy used took me off guard. Those would have been considered poor form where I'm from." He noticed calluses on May's hands as she held a fried chicken leg daintily in her fingers.

After Clarence paid, he stood with her on the boardwalk for an awkward moment. "Can I walk you home?" he asked.

"No, thank you," she said. She had to wonder what he meant by that. He had been a perfect gentleman so far, but she had seen them blink and become predators. Still, she didn't want to part company just yet. If ever there was a time to harness that mystery that made men desire her, this seemed to be it. "Actually, I don't . . ."

Clarence waited. "Yes?" He saw that she felt uneasy and embarrassed, and the truth dawned on him. "You don't have a place to stay, do you?"

She shook her head. This was very risky. She was vulnerable now. "Don't you worry about me. I'll make out all right." She felt ridiculous. What could a college boy from Vermont possibly see in her?

"Do you have any money?"

She shook her head again.

He reached into his pocket.

"No," she said, surprising herself with the firm tone. "You've done enough for me. I won't take any more from you." She would go back to that house of red curtains before she became a beggar.

Clarence let his money drop back into his pocket and put his hand on his chin. "I can't very well leave you out here on the street."

"I'll take care of myself. You don't need to worry about me."

"Wait a minute," Clarence said. "I may have an idea. Are you determined to stay in Denver?"

She shrugged. "I don't have to stay anywhere."

"Are you religious?"

May's eyebrows pushed together, her curiosity sharpening. "I used to like to go to church. Why?"

"I hear there's a group of pilgrims camped up on Clear Creek. They're going over the mountains to establish a new town. What if we go up there and see what they're about? Maybe they'll take you in."

May tilted her head forward and looked at him. She felt the dry air parching her lips. "Pilgrims?" she said.

"It's a church. They're on a pilgrimage to find a new town site. That's all I know about them, but it wouldn't hurt to find out more, would it?"

"I guess not." It was a hope worth considering, only she didn't feel much like walking all the way up Clear Creek with her feet smarting so.

He took her by the elbow and guided her to a bench on the boardwalk. "Wait here."

"Where are you going?" she said. It felt good to get off her feet, so she sat down.

"I'll be right back." He trotted away down the street and turned a corner.

May didn't know quite what to make of Clarence Philbrick. First he wants to walk her home, then he wants to give her over to a bunch of pilgrims. She had heard about the group on Clear Creek. She read something in the paper, too. An editor had ridiculed them, calling them "curistians" because they allowed mingling of the races. They had even taken in a Mexican Catholic since arriving in Denver.

She sighed as a man passed her on the boardwalk, glanced up and down at her, and tipped his hat. She ignored him. Where had Clarence gone, anyway?

It was true that she had enjoyed going to church before. People were nice there. Men were on their best behavior. She liked the music, too, though she sang in such a small voice that she could scarcely hear herself. What would it be like to establish a town? A lot of hard work, probably, but she was used to that from the farm.

She had sat on the bench for several minutes when it dawned on her that maybe Clarence wasn't coming back. That was odd. He had seemed so sincere. Well, now she was on her own tonight. Her feet were too sore to walk all the way up Clear Creek to the campground of the Church of the Weeping Virgin. Where was she going to sleep? God, not the wagon yard. The thought sickened her now for some reason. Dark was coming on quickly, though, and she had to think of something.

She heard a buggy whip crack and saw a nag pull a runabout around the corner. Clarence had the reins! She stood to meet him, forgetting her aching feet. He drove the horse to the edge of the boardwalk and pulled in the reins.

"Where on earth did you get that?" she said, a genuine smile showing her rows of perfect teeth.

"Hired it. Come on, let's go meet the pilgrims."

She took her skirt in her hand as she stepped into the buggy. "How much did it cost?"

"A rattletrap like this? Not enough to worry about. I didn't expect you to walk all the way up there with blisters on your feet."

He cracked the whip, and May surged ahead with the Vermonter, feeling like a gliding hawk moving effortlessly through the clapboard canyons of Denver.

SEVEN

It was almost dark when Dee Hassard carried his bottle from the saloon and looked at the sky. The first stars were out, wavering from his point of view, and carousers had taken over the streets. He smacked his lips and stepped down to the dirt to take his mule's reins from the rail.

"One more ride up the hill, Henrietta," he said, "then I'll be done with you." He tightened the cinch around the weary beast and mounted, holding the bottle atop his thigh like a carbine. The photographer would be long gone now, and Hassard could collect his diamond field earnings. He had had a notion about those religious fanatics earlier, but Carrol Moncrief was coming to lead them. It was better to go back east now, and let the pilgrims alone.

As he plodded toward Clear Creek, he noticed a voice filling the street somewhere ahead of him. It sounded like the rant of a hellfire and brimstone preacher, but this wasn't Sunday, and no churches stood on this street. He squinted through the twilight and located the source of the tirade.

It came from a big man in a black suit standing at the door of a saloon. The man wore a dusty hat at an angle over his forehead, a gun belt at an opposing slant across his hips. He held a Bible in one hand and a glass of whiskey in the other.

Hassard knew who it was at a glance. The resemblance to the man he had killed in South Park was unmistakable. It could be none other than the Reverend Carrol Moncrief—the Fightin' Parson.

". . . so go ahead and drink, you scoundrels!" Moncrief was saying. "By all means, drink, and I'll drink with you! Jesus loves a drunk as much as a parson. Take your toddies and your highballs, your juleps and smashes, your punches and cobblers and sours . . ."

Hassard pulled his mule up in the street, buttoned his coat to make sure Frank Moncrief's pistol and holster were covered. He put a forearm on the saddle horn and leaned into the most unusual sermon he had ever heard.

". . . but for the love of God Almighty! Don't let the devil take the stool next to you! There is a better way!"

Three men tried to enter the saloon, but the preacher stepped in the doorway.

"Sir," he said, raising his glass and singling out one of the men, "give your life to Jesus now, and I'll drink to your salvation."

The man stepped back and smirked. "Tell you what, mister. You buy me and my pals a bottle, and Jesus can share it with us." He laughed with his friends beside him.

"You can't buy your way into the Kingdom of Heaven

as easy as you can buy a bottle, friend. And let me warn you: Hell is dry."

"Now, that ain't so. I've been to Dodge City, and there's liquor there to drown an army. In fact, the army drowns in it pretty regular."

The preacher shook his head slowly and began to tip the shot glass in his hand. "Your soul is poured out like this jigger," he said, watching the drink splatter on the board-walk. He tossed the shot glass to the man. "You're empty, friend."

"What do you think we come here for?" He pushed his way past the preacher and led his group into the saloon.

"Hey!" A man in a bartender's apron stepped into the doorway and glared at the parson. "Why don't you go preach in church where you belong?"

"Anybody can preach to saints and hypocrites. I serve those who need it most: the honest sinners."

"Well, you've served here long enough. Go preach somewhere else now. You're drivin' away my customers."

"I'll stay here until I save a soul, then I'll move on," Moncrief said.

The bartender's lips curled under with frustration. "You'll move on now," he said, stepping from the saloon. He grabbed the parson by the collar.

Moncrief drew the revolver from his holster—smoothly, quickly—cocking it as its muzzle pressed against the throat of the bartender, whose eyes grew with surprise. "Don't stand between me and the work of the Lord," the parson said.

"Whoa, Preacher," the bartender wheezed. "Stay as long as you like."

"God bless you," Moncrief said, grinning as he let his pistol down. "I believe you've seen the light." He shoved the bartender back into the saloon as his eyes landed on Dee Hassard, straddling the mule in the street. "You, sir!" he cried. "I'll make you a deal for that bottle on your knee."

Hassard lifted the half-full bottle and looked at it. "What kind of deal?" He felt Lady Luck smiling on him, but this was a little spooky. Carrol so favored his dead brother that it seemed Frank was looking at him now.

The parson stepped into the street. "Throw it straight up in the air and give me one shot at it. If I miss, I'll buy you a full bottle. If I hit it, you get on your knees and give your soul over to Jesus."

Hassard looked at the bottle. "Can I take one more swig first?"

"Long as you don't swig it all," Moncrief answered.

Hassard pulled the stopper on the bottle and took a long draw. Replacing the cork, he sucked a fiery breath down his windpipe and looked at the preacher misty eyed. "Ready?" he said.

"The question is, friend, are *you* ready? You lose the bet, and Jesus wins your soul. I'll see you on your knees in this road of mud and manure if my bullet shatters that bottle."

"That'll take a miracle in this light, Preacher. Now let's see if you're really in the miracle business."

The preacher nodded, and Hassard lofted the bottle high above the false fronts of the buildings. Moncrief watched the clear glass glint in the starlight, whipped his piece from the holster, and paced the target until it reached its zenith, hanging for an instant. The Colt erupted, and glass burst from the bottle like a round of canister.

"Praise the Lord, Preacher!" Hassard dismounted as pieces of glass peppered his hat brim. When he got both feet on the ground, he stood agog and let his mouth drop open. "By golly, I feel different. I think I really do, Preacher!"

"Get down on your knees, friend. Quick, before the feelin' passes!"

Hassard pulled his hat off and dropped to his knees as if ax-handled. He went so far as to fold his hands and look up breathlessly at the preacher.

Moncrief sank to one knee beside the swindler and put his hand on Hassard's shock of red hair. "Do you renounce the devil?"

"I do!" Hassard said.

"Do you take the Lord Jesus Christ into your heart and into your life?"

"You bet!"

"Hallelujah! You can get up now."

Hassard stood and made his knees tremble. "Amen!" he shouted.

"How do you feel?" Moncrief asked.

Hassard paused and looked cockeyed at the street, as if trying to sort out some new emotion coursing through him. "I feel like I need a bath," he declared. "I'm all clean inside, and filthy on the outside."

Moncrief smiled and clapped the convert on the shoulder. "Come sit down, friend. Let's talk."

They moved together to the boardwalk and sat with their feet on the dirt street.

"Tell me," Carrol said. "How do you plan to do the work of Christ now?"

"I don't know," Hassard replied. "I've only just been saved. I reckon I don't know what I'm supposed to do. What's it like, being a Christian?"

The fighting parson breathed deep and looked at the sky. "Son, it's like all your life you've had an outlaw hoss by the tail, draggin' you around, and that tail was full of burrs. Now, all of a sudden, you just let that hoss go, and dang if it don't feel good!"

"Yeah, but the reason I was hangin' on to that hoss is 'cause I wanted to ride."

Moncrief smiled and looked his convert in the eye. What he had here was a philosopher. "You can still ride. Your new mount might seem slower than that outlaw hoss at first, but just wait till you get up to speed. This hoss has wings, son!"

"Which hoss is that, Reverend?"

"The love of the Man Upstairs, and the forgiveness of His only son, who died on the cross for you." He poked Hassard in the chest with his finger. "I know you done some bad things in your past. You ought to know what all I done before I changed hosses. But the Good Lord makes all things happen for a reason."

Hassard chuckled. "That's what I hear, but I don't savvy much of that talk. The things I done, I don't think you'd see much reason to 'em, Preacher."

"It ain't for me to see, son. I'm just as mortal as the next man. The Good Lord sees more than you can ever wish to imagine." He rose, looking down the street for another wayward soul. "Let me warn you, friend. The devil can eat back into your heart. Bein' a Christian is hard work, but it's worth it for the way it makes you feel."

"I can do it," Hassard said. "I've been lookin' for this day. Hard to explain, but I've been searchin' for somethin', and this is it. I can feel it."

"Bless your soul," the parson said, "and go do the Lord's work in life."

Hassard shook his hand, and Moncrief turned away renewed.

"Wait, Preacher!" Hassard said. He watched the big man turn on him. "You're him, ain't you? The fightin' parson?"

"I've been called such."

"You're the Reverend Carrol Moncrief."

"I am."

Hassard curled his hat brim in his hand as he approached the preacher. "Well, Reverend Moncrief, seein' as how I'm saved now and all, I guess I might as well start the Lord's work with you. I know you're hurtin' over what happened to your brother, Frank, and I just want you to know that I feel for you, and if there's anything I can do . . . Maybe say a prayer or somethin' . . ."

Moncrief squinted. "What the devil are you talkin' about?"

Hassard sucked in a gasp. "Oh, Lordy, don't tell me you haven't heard. I'd have broke it easier if I thought you hadn't heard." This was so much fun that he had to fight back the smile.

"Heard what?" the preacher roared.

"Your brother's dead," Hassard said, casting his eyes to the ground.

Moncrief snorted a laugh. "You don't know Frank. He's ornerier than that."

"I know you don't want to believe it, Reverend, but I was passin' through Fairplay a while back, and I was there when they brought his body into town. They found him shot in the head somewhere out in South Park. Said he left to take some prisoner to Cañon City and never come back."

Moncrief gritted his teeth and grabbed his convert by the lapel of his dusty coat. "You better be sure of what you're sayin'." His heart felt as if it were sinking red hot into his guts.

"I wish it was somebody else tellin' you, Reverend. It ain't fair. You've just given me a new look at life, and I've got to be the one to break this news to you." He put his hand on Moncrief's fist. "Just remember, Carrol, he's gone to a better place."

The preacher opened his fist and drew away from the confidence man. "Who was the prisoner he was taking to Cañon City?"

"I couldn't tell you," Hassard said. "Didn't stay in town long enough to find out. Now, if there's anything I can do, Carrol. Anything at all . . ."

The parson pulled a watch from his pocket and turned its face to the light from the saloon. There was a train going south tonight. If he caught it he could ride to Colorado Springs, then buy a horse for the trip to Fairplay. His head was throbbing, not knowing what had happened. "I've got to get down there."

Hassard stuck his lower lip out and looked at the ground. "Well, godspeed, Carrol. I'm sure sorry you had to find out this way." He turned toward his mule.

"Wait," Moncrief said. "There is somethin' you can do."

"Name it."

"There's a bunch of pilgrims from back east camped somewhere up Clear Creek. They call theirselves the Church of the Weeping Virgin. I was supposed to meet 'em and guide 'em over the mountains. Go find 'em for me. Tell 'em they'll have to get somebody else."

Hassard smiled. "Consider it done, Carrol." He watched the reverend walk away down the street and wondered at the gullibility of man. Imagine, the likes of Dee Hassard falling for that old line of Christian nonsense. Give your life to Jesus? What in the hell did it even mean?

He was beginning to think these Moncrief brothers would fall for anything. They had gun savvy, all right. They had guts. But, for the love of God, did they trust every snake that didn't rattle?

"If there is a god," Dee Hassard said to himself, "he's smilin' on you today, boy."

EIGHT

The runabout lurched over obstacles in the moonlit road, jostling May against Clarence from time to time on the seat. She was relieved that the Vermonter possessed the gift of conversation, or the ride up Clear Creek would have felt awkward.

They passed around a camp of men with pack saddles and strange black boxes stacked everywhere. A fine white mule caught Clarence's eye, but as the men there didn't look like pilgrims, he drove on.

When finally the campfires of the pilgrims came into view, Clarence began to feel a little uneasy. He realized that he was going to have to leave May's company here if she found the group agreeable, and he began to sense complications in his adventure. "That looks like them," he said, pointing ahead.

"My, there's a good bunch of them," May replied. She saw some children chasing one another among the wagons.

As he drove the runabout near the camp, a man with a rifle stepped from the shadows and blocked the road.

"Whoa," Clarence said, reining in the livery horse.

"Who are you?" the guard demanded, holding his weapon ready in front of him.

"I'm Clarence Philbrick. This is Miss May Tremaine. We'd like to speak with the leader of your group."

"You want to join us?"

"We just want to ask some questions right now."

"You got guns?" the man said.

"Not on me," Clarence answered.

"Get out of the buggy and walk up," the guard ordered.

Clarence looked at May. Neither felt eager to get out of the vehicle under the circumstances.

"Ain't no harm gonna come to you," the guard said. "We got to be careful, that's all. Been attacked in some places."

Clarence looked for May's approval.

She shrugged. "We came this far. We might as well talk to them."

As the guard escorted them toward the camp, May noticed something odd about the circle of people around the nearest fire. It first struck her as a writhing. Every hand was busy working on something. One man was oiling harnesses. Another was braiding a bullwhacker's whip. A woman bounced a baby on her knee as she mended a quilt. There were faces of all colors, some ruddy, some pale, some dark.

Clarence noticed an Indian woman, her hair long and straight, parted in the middle. A necklace of teeth and claws lay across the bodice of her faded print dress.

Next to her sat a black man who was whittling a walking stick. He had to be six-foot-six and couldn't weigh more than a hundred fifty. The man sat on a stool with his legs crossed, yet both feet lay flat on the ground. He looked up as the arrivals came near, and Clarence found a full head of gray hair and a large white mustache contrasting with his dark brown skin, a twinkle in his eyes struggling through reflections on his spectacles. He stood. "Is this him?" he said to the guard.

"Nope," the guard answered.

"You were expecting somebody else?" Clarence said.

"A Reverend Moncrief was supposed to meet us here tonight. He's to guide us over the mountains. But that's not for you to worry about. I'm Elder Hopewell. What can we do for you?"

Clarence saw a bunch of children spying on him from under a wagon. "Miss Tremaine would like to know a little about your group. She's all alone and looking for a place to settle out here."

"What would you like to know?" Hopewell said.

May swept her eyes across the faces peering up at her. "This is a Christian church, isn't it?"

The group around the fire raised a round of low laughter.

"We are *the* Christian church," Elder Hopewell replied, his teeth showing under the full white mustache. "All others have fallen into disfavor with the Maker and will have to be reconciled."

"According to what authority?" Clarence said.

"According to the Holy Virgin."

"Has she told you so?"

"Not me," Elder Hopewell explained. "The late Pastor Wyckoff received the visitations. It started seven years ago in Philadelphia. The Angel of Mary came to him in the night as he prayed. She was crying over the sad state of humanity, especially those who call themselves Christians yet obey the wicked laws of government and materialism over the laws of God. The Weeping Virgin told Pastor Wyckoff to gather the downtrodden faithful among the many races and repair to a new promised land. We are the New Order that will bring all the peoples of the world together."

"Amen," someone in the circle said. They had all nodded as Elder Hopewell told the story, their hands remaining busy with their tasks.

"Now, if you want to travel with us," Hopewell said, "we'd be happy to take you in. But if you want to truly join us, you have to give all your material possessions to the church."

"I don't have any material possessions," May said.

"Will you give your service to the church?"

May's eyes shifted. "What kind of service?"

The elder pointed to the people around the fire. "Like these folks are doing. Fix what needs to be fixed. Build what needs building. Everything we do is for the good of the church, and no time is spent idle."

"I don't mind work," May said.

"You'll have to read Pastor Wyckoff's book," Hopewell said. "And when you're ready, you will renounce all other authority and become a vested member of the Church of the Weeping Virgin. Until that time, you are welcome to share our company, our food, and our friendship." He looked at Clarence. "What about you, young man? Will you come with us, too?"

Clarence shook his head. "I have business in New Mexico." He took May by the arm. "Will you excuse us a minute?" He pulled her a few yards away from the circle of pilgrims. "I don't know if this is such a good idea," he said.

"They seem like nice folks," she replied.

"What about this business of the visitations and all? Sounds a little strange to me."

"Yes, but that was their pastor, and he's dead. These people look all right."

Clarence glanced over May's shoulder at the congregation, then looked back down at her face. She was looking up at him, as if waiting for his approval. He could see that she was going to go with them. She had nowhere else to turn. She couldn't go with him to New Mexico, could she? No, of course not. What choice did she have? She was going to join these pilgrims. He could leave her with doubts and misgivings, or he could bolster her confidence.

"I believe you're right," he said. "They seem like nice people, and there are enough of them to offer protection. You'll be all right with them."

May smiled again, her eyes twinkling gratefully. "Thank you for everything you've done. I won't forget you."

Clarence shuffled his feet. "When you get settled, I want you to write me a letter. Send it general delivery to Santa Fe. Let me know where you've settled so I can come check up on you someday."

She looked away, her face flushing. She began to speak, but a rattle of rocks across the creek interrupted her.

A mule splashed through the shallow stream and into the firelight as the guard stepped forward to challenge the rider.

"Howdy, brothers and sisters in Christ!" a red-haired man shouted from the back of the mule.

"Who are you?" the guard demanded.

"Put your weapon away, friend. I'm your guide. I'm to take you over the mountains."

Elder Hopewell approached the stranger and stood beside the camp guard. "You're Reverend Moncrief?"

"The good reverend couldn't make it. His brother's been murdered in South Park. He sent me in his stead. I'm Deacon Dee Hassard." He got down from the mule and held a hand out to the elder.

"When will Reverend Moncrief join us?" Hopewell asked.

"I have a feelin' he'll be huntin' his brother's murderer for a spell. You'll have to make do with me. He had to go to Fairplay while the trail was still hot." He looked past

Hopewell at the crowd around the nearest campfire. "Carrol didn't have much time to fill me in. How many people have you got here?"

"Almost two hundred, counting the children."

"And about the money. Five hundred?"

"We have it, as we promised."

"No offense, but I'd like to see it."

Elder Hopewell motioned for Hassard to follow and led the new arrival to the tailgate of a broken-down wagon. He pulled a pair of saddlebags out and opened one flap.

Hassard craned his neck to see by the light of a lantern hanging from a cottonwood limb above. When the elder pulled a roll of bills out and handed it over, Hassard glimpsed more currency deeper in the pouch. He saw the glint of gold and silver coins, heard them chink. Glorious thoughts of larceny rushed by like ripples in the nearby creek.

"Carrol said you'd be ready to go." Hassard slipped the roll of bills into his pocket.

"We are," the elder replied.

Hassard snorted. "Not with these wagons." He approached the pilgrims around the nearest fire. "Friends, we've got work to do, and we'd best get started right now if we want to leave tomorrow. First thing we do is load the wagons with anything that won't travel on a pack mule. We'll drive into Denver at daybreak and sell the wagons and everything in 'em."

"Now hold on there, Deacon," the elder said. "We've got household items in there. Tables, chairs, beds. Things of necessity."

Hassard twisted his face. "I thought you folks wanted to go across the divide to the Promised Land."

"And we will," the tall man said.

"Elder Hopewell, there are no roads where we're goin'. Wagons won't make it. It's best to convert all those material possessions to cash. Better yet—gold. Your church can use it to pay homestead fees or buy government land. Besides, it's a land of milk and honey over there, brothers and sisters." He turned to the people in the camp, speaking loudly. "You can build your own household goods from the bounty of God's green earth!"

"You've been to the Western slopes?" Elder Hopewell asked.

"I have, brother, and it is the most beautiful spot in the world. But gettin' there's gonna test your faith, and we've got to get started as soon as practical."

The elder caught some of Dee Hassard's false enthusiasm and smiled back at the congregation. "What do we do?" he asked.

"Get those wagons loaded with everything we don't need," Hassard cried. "Keep only your clothes, your weapons, and your tools. We'll sell everything else in Denver tomorrow and start west."

Elder Hopewell raised his hands, reaching high in the air. "It's time," he said. This was a relief. They had been waiting here too long, and everyone had looked to him since Pastor Wyckoff's murder. Now there was someone here who knew where to go. "Let's get ready!"

The people rose as if bolting from Sunday services.

"One more thing," Hassard shouted. "Remember

Reverend Moncrief in your prayers tonight! His brother's been murdered."

"Amen!" someone shouted, and the camp surged for the wagons to separate everything that wouldn't fit a pack saddle.

"I think I better go help them," May said. She and Clarence had watched the arrival of Deacon Hassard in silence.

"Good luck," Clarence said, taking her hand, releasing it reluctantly.

She joined the pilgrims, and he turned to the rented buggy. It didn't feel right leaving her there. It wasn't that she was in any danger. No, it was something else. He was going to miss her. He had only known her a couple of hours, yet he already regretted parting ways with her.

As Clarence Philbrick drove through the night back to Denver, he began to wonder what lay waiting for him in New Mexico. Was the Ojo de los Brazos as easy to look at as May Tremaine? Would it be worth the journey?

He began to compose his nightly journal entry:

I once went hunting for ducks and killed the largest brace of grouse I had ever bagged. I arrived at my duck blind very late, yet found fine sport there as well.

Is May Tremaine a bird of serendipity—a pleasant diversion along my way to fortune? Or is she a siren who tempts me to stray from my course, onto the rocks of ruin?

NINE

It was an embarrassment. Ramon del Bosque could still hear the jeers of his friends, even though he was a long day's journey from Guajolote.

"Adios, Padre Ramon," they had said, taunting him as he left the village, leading Sister Petra's burro. One of them had run into the street to give Ramon a whip made of yucca fibers so he could flagellate himself like the *penitentes*.

"What do you have that *disciplina* for?" Petra had asked.

"For the burro," Ramon had said, striking the animal a light blow across the rump with the whip.

It was bad enough that Ramon's father was always saying he was going to send Ramon to the school in Santa Fe to become a priest. That claim had caused Ramon no end of consternation: his friends constantly coming to him for confessions and calling him "Padre Ramon." But this was a humiliation almost too severe to endure.

God had spoken to Sister Petra. At least, that was what Sister Petra claimed. She had been praying nine days, not getting enough food or rest. She had fainted in her room and had had a dream. That was all. It was her own mind, not God, that had said, "The cross awaits you on the mountainside."

Ramon thought he must be the only one in Guajolote to remember that Sister Petra was, after all, an Anglo. Yes, she spoke Spanish perfectly, but she had green eyes, for heaven's sake. Why was this crazy Anglo to be taken so seriously? She was not going to save Guajolote. The

Anglos were going to get it, and people were going to be thrown out of their homes. Why was he the only one who could see that?

Sister Petra's claim had thrown Guajolote into turmoil, and no one had gotten more excited than Ramon's father. "I will send Ramon with you to find the cross on the mountain!" he had blurted. "Ramon is going to be a priest, you know. He will be your disciple, Sister Petra! You can use my burro!"

Now he was farther from home than he had ever been—a day's walk north, approaching the village of Chacon. Sister Petra had interpreted her dream to mean that she was to go to one of the hills on which the *penitentes* held their mock crucifixions every Easter. The nearest *penitente* chapter was in Chacon, and so that was where Sister Petra had decided to begin her search.

As he got his first glimpse of the village, Ramon simply could not take the pace any longer. "Sister Petra," he said. "Can we slow down now? We are almost there."

She was several steps ahead of Ramon and the burro, and she stopped to let them catch up, glaring at him with those green Anglo eyes. "You have been complaining since the moment we started yesterday," she snapped.

"But I have a cramp right here," he said, putting a hand over his stomach.

"You shouldn't have eaten so much breakfast this morning. You knew we were going to have to walk."

"We haven't been walking. We've been trotting like coyotes."

"How old are you?"

"Fourteen."

"I am more than twice your age. You should be able to keep up with me."

"I can keep up with you. I just don't want to."

Petra put her hands on her hips and scowled. "You don't believe in what I'm doing, do you?"

"No. What do you think you're going to find when you get to this cross on this mountain?"

"I don't know. I just know that God has instructed me to find it."

Ramon scoffed and rolled his eyes.

"If you prefer, I can send you back to Guajolote right now," Petra warned. "You've only been slowing me down."

The thought of returning in ridicule quickly sobered Ramon. His father would not be happy, and his friends would heckle him for days. It was better to let the excitement die down and return in a week or so. "All right, I'm sorry," he said.

"Throw that *disciplina* away," Petra ordered. "Juan will think you have it to make fun of him."

They proceeded into the village, Petra going directly to the shop of Juan Hidalgo, the carpenter in Chacon, and the *hermano mayor* of the *penitentes* there.

"Hello, Brother Juan," she said, finding him around the back of his shop.

Juan stopped sawing the cottonwood beam he was fashioning into an axle for his *carreta* and looked over his shoulder. "Sister Petra!" he said, his eyebrows gathering droplets of sweat into the creases of his forehead. He lay his saw down and came forward to take Petra's hand in his. Sawdust clung to his hands and his sleeves, and he dropped to one knee and bowed before the sister. "What brings you to Chacon?" he asked.

"I have prayed a novena to save our village," Petra said, "and God spoke to me."

Juan gasped and seemed so excited that he didn't even notice young Ramon del Bosque leading the burro around the corner of the adobe. "What did God say to you?"

"He said, 'The cross awaits you on the mountainside.'"

Juan touched the points of the cross on his forehead and body. "Do you think the cross on the mountain means our *Calvario* where we stand the cross during Holy Week?"

"I don't know," she said. "I am just beginning my search."

Juan nodded, smiling at the boy with the burro. "Who is this young fellow with you?"

Petra fought the urge to tell Juan that this young fellow was a pain in the neck sent by God to test her. "This is Ramon. His father sent him to help me search."

The carpenter put his hand on the boy's shoulder. "You should be proud. Not every young boy like you gets to go on such an adventure. I only wish I could go with you, but I have the people to take care of here."

Ramon drew away uncertainly from the carpenter. In Guajolote there were no *penitentes,* and he only knew what he had heard. He knew it was true that during most of the year, the brotherhoods accomplished charity works in their villages, helping those in need, counseling those who suffered. They lived normal lives, doing Christian works.

But during Holy Week, the *penitentes* would allow a *sangrador* to cut slashes across their backs with a knife. They would whip themselves with the *disciplina* made of yucca fibers, causing blood to flow from the knife wounds. On Good Friday, some of them would carry huge wooden crosses to the *Calvario*. And, every year, one would be chosen to crucify. His brothers would tie him to a cross and raise it into place, leaving him there until he lost consciousness. Ramon had even heard that some of the *penitente* chapters used real nails instead of rope, and that some men had died on the cross.

He looked at the hand on his shoulder and didn't see any nail scars through the sawdust but still felt uneasy enough to pull away.

"Which is the hill that your *morada* uses as its *Calvario*?" Sister Petra asked. She was anxious to see her quest through, to save her village, and to please her god.

Juan turned on Ramon and glared at him. "I will take you to it, but you—young man—you must promise never to tell anyone which hill we use. It is getting harder for us to keep outsiders away. They want to come and watch us perform the penance—especially the *Americanos*. They think we are some sort of *locos*."

"He won't tell anybody," Sister Petra promised. "I will make sure of that."

Ramon resented Petra's speaking for him, and he smirked at her. "I won't tell," he said to the carpenter.

They tied the burro at a water trough made of a hollowed-out log and followed a well-worn trail into the foothills. Sister Petra seemed excited, walking faster than ever. The carpenter matched her pace, and Ramon lagged only a few strides behind. He might have stayed in Chacon with the burro, but he was curious about the *Calvario*, where men hung from crosses. Perhaps the story of it would silence the jeers of his friends for a while when he got back to Guajolote.

"This is the place," Juan Hidalgo said, gesturing to the hill.

Petra paused at the bottom to catch her breath, then scrambled up the trail to the summit. When Ramon reached the top of the little mountain, he found the nun on her knees. He turned away from her and looked back toward Chacon. He couldn't see the village. The *Calvario* was secluded, so that the ritual might remain hidden from outsiders.

Mopping his sleeve across his brow, he searched the ground for signs of blood, maybe a nail or a crown of thorns or something. He felt the carpenter looking at him and met the pleasant gaze of Juan Hidalgo. The *penitente* motioned toward a small piñon tree near the summit, and Ramon joined him in its shadow, sitting side by side on the shaded rocks. They waited in silence only a couple of minutes, then heard Petra shuffling through the gravel.

"This is not the place," the nun said.

Juan rose from the shade of the scrubby tree, obviously disappointed. "Are you sure? If you want, I will build a cross and get the brothers to help me raise it here. Didn't the voice of God tell you to seek the cross?"

"It wouldn't do any good," Petra said. She sighed and looked northward. "This is not the place."

Juan felt deeply disappointed. "Where will you go now?"

"To the north," Petra said. "I feel that is the way to go. I feel the mountain is higher. I will search among the brotherhoods farther north, and higher up. I think that is what God wants me to do."

Ramon scrambled to his feet and stared at the nun. "But

how far are you going?" he asked. "How long is this going to take?"

She shrugged. "Who can say? You can go back home if you want to, Ramon. But I am going to take your father's burro with me." She walked past the carpenter and tramped down the trail back toward the village.

Juan chuckled. "You should go with her, Ramon. She is going to go high up into the mountains where it will be cool. I bet you are going to see a lot of new things you have never seen before. It will be an adventure to shape the rest of your life."

Ramon shook his head and looked up at the rising flanks of the Sangre de Cristos. "She thinks she is going to keep the Ojo de los Brazos grant from being sold," he said. "I don't know what she expects to find up there."

"God speaks to her. I believe it. She might need you, Ramon. Are you going to go with her?"

Ramon shrugged, his shoulders pushing out a sigh as they fell. "I guess so. A little farther, anyway."

The carpenter slapped the boy on the back. "You are going to see something wonderful, Ramon. Now hurry up before she leaves without you."

TEN

Clarence could hear his father talking: "Good God, boy! If I'd have been as naive as you in California . . . irresponsible is what it is . . . most foolhardy thing I ever heard of . . ." The old forty-niner would have lectured for hours.

But as Clarence stared at the Denver and Rio Grande schedule posted in the depot, he knew he was not going to buy a ticket. He was not going to ride the rails south, toward New Mexico and the Ojo de los Brazos grant. He still intended to get there sooner or later, but it didn't feel right going just now. Not with May Tremaine taking a different trail west. And, anyway, Clarence's father wasn't looking over his shoulder here. He could do anything he wanted.

He had seen Deacon Dee Hassard and several of the men from the pilgrim camp hawking wagon loads of goods early this morning. They had sold everything, bought burros and pack saddles, and trailed out of town. They were taking the road into the mountains, pushing toward the mining camps, and ultimately into unsettled lands.

Clarence didn't care what his father would say. All he knew was that he had left May too hastily. Some people called them fanatics, after all. He was responsible for whatever happened to her while she was with them. He had to be sure.

He gripped the Remington rifle by the octagonal barrel, resting the breech across his shoulder. Stooping, he grabbed his traveling bag and marched out of the depot. He felt like he ought to run in order to catch up, but he settled for a fast walk. By the time he reached the edge of town, he was only slightly winded, and just getting his legs warmed up.

The grade started to pitch uphill along Clear Creek, but Clarence only strode longer. He stopped when he reached the former campground of the Church of the Weeping Virgin, took off his heavy coat, and put it in his bag.

Only ashes shifted where last night the pilgrims had sat

mending and making things. The silence and emptiness made the Vermonter anxious to catch up, so he picked up his things and stepped briskly up the path.

The trail veered onto the Georgetown Road. Clarence could see footprints and burro tracks in the dirt. He figured he would catch them in camp at Golden. They wouldn't try to get too far the first day.

He climbed as the day warmed, stopping occasionally to look eastward, across the plains. He had hunted the Eastern mountains, taken in the scenery from various promontories. But this vista was unlike anything he had ever seen. The country was so big here, the view so long through the thin air. A body could see miles and miles of wide-open range, nothing like the shrinking pockets of dark forest wilderness back east.

Two days ago he had been a buffalo skinner in a treeless infinity of rolling grass. Now he was climbing ever higher among scattered pines and rocky passes. If he had known about this place, he would have come long ago, with or without his damned trust fund. The air here was so fine that a body could almost live on it like fuel.

When he approached Golden in the early afternoon, he sensed clouds gathering in the pass. By the time he reached the town, rain was falling in sheets. He took refuge in a wagon-yard barn and ate some grub he had packed for the day's hike.

"Goin' prospectin'?" the man in the barn asked, himself taking a break from the weather.

"No," Clarence answered. "I'm trying to catch up to a party of pilgrims. I'm going to help guide them across the mountains."

"They passed through town a couple of hours ago. Their guide traded mules with me. Said they was gonna try to get to Idaho Springs today."

"How far is that?" Clarence asked, holding his tin cup in the rain to collect some water.

"Better part of twenty miles."

Clarence's eyes bulged as he turned to the stable man. "That far?"

"That guide was hell-bent on coverin' some ground today."

The Vermonter stood immediately, put on his hat, and buttoned the oilskin coat harboring his fortune. "I'd better cover some myself then." He picked up his Remington and stepped toward the downpour cascading from the eaves of the barn. "You wouldn't have a ten-dollar horse for sale, would you?" he said, thinking of the miles that lay ahead.

"Got a three-year-old. Last year's bronc. He's gentled down right nice since we cut him. You won't get him for ten dollars, though."

All Clarence could think of, as he rode his new twelve-dollar mount up the slippery road, was poor May's feet. How was she going to walk twenty miles today with those blisters? He only hoped they would let her ride a burro part of the way, otherwise she would be miserable. She didn't even have a slicker to turn the rain.

The road continued to climb, and Clarence noticed that his gelding had a bad habit of tossing his head. He could fix that with a piece of rope tied between saddle girth and headstall, but he didn't have a piece of rope just now. The pilgrims would, he thought.

The rain stopped, clouds broke, and shafts of sunlight began to light circles on the mountainsides. He reached the edge of a mountain forest and stopped for one last look across the plains, sensing that the great ranges were about to engulf him.

After a couple of hours, the tracks of the pilgrims became clearer in the muddy road and Clarence knew they had passed here after the rain. He didn't see many small tracks and figured the children had given out and were either riding burros or their parents' backs.

He was having misgivings again. What business of his was the life of May Tremaine? Here he was carrying a fortune in gold into a wilderness. Perhaps he should have put it in a bank back in Denver, for safekeeping until he decided to head south. Too late now. The plan that had seemed so clear when he left Vermont was starting to break apart like melting ice on a river. If he lost that gold, his father would never let him forget it.

He stopped on a hill and saw several trails of smoke below where miners had carved a town into the valley. This had to be Idaho Springs. The near slopes stood divested of timber, which had been made into buildings for the ungainly town. He could see rude log cabins ringing the settlement, a few painted Victorians in one quarter bespeaking mineral wealth.

He wondered if the Ojo de los Brazos would look the way this place had before the mines—the high rocky peaks cradling forests and green valleys. He hoped so. He could imagine driving May up to the gate in a carriage on a sunny day.

What was he thinking? He barely knew this woman.

Clarence swung down from his horse and squatted at the side of the road. The cheap saddle he had bought was going to make him sore if he didn't walk the rest of the way. He put his rifle butt on the ground and gripped the barrel to steady himself as he balanced on the balls of his feet. What if New Mexico didn't look like this? What if May had no intention of going with him there? What would he do then? Give his earthly possessions to the Church of the Weeping Virgin? Become a religious fanatic?

Maybe he should have bought that train ticket this morning. He could have been in Pueblo by now. Well, no choice but to find the pilgrims and go over the mountains with them at this point. Come on, Clarence, you've got to see something through.

He led his horse into Idaho Springs and found out that the pilgrims were camped just up the creek from town. He was hoping they would give him food and take him in when he got there, but he knew no guarantees.

The burro tracks took him to the edge of the stream, where he found the pilgrims engaged in various forms of industry, though with little spring left to step with.

"Howdy," a guard said when he saw Clarence approach camp. "Good to see you again."

"Look!" someone else shouted. "It's Sister May's friend!"

Clarence took his bag down from the saddle horn and stared with wonder at the people stepping forward to greet him. May's friend? It was as if she had been among them for years.

"She told us how you helped her out in Denver," a

woman from Pennsylvania said. "God bless you, Clarence."

He spotted Deacon Dee Hassard sitting against a tree trunk with a book in his hand. The pathfinder sprang to his feet and came toward him.

"May!" someone was shouting. "Clarence is back!"

"What brings you back?" Hassard said, smiling as he offered his hand.

"Thought I might help you take these folks over the mountains," Clarence said, pulling his coat from the loop handles of his traveling bag before someone picked it up and felt its heft.

"What for?"

Clarence shrugged. "Never been over the mountains before. Thought I could help these people get there, see some new country."

"Well, you've got a good rifle," Hassard said. "How would you like to scout ahead and hunt for meat?"

Clarence fought the smile back. "All right." He noticed a teenage girl leading May up from the creek.

"Elder Hopewell!" Hassard cried. "Get another copy of Pastor Wyckoff's book for Brother Clarence, if you please." He turned back to the Vermonter and shook the open book in his face. "You've got to read this," he said. "It'll open your eyes," and he turned back toward his tree to continue reading.

The girl led May to Clarence and turned away, giggling. The other pilgrims smiled coyly and went back to their chores, leaving the couple alone at the edge of camp.

"They do make a fuss, don't they?" May said, blushing.

Clarence nodded. "It's welcome after that long walk. How did your feet hold out today?"

May smiled and stuck a toe out from under her hem. "That Comanche woman—her name is Mary Whitepath—she gave me these moccasins. They don't hurt at all."

Elder Hopewell approached the couple on his gangling legs and towered above them. "Here's your book, Brother Clarence."

"I'm not sayin' I want to join your church," Clarence explained. "Just thought I might see some new country with you and help you find a place to settle."

"Will you read the book?"

"I don't see any harm in that."

"That's all we ask. I hope you will learn to walk in the way that leads to light." Elder Hopewell gave him the book and turned back toward camp.

"I've been readin' that book," May said. "Some of it's all right, but other parts . . ."

"What?"

"It's just hard to believe."

Clarence raised his eyebrows and looked across the campground at the busy pilgrims. "Did you ever expect you'd fall in with a bunch like this?"

"I didn't know there was such a bunch as this."

They stood looking at each other—the Vermonter and the runaway wife—neither feeling quite awkward enough to break the stare.

ELEVEN

The eyes were wide open under Dee Hassard's hat. His head lay on a packsaddle, the edge of a blanket curled under his chin. Pastor Wyckoff's book, *The Wisdom of Ages*, lay open on his chest, and one hand rested across its spine. His lungs drew deep, as if he had fallen into the rhythm of sound sleep, but his mind was conscious, plotting, rehearsing.

The late Pastor Wyckoff was a genius, he was thinking. Hassard only wished he had thought of the scam himself. To an eye honed for deception, it was all laid out like a thinly disguised recipe for fraud in *The Wisdom of Ages*.

He held a reverent smile under his brim as he walked mentally through the formula again. Wyckoff's first step: he makes himself a pastor—the easy way. Creates his own religion. No Bible lessons, no seminary.

Only in America.

Hassard couldn't imagine why he hadn't seen it before, but religious freedom had opportunity written all over it. You conjure a revelation, proclaim yourself a prophet—bang, you're in business.

According to *The Wisdom of Ages*, Wyckoff's revelation arrives in the image of the Virgin Mary. She appears weeping over his bed one night, lamenting the sorry state of the wicked world. She tells Wyckoff to gather the poor downtrodden faithful from all the races and start over. Presto, there's your congregation.

It helps to be a good writer, Hassard thought. That Wyckoff could really mold the lingo, yet *The Wisdom of Ages* read like a dime novel, in simple language, with its philosophies easily understood. There was a reason for that. The book was designed to appeal to the poorly educated.

This part is hard to figure, Hassard thought. Wyckoff goes after poor people with little schooling. Where's the logic in that? Poor folks have no money to steal. It makes no sense at first. But that's why it's good—it's hard to figure.

Wyckoff isn't after just any poor folks. He wants honest, hardworking, trusting Christian souls—"the generous poor" as he calls them in his book. They don't have money to take, but they'll work. What a thrust! Didn't the Virgin Mary tell Wyckoff in his vision that all members of the New Order must work every waking moment to keep the devil from infesting their souls? No hand was ever to lie idle for even an instant.

Hassard could hardly stay still thinking of it. Take the church's built-in tenet for constant work, and add to it the Virgin Mary's order that every member give every penny earned to the church, and you have an organization that can only get richer. Wyckoff sits back and counts money while his new recruits keep chipping in their meager earnings.

Next step, publicity. Distribute the book, give a few sermons, convert a few souls. Let it build. Wyckoff is bound to run into opposition, of course. He's telling everyone to renounce money, government, and all other symbols of man's authority—especially other religions. He goes so far as to claim that the Bible is incomplete without *The Wisdom of Ages*. His is the only true Christianity.

But the preachers and priests and parsons won't stand for some upstart prophet shaving off pieces of their pie. They condemn Wyckoff, stir the resentment against him, foment the festering hatreds. They all but condone acts of violence and vandalism perpetrated against the Church of the Weeping Virgin and its members.

So what does Wyckoff do? He takes it like a true martyr for a while, raking in sympathy and new members. Religious fanatics feed off of persecution. It pulls them closer together. Then, when things get really bad, Wyckoff heads west, to new country, where no clergy rule. There his church will work for him, make him wealthy, carve his domain.

But he makes a fatal mistake. On the way west, Wyckoff probes the Old South for converts. Hassard rocked his head on the pack saddle at the folly of it. Wyckoff has grown too cocky at this point. He's been lucky so far, and now he's pushing it. Some white folks in Arkansas take issue with Wyckoff's marrying colored to whites, and they lynch him. You don't mess around with those Southern boys.

The mixing of the races is not a bad idea by itself. It excludes no one, appeals to immigrants. And people who will stand for it don't hate anybody. They're harmless. But Wyckoff should have been smart enough to know it would never go over in the South. Audacity has to be reined in somewhere.

Now he's a poor, dead, fake martyr. He could have had his own kingdom out here. And if Carrol Moncrief wasn't coming back after my hide, Hassard thought, I could pick it up where Wyckoff dropped it. As it lies, I can only take the Church of the Weeping Virgin for what it's worth now, and it doesn't have over a thousand dollars in its coffers.

The swindler shifted on a rock that was poking up into his back. The important thing, he had decided, was knowing the strategy of the scam, and there was still one aspect of the church he hadn't been made privy to: the initiation.

This was something they only whispered about, but he had gathered a little. When a new recruit had read *The Wisdom of Ages* and had decided to join the church, several of the congregation members would put the recruit through a three-day initiation process of some kind. Browbeating and lecturing, Hassard suspected. Whatever it was, it worked. Weeping Virginites were loyal to excess and kept the initiation rites a secret.

Anyway, once he figured out how to conduct the initiation, he could swindle the pilgrims, stay one step ahead of Moncrief, and go somewhere else to put his own twists on Wyckoff's grand swindle—maybe Canada or Australia.

Earlier today he had thought about just grabbing the money and making a run for it in the night. Then that greenhorn from back east showed up—Clarence what's-his-name. He looked just brave and dumb enough to give chase. Hassard had heard May Tremaine tell how Clarence had fought off the cowboy in Denver for her. All he needed was a college boy putting practical thoughts into the heads of his pilgrims. That was why he had made the Vermonter a hunter. To keep him away from the congregation.

Keep him away from Sister May, too. Dee Hassard knew that look. She was no weeping virgin. That gal had used what God gave her to get by before. Now that Clarence had come back, it looked as if he was going to have to string this thing out a little longer than he had at first planned. That was all right. Maybe he would find time to discover the secrets of the initiation rites and have a religious experience with Sister May.

He snorted, forcing her out of his thoughts. The cold mountain air streamed under the hat, into his nostrils. He heard Clear Creek boiling among its time-rounded boulders, the wind rattling twigs against the starry sky. The time was right. Dee Hassard was about to show the ghost of Pastor Wyckoff a thing or two about audacity.

He bolstered his gall, chose his opening line. Coiling his resolve like a twisted spring, he held a breath and waited for the release.

"Great God!" he shouted, springing up from the ground. He threw the blanket aside, staggered, and fell across the gangling legs of Elder Hopewell. "Wake up, everybody!"

The elder flinched as he woke and scrambled out from under Hassard. "What is it?" he said, groping for his sensibilities.

"It's a wonder!" Hassard shouted. He pulled his knees under him, clasped his hands, and made out like he was searching the heavens.

One of the pilgrims rose a short distance away. "Everything all right?"

"Yes," Hassard moaned. "It's wonderful."

"What's got into you?" Elder Hopewell said.

Hassard jumped to his feet. "Everybody, wake up!" he shouted, waving his arms. "I know what to do now!"

Voices began to mutter and pilgrims sat up in their blankets. A few of the more curious came trotting to Elder Hopewell's fire, and Clarence Philbrick arrived in stocking feet with his Remington rifle in one hand and his coat under his arm.

"Settle down," Hopewell said, putting his hand on Hassard's shoulder. "Tell us what you're talking about."

Hassard had made his eyes moist and used them now to catch the moonlight as he stared up at the elder. "I was meditating on Pastor Wyckoff's book," he said, his voice shaking. "I sank into a deep state, like nothing I ever felt before. And *she came to me!*"

"Who?" someone said, pushing into the circle that had formed around Hassard.

"Just like the book said. It was the Weeping Virgin! She told me where to lead the faithful!"

Clarence put the butt of the rifle on the ground and searched for May, finding her approaching the ring of pilgrims to his left.

"Are you sure you weren't just dreaming?" Elder Hopewell said.

"Dreamin'!" Hassard said, glaring up at the tall man. "No dream feels like that. I'm tellin' you, the Virgin spoke to me! She told me where to lead this church!"

"Well, where?" asked a man in the crowd. "Where are we going?"

Hassard wheeled slowly and looked at his listeners, raising his hands slowly. "There's a peak high up in the Sawatch," he said. "I've heard of it before. Thought it was only a legend. But the Virgin Mary told me for sure, and now I know. It's there, and that's where she wants us to go."

"What peak?" Clarence asked.

"I've heard of mountain men and prospectors seein' it," Hassard said, building on the curiosity around him. "Never met anybody who actually found it. It lies against the wall of a high basin above the timberline. The basin is small— just a few miles across, I guess. You can only see it from a few places along the north rim."

"See *what*?" Clarence demanded.

The swindler imagined the lucre he would win as Pastor Dee Hassard, and let the light of wonder fill his eyes. "The cross," he whispered. "A giant cross of pure snow driven into the crevices of the mountainside. I've heard it's a thousand feet tall, three hundred wide, with arms lifting toward heaven." He flattened his palms and spread his arms, turning in the circle of pilgrims, relishing the looks of stupor on their faces. Then his eyes crossed the skeptical glare of that damned Vermonter. "It's the Mount of the Snowy Cross."

"If you've never seen it, how do you know what it looks like?" Clarence asked.

"The revelation, boy! The Weeping Virgin! She's seen it!" He stepped toward the west curve of the circle around him and walked a few steps into the congregation, the pilgrims making way for him. Suddenly he pointed over their heads. "It's that way!" he cried. "That's the way we're to go."

Clarence smirked. "That's the way we've *been* going."

Hassard wheeled, spread his arms, smiled. "Now we know why."

The pilgrims began to mumble, and Elder Hopewell spoke above them. "All right, let's go back to bed," he said, calming the people with strokes of his long fingers over their heads. "We've got to rise early."

"As Elder Hopewell says," Hassard agreed. "We've got another long day's march ahead of us." He picked up his blanket and his book and went back to his packsaddle, lying back against it as the pilgrims dispersed.

He could tell by the looks on their faces that he had hooked them. Elder Hopewell was a little skeptical yet, but he would come around. The problem, if there was going to be one, would come from Clarence what's-his-name.

He rolled onto his side as he pulled the blanket up to his chin. Looking across the campground, he watched the pilgrims shuffling back toward their beds. And there was Clarence—talking with Sister May. He was swaying her, too. Look at her, peering up at him, hanging on his every word. What a form she cut in the moonlight! Young Clarence was going to require special treatment. And so was Sister May.

TWELVE

It was an ugly hump in the ground—fresh dirt sculpted by a recent rainfall. Carrol Moncrief compared it to the surrounding plots in the young Fairplay cemetery. Most of them were grass covered, and flat or concave. Frank's was mounded high, bare of vegetation, sun cracked.

He had never thought about the life of a grave before,

but it was suddenly obvious. The pine box buried below him would someday rot and collapse. This mound of dirt would fall in on his brother. The ground would sink, collect water instead of shed it, and grass would sprout.

The marker at the head of the mound was just a wooden cross with Frank's name carved on it. Carrol figured the county would put up a good stone one, seeing as how Frank had been sheriff.

His horse, tied behind him at the fence of pine pickets, jingled the bridle and stomped a foot, fighting off flies.

Carrol sank to his knees. Thank God Frank was underground where the flies couldn't get him, instead of lying out there in South Park. A hot coal in his chest rose and tears burst from his eyes. He sobbed alone, watching the blurry road to Fairplay for riders. No one was going to catch Carrol Moncrief blubbering.

"God, I'm a wicked, selfish sinner," he moaned. "I want my brother back. I'd drag him out of the ground to have him back. I'd deprive him his reward, God. Forgive me."

His eyes ran dry, but he still felt the sick, hollow heat in his chest. He tore his hat off and threw it to the ground. Shifting his weight, he rolled to the ground and straightened his legs. He lay on his side, watching the road to Fairplay over the mound of Frank's grave.

"He was a better man than me."

How could this have happened? Frank was careful, professional. The convict who did this must have been some kind of cowardly sneak. Oh, when he found out . . . When he caught up to the bastard . . .

"Vengeance is mine, sayeth the Lord," he muttered. He had to get on top of that kind of thinking, or he would sin for sure. What would Frank do? Bring him in alive. Let the courts have him. Let God judge him. Oh, the Lord knew how to test a man.

A glint down the road caught his eye, and he pulled himself up quickly and began dusting himself off. By the time the buckboard came into view, he felt as presentable as his hard trip from Denver would allow.

A large cream-colored horse and a small black mule pulled the wagon. The sideboards bore the faded remnants of a painted sign that said SOUTH PARK SALT WORKS. Carrol knew the driver.

"Hello, Vernon," he said.

The driver flinched and peered through the tiny glass circles of his spectacles. The lenses must have caused the glint Carrol had seen down the road, for nothing else on the outfit shone. "Who's that?" he demanded.

"It's Carrol."

The scowl left Vernon's face, a look of sympathy taking its place. "Good Lord. Didn't expect you so soon." He set the brake on the wagon and felt his way down, reaching over the sideboards for a spade, a shovel, and a pickax as he lit.

"How's the salt of the earth business?" Carrol asked.

Vernon had come to South Park as a prospector, but settled for a claim with a salt spring on it and started evaporating brine in a cast-iron kettle. His salt was used in gold refining, and on dinner tables. For extra income, he contracted his grave-digging services to the county. "Dryin' up," he said. "Freighters startin' to haul salt in cheaper than I can make it."

"What do you figure to do about it?"

"Never mind," Vernon said, passing the graveyard gate.

"I'm worried more for you than myself. Terrible thing that happened to Frank, but he's gone to his reward, and you don't need to worry about him."

"I know," Carrol said. "All I need to worry about is who did it."

"It was a fellow by the name of Dee Hassard. Said that was his name, anyway."

"Where was he from?"

Vernon squinted through his grimy lenses, found the place where he was supposed to dig. "Who knows?"

"What did he look like?"

"I didn't never see him close up, and my eyes is poorly, anyway. But there's a picture of him in the sheriff's office. A photograph."

"Photograph? There ain't no photographer in Fairplay, is there?"

"No, but you remember that government survey team that passed through the territory last summer?"

"Yeah."

"Remember that photographer among 'em?"

"Yeah. Fellow named Jackson."

Vernon threw his spade and shovel down and tested the handle of his pickax. "Well, he passed through town with his photographic party the other day, headin' down to the San Juans this year. Happened to be here the day we brought Frank's body in. When he heard the name of Dee Hassard, he says, 'Wait just a darned minute! I made a picture of a fellow called Dee Hassard up at Denver 'while back.' Sure 'nough, he pulled the picture out, and it was the same little crook Frank was takin' to Cañon City when he got kilt."

Carrol nodded ominously. "What was Frank takin' him to prison for?"

"He swindled a bunch of gold dust from Sam Cornelius. Convinced Sam that he had discovered a diamond field in South Park, and Sam bought his claim." He spat on his hands, getting ready to dig.

"Diamonds?" Carrol said. "Sam fell for that?"

"This Dee Hassard was pretty slick. He almost got away with it, but they caught him in Denver and brought him back for trial." Vernon snickered and took his first swing at the ground. "He had already lost all Sam's money in a poker game."

The second thud of the steel point in the ground made Carrol shiver. "Whose hole you diggin' there?"

"Sam Cornelius's."

Carrol gawked at the grave-digger. "That flimflam artist got him, too?"

"No, a mountain lion kilt him over on the Tarryall."

"Mountain lion!" Carrol blurted. "What was Sam doin' over on the Tarryall, anyway?"

"Chousin' Dee Hassard. He got madder than get-out when he heard Hassard killed Frank and escaped. Took off trailin' Hassard and got et by that lion. Funny how the Lord works, ain't it?"

Carrol snorted. "Sometimes. Sometimes it ain't funny at all." He pressed his hat down on his head. "Take care, Vernon."

"You too, Carrol."

The preacher mounted his horse and rode at a trot into Fairplay. He hitched his mount in front of the sheriff's office and walked in to find a deputy he did not know. "Howdy," he said. "You in charge here?"

The young man looked up from the load of paperwork he was shuffling through. "Yes, sir." He put his pencil down. "I'll bet you're the Reverend Carrol Moncrief."

Carrol smiled, touched by the recognition. "Wouldn't pay me to take that bet."

"You favor Frank a great deal."

"Only in appearance, I'm afraid. I've got some catchin' up to do in character."

"We all do, Reverend." The deputy stood and reached across the desk to shake Carrol's hand. "We didn't expect you this soon. We didn't know where to contact you. How did you find out?"

"A stranger in Denver told me. He had just come from here."

The deputy nodded and made a gesture inviting Carrol to sit. "Is there anything I can help you with?"

Carrol rattled the polished oak chair across the rough-sawn floor and sat down. "I was wonderin' about the head-stone."

"The county's gonna pay for a big marble marker. We've been waitin' on you to approve the inscription." He reached into a desk drawer and removed a sheet of paper, which he handed to the reverend.

Carrol checked the name and dates, read aloud the part that said KILLED IN SERVICE TO PARK COUNTY. He nodded approvingly. "His favorite psalm was one hundred eighteen, verse six. I want you to put that on there, too."

"All right," the deputy said, reaching for a pencil and a

piece of paper. "You'll have to refresh my memory, though. What does that verse say?"

"It says, 'With the Lord on my side, I do not fear.' But don't put the verse itself. Just put 'Psalms, One-eighteen: six.'" He stroked his fingertips across thin air, as if the polished marble stood between him and the deputy. "That way some curious soul might look it up every now and then, and Frank will draw somebody new into the Good Book."

The deputy shrugged. "If that's what you want."

"That's what Frank would want. Now, I understand you've got a photograph of the man who murdered my brother."

The deputy opened another desk drawer and pulled out a file folder. "It's in here somewhere." He began thumbing through the large photographs in the file. "That photographer, Jackson, brought us a whole mess of pictures he made of Fairplay last year." He removed one print and flipped it across the desk to Carrol. "Here's one of the Snowy Cross," he said. "Figured you might want to see it, you bein' a preacher and all."

Carrol glanced at the picture once, then felt his eyes pull harder toward it the second time. He had thought Jackson some kind of fool for chasing after the legend last year, wasting taxpayers' money. But here was proof of Jackson's instincts and abilities.

And what proof! Where did such a mountain stand? Such a scene! It stirred the parson, accustomed though he was to mountain views. Those pure lines of white in that stark wilderness seemed to tell him something. Seemed to call his name!

"Here he is," the deputy growled. He handed the photograph of Hassard across the desk.

When Carrol pulled his eyes away from the Snowy Cross, the face of Dee Hassard all but shouted at him, and his brain raced to place the features. He knew this man. But . . . Where?

"The name he used here was Dee Hassard," the deputy was saying. "No tellin' what he's goin' by now . . ."

The moment rushed back at Carrol like a gunshot. He saw Dee Hassard outside the Denver saloon, kneeling, pretending his rebirth. A moment later, breaking the news of Frank's death. Fool! You stupid, trusting fool!

"Reverend?" the deputy said. "You all right?" The big man had begun to tremble in front of him, his brown face darkening, one hand on the Snowy Cross, the other on Hassard.

Carrol looked up at the deputy. "I laid my hand upon his head. I blessed him. He didn't let on. He didn't show nothin'."

The deputy's mouth dropped open. "You've seen him? You've seen Hassard?"

Carrol twisted his features, fighting the hatred. "*He* told me about Frank." His fist clenched, crumpling the photograph, bending Dee Hassard's mouth into a cruel smile.

THIRTEEN

Ramon stopped on the trail and let Sister Petra walk ahead. He wasn't tired; he just wanted to take in one more view of the San Luis Valley before hiking back into the village of Del Norte. This was a wonderful basin of green waving grass: too broad to cross in a day afoot, so long that it rolled over the horizons and disappeared to the south and north. White-topped peaks gathered it in, marked it, made it a world unto itself.

The little nun was well ahead of him now on the path that led back to Del Norte. He paused another moment to let his eyes sweep the valley. He would catch up with her easily before they reached the village.

It was as if Ramon had grown on this trek. His legs seemed to have lengthened, and now he could challenge Sister Petra's gait for hours a day. And he had grown in other ways. He had learned that the *penitentes* were really quite ordinary men. Before, he had thought of them as fiendish fanatics who nailed one another to crosses. But now he could greet the members of the brotherhood in each new village with neither fear nor prejudice. They were just men.

With Sister Petra, Ramon had sought the *penitente moradas* throughout the villages of northern New Mexico, and into southern Colorado. He had never dreamed so many towns existed in those hills and mountains. In Taos, he had simply stared in wonder at the sheer numbers of people, writhing in the streets like hornets on a nest.

"What are they all doing?" he had asked Petra.

"What do you mean?"

"Where are they all going? What are they doing?" It had aggravated him that he did not know, as he had understood all the comings and goings in Guajolote.

"They have their lives," Petra had answered.

"Yes, but . . . Like that man, there, with the wheelbarrow. Where is he going?"

"I don't know," she had snapped. "Am I supposed to know everyone's business in the world?"

They had continued north, out of the low sage and up to this high green valley of farms, grasslands, and remote Mexican villages.

It had been a kaleidoscope of places and people, but this was certainly the end of the journey, and Ramon was ready to turn homeward. They had come to the northernmost *morada* of the *penitentes* at the village of Del Norte, Colorado. They had followed the trail to the *Calvario* where each year one of the brothers would hang from the cross. Sister Petra had knelt to pray. She had received nothing from God. It was over. Everything northward was Anglo domain. There were no more *Calvarios* to climb. Guajolote was lost.

Perhaps God had taken a hand in it after all, Ramon thought as he broke into a trot to catch up with Sister Petra. Now he knew that there were other places to live. He could go back to Guajolote and comfort the people. Yes, they would lose their homes, but the world was a big place. They would find new places to live.

When they reached the edge of the village, Brother Hilario rose from the ground where he had waited, leaning against the adobe wall. "Did you find what you were searching for?" he asked, a look of incredulity in his eyes.

"No," Petra said curtly. "I am going to pray now. I don't want to be disturbed."

She disappeared into the adobe Brother Hilario had provided for her stay, leaving Ramon with the local *penitente* leader.

Ramon put his hand on Brother Hilario's shoulder. "She

is disappointed," he explained. "We have no place else to search, and still we haven't found the cross on the mountain. I think she is a little bit upset."

Hilario nodded. "Well, she has walked a long way for nothing. I didn't think she was going to find anything up there."

Ramon bristled a little at Hilario's tone. "Sister Petra believes in what she's doing. She doesn't pretend."

"I never thought she was a pretender, only a lunatic." The brother pulled his shoulder out from under Ramon's hand and turned back toward his home in the village.

Ramon glared at the back of his head as he walked slowly away. "I hope they hang you from the cross next time," he muttered under his breath.

They were strangers here. This was far from home. Nobody in Del Norte had even heard of Guajolote. It was time to turn back.

Ramon walked down the street and led his burro from the trough to the adobe where he and Petra would stay the night. Methodically, he began unpacking the *aparejo*. It had become a routine with him at each new camp or village. He had learned to travel well, and he was proud of it. Sister Petra would praise him to his father when he got back home.

Ramon and the green-eyed nun had arrived at an unspoken truce after a few days of travel. He had stopped questioning her, and she had ceased to harangue him for laziness. There was respect between them now, and they traveled well together, though they knew little more about each other than when they had left Guajolote.

It made Ramon feel a little sad that Sister Petra would

not find her cross on the mountain. This was important to her. It was real. He still found it a little difficult to comprehend. Nothing had ever been that crucial to him. He had no ambitions of achieving anything the way Petra felt she had to find that cross she thought God had told her about, in order to save a tiny village from being sold out from under its people.

"Good, you're unpacking the burro," she said suddenly, catching Ramon off guard. "Bring the beans and flour in, and we will make something to eat."

He lifted the sacks of food, turned, and noticed the smoke trailing from the adobe brick chimney. This was strange. Petra seemed in rather high spirits—almost renewed. She had built a fire. She had an appetite.

He brought the food into the adobe and put it on a table of rough pine boards. These were the rudest accommodations they had been given at any village. One window was covered with parchment, and another with some kind of animal skin—coyote, he guessed. But the fire in the beehive fireplace gave sufficient light, and they would only be staying here one night.

"Well," Ramon said, "what are we going to do now?" He would not mention going home. He had learned that it was best to let Petra think she was making all the decisions. He simply tried to steer her down the right path through suggestion.

"I don't know," she answered, "but I have prayed for direction, and I have faith that I will have my answer by morning."

Ramon nodded, carefully testing the ground of this conversation. "What do you think the answer might be?"

Petra smiled and took the bag of corn flour from him. "You have been very patient, Ramon. Don't think I don't appreciate it, just because I haven't told you so."

"Yes, but . . ."

"I know, I haven't answered your question. I believe God will send us a sign in the morning, telling us where to search next. I don't know what the sign will be, but I have a feeling—just a feeling—that we are to continue going north."

Ramon dropped the bag of beans, spilling some across the pine table. "North!" he blurted. "That is Anglo country. That is fine for you, because you are Anglo. But what about me?"

Petra rolled her green eyes in the dim light of the adobe. "For your information, I am not Anglo. My grandparents came from France. *Anglo* means from England."

"You speak English, and that makes you Anglo. Besides, your skin is not brown, and neither are your eyes. You are *Americano*."

"Whether you know it or not, Ramon, you are American, too. You were born in New Mexico, a territory of the United States since 1848. I don't know what you're afraid of. You survived all those Americans in Taos, didn't you? You might as well get used to them. They're not going to go away. Traveling to the north will be good practice for you."

"But, I want to go home!" Ramon cried. "We are not going to find any cross on any mountain. Haven't we gone far enough?"

Petra's green eyes turned cold. "Go home if you want

to. The brothers will help you find your way. But I am going to keep searching. God has told me what I must do."

Ramon flailed his arms and turned a circle in the dusty room. He didn't look forward to walking home alone. But what was worse? Following Sister Petra indefinitely northward? His face pinched in a scowl, and he lost his temper. "Oh, God has told you what to do! Just like my father's burro was talking to me just now outside!" he blurted.

Petra gasped and stared openmouthed at the boy. Then her face hardened like a chiseled statue and she pointed stiffly to a stool beside the table. "Sit down!" she ordered.

Ramon cowered under the little woman's glare and sank obediently down on the stool.

"I'm going to tell you something, and I don't care whether you believe me or not." She bent at the waist, the better to glare down at him. "All my life I have faced doubters, including my own friends and family, but I know what my calling is, Ramon, and your sharp tongue does not shake my faith. Now listen, and I will tell you why I have given my life to God."

The boy swallowed and looked at the fire to escape the sister's harsh glare.

"I was only twelve years old when I first heard the voice of God," she said. "Only, I did not just hear it. I felt it, absorbed it like a tree that is struck by lightning. My name then was Julie. I was fetching a bucket of water for my mother, and I was thinking about things a girl might think of. Like dresses, and friends, and school. Then the voice of God came at me from everywhere at once, swift and hot as a ray of sun, and it knocked me to the ground, and

I spilled all of the water. And the voice had said to me: 'Serve them.' "

Ramon shifted his eyes suspiciously. "Serve who?"

"Be quiet. I am not finished." She braced her fists on her hips and looked down her nose at him. "After I heard those words, I forgot about friends, and new dresses, and school lessons, and I thought only about what God had said to me. I told my mother, and she did not believe me. She told me I had taken a heatstroke. It took me two years to convince her that I had heard the voice of God. And every day of those two long years, the children around me mocked and made fun of me, for I told everyone. I wasn't ashamed or embarrassed. Not like you, Ramon, when your friends call you padre. It was a great glory to me, and I knew I had to find out whom it was that God wanted me to serve.

"There was a convent, the Sisters of Loretto, at Nerinx, Kentucky. My mother took me there, and I gave my life to God. I became Sister Petra.

"I was twenty-one the next time I heard the voice of God. I was working in the vegetable garden, and something struck me down. Not painfully, like a blow, but swiftly and powerfully, as if I had been near an explosion. But there was no sound other than the voice. And when I awoke, I was on the ground, and dirt was sticking to the sweat on my face, and I remembered what God had said to me: 'Seek the blood of Christ.' The *Sangre de Cristo*."

"The mountains?" Ramon said.

"Yes, but I had never heard of the Sangre de Cristo Mountains then. It was another year and a half before I figured it out. Bishop Lamy came from Santa Fe seeking more nuns to serve in New Mexico, to teach in the schools and nurse the sick. This wasn't new to the Loretto convent. Sisters had gone west with Bishop Lamy before. The bishop was telling us about New Mexico, and he mentioned the Sangre de Cristos. I asked him what the name meant, for I was enchanted with the Spanish language. And when he told me, I knew that I was to go with him.

"I spent a while in Santa Fe, then I volunteered to serve at Guajolote, because there was no priest there, no chapel, no school. You may not remember how poor my Spanish was when I arrived five years ago, but I learned, and I served, and I waited again to hear that voice of light and power. And now I have heard God speak to me again, and he has told me that the cross awaits me on the mountainside. So you see, I must continue to search. I believe that God wants to save the village of Guajolote. And that is why he has spoken to me these three times in my life. I must serve him."

Ramon looked at the dirt floor of the adobe hovel. "But why would God choose one village? Why Guajolote?"

"That is for God to know. The Bible says that we will hear, and not understand; that we will see, and not perceive. I only do what God tells me to do. I have no choice. It is my life. I have heard the voice of God. I don't blame other people for not believing what I say, but I am not a perfect little angel, Ramon, and I get tired of it. So if you think I am lying, you can just go on back to Guajolote. I must continue." She turned her glare on the fire now, releasing Ramon.

He glanced up at her, saw the fire reflecting in her sharp eyes. "It's a shame," he said.

"What is?"

The boy shrugged. "You're not really that bad looking. I think you are too old to get a man anymore, but you have a pretty face, and nice long hair. You're almost too skinny, but that is better than being too fat. It is a shame you have to be a nun."

Sister Petra blushed and pushed a strand of hair back from her cheek. "Maybe you are trying to be nice now, but you are wrong. It is not a shame, Ramon. It is an honor. It is a glory. It is a burden and a responsibility, but it is not a shame. It is like nurturing a child, but the child is all of humanity. It is a labor, but it is a labor of hope and love. It is a blessing to be called, not a curse."

She looked at the boy and found him staring back at her, his brow wrinkled in the firelight. How much of this could he understand? She smiled. "I'm sorry I snapped at you. Tomorrow, if you decide to go home, I will understand. But that will make my journey more difficult, because you have become a big help to me."

Ramon looked away, feeling ashamed now for some reason.

"Do something for me if you will," Petra said.

"What, Sister?"

"Tonight, pray for direction. God hears all voices. If you pray, you will know what to do."

Ramon made a furrow in the dusty floor with his toe. It was not so much to ask for. Petra's style was to influence by example, not by directive. If she was coming right out and asking him to say a prayer, she must want him badly to do it. It wouldn't hurt anything.

"All right," he said. "I will."

FOURTEEN

Petra woke when she sensed the morning light struggling through the parchment and animal-skin window coverings. She hadn't slept past dawn the whole trip, and she felt more than a little indolent for letting it happen today.

As she put on her shoes, she thought about waking Ramon and having him pack their things on the burro. But she had nowhere to go just yet. Perhaps it was better to let the boy sleep a while this morning. Maybe she could borrow some eggs or cheese and make Ramon a big breakfast.

She closed the pine door quietly behind her as she stepped out into the gray light of early morning. The sun had not yet risen over the Sangre de Cristos, far across the valley. She stepped around the corner of the adobe to take in the view of the basin and her eyes pulled northward.

The first ray of sun suddenly streaked through a faraway mountain pass and fell on a patch of whiteness above the village. It seemed to flare, like the burning bush on the mountainside. A body of motion took form around it, and Petra made out a rider on a white mule leading a party of men toward the village.

Something made her shiver, and she took a step toward the travelers. She counted them as they came nearer. There were seven men, each riding a horse or mule. A pack train of four mules walked among them. A couple of the beasts carried large black boxes such as Petra had never seen. She met the party beyond the outskirts of the town, and the riders pulled up their mounts to converse.

"*Buenos dias,*" the bearded man on the white mule said. He looked wise for his years, gentlemanly. His accent was terrible.

"*Buenos dias,*" Petra answered.

"Do you speak English?" the rider asked, his eyebrows rising hopefully.

"I ought to," Petra said. "I grew up in Kentucky."

The man smiled, swung down from the handsome white mule, and held his hand out to Petra. "Forgive me. I mistook you for one of the locals."

"I'm just a visitor here," Petra said, taking his hand.

"This is the village of Del Norte, isn't it?"

"Yes."

"I'm William Henry Jackson, chief photographer of the U.S. Geological Survey. This is the photographic party." He gestured toward his men.

Petra nodded at the riders, who tipped their hats. "I'm Sister Petra, of the Loretto convent in Santa Fe."

Jackson's eyes widened. "You're a nun?"

"Yes."

"What brings you here from Santa Fe?"

"I'm searching for a cross on a mountain."

Jackson smiled, his eyes twinkling. "You've seen my photograph."

"Pardon?" Petra said.

"I'm the one who made the photograph of the cross. It was on last year's expedition."

Petra felt her heart flutter. "You know of a cross on a mountain?" she asked.

The photographer wilted. "You haven't seen the photo-graph?"

"No."

"But you've heard of the mountain?"

"I've been told to seek the cross on the mountain. Could you tell me how to get to it?"

Jackson scratched the back of his head, tipping his hat down over his forehead. "Well, sure, but . . . What do you want to go there for? Some sort of pilgrimage?"

Petra's breath was coming in anxious gasps, but she was trying to appear calm. "I've been sent there."

"By whom?"

"God."

Jackson stifled a smirk when he read the conviction in the nun's eyes. "It's not an easy climb, Sister. It's in rough country, and you can only see the cross by climbing above the timberline."

"Who put it there?" Petra asked, trying to envision a cross on the high, barren slopes.

"*Put* it there?" Jackson shifted his eyes to his men around him.

"Yes. How did they get it so high up on the mountain?"

The photographer folded his arms across his chest and cocked one hip, as if posing for one of his own cameras. "Sister, what do you know about this cross?"

"Only what God has told me: that it awaits me on the mountainside." Her patience was teetering, but she paced herself.

"The cross I'm talking about was put there by God, Sister. It stands a good thousand feet tall. It's made of snow packed into crevices in the mountainside. I wish I had a print of my photograph to show you, but I gave the last one away in Fairplay."

Petra had raised her palms to her cheeks and was staring with her mouth open. This was better than the time Bishop Lamy told her the meaning of *Sangre de Cristo*. She said nothing for a moment, wanting to taste the glory. Her heart was thumping in her chest, causing her to tremble. "How do I get there?" she finally asked.

Jackson pointed over his shoulder. "Well, you go north from here, up the San Luis, and over Poncha Pass. Drop into the Arkansas Valley and go upstream to Tennessee Pass. Now, there's an old Indian trail leading from Tennessee Pass to the base of Notch Mountain. Climb to the Notch Mountain Divide just south of the summit. You go above the timberline, and when you get to the top of the divide, you see the cross. That is, if it's not too cloudy up there."

Petra smiled, her eyes glistening. "How far is it from here?"

"If you came from Sante Fe, I'd say you're about halfway there. But it won't be easy, Sister. You'd better think twice about it. No white woman has ever been there. No woman at all, as far as I know. We had a devil of a time climbing there last year. Two helpers and I had to carry forty-pound packs to get the photographic equipment to the divide. It was too rough for the mules."

Petra waved his warnings away with a brush of her hand. "If you can make it with forty pounds on your back, I can surely succeed. I go with the strength of God. Now"—she clasped her hands before her and smiled at the messenger—"tell me the way again. Tell me what the cross looks like."

Ramon stepped from the dusty earthen house and rubbed his eyes. What was the nun up to this morning? Why hadn't she wakened him? He squinted as he searched the winding dirt streets, the cottonwoods along the river. His eyes swept across the San Luis Valley, past the glare of the rising sun, and northward, where they locked in on a group of men and beasts.

There she was! Who were those men she was with? She was listening intently to one of them, her hands folded before her as if in prayer.

The man in front of her wore a beard, neatly trimmed, and gestured with his hands a great deal. He was describing something big—as big as a mountainside. His palms swept the morning air like the brushes of a reckless painter. Now he made fists, flung them open like bursting shells. Facing the nun, he put his feet together and leaned as far back as he could without falling. His arms rose at his side, straight and stiff as timbers. They leveled out, made a perfect cross of his body, then kept lifting, slowly, until his palms had risen just above his shoulders.

Sister Petra bounced on her toes like a little girl, lunged at the man, and hugged him under his uplifted arms.

FIFTEEN

The drunker he stayed, the meaner he felt, and Charlie Holt liked the way the anger seethed. He knew that if he sobered up he might lose his resolve, quit the search for his runaway wife, go back to Kansas to be laughed at.

But if he stayed primed, he would have purpose. Maybe he would find her with another man. What would he do then? He had a notion. Maybe he would do some killing and turn outlaw. The thought appealed to him here in the saloon across from the shoe store. He saw it in hazy glimpses, like chapters of a dime novel he might have read once. There were gunshots, dead bodies, lawmen coming after him. Women who courted danger would open their doors. Men would stare in fear at his poster. Yes, Charlie Holt would have his own poster.

It had been easy to trail May this far. She was the kind of woman who caused the gazes of men to linger over her as she walked away. She had been remembered by the stage driver who gave her a ride into town in the middle of the night, the ticket agent who sold her the fare to Denver, the conductor who saw her enter the wagon yard near the depot.

Charlie had arrived in Denver yesterday, found the wagon yard she had stayed in a couple of nights. The man seemed nervous talking about her but said she had worked at a shoe shop a few blocks away the last he heard.

Charlie had been sober this morning when he found the

shoe shop. Sober and weak of will; unsure of his ability to handle an unpredictable woman. He had sat in the saloon across the street for three hours now, watching the shoe store through the grimy glass. He was ready. Whiskey had stoked a fire in his belly. To hell with that farm. This could turn out to be the best thing that ever happened to him.

He remembered something his father had told him: "The true mark of a man lies in his ability to profit from his misfortunes." That was before his father died and his mother married that mean bastard with the hog farm.

He got up suddenly, pushing the chair out hard behind him. He slipped the half-full pint bottle into his breast pocket, slapped his dirty farmer's hat on, and strode for the door. The fire in his belly roared like a furnace. It was time for Charlie Holt to make some profit from the misfortune brought upon him by marriage to the faithless May Tremaine.

Stepping long across the street, Holt came to the door of the shoe shop and burst in, causing a cowbell on the transom to clang.

The cobbler glanced up as a customer counted coins and dropped them into his waiting palm. "Thanks," the cobbler said, casting the coins into a cigar box, which he closed and placed under his sales counter. "What can I do for you?" he asked, turning to Holt.

Charlie waited until the customer had left, then stepped up to the counter. "I'm lookin' for May Holt—or May Tremaine—whatever she's callin' herself."

The cobbler's smile dropped. "She don't work here no more."

"Where'd she go?" Hold demanded.

"Now, look here," the cobbler said. "Who are you to bust into my shop and start askin' questions?"

"Name's Charlie Holt. I'm her husband."

The cobbler's eyes flashed once, then shifted nervously. "She never said she had no husband. I never heard nothin' 'bout no husband."

Holt sighed impatiently. Talking of May made all the men whose paths she had crossed turn nervous. He had his ideas as to why. "Just tell me where she went."

"Didn't show up for work one day. Hell if I know why. Next day I seen her with them pilgrims when they come into town to sell their wagons."

"Pilgrims?"

"Yeah, a bunch of fanatics called the Church of the Weeping Virgin. They put a pack string together and headed west toward Georgetown. Goin' over to the West Slope, I heard."

Holt sneered, but felt empowered by the news. He touched his brim and started to turn away.

"You want her things?" the cobbler asked.

"What things?"

"She left a shawl and a hairbrush and some other things."

Holt grabbed his lapels and glared. "She *stayed* here?"

The cobbler swallowed, sweat beading his brow. "Well, why not? Had to stay somewhere. I'll go get her things."

When the shoe man stepped into the back room, Charlie Holt felt an impulse sweep him up and knew he had to act on it or lose it forever. He reached over the counter and felt for the cigar box. Finding it, he lifted it into view, placing it on the counter. He flipped the lid quietly, his heart thrilling. He took the paper money first, wadding it in his pants pocket. Then he plucked a few gold coins, wincing at a metallic chink they made in his palm. He heard footsteps, closed the box, slipped it back under the counter.

"Don't know why she didn't come back for it," the cobbler said as he returned. He saw the man straighten and noticed the wild look in his eyes, mistaking it for anger.

Charlie closed his hand around the gold and crossed his arms, shoving both fists under his armpits. "Oh, hell, just keep that shit," he said. "Like you say, if she didn't come back for it, that's her own damn fault."

The cobbler felt awkward holding the handful of women's articles. He shoved them into his left hand and held his right over the counter. "Well, good luck findin' her," he said.

Charlie Holt felt several gold pieces in his right fist. He curled his lip and hissed at the cobbler with disdain. "Hell with her. I'm goin' back to Kansas." Turning toward the door, he pushed the fist into his pocket. It would be a good idea to get out of town about now.

SIXTEEN

Dee Hassard slung his blanket into the pine branches and tripped across a body in the dark. "Wake up!" he shouted.

A dream snapped in Clarence Philbrick's mind, and he sat up without thinking, his hand falling on the breech of his Remington.

"She came back!" Hassard was shouting. He stumbled shoulder-first into a bank of orange embers, rolling quickly away, regaining his feet. "Praise God, she spoke to me again!"

Elder Hopewell stirred with the pilgrims, annoyed at the disturbance of his much-needed rest. Yesterday they had crossed the Great Divide in a freezing rain by a mountain pass that stood above the timberline. His first look at the West Slope had been a frightening one, for he could see only bare rock below him in the storm. They had since descended into a deep valley of verdant grandeur, waterfalls plunging from rocky places in ribbons of froth. Hassard had pushed the party hard—too hard, Hopewell thought.

They had built a log ferry to cross the swollen Blue River, not even pausing to rest on the west bank. They had marched right through the new mining town of Frisco— the last settlement they would see. They had passed beaver ponds where the elder had hoped they might linger. Hassard had driven them relentlessly through a winding and sheltered valley that looked to Hopewell like a good place to settle. But the new prophet of the Church of the Weeping Virgin seemed to think of nothing but his pilgrimage to the Mount of the Snowy Cross.

The trek had been exhausting. And now this—to be woken from a sound sleep in the chilly night. Hopewell gathered his gangling legs under him and willed his eyes to focus in the dim moonlight, catching sight of the hysterical Deacon Dee stumbling across the congregation.

"I know what to do now," Hassard cried. "She told me!"

"Whoa, Deacon, whoa," Hopewell said, as if calming

a skittish horse. He reached a long thin arm far across the camp as Hassard stumbled near him and grabbed the man firmly by the collar. "You're unsettlin' the people like that."

"Hopewell!" Hassard said, seemingly startled to find the elder there. "The Virgin came back! Where's the money?"

Clarence felt his coat for coins. Yes, it was still laden with gold, pressing heavily down on him as he got to his feet.

"Now get ahold of yourself," Hopewell said. "You're not making sense."

"It makes perfect sense," Hassard said, gripping the elder's arm. "It's just like Paster Wyckoff wrote in the *The Wisdom of Ages!* The faithful have to renounce everything that pretends to take power from God. That includes government, all those other false religions, and—money!"

"We have renounced all that," Hopewell said. "That's why we came out here, away from government power. Away from those other denominations. And we've given our money to the church."

Clarence stepped around the dazed pilgrims and stopped with the rifle stock on his hip. He looked back for May, remembering where she had bedded down on the spruce boughs he had cut for her. He saw her rising in the moonlight, as fine a sight as he had ever seen.

"And now it's time for the church to renounce that money!" Hassard yelled, raising his arms and laughing. "We're finally to be free of that 'evil mammon'—that's what Pastor Wyckoff called it. The Virgin came to me again tonight, Hopewell. Just now. And she told me why

we're to make our pilgrimage to the Mount of the Snowy
Cross. We're to sacrifice that money to God, there on the
mountain. We're to give it up and trust in his will to get
us by!"

"Wait a minute," Clarence said, stepping forward.
"When you had these people sell all their wagons and
things, you told them the money would be used to file on
homesteads or buy government land."

"That was before the revelation!" Hassard hissed, waving his hand at the Vermonter. "Now I know better. What
do you need money for? The wilderness will provide us
everything. Now, where's the money, Elder Hopewell?"

"Hold on," Clarence said. "I see where you're entitled
to a certain amount of authority as guide of this party, but
that money belongs to these people. It's up to them to decide what to do with it."

"But it's not up to them," Hassard said. "It's not up to
me, and it's not up to you. It's up to God, and God has sent
his angel, the Virgin Mother of his only son, to tell Pastor
Wyckoff, and now me, what the faithful are to do to save
mankind!"

"But legally—" Clarence began.

"Legally?" Hassard stomped toward the Vermonter.
"Brother Clarence, you haven't embraced what this church
is all about. There is no law but God's law!" He seethed
with a rage almost real in its vehemence.

Clarence remained unmoved. "If it were your money,
you could do whatever you wanted with it. But . . ."

"Look," Hassard said, tromping off toward his saddle
on the ground. "I understand your reservations. You
haven't seen the Virgin weeping in your dreams." He fum-

bled excitedly with the flap of his saddlebags. "But maybe this will convince you."

Clarence scarcely saw the articles Hassard lifted from the saddlebags in the moonlight, but he could tell by the way the man handled them that they carried considerable weight for their size.

"I've got almost two thousand dollars' worth of gold dust here from my mine in Tarryall," Hassard said, carrying the two leather pouches to Elder Hopewell. "I didn't mention it before, because I was greedy. Thought you might want some for your church. But now I'm willing to give it all up!" He placed the two bags of dust in Elder Hopewell's hands.

"What do you want me to do with it?" Hopewell said.

"Add it to the church coffers." He took the roll of bills from his coat pocket and handed it to Hopewell. "Put this with it. And when the time comes, I hope you'll see fit to dedicating it to the Lord."

"Just what do you mean by 'dedicating' it?" Clarence asked.

"I am to find this mountain—the Mount of the Snowy Cross. I am to lead the faithful there. And we are to leave all our evil mammon at the place where we first catch sight of the cross. Those are my instructions from the Weeping Virgin. That is dedication, Brother Clarence. That is the dedication of the faithful!"

"That's throwin' money away on a mountaintop if you ask me."

A look of suspicion swept Hassard's face. "Maybe you'd like to have your share of the money back," he said. "Is that it, Brother Clarence?"

"No, that's not it, because I never put any money in there. I'm just against throwing money away when it might be put to some kind of good use."

Hassard put his hands on his hips. "Have you read *The Wisdom of Ages*?"

"Not all of it," Clarence admitted.

"How much have you read?"

"I only got through the first chapter."

"Brother Clarence, how do expect to become a member of this church if you don't read Pastor Wyckoff's book?"

"I never said I intended to become a member of this church—no offense to any of these folks. You just hired me on as a hunter for this trip."

"So you're here to make money, not to dedicate it. You seem to be struggling with inner greed, Brother Clarence."

"No," May said, the heads turning to look at her. "Clarence was real generous to me. He bought me supper in Denver when I was hungry and didn't have a place to stay."

In the sparse light, Hassard saw the eyes of the pilgrims shift from May to Clarence and knew he needed to add nothing to their suspicions. "I don't doubt he did. But he's said he doesn't intend to join the congregation of the Church of the Weeping Virgin, he's offered no money to the church coffers, he's failed to read past the first chapter of *The Wisdom of Ages,* and yet he thinks he has the authority to tell these people what to do with their money?"

"You're the one who's trying to tell them what to do with the church money. I'm saying it's up to them, not you."

Hassard took a few steps toward Clarence. "I'll tell you

one thing I have the authority for. That's gettin' these good people safe to their promised land. To do that, I have to keep them fed, and I haven't seen you bringin' in any meat."

Clarence shifted the rifle in his hand. "Game's been scarce. Prospectors must have spooked everything out."

The deacon snorted. "You've got tomorrow to bring some meat in, or you're fired. Now, I'm goin' into the woods to pray. I'll say a special one for you, Brother Clarence. You need it." He walked through the throng, which parted to let him pass into the trees.

When he had skulked far enough into the timber, he stopped to urinate on a tree trunk, then grinned as he buttoned his trousers back. That Clarence from Vermont really thought he was something. He almost hoped that smart-mouthed kid did kill some meat tomorrow. Pulling this thing off would be a lot easier without him around, but it would definitely be more interesting with him.

He found a log on the ground and knelt beside it, lying across the top of it. He would sleep there, and someone would come to wake him before dawn and find him as if he had fallen asleep in prayer.

Oh, young Clarence was full of himself. But Dee Hassard had made fools of brighter men than him. If he couldn't get rid of the damn nuisance, he would just have to put a ring in the Vermonter's nose and break him to lead. And if that didn't work, there was always the rust-pitted Smith & Wesson or the fine blue Colt taken from the corpse of Frank Moncrief.

SEVENTEEN

Clarence sat against the trunk of a ponderosa pine, watching a small meadow take shape in front of him. His Remington rifle lay across his thighs, his right thumb on the hammer, left palm cupped around the forestock. Dawn was making the strange terrain known to him. He did not expect game.

This was lunacy. He should be in New Mexico by now, surveying his new domain, instead of lounging indolently in this strange forest. The Ojo de los Brazos waited to embrace him. Did the arms of May Tremaine?

The weight of fifty-six hundred pressed against his lungs, pulled at his shoulders. He felt like a fool right now. He was wasting his time. What if some other investor was snapping up the Ojo de los Brazos at this very moment? When his father found out, he would never hear the end of it. He wished at this moment that he had come west without the damned money. Look how far he had gotten on his wits. The money was only tormenting him, hurrying him through places were he might otherwise linger.

"Get the game, or go," he muttered to himself. This wilderness would decide for him. If he did not have meat on the ground by the time the sun bathed this meadow, he would leave the Church of the Weeping Virgin to fend for itself, and he'd turn south toward his destiny. He would not even rejoin the party. May would be with them. He would see her graceful limbs, meet her eyes, and lose his resolve.

I will have forgotten her by the time I reach Santa Fe.

Good-bye, May Tremaine. Good luck. What will become of you while I build my kingdom down in New Mexico?

A sound swelled up under him, as if a heart had begun to beat in the bosom of the earth. His eyes searched as the Remington rose. The heartbeat thumped under him again, and he saw the buck deer bounding on four stiff legs at once. He pulled the hammer back, and the hooves came down again: the third heartbeat.

He shifted into shooting position as the buck landed broadside and froze. The irons found the shoulder. Black powder stained the air. The buck flinched and fell, quivering now on the ground.

The rhythm of the earth's heartbeat continued, coming now from the Vermonter's own chest. His ears rang, but he heard the echo of his shot glancing off some distant rim. The curve of an antler—bulbous and velvet-covered this time of year—stood above the grass no more than fifty paces from where he sat.

He got up and strode slowly toward the dead deer. From whence that buck had come, he could not say. It seemed to have sprung from the soil, surprising him. He had seen this happen with deer before, seen them materialize where moments before nothing had stirred. But this was fresh magic.

He approached the carcass and stood over it. A big deer compared to the whitetails he had hunted back in Vermont. What had made him start bounding like that—drumming the earth with all fours like creation's own heartbeat? He had read in the sporting magazines that this was the way with blacktailed deer, hopping on four legs at once, but he had never dreamed it would shake the ground so.

He knelt, felt his grip take in the velvet antler, dreamed of riding into camp in glory. His doubts evaporated, and as he reached anxiously for his gutting knife, he knew he was in the right place, the right time. He was sick and tired of trying to live up to his father's expectations. This was where Clarence Philbrick belonged, whether there was any money in it or not.

Dee Hassard had turned the pilgrims onto a trail recently widened by the axes of prospectors . . . a trail used for centuries by dark-skinned huntsmen . . . a trail as old as the migrating herds who had trodden it bare long before any human shadow fell upon its ground. It led the faithful along the flanks of the Sawatch Range, toward Notch Mountain, where the view of the Snowy Cross supposedly awaited them.

May walked near the rear of the party this morning, glancing often over her shoulder. Her feet had healed and toughened nicely, thanks to the moccasins Mary Whitepath had given her. She might have paced the sojourners at the head of the pilgrimage, as she usually did, but something caused her to drop back today.

Strange how the pilgrims daily took their regular places in the processional, May thought. Some kept to the head of the line, some lagged, others habitually gravitated toward the middle. Back here, May was getting acquainted with a whole new set of believers. Faces she had seen around camp took on names, loosed voices.

"Are you plannin' to go all the way up to see the cross?" one said.

May looked into the tired but hopeful eyes of a young

mother walking beside her. She couldn't place the accent. Scottish or Irish, she guessed. Maybe Welsh. She wished she knew more about the world. "I don't know what I'm plannin'," she admitted.

The immigrant woman carried a baby in one arm, had a misshapen bag looped across one shoulder. Her other hand led a child tired of trotting, begging to be carried. "I'll follow Deacon Hassard there if I'm able," she said.

May glanced at the trail behind her. "Let me carry that baby for you," she said. "I don't have a load to pack."

"Thank you," the mother said. She handed the baby to May, swinging the heavier child up into her arms. "Are you ready to join yet?"

"I don't know that either. What all do I have to do?"

"You have to go through the initiation."

May drew her lips together. She was hearing more about this initiation all the time, the references always vague. "How come I can't just join?"

"Oh, there's things you can only learn in the three days. It's a secret. I can't tell you. But you'll be exhausted by the time it's done, I'll warrant that!" The little woman laughed at May, her eyes sparkling.

They strode on, May listening apprehensively to the immigrant woman make sketchy hints about the nature of the initiation. She would get no sleep, she would be starved, and she would be broken down to tears before it was all over.

"Why would anybody want to do that?" she asked, and the woman only laughed at her. She suddenly felt a thousand miles from civilization, caught up in something she didn't want or understand. Clarence was the only hope she had, and Dee Hassard had given Clarence the ultimatum.

As they came around a giant fir tree at a crook in the trail, May looked over her shoulder, and when she turned back to the way ahead, she found Dee Hassard in her path. She gasped, instinctively shielding the infant in her arms from the red-haired prophet.

"He ain't comin' back, Sister May," Hassard said.

She blushed. "Who do you mean?"

"You know. The kid from back east." He looked disapprovingly at the baby in May's arms, noticed the mother standing nearby as the rest of the party trudged on around them. "Brother," he said to a poorly clothed young man with several teeth missing, "carry this baby for this good mother. I want to talk with Sister May."

Reluctantly, May gave up the child as the mother drifted on up the trail with the rest of the party.

"I don't expect to see Brother Clarence ever again. He packed all his things with him and rode his own horse out this morning."

The tail end of the pilgrimage was coming around the bend in the trail now, shortly to leave May alone with the prophet.

"Did you see that in one of your visions?" she said, unable to mask her sarcasm.

Hassard smiled. This girl had seen and done more than she let on. "You don't believe in the Mount of the Snowy Cross?"

The last pilgrim, an old woman, limped around the crook in the trail, casting a parting glance at the pair—a fearful glance, it seemed to May—almost a warning.

"I don't know," May said, feeling vulnerable. She began walking again, but Hassard grabbed her by the arm.

"Wait," he said. "I want to talk to you about something."

She pulled timidly away, but he refused to release her. "Turn me loose," she said.

"Just a minute." He smiled, tightened his grip. "I won't hurt you, Sister May. I just want to talk."

She glanced down the back trail. No one was coming for her. Hassard was right. Clarence would never return. She was alone here with this stranger, deep in the forested mountains. The familiar fear surged all around her, the helplessness her aunt's husband had first introduced her to years ago.

"What do you want?" she said, her voice shaking.

"I want you to help me lead this rabble," he replied, testing her like strange snow-drifted ground. "People think more of a man when he has a beautiful woman by his side." He smiled, a thin expression of his power over her.

"They think enough of you already. You and your revelations. You don't need my help."

Hassard turned her toward him, his hand still firmly grasping her arm. "I know what I need, Sister May. Now, you think about it. This church will be the richest thing in the mountains before it's all over."

"I thought you were going to make them give all their money away."

"I mean land rich. God's green earth possesses more value than man-made coin. These people need a female model they can look up to. I think you fit the mold, May. You'll have everything."

"I don't know what you mean," she said.

"You know exactly what I mean. Ol' Deacon Dee has been around, Sister May. Enough to recognize that you have, too." He put another hand on her, crept his palms slowly up her arms, pulling her slightly closer to him.

May quivered, felt her disgust of the man being squeezed between them. Why did men like him always treat her this way? Damn him to think he could do this to her, lay his hands upon her, hold her here against her will! "All right, I'll think about it," she said. "Just let me catch up with the others."

"I will, May." He showed her how strong he was, pulling her toward him until her palms pressed flat against his chest. "But you've got to make up your mind soon. I go out in the woods to say my prayers every night. If you decide you want the easiest life in these mountains, you come on out and join me there. If you don't, this wilderness could be a little hard on you."

As his leer descended on her, she drew her face back, then turned her head sharply away. She thought she would burst with shame and hopelessness until she saw the figure rise from a dip in the trail downhill. "Clarence!"

Hassard glanced and felt his grip melt from her arms as she pulled away. He saw the antlers jostling, the broad body of the deer slung over the saddle. The hunter was leading his horse, grinning at May as she trotted to meet him. The Vermonter swept his hat from his head, its brim rolled in his hand.

"Damn!" Hassard muttered. He backed away as May reached the hunter. He stepped around the big fir in the crook of the trail. How had that kid managed to kill that deer? Sister May wouldn't be coming to join him in the woods tonight—he knew that. They meant trouble now—both of them.

Every scam he had ever had fail had failed because of a woman. Even that diamond field fiasco. He would never have gotten caught in Denver if he hadn't stopped at that whorehouse to gamble and fornicate.

Now Sister May had taken a peek under his prophet costume. How much would she tell young Philbrick? Damn those inviting eyes!

EIGHTEEN

Carrol Moncrief stalked slowly down the street, his eyes searching for bits of shattered glass. This was the place to begin trailing Dee Hassard. Not so much as a reader of sign, but as a calculator of men.

The hooves of a hundred horses had broken this ground since Hassard knelt upon it. A thousand drunken miners, cowboys, and vagabonds had obliterated the tracks the swindler had made leaving this street. Still, this was the place to begin, where they had stood together, the swindler hoaxing the preacher, the preacher deceiving himself.

A shard of glass twinkled in the noonday glare, and Moncrief squatted to pinch it between two toughened digits. Once he found the first, others seemed to sprout all around him—like gems in Dee Hassard's ludicrous field of diamonds. This was where the whiskey bottle had rained down on them in pieces. Where Carrol had met his brother's murderer.

The question was why. Why had Hassard made himself known to Carrol that night? He had shown his face, given the preacher a firsthand sighting, a lead. Was Hassard simply so mean that he wanted to see the look on Carrol's face when he broke the news about Frank? Or was he clever?

Let's assume he's clever, Carrol thought. No, more than just clever. Sly. Treacherous to the point that he didn't mind getting on his knees in the sight of God and everybody else in order to draw a victim into a snare.

But which snare?

Hassard had wanted him to go back to Fairplay for some reason. Carrol rolled the jagged piece of glass between his fingers until a new facet glinted at him. Maybe he had been looking at this thing wrong. Maybe Hassard didn't want him in Fairplay so much as he just wanted him out of Denver.

Still, why?

Moncrief felt his fingers tightening with frustration until a sharp point cut through his thick skin. He flinched, flicked the shard of glass aside.

All right, let's start over, he thought. What does a confidence man want? He wants something you've got. Something valuable. He wants it so bad he's willing to work for it, and work hard. Most people don't realize that a swindler is not a lazy criminal. Deception is hard work. Hassard's motivation lay not with indolence, but in the taking—the actual theft by swindle. It gave him a perverse sense of mastery to so smoothly steal.

He strode slowly toward the board sidewalk, mulling it over, stopping only to let a buggy pass. What did he have that Hassard would want? Where would Hassard go to get it? He kicked the board sidewalk where he and Hassard had talked religion. What were the last words that had passed between them? He had asked Hassard to inform the Church of the Weeping Virgin that he would not be available to lead them over the mountains.

So what? It wasn't as if Hassard would actually do him that favor out of the goodness of his heart, for not even the hole where his heart should have been held any goodness.

What had ever happened to that bunch of fanatics, anyway? Whom had they hired to lead them over the mountains? Oh well, that wasn't his concern. He had to catch Hassard. But there were no leads. The man could be anywhere.

The coward had killed Frank in cold blood and all but boasted of it to Carrol's face.

He spat in the street and fought an urge to utter a cuss word that was whirring in his head like the wings of a locust. Investigating had been Frank's strength, never his own.

In his old days of lawlessness, Carrol Moncrief had shaken many a lawman and vigilante from his trail. It was so easily accomplished. Only Frank had succeeded in riding him down, jailing him, seeing him to the penitentiary.

He had hated Frank for it at the time. "You ain't no brother of mine," he had told him. Now Carrol knew that he would have been dead and in hell by this time if Frank hadn't taken him down that hard reality road.

How had Frank done it? In those days no one could ride harder than the outlaw Carrol Moncrief. And yet his own brother had managed to bring him in. How? Simple enough. He made it more than a job. He made it personal.

He just kept coming. That was what Carrol would have to do to catch this Dee Hassard, or whatever his real name was. Never quit, never stop thinking like a confidence man. Just keep coming.

He smacked his lips and looked at the sign on the saloon front. Parting the double doors, he stepped in, his eyes meeting those of the bartender almost instantly. "Remember me?" he said, his spurs singing loud against the board floor.

The bartender's quick glance lashed his shotgun under the bar, then returned to the preacher. "You've got sand in your craw to come back here after pullin' that hog leg on me."

"Dry sand," Carrol said, throwing a coin onto the bar.

"You think I'll pour you good whiskey?"

"One thing I've learned about bartenders," Carrol said, hooking his heel on the foot rails. "You're forgivin' souls. I guess you've got to be when your best customers are drunks." He smiled with genuine warmth.

The bartender smirked, reached for a bottle and glass. "You're the damnedest preacher I ever saw. I thought the Good Book was supposed to be against drink."

"Against drunkenness, not drink. Jesus himself changed water to wine. Man's got to know when to quit, that's all."

"I hope you don't aim to hang around here all day and go to preachin' again."

Carrol took a sip and shook his head. "Just came to clear the cobwebs. I'm lookin' for somebody."

"Who?" The bartender's eyes brightened, hoping he could help move the preacher on.

"A fellow named Dee Hassard. Little redheaded pecker-wood was here last time I was."

"Not the one you Christianized out there in the street?"

Carrol set his glass on the bar. "You remember him?"

"I heard the shot, like everybody else. Looked out the window to see what was goin' on. Saw that redheaded feller on his knees. You must have put the fear of God into that soul, Parson."

"How's that?" Carrol was straightening, sensing a fresh turn in the trail.

"He up and joined that bunch of fanatics the next day. You know, the pilgrims goin' over the mountains. Came into town with some of 'em to swap their wagons for mules and burros. Hell, looked like they was joinin' him, instead of him joinin' them."

"What do you mean?"

"He was ramroddin' the whole outfit. Had 'em sellin' wagons, furniture, all sorts of things. Later on I seen 'em leadin' a pack string back up toward Cherry Creek. That redheaded feller was on the lead mule."

Carrol smiled and picked up his glass. "Friend," he said, pausing to throw the last of the whiskey down his throat, "I'm sorry I ever pulled my pistol on you." He faced the handful of men in the saloon, raising his hands as he turned. "Bless this saloon!" he cried, closing his eyes tight. "May God bring only health and prosperity to all who enter its portals!" He made his head tremble for empha-sis. "May every jigger poured here cleanse the soul of he whose veins it courses! Amen!"

"You ain't gonna start preachin' to my customers again,

are you?" the bartender asked as Carrol Moncrief strode long for the door.

"Nope."

"Where you goin'?"

Carrol stopped at the door, his eyes flaring as they shot back across the barroom. "Over the mountains, brother bartender. I think it's time I went on a pilgrimage."

NINETEEN

The town was called Buena Vista, but the view did not look so good to Ramon. He hadn't seen one brown face since he arrived, nor heard a single word of Spanish—not even from Sister Petra. She had been murmuring that gibberish called English to virtually anyone who would listen.

The surrounding mountains were spectacles such as Ramon had never seen, hence the name of the bustling mining town. But the name was the only thing Spanish about this place. The peaks were not like the ones that rose above Guajolote. These were American mountains. Not Spanish, or Mexican. They didn't even seem like Indian mountains, though Petra had told him they belonged to the Utes. This was strange country—white man's domain—and he did not belong.

The people here gawked at him as if they had never seen a Mexican. Perhaps it was not Ramon, himself, so much as it was the trio—the boy, the nun, and the burro. It appeared to Ramon that word of them had spread since they arrived an hour ago, and now every soul in town wanted to get a look at the strange little party that sought the cross on the mountain.

They were on their way out of town now, which gave him some relief. But they were heading ever farther north, which only made him feel sick for the familiarities of home. Everything had slipped hopelessly beyond Ramon's control. There was no way he could abandon Sister Petra now and make his own way back to Guajolote. He didn't speak the language of this place. There were no friendly societies of *penitentes* to provide him with direction and sustenance. He hated feeling this dependent on the nun, but he clung to her like a child to its mother.

Worst of all, the bitterness and homesickness he felt was beginning to make him doubt her. They had actually gotten along very well since Del Norte—working together, entertaining each other with conversation and stories. Still, he was beginning to have an evil thought.

It had first occurred to him when they crossed Poncha Pass, leaving San Luis Valley and all its Mexican settlements behind. It struck him then that the Anglo photographer they had met in Del Norte had spoken only English. Sister Petra had been the only one in the village able to translate for him. What if she had lied about what the photographer said? What if she had simply made up the story of this white man photographing a cross on a mountain? How would anyone know the difference? Petra was the only one who spoke the photographer's language.

This was the idea that burdened Ramon with guilt—the notion that Sister Petra was a liar. It was a sin to think such a thing of a nun, but he couldn't help it. She could have been lying to him all along for all he knew. God might never have spoken to her in the first place. Maybe she was just plain crazy.

The road led them out of town and up the rocky valley of the Arkansas River, a stream of white water, rushing like the Anglos back in Buena Vista who seemed ceaselessly to scramble for wealth or influence, or whatever it was that drove them so.

"What's wrong with you today?" Petra said to him as they mounted their familiar gait—an easy rhythm, efficient in its regularity.

"I'm keeping up," Ramon said defensively.

"Not that," she replied. "You haven't spoken in hours."

He turned his head from her and sighed. He really didn't want to talk about it. "Did they say anything about the cross back there?"

"Oh, I'm sorry, I should have told you," she said. "Yes, everybody around here has heard of it, though I met no one who has actually seen it. They said the Indians first spoke about it, but they didn't really believe the Indians. Then, several years ago, an old prospector got lost—turned around up in the mountains—and he went above the timberline trying to find his way. As he came over a divide, he suddenly saw the cross. And then, he found his way all of a sudden, like magic!" She beamed her pretty green eyes at him.

Ramon looked away. "And where is this old prospector now?"

"Oh, he wandered away long ago. That is the way with prospectors, always searching for new diggings."

He rolled his eyes a little, almost hoping that she noticed. "And what about the photographer?"

"They didn't know of him, but that is because he never came through Buena Vista on his expeditions. One man I met had heard of the geological survey, though—the Hayden Survey, as he called it."

Ramon slapped his palms against his thighs, flailing the lead rope of the burro that had plodded so stupidly along with him on this ridiculous quest. "So we still have no guide to take us to this mountain, this cross, this vision of yours."

"It was never a vision," she said, her voice hardening. "And we do have a guide, of sorts. We have the directions given to us by the photographer."

"Given to *you*," Ramon blurted. "I heard only *Ingles*."

"But I translated it for you," Petra said. She stopped in the road. "You believe me, of course."

Ramon took a few steps, then stopped. He did not turn to look back at her.

"Ramon? You *do* believe me?"

He wheeled, glared at her. "Of course! You are Sister Petra, the Divine. God talks to you, like me talking to this stupid burro to hurry up, or to get his foot off of the rope! You could not be a liar. You are too perfect."

She felt suddenly disappointed in him. He hadn't thrown a fit in many days, and she had come to think that he had grown beyond that. Now he was acting like a little boy again. She stalked off the road, toward a big rock near a slow bend of the river, in the shade of a cottonwood. "I am no more perfect than you are," she insisted as she passed him. "We will eat our lunch over here. Maybe we can catch some fish for tonight."

"Wouldn't that be *perfect*," he grumbled.

"Stop that!"

"I can't. I'm not a perfect angel like you. I have sins in my heart. Great big ones! Maybe one of them thinks you are a liar, but that could not be, because you are so perfect."

"Then why am I mad enough to pull your little nose off?" She clawed at the packsaddle, looking for the dried meat and fruits.

"You know what!" he said. "It would have been easier just to leave Guajolote and move to some other village than it is following you all this way on this stupid trip."

"I am not interested in what is easiest for you. I am interested in what God tells me I must do."

"Why? To save a little village nobody even cares about? Not even the church cares about it, because if they did, they would send us a priest instead of just a nun. Why would God want to save a little place like Guajolote, anyway? It doesn't matter to anybody. What do you think you're going to find, if you ever see this cross? How is it going to help?"

"Neither you nor I know how God works. We must simply do his will."

"No, *you* must because you are so perfect. I am only here because my father made me go, and I was too stupid to disobey him."

"For the last time, Ramon, I am just as human as anybody else. Quit called me perfect, or I will prove to you that I am not!" She raised her hand threateningly.

Ramon was beyond fear of the little woman. Maybe she would slap the devil out of him, but he was willing to risk it in order to speak his mind. "What sin did you ever commit?" he said. "I bet you never even had a thought to do anything wrong."

"You want me to brag about my sins? That is preposterous! I don't have to prove my humanity to you by my sins!"

"Ah!" he shouted. "That's what I thought. You don't have any to brag about!"

She gathered her lips together in frustration and pounded a half loaf of rock-hard bread down on the boulder. "All right, Ramon! If you really must know, I will tell you one. Oh, you want to hear a *big* sin, don't you? Well, fine. I will tell you one. When I lived in Santa Fe . . . When I was at the Loretto convent there . . . Well, it was a very difficult time for me, and . . ."

"And what?" Ramon demanded.

"I had impure thoughts!"

His face writhed in wicked laughter. "Not *thoughts*!" he cried. "Now you are going to hell with the rest of us, Sister Petra!"

"It was not just the thoughts! I *acted* upon them!"

The mocking leer dropped from Ramon's face. "*Impure* thoughts?" he said quietly.

"Now you see that I am just as wicked as everybody else, don't you?" It was a little like bragging, she realized. It did suddenly put her on more even footing with Ramon, and that was what was needed.

"Wait a moment," he said, still uncertain as to whether or not he and Petra understood each other. "What exactly happened?"

She hesitated. The truth was she wanted to tell him. She had always wanted to tell somebody but had been too afraid. She had never even confessed it to a priest, which had driven her guilt even deeper. But she had come a long way with Ramon and gotten to know him well. Perhaps she owed him this. He was a good boy. They were friends now. Maybe this would help him to keep going somehow. She felt one thing for certain: Ramon might not agree with everything she dragged him through, but she could trust him.

"You have to promise never to tell anyone," she said. "Ever. If you do, I will commit another sin when I get my hands on your neck!"

"I won't tell," he said, sitting on the boulder to break a piece of bread.

She looked away from him. "You must understand that it was not an easy time for me," she began. "I had grown into a woman and was starting to regret that I had never done the things most girls do. I was beginning to doubt. The words God had spoken to me before seemed like a dream. I began to think maybe I had imagined them or something. Like my mother said: a heatstroke. I didn't know if I was supposed to be a nun all of my life. I was alone in Santa Fe, and I was confused."

"Yes, yes," Ramon said, urging her along with gestures. "Get to the impure thoughts."

She frowned at him. "I was teaching at the orphanage for girls, and there was a carpenter who came there to build a new staircase. He was an American from Kentucky, like me. His voice reminded me of home, and I liked talking to him. He was about my age—about twenty-five—and he was very good looking.

"Well, we became friends, and I started thinking about

him all the time, wondering what I had missed. So I decided to find out. I knew it was wrong. I knew it went against my vows. But that is the way with sin. It makes you enjoy your betrayal of God. That is the true evil of it."

"So . . ." Ramon said, trying to avoid the sermon and get back to the story. "What did you do with the American?"

"I told him the truth. That I wasn't sure I wanted to be a nun anymore. He told me he would help me find out. He rented a room. We met." She shrugged as if she had said all she intended and picked up a piece of cured meat.

"But what did you do together?" Ramon demanded.

"Oh, come now. Your father raises chickens and goats, does he not? You know about the birds and the bees."

"Ay!" The boy gasped with quiet astonishment, as if he were talking now to some explorer returned from exotic lands. "How did you know what to do?"

"I didn't. I was terrified. I felt clumsy and foolish. But he knew."

Ramon chewed a piece of jerked beef for some time in silence. "What happened after you met the American there?"

"I was a little disappointed, once it was done. It wasn't all I had expected. I felt guilty, too. Ashamed that I had broken my vows in such a way. And yet, the pure thrill of sinning was part of me now, and I didn't want to let that thrill go."

"Did you meet him again?"

"Yes, I met him every now and then, when we could arrange it. Our affair lasted about two months." Embarrassed, she put her fingertips against her forehead to shield her eyes.

"What happened after two months? Did somebody find out?"

"No one ever knew but he and I. He was a decent young man, as some sinners are, Ramon. He was just led astray. By me, I suppose. Anyway, after two months went by, I realized something. I had been waiting for a feeling that would tell me I should quit the order to marry this man. I was waiting to fall in love with him, in other words, but it wasn't going to happen, and I knew it."

Ramon shook his head. "I bet you broke his poor heart."

Her eyes cut toward the river. "That was the greatest sin of all. And for that I felt so terribly shameful, Ramon. You will never know. It was a terrible thing to do to another person, to myself. And most of all, to God. I had made promises, Ramon, and had broken them in the most self-ish way—right in the sight of God!

"I dictated my own penance, and I was more severe on myself than any priest or bishop would have been. Even the pope!"

"What did you do?" Ramon asked, thinking of the phys-ical rigors the members of the brotherhood forced them-selves to endure.

"I banished myself to Guajolote. Where there were no handsome young men who spoke in Southern drawls. Where there were no markets, or artists, or grand festivals. I banished myself to that dusty little village of yours and begged God that some good might come of my sins.

"And some good will come of it, Ramon. My faith is restored. God has forgiven me. And I have learned to love that remote little place. It is strange how the Good Lord works. It is almost as if he wanted me to sin." She shook her head. "It is more than I can understand."

"Maybe it's better that you committed that sin," Ramon said. "If you hadn't, you would always be wondering. I know I would."

"Ah, but that is the nature of faith, Ramon. You accept the road God gives you. You have faith that it is the right and only path for you. And you do not wonder anymore."

The boy dusted some bread crumbs from his shirt and remembered what she had said about fishing. There was a line and a hook in the pack, and various bugs around to use for bait.

"I'm going to try to catch a trout," he said. "You might as well take a siesta. It doesn't take two people to catch a trout."

He secured the line, caught a grasshopper. Before he went to the river's edge, he saw Petra spreading a blanket to lie on under the shade of the pine. "Sister," he said. "I am sorry I called you a liar."

She smiled, waved him away with her graceful little hand. "There will be none of that." Kneeling, she added, "Ramon, I have not had a friend like you in a long time. A very long time."

TWENTY

Easy money spent fast. This Charlie Holt had learned by the time he got to Frisco. He was all but broke when he left the café, but his stomach was full of venison steak and fried potatoes, and he had just enough stolen cash remaining from the shoe store till to get mildly drunk, which was exactly what the outlaw in Charlie needed right now.

The valley lay cooling as he walked to the nearest saloon, the sun having plunged beyond the Sawatch Range. This wasn't like Kansas, he thought, where the blazing summer daylight scalded you hour upon hour in the fields. This was life such as Charlie had only dreamed of. This was the outlaw trail. Why he had ever lived another way was a mystery to him.

He was only three or four days behind the Church of the Weeping Virgin and closing ground fast. The pilgrims seemed to be moving at a pretty good clip for a party afoot, but Charlie had been riding hard, swapping for fresh horseflesh at every mining town. The roads up here were mere ledges carved out of mountainsides, but they tended to channel most travelers through the same passes, down the same valleys. The church had been easy to follow. With one more fresh mount, Charlie would be on them.

Lordy, but May was going to be surprised to see him. She was likely to piss herself. He would make her regret running away when he caught her.

The only problem was that Charlie was nearly broke. He didn't have enough money left from the "Denver Job," as he had come to think of it, to purchase a fresh mount plus the supplies he would need to push into the wilderness. Frisco was his last chance to get outfitted.

He stepped through the open door of the saloon and returned the suspicious gazes of the men who sat hunched over their drinks. It was a shotgun-style frame building—narrow where it fronted the street, running deep under a low ceiling. Two windows allowed a little grime-filtered daylight into the front of the saloon, but the back seemed dark as a bear cave, the bartender having not yet lit the coal-oil lamps.

A pair of townsmen broke their conversation to watch Charlie walk past their table at the window. They wore garters on their white sleeves. He strode the narrow path between the long rough-sawn bar and the two-seater tables against the wall. None had more than a single man sitting at it—dirty miners, most of them. Beyond the bar, calls and raises slowly circled a big table in a torpid poker game. Behind the big table, a back door led to a small dark space of some kind.

Charlie found a single high stool at the end of the bar and sat with his back to the poker game where he could watch the front door, drink, and plan his next job. He slapped a three-dollar Indian-head gold piece against the bar. "Give me a bottle of your slowest-sippin' whiskey. I've got time to kill."

"You come to the right place," the bartender said. "We've kilt more time here than Congress." He plucked the coin from the bar as he lay a glass in front of the stranger. "You must have come up from below with that government coin."

Charlie nodded, noticed where the bartender threw the three-dollar piece. "Kansas."

The bartender chortled as he poured the stranger's first drink for him. "Come to get rich off the diggin's?"

Charlie shrugged. "One way or the other."

As dusk came on, the saloon man lit the lanterns, and new customers sifted in off the rutted street. A comforting hum began to chase the tense afternoon silence from the room. Every now and then, Charlie noticed the bartender cutting notches into pieces of board that he kept stacked under the bar. He didn't know why and didn't really care.

After dark, he inquired about a privy, and the bartender pointed to the back door beyond the poker game. The door led to a small dark landing at the bottom of a flight of stairs. The stairs led to the saloon owner's room, he guessed. He turned the other way, went outside, and found the outhouse.

Returning to the saloon, Charlie found his stool taken, so he stood at the bar and watched men swap gold dust for drinks, the bartender measuring each purchase on a set of scales.

This saloon couldn't be old, Charlie Holt mused, for the paint had yet to peel anywhere in the whole town of Frisco. But the ceiling was already smoke stained, the walls whiskey spattered, the floor heel gritted. He wondered if he would be the first to rob the place.

He had already figured out how he would do it. The bartender-owner lived upstairs, he had learned, and usually closed his doors around dawn to catch some shuteye. Charlie would leave by the back door some time tonight, as if he were going to visit the outhouse again. But instead, he would go upstairs and wait for the tired barman. He would use his gun barrel on the bartender's head. He would have just enough time to raid the till, buy his supplies, and get back on the trail of his wretched runaway wife before somebody found the bartender bound and gagged.

"What?" the bartender said sharply, turning to a small tarnished mirror behind the bar. "Have I got lice on my head or somethin'?" He began searching his scalp for vermin.

Charlie poured another glass of whiskey, realizing he had been staring at the bald spot on the bartender's head—the spot he would split open with his pistol barrel. "Maybe just a nit," he said. Someday when the name of Charlie Holt was known all over these mountains, this bartender would entertain his customers by showing them the scar the outlaw scribed on his head.

"Block and tackle." The voice came like gravel slung from a prospecting pan.

Charlie glanced to his right, found an ancient miner there, dirt clinging to his shirt where it had stuck to sweaty places. The old man had dusted his clothes of everything that would shake loose, washed his hands and his white-bearded face. He smiled as his burled hand took a brimful glass from the bartender, and his face wrinkled like a map of the bad lands.

This fellow was a regular here, Charlie thought. The bartender didn't take any money or dust from him, just made a notch in a board with a pocketknife. The board had the name BILLINGS written on it in pencil.

"Block and tackle?" Charlie said as the prospector took his first drink.

The old man grinned. "Make you walk a block and tackle anything." He thrust his open palm toward the stranger. "Jules Billings."

"Charlie Holt," he said shaking the hand.

As the night wore on, they got vaguely acquainted, the

bartender adding notches to Jules's wooden bar tab. By midnight, Charlie's bottle was half full and Billings was misty eyed.

"Prospectin' up here?" the old-timer asked.

Charlie scoffed. "Don't know the first damn thing about it."

"Tell you what"—Jules Billings was feeling the magnanimity of drink—"you can come to work for me till you learn the trade."

The outlaw Charlie Holt chuckled. "Learn prospectin' from a man who pays for his drinks with notches on a stick?"

Jules looked over both shoulders and leaned toward the stranger to speak low. "Boggs don't know it yet, but I'll settle my tab with him tomorrow. Ol' Jules Billings pays his debts."

"With what?"

"I finally hit a good one, Charlie," he said, as if they were old friends. "Filed the claim on it today. Sure, I've had some strikes play out on me before, but this one's wide as a gate. I worked it three days to make sure. Washed more than a hundred dollars' worth of dust a day with just a pan and a shovel."

"No shit?" Charlie said. "Gold dust?"

The prospector grinned and hoisted his right leg. He lifted his trouser leg over his boot top and made out as if scratching an itch on his calf. "What do you think of that? It's plumb full of gold dust."

Stuck into the top of the rawhide-laced boot, lashed tight against the prospector's leg, Charlie saw, was a small drawstring pouch bulging with its contents. He grinned out of one side of his mouth. "Boss," the outlaw said, "I'm with you."

"Let's go somewhere we can talk over terms," Jules said. "Hell, I might make you a partner if you'll carry your half."

Charlie grabbed his bottle by the neck. "Where do you want to go?"

"There's a quiet little whorehouse on the edge of town," he said. "Hell, half the business deals in town get cinched there." He tossed his head at Boggs, pulled his hat down on his brow, and stepped back from the bar.

"Let's go out the back," Charlie suggested. "I need to visit that privy."

Jules Billings shrugged, gestured toward the back door, and fell in behind Charlie. This was more than the old man had hoped for. After so many false mother lodes, his reputation as a prospector was such that he could scarcely hire an employee, much less get one to throw in with him on shares. He knew when he came to town that he was going to have to find a greenhorn so new to these diggings that he had never heard of Jules Billings's dubious reputation.

This Charlie Holt is perfect, he thought, grinning as he peeked at the poker hands around the big table. The man has calluses on his hands—no stranger to hard work. He said he was broke, needing a stake. He'll settle for a quarter interest, sure. Hell, that'll make Charlie Holt richer than just about anybody in town. Except for me, that is.

He felt a blast of glory surge through him as the cold night air filled his lungs. He thought of his claim again— the best he had seen since California in forty-nine. This secret had been roiling in him for days, now stirred by the stout drink. He slammed the door behind him, leapt from the wooden steps, and pushed a wolf song up his throat.

"What the hell?" the outlaw said, startled, reaching for his pistol.

Jules laughed. "Tonight's my night to howl, Charlie." His head fell back and he took in the field of stars above, so bright through the thin air of the moonless mountain night.

"Shit," Charlie said. "I thought you'd gone loco." His heart was pounding like a monster's.

"Just feelin' close to God. Like the song says: 'I once was lost, but now am found.' "

"Which way is that outhouse?"

"Over yonder," Jules said, pointing.

"Lead the way, will you? I don't know this place."

"Come on, I'll get you downwind of it, then you'll find it easy enough." He laughed as he strode down the slope toward a little draw.

Charlie Holt's hand was still on his pistol grip, and now he eased the weapon quietly from the stiff leather holster. He had to step quick to come close behind the old prospector. The man began to whistle. Perfect. The poor idiot had no idea. Charlie's chest burned like a furnace as he reached for Jules Billings's hat brim, his pistol hand already swinging overhead like a windmill blade.

The cold air and the blue steel struck Jules's head together as he tried to turn, and he fell to his knees. The outlaw struck him again, grunting with the effort he put into the blow, feeling the body give under the impact, hearing the sick thud that gave him such twisted satisfaction. The old miner fell on his side, unconscious.

Charlie Holt put his pistol back in the holster, drew it

again, pointed it at his victim, shook his head, put the pistol back in the holster. He turned toward the back door of the saloon, then back to Jules Billings, his whole body shaking with a nameless fury. He knelt and clawed at the pants leg. No, not yet. Not here. Hide the body first.

He dragged Billings across the rocky ground to the brush that fringed the edge of the draw. Pulling the limp body behind the bushes, he collapsed and began yanking at the right pants leg. Hiking it above the boot top, he felt the pouch, groped at it until it came free. The weight was like a trophy in his hand, and he smiled.

But now what? His chest was burning as if he had run a mile at full sprint. What was he going to do with Billings? What if the prospector came around before Charlie could get his supplies in the morning? Damn, he hadn't thought about that! Maybe he should have stuck to the saloon plan. Hell, maybe he should have just broken into a store and stolen his supplies.

He looked down at Jules Billings. Tie him up? No rope. Gag him? With what? "Shit," the outlaw said.

Jules Billings groaned. A leg moved.

The outlaw Charlie Holt jumped back, pulled his pistol. No, don't shoot, he thought. Damn, what was he going to do?

The back door of the saloon opened, and a trio of laughing young men poured out. Billings groaned loud, put a hand to his head. He was trying to sit up!

Charlie's pistol came down hard on the miner's head as he heard the three men hooting. He struck old Jules again. Again, and again. He paused, then lay three more crushing licks across the battered head.

He looked toward the saloon, saw the three men standing in a row, urinating. They laughed, then set up a chorus to rival the wildest pack of timber wolves in the mountains. Old Jules Billings had been wrong. It was not his night to howl.

TWENTY-ONE

As far as Carrol Moncrief knew, he was the first and only preacher to have ever set foot in Frisco, Colorado. He enjoyed a monopoly here, and never did he need it more than today. As he trotted his tired horse into town, he found himself hoping for a prayer meeting, a funeral, a shotgun wedding—any excuse he might find to pass his hat.

It was not Sunday, so only a few miners were in town from their claims, and fewer would likely be in a frame of mind to worship. It was not even Wednesday, on which evening the Frisco Christian Society met in the vacant second story of the newspaper office. It was Thursday noon, and Frisco lay as fallow for the gleanings of a circuit preacher as it would all week.

"Now, Carrol," he said, admonishing himself. "The Lord will provide."

He rode first to the general store of Edgar Dreyer, who served as the town's undertaker by virtue of the fact that he sold pine coffins. Carrol might have simply asked Dreyer for credit, except that he already owed the man nearly a hundred dollars. He had planned to repay Dreyer with part of the five hundred the Church of the Weeping Virgin had promised him, but Dee Hassard had destroyed even that intention.

"Howdy, Edgar," he said, stepping into the general store.

"Carrol! Goddamn, it's good to see you."

The preacher winced. "Now, Edgar, you promised me you'd work on your language."

Dreyer gritted his teeth. "Shit," he said, then clapped his hand over his mouth, his face bug-eyed. He turned to a slate behind his counter, and with a piece of chalk rock made two hash marks, one on either side of a dividing line. "Well, that's only three blasphemies and a half a dozen profanities so far today. I'm under the average, Carrol. That tally board you give me helps."

"Try a little harder, Edgar. Learn to say 'fiddlesticks' or 'dagnabbit' or somethin' that ain't so offensive." He glanced around the empty store. "How's business?"

"Slack. We need a fresh strike around here. All the diggin's are dwindlin', dagnabbit. What brings you around? Didn't expect to see you till next month."

"Some little redheaded flimflam artist stole a church from me."

Dreyer's eyes shifted. He had seen the redhead lead the strange congregation hastily through town a few days ago. "You don't mean them pilgrims, do you? The fanatics?"

"That's them. I was supposed to guide 'em into the mountains, but a fellow named Dee Hassard jumped my claim and took over the whole congregation. How long since they been through here?"

"Just three or four days. We was all hopin' they'd settle

near here, maybe pick business up some, but they didn't even stop for a day. Didn't buy no supplies or nothin'. Just plowed right on through town like they was in a big hurry. I see why now, if you was after the leader."

"He was still with 'em when they came through here?"

"Yeah, a little redheaded feller."

Carrol nodded grimly. "Well, he'll probably be long gone by the time I catch up to the pilgrims, and I'm sure he'll get away with every penny they've got, too. I'll keep after him, though. He did more than cheat me out of that five hundred, Edgar. He killed my brother, Frank, down in South Park."

Dreyer's mouth dropped open, then he scowled. He snatched up his piece of chalk rock and made an angry swipe at the side of the slate designated for enumerating profanities. "Why, that son of a bitch!" he said.

Carrol looked back toward the pine boxes. "I'll allow you that one, Edgar. Got any work for me?"

"Got a feller needs buryin' back here, but I doubt anybody'll turn out to pay for you prayin' over his grave."

Carrol shuffled curiously toward the coffins, feeling drawn to one in particular with the lid on, but not nailed down yet. "Who is it?"

"Old Jules Billings. Got hisself killed last night. Somebody beat his head in."

Carrol lifted the lid, squinted his eyes a little at the shape of the dead man's head. "Any idea who?"

"He left through the back door of the Eagle Saloon last night with some stranger. Somebody found him out behind the saloon this mornin'."

"Where's the stranger?" Carrol asked, quietly lowering

the lid on the coffin, as if he didn't want to disturb the man who rested within.

Dreyer shrugged. "Some of the boys looked around. We figured he hightailed it back toward Georgetown. Did you see anybody suspicious on your way up this mornin'?"

Carrol shook his head. "Didn't see anybody at all. He must have headed south for Buena Vista."

"The funny thing is, we can't figure out why this stranger killed poor ol' Jules. He wasn't robbed. Still had his watch in his pocket. He never had no money or gold, anyway. He was buyin' drinks on credit last night, just like always."

"No family?"

"Story he used to tell was that he run away from an orphanage in Alabama when he was just a kid. Claimed he stowed away around the Horn to California and got rich in forty-nine. Been prospectin' in these mountains for years. Everybody liked him, but he was sort of a crank. Did you ever hear his story about the cross?"

"What cross?" Carrol said.

"Ol' Jules claimed he got lost up in the Sawatch years ago. Wandered above the timberline and found a huge cross made out of snow on the side of a mountain. Said that's when he took religion, and found his way out of the mountains like he'd growed up there." Dreyer shook his head, chuckled, and rolled his eyes. "He was a crazy old codger."

"Don't laugh too hard, Edgar. That cross is up there. The photographer for the Hayden party made a picture of it last year. I've seen the picture myself."

Dreyer looked at the pine box and smirked. "Well, I'll

be switched. I just figured Ol' Jules was stretchin' the blanket, like all them stories he told about the claims he's filed on. He was always hittin' these big mother lodes that'd play out on him. Owed everybody in town."

Carrol grunted. It wasn't much to work with, but it was something. "And everybody in town owes *him,* Edgar. If the old man was well liked, his friends ought to turn out to see him buried. Is the grave dug?"

Dreyer looked at his watch. "Should be by now, I'd say."

"Nail that coffin shut and get ready for the funeral. I expect you to sing loudest."

The preacher left the store and angled across the street toward the Eagle Saloon. Stepping in, he waited until the eyes of the seven or eight occupants were on him. "I need six men," he announced.

Boggs frowned from behind the bar when he recognized the preacher. "I've warned you about harassin' my customers, Moncrief. You leave these men alone."

Carrol ignored the bar owner. "Six men with strong backs," he said.

"What for?" a customer said.

"Pallbearers for Jules Billings."

"That's enough," Boggs said, reaching under the bar for his shotgun. "Get out while you can, or I'll fill your hind end with pellets."

Carrol Moncrief put his grip around his pistol butt, drew the weapon calmly but quickly from the holster, all the while keeping his eye on the bartender. He leveled the barrel as Boggs lifted the shotgun, let a round go into the wall before the bartender could get a thumb hooked over a hammer. "Drop it!" he ordered.

Boggs tossed the scatter gun onto the bar. "Whoa, Preacher," he said.

Carrol smiled wickedly through the smoke, turned his muzzle upward, and let another two shots fly, causing dust to rain from the ceiling. "You sinners have been neglecting your Christian duty! A good man's been killed. Murdered by one of your customers, Boggs. Everybody get up now, we're gonna have a funeral!"

The customers rose and shuffled toward the door.

"You boys go get the coffin," Carrol said.

"Yes, sir," a man replied, grinning and tipping his hat.

Boggs came around the bar, a scowl on his face. "Damn you, Moncrief, you've gone too far this time!"

Carrol clicked the cylinder of his revolver, punching out empty shells. "Where's your business sense, Boggs? We'll get half the town down to the graveyard, say a few words for Old Jules, sing a hymn, then you announce first round on the house at the Eagle Saloon. You'll have the Thursday of your career."

Boggs contemplated a moment, then smirked. "Maybe I'll even pay off Jules's bar tab. All right, Moncrief, I'll go along this once." He shook his head as he walked out of the bar. "You're the damnedest man of the cloth I ever laid eyes on."

Carrol marched down the street in advance of the funeral procession, shouting into open doors, knocking on closed ones. It was a beautiful, warm mountain day, and for that he gave thanks. It would have been difficult herding these mourners into a muddy street. He limbered up his vocal chords as he made his way through town, railing by the time he had reached the outskirts.

Behind him, Edgar Dreyer had started a verse of "Shall We Gather at the River," which seemed appropriate, for the young Frisco cemetery lay hard by the banks of the Blue. By the time they reached the narrow hole in the ground—the grave-diggers still on hand with their picks and shovels—the procession had taken on a long trail of curious townsmen, friends of the late Jules Billings, bored merchants relishing the change in routine, busted miners anxious to forget their troubles long enough to celebrate life over the grave of one less fortunate, even a couple of weeping harlots who had known and liked old Jules.

Carrol read the Scripture loud and fast as the frothing Blue rushed by in kind. He wished the soul of poor Jules godspeed on its journey to the reward. ". . . and, God most merciful and wise," he prayed at last, his eyes welling up with real tears, "help us find it in our hearts to forgive even that cruel and wicked servant of the devil who so viciously murdered our friend. Oh, this is the greatest task you give us, Lord, for we loved Jules and will miss him. But yours is to judge, and ours is to trust in your wisdom. So be it. Amen."

Carrol Moncrief saw a tear drop on the clod of dirt he held in his hand. As the pallbearers lowered the box into the hole, he tossed the clod in, hearing it drop loudly on the planks. "Amazing Grace" was sung as the preacher stared into the grave and wept, but a few of the mourners were able to blink back their tears.

It was so hard. So very hard to forgive. Carrol tried to find the forgiveness his heart. He searched and prayed for it, but it wasn't there. He hated Dee Hassard. Hated him with the ire of the devil.

Edgar Dreyer passed his hat, seeing that Carrol had forgotten, and it swelled with contributions as the last chorus was sung. Even the grave-diggers pitched in their wages.

"First round on the house at the Eagle!" Boggs shouted. "In honor of Jules Billings!"

It was later, in the store of Edgar Dreyer, that Carrol Moncrief counted the money and weighed the dust, giving most of it back to Dreyer in exchange for the supplies he needed to stay on the trail of Dee Hassard.

"You might as well have this, too," Dreyer said, handing a certificate to the preacher.

"What is it?" Carrol asked.

"A new claim Jules filed just yesterday."

"Is it worth anything?" Carrol asked.

Dreyer began to chuckle. "I wouldn't piss in the rain with a slicker on for half a dozen of Old Jules's claims. He didn't know squat about prospectin' these mountains."

Carrol put the certificate in his pocket. "There goes your language again, Edgar. You've got to try harder."

Dreyer bunched his eyebrows together and ran through what he had last said. " 'Piss' is profane?" he asked.

"Yes, it is," the preacher answered. "And offensive, too."

"I didn't know that," the store owner admitted, and apologetically made another hash mark on his slate.

TWENTY-TWO

Dee Hassard was fighting a familiar compulsion. Every time a big job got this close to the final thrust, he took an urge to grab the money and run. Somebody would be getting suspicious by this point, even if nobody showed it. Some detective or former victim might be catching up to him, for he had used the same alias too long, worked the same mark. The temptation was to take part of the loot—enough to carry him for a while—and clear out of the territory.

In this particular case, Hassard knew Elder Hopewell harbored doubts. He knew Clarence Philbrick was downright suspicious. He could feel Carrol Moncrief sniffing his ever fresher trail. But Hassard was a professional. He would plan this thing to the last beat, stick to the plan, and escape unscathed as he always did. That was what separated him from the common sneak thief.

Sure, he was nervous. A little worried, too. Nothing wrong with that. That was what made it interesting. If anything went wrong, he could always sneak out or change the plan. He had learned to think quickly over the years. It was second nature to him by now to constantly calculate.

He had made up his mind. He was going to pull this thing off, then use Wyckoff's scam in Australia—start his own church there, rake in tens of thousands.

He had badgered enough information out of these pilgrims now that he even understood the three-day initiation. Just a bunch of preaching by the congregation members, working in relays, spelling each other in order to harangue the recruit nonstop with Christian propaganda. The key was to get the recruit to dredge up a bunch of past failures and humiliations, and then to keep repeating them as a reminder of how awful life is outside of the Church of the Weeping Virgin. It's different inside the church, of course. Give yourself to the church and you will be cared for the rest of your life, in spite of failure or humiliation.

The odd twist was that getting initiated like this automatically trained the new member in how to initiate the next recruit. And they believed it! These fanatics actually thought that this scam in the guise of a church could manufacture some kind of emotion akin to a mama's love or something.

This was really nothing new in the ancient art of the swindle. One of the easiest ways to win trust was to listen to a victim's worst experiences and act as if you gave a damn. That's all the Church of the Weeping Virgin was doing, only its members didn't even know it.

Australia was prime territory for a Weeping Virgin–style sect, and there Hassard would set up shop. It took money to get to Australia, though, and the swindler was determined to travel in style after this wilderness ordeal. He had earned it.

It was all going to have to fall into place within a couple of days, for Carrol Moncrief could not be far behind by this time. The thing Hassard needed most was something to occupy the pilgrims—a town site for the Church of the Weeping Virgin. And as he trudged around a bend in the trail, he found it.

The forest opened up to reveal a sloped clearing of about fifty acres. Near the bottom of the slope, the Eagle River shushed the wind in the mountain peaks. Around the rest of the grassy meadow grew firs, spruces, and pines. A cluster of aspens stood at the high end, their straight white trunks spaced regularly, like the teeth of an ivory comb.

It was a sight to take one's breath: the rocky, snow-streaked mountain rising above timberline in the distance. A huge bluff stood not far up the valley of the Eagle, looking like a lost precipice from some red desert canyon. High above, a hawk called, its piercing voice pricking Hassard's ears like a call to action.

A movement caught his eye across the meadow, and he made out a lone prospector striking camp along the tree line. Hassard broke into a trot, hailing the prospector as he approached.

"Howdy," he said, out of breath as he drew within earshot. This high altitude taxed his lungs. He reckoned he was close to nine thousand feet here, judging from the proximity of the timberline.

"Stop there," the miner said, swinging his rifle up.

Hassard showed his palms. "Don't want any trouble. Just wanted to talk to you before you broke camp."

The white-bearded miner spat a brown stream out of the left side of his mouth. "Well, talk, then."

"You have a claim here?"

The old man cackled. "Ain't no gold here. I'm on my way higher up."

"This place have a name?" Hassard removed his hat and slicked a sweaty strand of red hair back alongside his head.

"Utes call it Tigiwon. One of their campgrounds."

"Seen any of 'em around?"

The miner hissed, as if disgusted at the ignorance of this greenhorn. "They all went down to the Los Piños agency for their annuities. You won't see any of 'em around here for a spell."

"You know this area pretty good?"

The prospector nodded once.

"Have you heard of the Mount of the Snowy Cross?"

"Heard of it? Hell, I seen it! I seen it before them government surveyors come through here last year to photograph it. I was the first white man to lay eyes on it."

Hassard began to feel excited. This was a pilgrimage of sorts, even for him. This grueling trek was a tribute to his profession, his power over ordinary human beings, his supremacy over their silly codes and statutes. "How do you get to it?" he asked, sensing that the old prospector was anxious to leave.

The miner picked up his pack, pointed his rifle toward the snowy summit that rose behind him. "See that peak above the timber? That's called Notch Mountain. You see that notch in it, don't you? Well, you claw your way up that mountain—through the timber and across the creeks—till you get above the timberline. Then you keep goin', over the boulders and the snow fields, and you cross the divide to the south of the peak there. That's where you'll see the cross. It's a sight, son. It'll make your skin crawl." He turned his eyes back to the stranger, then squinted at something across the meadow.

Hassard looked over his shoulder and saw the ragged party of sojourners emerging from the woods. "That's my congregation," he explained. "We've come to see the cross, and to establish a town here."

The prospector sneered. "You won't see none of me no more. I'm goin' higher up." He turned his back and trudged up the trail.

"Hey!" Hassard called. He was curious now. Just curious. "How'd you ever come to find that cross in the first place?"

The old man stopped and turned to look at the stranger. "Like the song says: 'I once was lost, but now am found.' It's never too late, son." And he paced into the shadows, vanishing among shafts of sunlight.

Dee Hassard shrugged and walked back toward the center of the meadow. He stood there, cultivating an expression of reverence to wear for the pilgrims. It wasn't hard at this moment. He had found almost everything he needed. The town site was here, the fabled cross just a day's hike over the ridge, the gold in one lump on Elder Hopewell's burro. He needed only two things now: an escape route and a way to get rid of Clarence Philbrick.

He didn't want to have to kill that rich boy from back east. That would make things messy. But Philbrick was getting suspicious. The arrogant little snot thought he knew something, thought he was too smart, too educated. Well, there was only one way to handle a fool like that. Put him in your hip pocket. Keep him so close to you that he couldn't draw a breath to shout thief without you hearing him. And if he did draw that breath, you'd better be prepared to prevent him from ever using it.

"Are we gonna stop here for lunch?" asked a young black man who always walked near the head of the party.

"Yes," Hassard said. "We'll have lunch here tomorrow, too. And the day after, and every day of your life."

A red-faced woman dropped her pack. "You mean this is where we're to build?" She looked around her, mindful for the first time today of the grandeur of the Eagle River valley.

"We'll call the town Tigiwon," Hassard announced, sweeping his arms. "It's a Ute word that means 'sacred place.'" He didn't know what the word meant at all, of course. "This is where the New Order of Christianity will begin, and from here, spread throughout the world!"

Elder Hopewell approached, uncertain. Sure, he liked the looks of this place. Who wouldn't relish beauty like this? But wouldn't it get cold here in the winter? Wouldn't the snow last for months up here? "You sure?" he said. "How come this place?"

Hassard pointed at the notch in the summit to the southwest—a groove filed in a huge rifle sight, drawing aim on the Snowy Cross. "We're just a day's hike to the cross from here. I can sense it. We're going to be free here, Elder Hopewell. Free of everything unholy!"

The young Vermonter had stopped at Hopewell's side, joining him in his reservations. "Isn't it a little high here for a permanent settlement?" he asked.

"Nearer to God," Deacon Dee replied. "Besides, I've lived in a dozen mining towns higher than this."

"But there's nothing to mine here," Clarence said. "How do you expect people to make a living here?"

Hassard looked at the Vermonter as if the boy had lost his mind. "The Utes have made their living here for a thousand years. We'll learn from the red man. Don't we have red-skinned brothers and sisters in our own congregation? We'll hunt, gather the fruits of the wilderness, cultivate our own crops for our own consumption. We need only enough to exist, brother Clarence. We don't need to produce anything for sale. *The Wisdom of the Ages* and the dreams I have had make that clear."

Looking down on them, Hassard saw that he had most of them with him in this. But there was a clutch of doubtful minds clustered around Elder Hopewell, Sister May, and the Vermonter. It was time to address the problem. Meet it head-on.

"I know that some of you doubt me," he said. "I can see it in your eyes. But the Weeping Virgin has guided me here to this spot. In my dreams I have seen a cross of pure white snow on the face of a mountain over this ridge." He thrust his finger angrily at Notch Mountain. "Tomorrow I will take a party to find it, and when you see it, then you will surely believe, and we shall wash our hands of our filthy lucre! We'll leave it in sight of the Holy Cross and begin anew! If the cross is there, you'll know!"

"Amen!" shouted one of Hassard's believers.

"Now, what does *The Wisdom of the Ages* say?" Hassard continued. "We don't have a moment to waste in this life. Let's sustain ourselves with a meal, then get to work. We'll build the church first, up there on the highest point of the meadow!"

"Hallelujah!" a woman answered.

Hassard felt a tingle travel up his spine. This preaching business agreed with him. He was going to enjoy the hell out of this once he got to Australia.

TWENTY-THREE

The sun had dropped behind Notch Mountain when Dee Hassard approached the place called Tigiwon. There were still hours of daylight left but it was cool, shadowy, like the brink of nightfall in flatter regions—a high-country phenomenon he had never gotten used to. It made him feel that time was growing short, like daylight slipping away.

Maybe it wasn't the mountain's shadow making him feel that way. Maybe it was the fact that Carrol Moncrief had to be getting closer to him by the minute.

The confidence man had ridden a big red mule a few miles up the valley, hobbled the beast there, and walked back. He had hoped to overtake that white-haired prospector he had met in the meadow, get some more details about the climb to the cross. But the old man hadn't even left any tracks. No matter. He would find the way.

It was almost as good as done now. Hassard had his escape route planned: up the trail to Tennessee Pass on the big red mule, down into the valley of the Arkansas, to Buena Vista and points beyond. Everything was in place.

Everything but Clarence Philbrick. Hassard knew one thing for certain. Tomorrow, when he announced that he would take the gold up to the Snowy Cross for the dedication, Philbrick was going to insist on going along. The Vermonter had appointed himself watchdog of the church coffers.

What was he going to do about Philbrick? An accident

tonight? Too obvious. That would only arouse more suspicion. He didn't want to have to sacrifice Brother Clarence to the Snowy Cross tomorrow. He hated that sort of thing. Killing always made somebody hound him harder. And besides, it was sloppy—unprofessional.

He thought back to his education under the East Coast masters. They would say to keep Clarence in view. Know at all times where he was, what he was doing. Yes, the thing to do at dawn tomorrow was to *invite* Clarence to come along before he could insist on it. That might lower the young fool's suspicions.

Then, maybe . . . Just maybe the best plan was to leave all that money up there on the divide, like he had been promising to do all along. Yes, *dedicate* it! Really leave it there and come back to the town site. That would probably convince even Clarence. Nobody was going to bother the money up there.

Then, in the middle of the night, when Clarence and all the other doubters were asleep, Hassard would sneak back up to retrieve his wages. It just might work. He would have several hours' head start on them. He would come down the mountain where he had left the big red mule, and ride for Buena Vista. What a slick haul that would be!

"That you, Deacon?" The voice came from the trail to Tigiwon.

"Yes," Hassard said. "Just me."

The guard stepped into the open path, a burly youth with a single-shot squirrel gun.

"Good job," Hassard said, grasping the guard by the shoulder. "We must all stay alert, even in this wilderness, Brother . . ."

"James. James O'Rourke."

He patted the muscled shoulder. "I don't expect we'll have anybody bothering us a way out here, but you know what Pastor Wyckoff used to say: 'Prepare! For the devil lurks in the guise of Godliness!'"

"Yes," Brother James said. "What happened to your mule?"

Hassard began to laugh. "I was trotting up the trail, beholding the beauty of God's creations all around me, when that blessed creature ran me right under a tree limb. I landed on my rear end, and Ol' Red just kept trotting away. But, what did God give me legs for?"

"You want me to go catch the mule?"

"You have a more important job here. Don't worry about Ol' Red. He'll wander back to Tigiwon in a day or two." He smiled at the young guard and strode on toward the town site. "Hone your eyesight," he said. "I'll see you tonight in Tigiwon."

He loved that name. He loved the way these people looked up to him. This could be infectious. When he thought about it, Wyckoff's scam seemed to be one that actually benefited the victims. These people were like sheep. Hell, they begged to be swindled. He hoped he would find plenty just like them in Australia. But then, there was no need to worry about that. There were fools like this everywhere.

"You should have known Pastor Wyckoff in the old days," Hopewell said. He paused just long enough to straighten, sop the sweat from his eyebrows, and to glance at the beauty of the long-shadowed mountain slope.

Clarence and May helped him roll the log they were peeling for the new church.

"That character sure had a way with words," Clarence said, "judging from his book." The construction of this church was a ridiculous thing to him, but he was helping in order to stay close to May. Hunting had gone well since he killed that first buck, and he had some time to burn before the evening hunt.

"Oh, you should have heard Pastor Wyckoff preach," Hopewell replied. "He could hold a group breathless—I mean really breathless, to where they wouldn't even risk making a sound to breathe for fear they might miss him whisper. Then he'd roar something at them, and they'd bolt up like lightning struck them."

"Fast talk and leadership don't always amount to the same thing."

"You're skeptical," Hopewell said. "That's understandable. I was, too, even after I heard Pastor Wyckoff speak. Then I went through the initiation. That's when I realized that the Church of the Weeping Virgin was going to be God's salvation to the world. Give us a fair chance, Clarence. Consider joining the church."

Clarence snorted. "I'm not interested."

"Why not?"

"This initiation. Nobody in your congregation will tell me anything about it. They all act as if they know something I don't. Like they're flaunting it; proud of it; selfish with it. It's all too secretive and elitist for me. Everything I ever learned about faith is based on truth, light. Not darkness."

Hopewell shook his head. "I know it's hard to understand if you haven't experienced it. I wish you could talk to Pastor Wyckoff. He could convince you. We had true leadership when he was alive."

"What about you?" May said quickly. She could feel the religious conflict deepening between Hopewell and Clarence and didn't like the thought of them being at odds with each other. "You got the church from Arkansas to Denver after Wyckoff was lynched." She flaked a large piece of bark off with her draw knife and moved on down the log. "You could lead them as well as anybody."

The tall man straightened again, rising to his full height. He was standing above them on the slope, and he looked like one of the straight trees the pilgrims were felling in the forest, tall and slender, his white hair and whiskers like bundles of moss. "I'm no match for the likes of Pastor Wyckoff. I don't have his use of words."

"This rabble would be better off with you leading them than Dee Hassard," Clarence said.

"He's got a way of whipping people in behind him," Hopewell replied. "He's not as good with speech as Pastor Wyckoff was, but he's handy at it. He's got me worried. I can't say just why, but I think it has something to do with the money."

"You mean throwin' it away up on that mountain?" May said.

The elder nodded. "Pastor Wyckoff never had any objection to the church making or keeping money. To him, money was like this ax." He held the broad iron blade in front of him, a long arm's length away. "It can be a good tool, if you use it properly, the way it is intended. It can also be used to crush somebody's skull. It has nothing to do with any amount of holiness or evil in the instrument itself, but in the user. Same with money."

Clarence nodded. "I agree." He looked toward his jacket, which was lying within his grasp under his Remington rifle. "Same with guns. They can be used for protection or aggression. But if the aggressor's got one, the protector had better have one, too."

"A sad truth," Hopewell said. "One we have learned."

They worked the log in silence for a few moments, hearing the cadence of axes in the forest above them.

"What about Hassard's guns?" May said. "Have you noticed? That little pistol he wears tucked under his belt looks like it's been lying out somewhere in the weather. Then he's got that big pistol in that holster, all shiny and polished, and the gun belt has a new hole poked in it because whoever owned it before Hassard was bigger around than him."

Clarence contemplated, impressed by what she had said. He didn't know what it meant any more than May did, but there was something wrong with the deacon's whole getup. "Everything about him is suspect. Who is he, anyway? He says Reverend Moncrief sent him, but how are we to know?" He paused, looked up toward Notch Mountain. "I'm going with him when he takes the party to find the cross."

"I intend to go, too," Hopewell said. "But we'd better be careful. We'd better watch him every second."

"Clarence," May said. "What if there really is a cross up there?"

The Vermonter smiled. "The cross exists."

Elder Hopewell stopped with his ax above one shoulder and looked at the hunter.

Clarence nodded. "I've seen a photograph of it, taken last summer by a photographer for the U.S. geological survey. I don't know how Hassard found out about it, but it is just as he described it."

Hopewell lowered the ax. "Why didn't you say something?"

Clarence searched the ground, as if for reason. "I'm not sure. I felt there was some kind of advantage to my keeping quiet about it.

"There's something strange about all this. From the moment I saw that photograph, I knew I would climb Notch Mountain someday to see that cross. It was one of the final things that made me know I had to come west. I had planned to get situated in New Mexico first. It was only by chance that I met May, and we fell in with the Church of the Weeping Virgin. It's almost as if I were destined to come here—drawn here like some beast on a migratory journey." The Vermonter was virtually reciting the entry he would make in his diary that night.

A rifle blast suddenly ripped the wide-open air above the meadow. Axes fell silent, the rush of the river and the echo of the gunshot the only remaining strains. Clarence picked up his Remington, swung an arm into his jacket sleeve, and trotted toward the sound of the shot, on the trail that led north down the river valley. He ran into the timber flanking the trail below Tigiwon and soon saw a guard marching toward the town site—a lanky, rawboned man stalking angrily in front of him, his hands in the air.

"What's this?" Clarence asked.

The guard was named Dan Feather, a Kickapoo who had joined the church in Indian Territory. He had the stranger's gun belt slung across one shoulder. "He no stop," Dan said, "so I shoot."

"Who are you?" Clarence said to the man.

"Charlie Holt. I come for my wife."

"Your wife?"

Dan Feather scowled. "He want Sister May."

TWENTY-FOUR

May waited with Elder Hopewell, watching the open slope, trying to eke some sound out of the air. Below, to her right, she saw Dee Hassard trot into the opening. Seconds later, along the left side, a sight emerged from the forest that struck her with sudden terror.

"What is it?" Hopewell said, hearing her gasp.

She saw Clarence appear behind her husband. The Vermonter's eyes found hers immediately, even across the distance up the slope. They questioned her, and she knew she should have told him. Charlie Holt's eyes found her next, and he pointed accusingly. She put her hand over her mouth and felt choked with fear. She was his wife. They were going to make her go back with him.

"Sister May," Hopewell said. "Who is that?"

"My husband," she said.

"May!" Charlie Holt's voice rattled up the slope. "You come on down here. I'm takin' you home!"

The elder put his long flat hand across May's shoulders. "You stay here. I'll go see into this. Don't you worry, I won't let any harm come to you."

May took some comfort from his words, but good Elder Hopewell didn't know Charlie. She turned her eyes away from her husband and sat on the log she had been peeling, dread coursing through her like a fever.

Dee Hassard met the three men in the meadow and motioned for Dan Feather to lower his weapon. This was a relief. He had thought, when he heard the shot, that Carrol Moncrief might have caught up. He didn't see how that was possible. He had calculated the distances over and over. Moncrief would come hard, but couldn't possibly get here for a couple of days yet. For all he knew, though, this character might be some detective hired by a former victim, some bounty hunter, or a friend of Frank Moncrief's. He would have to be ready and stay alert.

"State your business," he said to the stranger as he strode to the group.

"I come after my wife," Holt said, and he pointed at May again.

Hassard's eyes flashed, and he glanced at Clarence, relishing the tortured look on the hunter's face. His mind raced. May was a runaway. There was opportunity here somewhere. This was some way to get rid of Philbrick and yet build himself in the eyes of the congregation. But how? "Would you like to join our congregation?" he asked, buying time to think, knowing well that this enraged husband harbored no spiritual bent.

"Hell, no," Charlie said, the taste of whiskey thickening his tongue. "I come to take her home, damn it." He glared at the gangling black man striding down the slope.

Hassard was racing back through the gospel according to Wyckoff. He wanted more than anything to give Sister May to this stranger. Clarence would follow, and he would be rid of him. But he had to consider what *The Wisdom of Ages* would say on the matter. This was no time to lose the confidence of the pilgrims. It took him only a moment to form the policy. "Sister May is a member of our family now. You can't take her from us against her will."

Holt fumed. "She's my wife, goddammit!"

"By the laws of an unholy government that we don't recognize. Now leave, and take your foul language and your blasphemies elsewhere."

"The hell I will," Holt said, and he started up the slope, pushing Hopewell aside. "I'm takin' my wife home."

Hassard flung his coattail aside, pressed his palm against the butt of the big Colt, and drew the weapon smoothly from the belt scabbard. He cocked and aimed, flexing his trigger finger as the irons settled on the crown of Holt's hat.

The outlaw Charlie Holt shrank to the ground like a quail when he heard the report and felt the bullet rip through his hat. "Damn you!" he said.

"Brother Clarence, you can let Sister May know that everything's all right now. This man won't come back if he knows what's good for him."

Clarence hesitated. "You want help with him?"

Hassard shook his head. "Don't need it." He looked at Dan Feather. "Was he mounted?"

The Kickapoo nodded and pointed his chin down the valley. "His horse down yonder."

"I'll escort him back to his horse alone. I want to have a word with him as he leaves." Hassard waved his pistol toward the trail the stranger had arrived on. "Come on," he said.

Holt scowled but obeyed and paced long into the forest. As he passed, Hassard took Holt's gun belt from Dan Feather's shoulder.

Clarence watched them disappear, then walked slowly up the slope toward May. Facing her was going to be awkward. He had thought he was beginning to know her well until her husband showed up. Now she seemed a complete stranger. She had kept secrets from him. This wasn't some trifling thing, either. It could have gotten him killed, judging from the look on Charlie Holt's face down there.

As he came to the place where she sat, she avoided looking at him and fidgeted in her embarrassment.

"He's gone," Clarence said. He waited for a reply, but she gave none. "He said you were his wife." His tone was rather accusing.

She nodded. "I don't want to go back with him." She looked at him, her eyes full. "I know I should have told you about him, but I didn't know how." Tears poured down from her eyes, streaked her cheeks. "Please don't let him take me back."

Clarence felt suddenly ashamed. Secrets? Wasn't he carrying a few up his own sleeves? She had been no less honest with him than he had been with her. He sat down beside her and put a hand on her shoulder. "You don't have to go anywhere you don't want to," he promised. "I'll see to that."

The axes began to chop again as they sat there.

Clarence didn't know anymore if he would ever get to the Ojo de los Brazos. Could it possibly possess more beauty than the Eagle River valley of Colorado? How long could he carry this money around in his jacket? Why had this Mount of the Snowy Cross interfered with his plans? Why did he feel this way for this woman?

I once heard of two fishermen—he thought this, thinking again of the night's journal entry—*who entangled their flies just as a fish struck, and both anglers hooked the selfsame trout. As one would not yield to the other, neither was able to properly play the fish, who threw both hooks and swam free.*

I am that trout. The Ojo de los Brazos pulls me one way; May Tremaine another. The lures they use are diabolical. Perhaps neither shall keep me in her creel.

TWENTY-FIVE

wonder what he wants," May said. She stood beside an ancient fir, wringing her hands nervously.

Clarence shrugged. "Curious, isn't it? I mean, that he would ask both of us to meet him here."

She nodded.

The Vermonter looked up the huge trunk of the tree and decided to change the subject. "How old do you think this tree is?"

May noticed the old valley monarch beside her for the first time, its trunk rising in tons of timber. "I don't know," she said.

"I'll bet it's seen a dozen generations come and go."

She smiled a little and wondered what made a man think such thoughts. He was different from anybody she had ever known. She wanted her own mind to work the way his did. She wanted to question things, study them. She had always been too occupied with survival to think of such things. But Clarence made her feel safe and let her mind run.

"Did you ever finish that book? *The Wisdom of the Ages*?"

"Yes."

"What did you think?"

"I think that old Pastor Wyckoff was a little touched."

Clarence chuckled and nodded at her in approval. It was good that she was able to question those religious ramblings. "What about joining the Church of the Weeping Virgin?"

"They keep pestering me about it, but I don't want to go off in the woods for three days with a bunch of strangers."

"Then don't."

"They keep putting the pressure on me heavier all the time. I don't think they'll let me stay on with them if I don't join up. I don't have much choice."

"You can come with me to New Mexico. I'll see that you get situated."

May felt almost embarrassed, almost as if she had maneuvered him into saying what she wanted to hear. "Thank you, Clarence. But Charlie will be out there looking for me, and he's some put out."

"You must have had a good reason for leaving him. I've got an idea what it was, and I don't blame you. If a man hurts a woman, he doesn't deserve to be called a husband. Don't you worry about anything. If you want to go, we'll go."

They heard boots scraping a gravelly stretch of trail and turned to see Dee Hassard coming from the town site.

"Good evening," he said, "thanks for meeting me here. Let's walk up the trail a little way. I want to talk to the two of you."

It was near dusk now, the valley darkening into shades of deep blue and purple. Clarence shrugged at May, and they followed Hassard up the trail at a stroll.

"I wanted to talk to the two of you about your future with the church. You joined this party together, and you've spent much time together since you've been with us." He grinned coyly at them. "I was wondering what your plans are now."

Clarence wrinkled his brow, wondering what the deacon was up to. He propped his rifle barrel on his shoulder. "I haven't made up my mind what I'm going to do."

"Me neither," May added quickly. She was making sure to keep Clarence between her and Hassard.

They came to the picket line, and James O'Rourke stepped into the trail ahead of them. "Evenin', Deacon," the guard said.

"Are you still on guard duty, Brother James?" Hassard replied. "I'm going to send somebody to relieve you as soon as I get back to Tigiwon."

"I don't mind," the youth replied.

"We're going to walk up the trail a way, but we'll be back directly."

James nodded, and the three continued their stroll.

"I was hopin' to help you both make up your minds," Hassard said. "Brother Clarence, we'll need a hunter with a good rifle until we get crops and herds established. I owe you an apology for doubting your hunting ability before. You were right; there just wasn't any game back among the mining settlements. Here you've kept plenty of meat hanging.

"And, May, about the other day, you understand that I was suspicious about your past and just tryin' to coax some information out of you. I had the feelin' you were on the run from something. I thought maybe it was the law. But I understand, now that I've met Charlie Holt."

Clarence glanced at May, for she had said nothing about that of which Hassard now spoke.

"By the way, I warned him about ever returning for you, Sister May. I believe I put a righteous fear into him."

"He's gonna come back," May said, a grim certainty in her voice. "If he followed me this far, I know he'll keep tryin'. He's gone downright wild. I could see it in his eyes."

Hassard shrugged. "I've doubled the guard below Tigiwon, just in case."

Clarence noticed movement on the trail ahead and saw Charlie Holt step from the trees with a drawn revolver. His rifle barrel was over his shoulder, and he knew better than to swing it into action, for Holt had murder in his drunken eyes. All he could do was step in front of May.

Hassard gasped when he saw Holt. He was truly surprised. Holt was supposed to fire in ambush a good half
mile up the trail. He wasn't supposed to show himself. He
wasn't supposed to be this close to the guards. Already the
fool had botched the plan, and Hassard knew he would
have to make drastic changes. "Holt!" he said, stopping in
his tracks. "You're making a big mistake."

"She's the one made it," Holt said. "You never should
have run from me, woman. Never should have laid me out
for good with that poker."

"It was the fryin' pan," May said, her voice less timid
than even she could explain.

"Shut up and step out from behind that boy, or I'll kill
you all."

Clarence used his free arm to hold May behind him.
"Put your gun away," he ordered. He could think of only
one thing. He had to take control. This helplessness was
death. His trigger finger slipped inside the guard, his
thumb found the hammer. Now, quickly, he thought, before your fear overcomes you.

May had never seen Charlie like this, and she instinctively knew it meant the worst. This was her fault. She had
led him here. She was going to make something happen.
She wasn't going to watch him shoot Clarence Philbrick
down. No time to think. Just act!

Clarence felt May bolt to the right side of the trail, saw
Charlie Holt's eyes and gun muzzle follow her. He slung
the long, heavy barrel of the Remington over his shoulder
without thinking, and Charlie Holt reacted, covering him
with the pistol. The hammer latched as the forestock hit
his left palm, and he tensed, seeing the pistol barrel swing-

ing toward him. Dee Hassard was diving for the trees to the left as Clarence jerked the trigger, knowing he had fired too soon, over Holt's head.

He scrambled to his left, and his boot slipped. The Colt pistol fired, only shattering a dead tree limb on the ground six feet away. Clarence took cover, thought about reloading the single-shot hunting rifle. Why wasn't Hassard firing, protecting May? Holt had missed him badly. The man was no *pistolero*. No time to reload the rifle. It was going to happen too fast. Holt would have May in seconds.

He stepped back into the trail, saw Holt peering into the forest for May. He ran at the outlaw, his rifle gripped tight in both hands. The Colt pistol swung on him again, but he pushed the heavy hunting piece ahead of him—hurled it sidewise at Holt with all the force his solid arms could gather.

The rifle hit Charlie Holt's forearm, spoiled his aim as he fired. Clarence collided with him as Holt cocked the weapon for another shot. He grabbed the outlaw's wrist as they slammed against the rocky trail. The heavy jacket constricted him, and Holt was stronger than he had expected, but he held his own, and now he knew Hassard would have to do something. Or would he? Who was this Dee Hassard? Where was he now?

Hassard cursed Charlie Holt from the deepest center of his guts. This should have been so simple that he figured even an amateur like Holt could pull it off. Hassard had done everything he was supposed to do. He had come up the trail at the right moment, stood far enough away from Clarence. Holt was supposed to kill the Vermonter, grab the girl, and ride like hell before the guards could come. But he had shown his face, and he had set his ambush too close to the guards, and now they were coming. Holt might talk.

Hassard drew his Colt and ran for the two men on the ground. They made a good match—about the same size, and both of them strong: Holt from farm labor, Philbrick from a rich boy's calisthenics. He was hoping this wouldn't look too obvious. Thank goodness he had raised all that talk about their future with the church—just in case something like this went wrong.

He could hear James O'Rourke's footsteps coming up the dim trail as he landed on the two men. His left hand grabbed Holt's gun, as if to aid Clarence. The muzzle of his own pistol pressed against Holt's chest. He saw Holt release Clarence's jacket—a strange look of fear and curiosity in his bloodshot eyes. Hassard listened to three of O'Rourke's foot beats, then fired.

May Tremaine screamed and sprang from the trees. She saw Clarence roll away from her husband as the bloody outlaw's eyes rolled toward her and locked onto her, staring forever.

Hassard sprang to his feet and dropped his revolver as if it were hot. "I had to shoot him," he said. "He was reachin' for my gun. He could have killed Clarence. He could have killed me." He was explaining this to James O'Rourke, who would take the news back to Tigiwon— James O'Rourke, who was posturing excitedly over the dead man with his weapon.

Clarence stepped over the outlaw Charlie Holt, breaking the death stare that held May. He glanced sideways at Hassard, who had handled everything poorly. Today in the meadow called Tigiwon, Hassard had acted swiftly and effectively, firing through Holt's hat. Here he had waited too long, then acted too rashly. Clarence had pinned Holt. The guard was coming. There was no need to kill the man.

He grabbed May's arm to lead her away, when, unexpectedly, she pulled her arm from his grasp and gripped his wrist instead. He found her looking at him as no woman ever had, and something indomitable came clear between them. She was tired of being weak, and he was making her strong.

"Wait," she said. "His things are mine. I'm his next of kin."

Clarence watched, amazed, as she knelt to unbuckle the gun belt from Charlie Holt's hips. She dragged the leather out from under the body, then took the pistol from the limp hand. She holstered the Colt, handed it to Clarence, then looked back at James O'Rourke. "Anything else he has, the church can own."

There was no Charlie Holt behind her now, and she wanted nothing more than to leave this place with the tall Vermonter. Yet it wasn't that simple with Clarence, and she knew it. He had arrived at a personal struggle with the man who claimed to be a deacon. It was as if they were arm-wrestling or something, and now they were growing weary of the contest and both desirous of an end.

She looked at them both, and they knew—they all three knew. They couldn't speak it, or even speak of it, yet it was there to resolve. Someone would have to prove something tomorrow.

* * *

Ramon looked at Sister Petra's face, her features aglow in the soft firelight. How could she sleep? He was too excited to even lie down, let alone sleep. They had met an old prospector who had seen the Mount of the Snowy Cross. Seen it with his own eyes! Ramon hadn't understood a word of his speech, but Petra had translated. This was the old prospector who had been spoken of in Buena Vista. That they should even cross his path was a miracle in itself.

He pulled his wool blanket tighter against his neck and it scratched his skin. It was cold here at night and always a bit musty smelling. He tried to imagine how warm it was in Guajolote right now. That was a wonderful place to sleep in the summertime—sleep with the windows open and the mountain breezes flowing down clean and dry from the pine forests. Maybe that little village was worth saving. Maybe the money to buy the Ojo de los Brazos grant would drop from heaven tomorrow.

He shook his head to rid it of such ridiculous thoughts. And yet, hadn't that old prospector told them of a ragged band of pilgrims camped several miles down the valley? A party of religious fanatics come to see the cross. It was fantastic. Sister Petra was not alone in her quest for this cross. There was something to it all, and he could not fight back the feeling that something wonderful was going to happen tomorrow.

Once he had been a normal boy, unconcerned with the prospect of anything happening to his village. It seemed like such a long time ago that he had been swept up by these wild happenings and carried along on this journey almost like a twig in a river. It had been only a matter of weeks, but he had changed so much and so rapidly that he didn't know how to measure it.

He was a small boy in a land of huge mountains, and he felt helplessly insignificant sitting by the campfire tonight. That he was here seemed almost an accident. This was a journey for more important souls than his own. He had contributed nothing, and in fact had burdened Petra as much as he had aided her.

Perhaps tomorrow he could atone for it. It was to be his last chance. The old Anglo prospector had assured them that the view of the cross was only a half day's climb up the mountain. Tomorrow he was going to climb as he never had before. And if he had to carry Sister Petra on his back to see that cross, he was going to do it.

He forced himself to lie back on his bed of spruce boughs. Sleep, Ramon, he said to himself. Sleep, you idiot. You must show your strength tomorrow. It is your last chance.

TWENTY-SIX

Hassard rose from the log where he had eaten his breakfast of venison steak and saw the eyes of several hopeful pilgrims following him as he reached for the coffeepot over the fire. They had risen to breakfast with him under the stars, in hopes that he might choose them to accompany him up the mountain.

He was getting anxious now. The time was near when he would have to deal with Brother Clarence.

He had Philbrick figured: Over educated and over confident. Morally responsible and physically formidable. A simpleton in terms of practical experience. His ideas of fair play would prove his downfall. He really had no inkling how far Dee Hassard would go. It might have been possible to dupe young Clarence before last night. But the Charlie Holt affair had taught him something. The boy had instincts that he was just too educated to know how to use yet. He would probably never get the chance.

Less than twenty-four hours from now, Hassard was going to leave this camp and head back up the mountain to retrieve the loot that he would leave there today. Philbrick would probably be watching him, waiting for him, and he would have to make silent work of the young Vermonter. This was the reason that Hassard now carried Charlie Holt's dagger. He disliked using knives, but it would have to be done. He would kill Clarence if he had to, get the money from the divide, locate the hobbled mule he had left up the valley, and ride for Buena Vista a half day ahead of Carrol Moncrief.

Carrol Moncrief: Dangerous. Vengeful. Possessed with affecting the capture or death of Dee Hassard. Weakness: Religious scruples. Yet, Moncrief had seen this side of the law. He might easily revert. It was imperative to stay beyond the big preacher's reach. The man was already mounted and riding by this time in the morning and would be at Tigiwon by noon tomorrow, no sooner. It was time to wrap this thing up.

He looked across the camp at the faces of the congregation. They were watching him so expectantly. Oh, glory, what a life to lead! To think that these wretched pilgrims would resign themselves to hard labor and prayer. He hated them. They were small, stupid, and gullible. They would only get what they deserved.

"I had another dream last night," he said, low and thoughtfully, warming his cup of coffee with a splash from the pot. "A visitation."

"From the Weeping Virgin?" someone asked.

Hassard nodded. "She gave me specific instructions to follow today, and I am afraid they will disappoint many of you. I don't understand why I am to do this, I only know I must."

"Do what?" Clarence asked. He was wearing the Colt revolver of the late Charlie Holt.

"I am forbidden to touch the money that we are to dedicate to the Snowy Cross today. Instead, I am to take a small party of faithful with me to carry the stuff and accompany me to the cross."

A murmur swept around the fire as the pilgrims shuffled uncomfortably.

"In days to come, you will all see it," Hassard insisted reassuringly. "I'm sure we'll make regular pilgrimages to it. It's the personal experience for each of you that counts, not who gets to go first. But today, I am to take only a few."

"How many?" James O'Rourke asked. He was certain that Hassard would include him, now that they were personally acquainted after yesterday's trouble.

"Three. The first is Elder Hopewell. The second is Sister Mary Whitepath. The third, Brother Clarence."

O'Rourke sprang to his feet. "What about me? I joined the church in Baltimore, before any of them, except Elder Hopewell!"

"I can't explain why these have been chosen," Hassard said. "I can't even explain why I have been chosen. I, too, joined the church after you, Brother James, only as recently as Denver. I only know what the Weeping Virgin has told me." He shrugged apologetically. "Try to remember what Pastor Wyckoff has written about personal sacrifice. Perhaps this is yours."

O'Rourke sat sullenly down against a tree trunk.

Dee Hassard picked up a hatchet and felt its edge with his thumb. "Elder Hopewell. The money."

"It's here," the elder said, lifting a heavily laden saddlebag. In it were all the monies Pastor Wyckoff had collected since the pilgrimage began, plus Dee Hassard's take from the diamond field fraud, and even a bag of gold dust recovered from the body of the outlaw Charlie Holt. No one had bothered to add it all up.

"Let's go," Hassard said, rapping his coffee cup upside down on a rock to knock the dregs out. "We've got several miles to climb."

In the dark, Clarence brushed by May as he turned up the trail. He squeezed her cool neck gently in his hand as he passed. And she touched him, too—her open palm pressing against the back of his hand, where she knew he would feel it, her fingers slipping away as he walked on.

"I'll carry the heavy stuff," Clarence said to Hopewell.

The elder handed the saddlebags to Clarence, then picked up a coil of rope and looped it over his head and one shoulder.

Mary Whitepath fell in behind them, her moccasins treading silently on supple blades of grass.

"Deacon Dee!"

The con man turned to look at James O'Rourke.

"God go with you," the youth said.

Dee smiled. "Bless you, James." With his hatchet he chopped a slash mark on an aspen tree—the first in a long line that would lead him back to the gold after today's sunset.

Sister Petra could look down and see last night's camp far below, the light of dawn showing the wisp of smoke rising through the pines. The sun hadn't even risen above the mountains to the east and already she had climbed a half mile. Her muscles were warm, the stiffness from the bed of spruce boughs gone.

Ramon was on her heels. "What are you waiting for?" he asked.

"Just looking down on the camp. We must not start too fast. We will have a long way to climb today." She smiled, for it was a joy to see him this excited about reaching the cross.

"We must not go too slow, either," he argued. "We don't know what we might run into."

They had found a game trail not far above their camp, but it had played out quickly, and now they were simply clawing their way up the steep slope, crawling under low limbs, over deadfalls and boulders. They couldn't see Notch Mountain for the trees, but knew it loomed over them, reaching high above the timber.

They worked upward for an hour, finally arriving at a minor ridge that branched off the main divide like a rib from a backbone. Working their way along the top of the ridge, they could move with relative ease among the trees, until they came to the broad flank of the mountain, where they had to negotiate steep grades again.

"Which way should we go?" Ramon asked.

Petra put her hands on her hips and saw her breath form a cloud in front of her. It was a wonderful day, sunny and warming. "The old man yesterday said to cross the Notch Mountain divide south of its summit. I think if we turn northward here and work our way gradually up the mountain as we go, we should come out above timber in about the right place."

Ramon nodded, took the lead. He didn't know why, but he felt like climbing today. His legs almost ached to be used. "Come on," he said.

Coming around a forested bluff some time later, Ramon stopped and could only stare as Petra came to his side. An avalanche had swept down the mountainside in front of him, carrying trees and rocks downward in what must have been an incredible spectacle as it occurred. Now it was nothing more than an ugly scar to cross, the footing treacherous for some sixty yards.

"I suppose we could climb and go over it," Petra said.

Ramon looked up the old avalanche. It was a long way in the wrong direction. "Look," he said pointing to a place not far above. "There's a path that some mountain sheep or something has been using."

Petra sounded nervous. "Yes, but could we?" One misplaced step could send either of them sliding hundreds of feet down the loose slope.

"One step at a time," Ramon said.

He climbed to the path the wild sheep had made and stepped onto it, testing every footfall for security. Stride by stride, he began crossing the landslide, pausing only once in the middle as a flash of something below caught his eye. He looked far downward and saw the sun reflecting in a beaver pond maybe two miles away. The avalanche had cleared a swath down through the timber, opening an incredible vista.

"Gracias a Dios," he muttered, taking in the eagle's view. Turning, he saw a look of wild terror in Sister Petra's eyes and knew he had better not ask her to look down. He moved steadily across the rest of the landslide, waiting for her on safe ground, offering his hand.

They spoke nothing, but moved on, ever upward, across the steep forested face of the mountain. Coming around another huge wrinkle in the topography, they heard water rushing not far away. As they got nearer, it grew to a roar, and soon they found the stream thundering over a precipice in a white froth.

They had to climb to get to the top of the waterfall, where slick stepping stones led them across the torrent of snowmelt. Ramon went first, leaping from one rock to the next with perfect balance. When he turned, he saw Petra still waiting across the stream.

"Come on!" he cried.

She answered, but the sound of the cascade swallowed her words. Uncertainly, she started, looking long at each successive step, gathering herself for the long stride repeatedly before chancing it. On the fifth stone, her foot slipped. The water was knee deep, cold, and swift enough to take her foot out from under her.

Ramon was in the stream in an instant, splashing toward the little nun, even though the current lacked the force to sweep her far toward the brink of the waterfall. He grabbed her by the arm and pulled her across the stream.

"I'm all right," she said. She sat down at the water's edge and caught her breath. "I didn't know it would be this hard. We've crossed nothing like this." Her eyes, for the first time since leaving Guajolote, showed her doubts.

Ramon rose and stepped back, aghast. *"Oiga,"* he ordered. "Listen to me, Sister Petra. Day after day I have followed you north looking for this cross. Now we are only a couple of miles away, and you are losing your nerve?"

"I haven't lost my nerve," she snapped. "I just didn't know it would get this dangerous. "I'm afraid one of us is going to fall off this mountain."

"Well, it's not going to be me," he said. "I'm going to find that cross. I'm going to see something that only a handful of people have ever seen. Do you want me to tell you about it, or do you want to come with me?"

Petra gritted her teeth as she rose. Something had come over this boy. How much he had changed since Guajolote. Giving orders now! *"Listo,"* she said. "I am ready," and the determination in her eyes convinced Ramon.

They trudged on at a steady grind, their legs falling into a slow rhythm. Taking a severe angle up the mountain, they covered ground more slowly, but gained altitude faster. Patches of snow began to appear in shady places, the patches growing larger as they ascended. It took thousands of wordless steps, their path wending among many obstacles of stone and wood, before they reached the timberline.

It came suddenly, the bright openness glaring down at them after the shadows of the forest. Petra looked for a path, but, of course, there was none. Ahead lay fields of snow, ancient rock slides.

"Is this Notch Mountain?" Ramon said. "Where is the notch?"

"We can't see it from here. We are too close to it. It all looks different when you are upon it."

It was cooler up here, but the sun was shining brightly, and the climb had kept them warm.

"It should be easier now," Ramon suggested. "No more dead trees to climb over."

"Yes," she answered. "But there will be more snow. We are going to have to go through it in some places. We still have a mile to climb, maybe two."

He took some dried meat from his coat pocket and began to chew on it as he led the way up the slippery alpine tundra. He stepped in a mushy spot where melted snow had seeped and felt the cold water almost immediately on his toes. His boots were worn out from the long journey. Petra's were in better shape, and they were high-topped lace-up boots. Ramon's were low, wide-mouthed boots. They would not serve him well if he had to cross fields of snow.

Petra looked northward and saw white clouds on some far-distant range. "I hope the clouds don't gather here. It would obscure the cross."

"You worry too much. We are almost there. What could happen now?" But Ramon was worried, too. Not about whether they would find the cross, but about what would happen then. Did she really think they would find money lying around on the rocks? This trip was meant to save Guajolote. Did she remember that? How was this Snowy

Cross going to save a tiny village hundreds of miles away? Petra was in for a disappointment. That was all there was to it. And she was going to be hell to live with all the way home.

TWENTY-SEVEN

This was the way Frank had done it. Years ago, when Carrol was the outlaw on the run, Frank had caught up to him unexpectedly at a cabin in the San Juan Mountains. Carrol had stolen a couple of dozen cattle, shooting and wounding a cowboy who had given chase. He knew the law—probably his own brother—would trail him, so he had ridden like the devil's own jockey for Arizona, stealing fresh mounts along the way.

He had come to the abandoned cabin in Ute country, probably the former home of some long-dead fur trapper. He had chanced a few hours of sleep there, knowing that no one could have ridden harder than he had.

And yet, not three hours later, Frank Moncrief burst into the cabin and clubbed his surprised brother over the head with the barrel of a navy Colt. It was weeks later that Frank explained how he had done it. They were camped by the Platte River in South Park, on the road to the state penitentiary in Cañon City. The same place where Frank would later die at the hands of Dee Hassard.

"Bet you wonder how I caught up to you in the San Juans, don't you?" Frank had said, the gurgles of the Platte keeping time with the cracklings of the fire.

Carrol had wondered, all right. There was no way any man could have ridden harder than he had after stealing those cattle and shooting that cowboy. But he wasn't going to give Frank the satisfaction of asking how.

"You were slippin' away from me," Frank admitted. "I was ridin' hard, but I had to trail you, and that slowed me down. Every time I'd get to where you had stole a fresh horse, I was a little further behind you. I had to try somethin'.

"So when I came to that ranch you stole your last horse from, I borrowed six fresh mounts. I tied 'em in a string, head to tail, rode the lead horse till he was near dead, then switched to the next one back. Every time I did that, I'd leave the jaded horse where I'd finished with him and take the fresher horses on. I knew you were headin' for Arizona, so I just rode. Didn't worry about trailin' you anymore. I was lucky to find that cabin. Spotted the smoke from the chimney. You never should have lit that fire."

Carrol had spat on the ground between himself and his brother and said, "I'll be damned if you'll catch me next time."

"Let me promise you somethin', brother," Frank had replied, the cold glare of determination filling his eyes. "When you get out of prison, if you decide to step back on that outlaw trail, I don't care if I have to kill every horse in Colorado. I will ride you down again. If you gallop all the way to South America, I will dog you like a hound on a damned coyote."

"You do, and I'll kill you," Carrol said, and he had meant it.

Thank God it hadn't come to that. He had found a new

way, in prison of all places. He had learned to place Frank
in higher regard than any man he knew. But now Frank was
dead, and he was closing fast on his killer, Dee Hassard.

He was glad now that he knew about the string of horses
that Frank had used to catch him years ago. The method
was working well here, because the pilgrims left such a
plain trail. Carrol could read it at a gallop. It was dangerous, though. Six galloping horses in a string was a wreck
looking for a place to happen, and he had been happy just
to drop the first tired horse from the head of the string ten
miles out of Frisco.

He was down to two horses now, having lathered four
mounts to near exhaustion. The last two were hardly fresh.
They had run all the way from Frisco, yet they had carried no man upon their backs, felt no cinch tighten around
their barrels. Each horse would carry him about five miles
before tiring. If he didn't overtake the pilgrims by then,
Hassard was as good as gone.

It was odd that Frank had used any horse this hard, for
Frank had always believed in treating his mounts with gen-
tleness, though he knew how to get the most out of them.
Carrol was only now realizing how desperate Frank must
have been on that ride, how much he must have hated hunting down his own brother: a shame and a duty in one
courageous act.

The parson changed his saddle to the last horse on the
banks of the Eagle River. He hadn't been saddle sore in
years, but this wild ride had chafed layers of hide off his
inner thighs and pounded his knees to aching mush. He
mounted and rode in a long lope upstream. The horse had
some gallop left in him, but Carrol decided to ride for dis-

tance instead of speed. He might get ten miles out of this horse at a lope.

As it turned out, he needed only six. He was following the wide trail trampled by the pilgrims, coming to the top of an incline, when he heard a voice and saw an armed man step into the path ahead of him.

"You stop!" the man demanded.

Carrol reined in the heaving mount and took a moment to size up the man in the trail. He appeared to an Indian, but wore the clothing of a white man, braids falling over his lapels. The preacher got down and gave his exhausted mount some slack in the saddle cinch. "Who are you, friend?" he said.

"Dan Feather. You?"

"I am the Reverend Carrol Moncrief. I'm looking for the Church of the Weeping Virgin."

Dan lowered his rifle. "Moncrief? Okay, you come on in." He motioned up the trail with his muzzle.

"Where is Dee Hassard?" the parson asked, leading his horse. Pain stabbed both knees after the hard ride, and walking felt awkward.

Dan Feather pointed his barrel upward. "Deacon Dee go up the mountain today. Go see cross. He take money."

"When did he leave?"

"Daylight."

Carrol nodded. Maybe there was time.

When they walked into the clearing, Carrol took a moment to judge what was going on. The place crawled like an ant bed, and the walls of a building at the top of the slope already stood four logs high. "What is this place?" he said.

" 'Tigiwon,' " Dan Feather replied.

"What's that mean?"

"Sacred place."

A look of disbelief swept his face. This Dee Hassard sure had some line of gab to get these people here, building a town this high in the mountains. "Do me a favor, Dan Feather. Walk my horse a while. Rub him down. He's been used hard."

"I take good care," Dan promised and led the horse away on a level trail.

Carrol looked for someone who might be in charge, settling on a young man who was peeling logs with a good-looking woman. The pilgrims had begun to take notice of him by now, and some of them gravitated toward the log church to see what he wanted.

"Who are you?" James O'Rourke said, cordially, when the big man in black trudged up the slope to him.

He tipped his hat to the lady. "Name's Moncrief. Where's Hopewell? He hired me by correspondence to guide this party."

"He went with Deacon Hassard and two others up the mountain."

Carrol sighed. He was tired. "I need to borrow a horse or mule so I can catch 'em."

O'Rourke's brow wrinkled. "You can't ride where they've gone. Too rough. They'll be back this evening, though."

"I doubt it. Which way did they go?"

O'Rourke pointed. "What's the hurry all about?"

He studied their faces. The woman looked concerned. Maybe she had suspected something by now. But the youth beside her had been taken in.

"Dee Hassard is no more a deacon that this log is," he said, kicking the felled timber. "He's a swindler and a murderer. He shot my brother to death not long ago in South Park, and I mean to bring him down for it."

He watched carefully. The woman sank to the log and put her hands to her face, growing almost instantly pale. A body couldn't fake fear like that. The lad's face, on the other hand, remained blank for several long seconds, then grew angry, and finally turned to scowl at the woman.

"You're in it!" he said.

May gasped, thought quickly, realized how it must look to them. She glanced at the gathering crowd, saw their eyes piercing her.

"You joined the same time Hassard did!" O'Rourke said. "So did Clarence. You're all in it!"

"No!" May cried.

The pilgrims closed in on her.

"What about that man who came here yesterday? Supposed to be your husband? He was in it, too, and you three killed him to get a bigger cut, didn't you?"

"No!"

She stood up, and O'Rourke grabbed her by the arm as if she were trying to escape.

"Let her go!" Carrol ordered. "Get aholt of yourselves! This ain't no time to be makin' rash accusations. We'll sort this whole thing out after I get Hassard." He pushed his way past several pilgrims, starting up the slope.

"I'm comin' with you," May said. She was getting mad now. She had been first duped by Hassard, now wrongly accused by these pilgrims, and she was getting tired of it all. She might have taken it meekly before she met Clarence, but she was getting stronger for having known him.

"I'm goin' alone," Moncrief answered, without looking back.

"You just try to stop me," she insisted, her voice grating as even she had never heard. She knifed one of her accusers with a glare and hiked briskly in Moncrief's footsteps. "Clarence has a gun. He'll be in trouble if we don't hurry. We can follow the blaze marks on the trees."

Moncrief slowed his pace, and the woman stormed past him. Lord, give me strength, he thought. He was tired—so tired. And now, to go up this mountain on foot. Maybe the woman would help. He didn't blame her for not wanting to stay with the pilgrims. Also, she knew what had been going on with Hassard, so maybe she could fill him in. Anyway, he had no time to argue.

"Moncrief!" the youth cried.

The reverend swiveled his tired eyes.

"Yesterday Hassard rode up the valley on a big red mule, but he came back on foot. He said he fell off and the mule got away."

Carrol's eyes searched the young face and understood. Maybe Hassard had already established his escape route. Maybe it would be better to ride up the trail, find the mule, and wait for Hassard to come down to it. For some reason, he could only briefly consider it. Maybe it was because he was so tired of riding. The trail ahead was hot. Perhaps the cross was calling him up the mountain.

He took a few deep breaths and turned up the slope behind the woman. If this failed, Hassard was gone.

TWENTY-EIGHT

They had climbed above the timberline for almost an hour now, and still the crest seemed a mile above them. Clarence was carrying the saddlebag full of money in addition to his own secret holdings in his jacket. Even with the extra weight, he stayed on Hassard's heels, and could have passed him if he had wanted. But Clarence preferred not to turn his back on Deacon Dee.

They came to the brink of a cliff that dropped untold hundreds of feet below them in a succession of narrow ledges scarcely fit for mountain goats. Clarence stopped for a moment and let Hassard trudge on up the trackless slope of cold rock and slick alpine tundra.

The view from the cliff spanned reaches that would require weeks of travel to fetch, and the Vermonter could not imagine why he had ever worried about the west filling up with people before he could get here. Across the many high peaks and forested valleys around him, he could see not one mark of settlement. Not a road, nor a field, nor a streak of smoke across the sky.

Hopewell came to his side and looked down the cliff, trying to gather in the sheer expanse of air below him, knowing now how the lowly world looked to the eagle.

"Did you ever think you'd see anything like this?" Clarence asked.

Hopewell shook his head reverently. "Didn't know there was such as this on all of God's whole earth."

"Let's throw a rock off," Clarence suggested, grinning at the elder.

Hopewell smiled boyishly, found a stone the size of a hen's egg. Clarence picked a like one, and they hurled them together as Mary Whitepath passed silently behind them. The stones arched unimpressively away from the precipice, then began plummeting downward, finally vanishing like flies into the sunlight. If they made a sound against something, it never reached the ears of those who had thrown them.

"Hey!" Hassard shouted from above. "Let's get goin' down there!"

Clarence saw a ridge above and climbed steadily toward it, containing his excitement. When he reached it, he found only a higher ridge beyond it. He knew they had to be near the divide, but here he was such a tiny speck on this vast mountain that he couldn't be sure which ridge was the highest.

He looked down toward Tigiwon but couldn't be certain where it lay anymore. The valley of the Eagle River—a long, straight furrow from the banks of the stream—had become invisible from here. It had shrunk away to a series of low dark places. The sun shone from on high now, and Clarence found bearings difficult to maintain in his mind. He was practically lost, turned so far around that he couldn't have hit Vermont with a rifle shot. Rationally, however, he knew that he must only continue upward to arrive at his destination. And they had left a trail of blaze marks and piles of stones to guide them back down the mountain.

He followed Hassard's lead, winding among countless

snowfields and fans of huge boulders where peaks had crumbled in ancient times. The wind wanted his hat here, and he curled the brim hard to keep it on his head. Cool air rushed in and out of his lungs, fueling him well even with its dearth of oxygen.

It seemed they were climbing to the top of the world, and Clarence looked up only occasionally now, between steps. Always the mountain loomed ahead of him, like a planet whose curve he could never traverse. But suddenly, rounding a small peak of huge stone rubble, he saw the entire sky open below and ahead of him where the mountain had lain before. Here the world fell away in every direction except for the ridge winding away to his right, which he suddenly knew was the summit of Notch Mountain. And here was its divide under his feet.

Hassard was standing ahead of him. Just standing, for the first time today, taking in some view. Clarence came further around the small peak, and then saw it. Like a faraway painting whose canvas trailed off into infinity. It seemed almost touchable, yet between its face and the Vermonter's eyes lay a void no cannon shot could span.

The paragon of mountain peaks rose high across a basin like a near-perfect pyramid of rock. Upon its face, in gossamer lines of pure white snow, the cross stabbed Clarence's eyes as a beautiful blaring trumpet might assault his ears. Its arms lifted upward like a conductor holding an orchestra at perpetual readiness. Far friendlier than any beams of square-hewn timber, the snowy lines of the cross reclined comfortably against the cold granite. And though they may have stood wide as a town square, from here the lines were mere brush strokes of snow driven into unbelievable crevices.

"That's God's own easel," Hassard said.

The voice startled Clarence, and he realized that he had let the deacon circle behind him. He turned quickly to look, but found Hassard sitting harmlessly on a rock in the cold sunshine.

It was not as if the thought hadn't occurred to Dee Hassard, too. His pistol was easily reachable inside his coat. He had made sure of that. Neither Hopewell nor the Indian woman carried a weapon. It would have been a simple matter to put a bullet through the Vermonter's back, chase the elder and Mary Whitepath back down the mountain, and then angle southward to find his mule. Hell, he might have left all three of them dead on this mountain and let that cross of snow serve as their ridiculous headstone. He was already on the run for killing Frank Moncrief. What would another body or two matter?

But Dee Hassard had his pride. A killing to him was messy. It showed a lack of professionalism. He was more meticulous than that. Besides, he liked letting them live, letting them know how badly he had fooled them. That was part of the game. No, that *was* the game. Often he had wished he could be there when the realization struck—to see the looks of anger, shame, and panic meld suddenly on their faces. Murder was sometimes necessary—take Frank Moncrief and Charlie Holt. No way around either one of them.

But not here. This was too perfect. Look at their mouths hanging open. Look at them gawking across this basin at that crooked snow formation. It was laughable, and in days to come, Dee Hassard would laugh hard over it. There was still a chance that he could pull this thing off without killing Clarence. He hoped they would all live long to think about this one.

"It's just like the Weeping Virgin told me in my dreams. Let your burden down, Brother Clarence. It belongs to God now." In a way, he actually meant it. Dee Hassard was his own god, and these mortals were sacrificing to him now and didn't even know it.

Clarence looked at Hopewell, but the elder's eyes were across the basin. To leave this money here was foolishness. But was it really his concern? They had allowed Hassard to leave this morning with the church coffers. They had prayed for him. It was their money—church money. The congregation had to decide what to do with it, ridiculous or not.

Oh well, he thought, letting the saddlebags slide off his broad shoulder, at least I won't have to carry it back down the mountain. He studied Hassard. The man was staring just as long and reverently at the Snowy Cross as Elder Hopewell or Mary Whitepath. Yet the Vermonter knew it was far from over. An unnamed tension stood between him and the deacon like a magnetic field: opposing poles pushing against each other. You must not turn your back on this man. He is not what he claims. He will return for this money, and then it will be your concern.

Mary Whitepath was on her knees, weeping silently, staring at the cross.

The others sat in silence for several long minutes, and Hassard paced through the logistics one more time. Tonight, after a couple of hours of sleep, he would sneak away from Tigiwon. Slipping past Clarence would be the hardest part, but he would have an excuse planned in case the Vermonter questioned him, and the dagger in his pocket in the event the excuse failed to satisfy. Back in the cities, he had learned how to stick a man so that he would not even cry out. He would only die.

Next he would climb back up here to retrieve his earnings, a half-moon to light his way. Had any man in his profession ever pulled off such a feat? By dawn he would be mounting his mule and riding up the valley, about the same time Carrol Moncrief arrived at Tigiwon. It would be grueling, but after Buena Vista, he could sleep in the stagecoach on his way to California.

He repeated each step in his mind until he began to feel the chill of his own sweat. "Well, let's get back to Tigiwon," he said, springing to his feet.

Clarence let the surprise show on his face. "Already?"

Hassard shrugged. "It's a long walk. We'd better get back before dark. The others will be waiting to hear about this." He started down the barren ridge without once looking back. "It's not as if we can't come back whenever we want to."

Clarence looked at the leather pouches stuffed with gold and currency and nodded. Yes, he thought. And Dee Hassard will want to come back tonight.

The snowfields had become so numerous around them that there was no other way. Going around them would mean retracing hundreds of feet back down the mountain, and neither Petra nor Ramon cared to lose any altitude at this point. Their path lay upward.

They had crossed some narrow streaks of snow already, but the one now in their path stretched almost a hundred yards and covered an old rock slide. Petra went first, wading into the field of white, crunching through its dirty surface.

"Be sure to feel for every step," Ramon warned. "You might fall into a hole or something."

"Yes," she said. "I will be careful."

After several steps, they sank waist deep into the drift, and snow was falling into the tops of Ramon's short boots, packing hard around his ankles. He said nothing of it, only wanting to reach the other side.

He paused to look around him. He had seen many new things on this journey, but this was something he had to remember. Here it seemed that some blight had lain waste to the whole warm world of trees and grass. Everything he saw was rock and snow, from the slick boulder under his heels to the distant ranges a hundred miles away. If there was still greenery below, he would never have known it from this vantage.

Coming finally out of the snowfield, Petra stomped the ice crystals from her legs and Ramon sat down to dump the packed snow from his boots. The nun happened to look at a chunk of ice Ramon cast aside and saw a crimson hue to it. "Are you bleeding?" she said.

The boy shrugged. "The snow packed in my boot and scraped me a little. It's nothing." He stood and looked up the slope. They seemed very near the top of the divide, but he had thought that many times today. "Let's look over this ridge."

He started slowly, letting Petra pull ahead of him. He

almost dreaded peering over the crest. What if they found another, higher ridge a mile away? How long could they keep going? They could not get caught here by darkness. Soon they would have to go below.

What was he doing here, anyway? The reason was so old and far away that he almost couldn't bring it to mind. The Snowy Cross—that was it. Why? To save Guajolote. How? How was any of this going to help? Does gold lie scattered atop this range in the thousands of dollars?

"Ramon?"

He looked up and saw Petra standing straight and rigid on the crest above eye level. A fresh wind was trailing her hair behind her, and she looked like some kind of conquering princess. She didn't look down at him, but her hand waved for him to join her.

Already his heart was pounding, for he knew what he would find when he scrambled up the last of the incline. Then his heart stopped as the vision struck him. It was like brilliant light shining through a cross-carved door into a darkened room. He felt Petra's arms around him, his own around her, as a power surged between them whose force was greater than the sum of anything they could have mustered apart. Then she sank to her knees, and Ramon was left alone.

For a long moment he stared at the Mount of the Snowy Cross, marveling at his arrival here. Then, suddenly, he thought of home. Guajolote, where warm adobe soaked in sunlight and spring water laughed from miniature cascades. And for a moment, he felt a glimmer of faith strong enough to cause him to look around—around his feet first, as if he would find gold coin stacked there waiting for him.

His eyes pulled to the right, following the ridge that rose to the summit of Notch Mountain. There was rough rock and patches of coarse snow—and something that glowed with the luster of time-smoothed leather.

He blinked hard and looked again at the object standing not fifty yards away on the ridge. A pair of leather saddlebags perched on the crest as if some hand had just deposited them there. He thought about the American photographer, Señor Jackson, whom he and Petra had met in Del Norte. The photographic party must have left this thing behind.

He left Petra and climbed an easy slope to the saddlebags. Stooping, he lifted the bags, finding them heavier than he had imagined. He dropped them and heard a chink of metal. What he was thinking wasn't possible, of course, but it made his stomach flutter nonetheless. He glanced at the Snowy Cross, looming across the high basin through a cloud-haze that was beginning to form. He looked at Petra, the quintessence of devotion there on her knees in this unlikely place. Was her faith alone sufficient?

He knelt and unfastened the buckle on one of the pouches. Slowly he lifted the flap and peered inside. For a splinter of a moment he knew what it felt like to have been brushed by the wake of angels passing nearby. He tried to call Petra's name, but couldn't speak. Ramon del Bosque was never again to know the careless indifference of boyhood.

TWENTY-NINE

They came to the place where Clarence and Elder Hopewell had thrown the stones into the void, and they paused there to look again across the uninviting mountainscape. They could see the dark forest from here, and Clarence longed to be back in its shadow, back where tall things grew. But it was impossible to pass this place without stopping to look over.

Hopewell and Mary Whitepath stood to his left, Hassard slightly downhill to his right, anxious to move on. Then Clarence saw Mary Whitepath's arm raise toward him, her finger pointing back down the trail toward Tigiwon. Clarence looked, and he saw climbers just above the timberline.

"By golly, that's May," he said, astonished. "Who the devil is that with her?"

Dee Hassard took one look and felt panic whir in his brain. How could that be Carrol Moncrief? He had underestimated the big circuit rider, but that didn't matter now.

Clarence saw Hassard begin to turn. He thought about Charlie Holt's pistol, strapped now around his hips under his jacket. He tried to get at it, but the jacket was buttoned. Hassard had come around to face him now, a hand inside his coat. Clarence tried to lift the bottom of his jacket over the gun grip, but the gold coins stacked on edge in the fabric slowed the attempt. It was too late now, anyway. He was looking down the barrel of Hassard's Colt.

He saw the orange flare and the smoke, but he never heard the report, never felt the slug.

Hassard watched, satisfied to see the Vermonter fly backward over the cliff. He trained his muzzle on Hopewell, then Mary Whitepath. No need. Neither could harm him.

"Don't follow!" he shouted, glaring wildly into their stares of horror and astonishment.

Dee Hassard shoved the Colt back into Frank Moncrief's holster and sprinted up the mountain. It was a footrace now, and one that he could not afford to lose.

It seemed to take him only a few minutes to reach the divide, but when he got there, his lungs were ready to rip. He scrambled around the peak of rubble and slid to a standstill, almost swallowing his tongue in his surprise. A small, pretty, dark-haired woman and a black-haired boy were hunkered over the money, counting, calculating. Pilgrims? No, he didn't recognize them from the congregation. What in the name of . . .

Dee Hassard fought for oxygen as he glanced back down toward Moncrief. He drew his Colt, the boy and the woman shrinking away from its muzzle. "Put it back in the bags!" he managed.

Sister Petra felt a calm come over her. The Snowy Cross was out of her sight over her left shoulder, but she felt its solid presence. She obeyed the stranger, methodically placing the cold specie, the paper notes, and the pouches of gold dust back into the saddlebag openings.

"Who the hell are you?" Hassard demanded, annoyed. Maybe it was a good thing he had been driven back up here, or these thieves would have gotten his earnings.

"I am Petra, and this is Ramon."

Hassard snorted and shook his head. This was too much to take in, and he really didn't care. The woman had finished replacing the money, and now she stood with the saddlebags draped over her right forearm. She stepped in front of the boy.

"Give them to me!" Hassard ordered.

"I cannot," she said. "This does not belong to you." It was so clear and simple that she didn't have to think about it. It was so obviously right that she didn't have to fear.

Hassard felt Moncrief too close behind. There was no time for this. He reached for the bag, grabbed a leather strap. The woman would not turn it loose. She possessed some grip, and Dee Hassard was tired. Could he wrestle her? What about that Mexican boy? Mexicans carried knives, didn't they?

Ramon had stepped to Petra's right, trying to see some sense in all this. What were they saying in that damned numb-tongued English? He was afraid of this orange-haired stranger, but Petra seemed perfectly at ease holding on to her prayers answered. He was about to tell her to let the stranger have the money when the gun fired and Petra crumpled backward onto the sharp rocks. The muzzle swung toward him, but he ignored it, falling on top of the good sister.

Hassard panted hard. The boy was no threat. He had to run now. Moncrief was too close behind him. He threw the winnings over his shoulder and smiled as he angled southward down the slope. Damn, what a couple of close ones!

*   *   *

Arriving at the bluff with May, Carrol found Elder
Hopewell and Mary Whitepath lying on their stomachs,
looking over the precipice.

"Don't move!" the gangling black man was shouting.
"Clarence. Don't move!"

May screamed and threw herself between them, looking over the edge. She saw Clarence lying on his back
some thirty feet below, his chest heaving. He rested on a
narrow gravelly ledge that sloped dangerously downward.
One arm and one leg hung over the edge. Below lay a series
of ledges, each too slim to stand upon. If the Vermonter
slid one inch, he would fall hundreds of feet, bouncing
off hard rock ledges all the way down.

Carrol gritted his teeth as he looked over the edge. From
below, he had looked up just in time to see the tall young
man take Hassard's bullet in the chest. It was amazing that
he had survived at all, but now he was almost surely
doomed. Either he would have to climb back up to the
ledge, or someone would have to climb down to put a rope
on him. The young man's chances were slim, but Carrol
did not feel good about leaving these two women and this
old man to handle it.

Then he heard the shot—a single pistol blast from
above. "Are there more of you up there?" he asked the
black man.

"No," Hopewell said.

May had sprung from the rocks to fetch the coil of rope
Hopewell had thrown from his shoulders.

Carrol made a hard decision. His job was to get Hassard, bring him to justice for killing Frank. Bring him in
or kill him. He was getting mad. May had told him about

the death of Charlie Holt, and he had just seen Hassard shoot this young man in cold blood with his own eyes. The con man had turned murderer and left a virtual trail of dead bodies all over Colorado. These three would have to handle the young man on the ledge. He turned and sprinted up the mountain.

Coming to the divide, Carrol drew his pistol and came around a cone of timeworn boulders. He heard a scuffle of feet on the rock and found it quickly. The boy looked at him with tear-filled eyes. In his arms was a woman whose blood stained the front of her frock in a hue of crimson bright as a cardinal. Her eyes were blinking, but her body lay limp. Trying to lift her, the boy caught sight of Carrol and gasped.

Quickly the parson put his revolver in the holster and came toward the unlikely pair. "Put her down," he said.

The boy replied in Spanish: "Help me. She wants to look at the cross."

"La cruz?" Carrol said, picking out the few words he recognized. He let his eyes focus for the first time on the distant mountain slope across the basin, and saw the lines of snow driven there. He put his arms under the woman, a slight creature whose green eyes glistened serenely at him. With help from the boy, he lifted her, turned her, carried her to the very brink of the divide and made her as comfortable as possible on the rocks.

Looking southward down the slope, Carrol thought of Hassard slipping away. If he reached the red mule he had left up the valley, he would likely go free. He sprang to his feet and ran a few yards along the divide. He could see no sign of the murderer. Trailing him would be slow, while

Hassard would be running like a mountain goat, widening the gap between them.

He could think of just one way. Return to that town those lunatic pilgrims were building, borrow a mount, and try to ride Hassard down somewhere on the trail.

When he came back to the dying woman, the boy with her had dried his eyes and was listening to her. Carrol understood little, for she spoke only Spanish, though she didn't look Mexican—not with those green eyes.

"My life has been a glory," Petra was saying, holding Ramon's hand, glancing away from the cross to him. "But I will not leave this place. Now it is up to you. You must save Guajolote."

"But, Sister," Ramon said. "The money is gone. That man took it away."

She smiled. "Have faith. The Lord will provide. You must not go home until you know how to save your village."

THIRTY

H e could hear May's voice echoing across the mountains somewhere, far away. "Grab the rope!" she was saying.

Clarence tried to make sense of it. His chest felt as if someone had driven a wagon over it. Sharp things poked him in the rear end. An arm and a leg dangled off something, feeling cold, and he was gasping for breath.

"Damn you, Clarence Philbrick! You grab ahold of that rope!"

What was she talking about? There was something flopping around on his stomach. It felt like a snake, but he knew somehow not to move. Slowly he opened his eyes and saw the rock rising above him to his right, felt the emptiness to his left. The rope was undulating above him. There was May's face, looking angrily down at him. Sister Mary Whitepath and Elder Hopewell were there beside her.

Now he remembered the loud blast from Hassard's pistol and gathered where he was. His chest hurt like hell, but he felt no blood warmth, no bleeding inside. The coins, lined in pairs up and down his jacket must have saved him. He had always heard stories like that—men surviving shoot-outs and pistol duels when bullets glanced off coins or whiskey flasks or pocket watches.

"Clarence!" May repeated. "Grab the rope. You're about to slide off!"

Sure enough, the Vermonter could feel his body pulling away from the face of the cliff, wanting to roll on the gravel. He raised his right hand slowly and put it on the rope, taking a wrap. But he couldn't imagine even sitting up right now, much less climbing twenty feet of line.

"Good," May said, though she hardly sounded as if she approved. "Now, you've got to tie yourself on."

Suddenly he felt himself slide and found an instant store of strength. His cold left hand swung to the rope and pain like a knife wound tore into his chest. He slid over the little ledge he was on, and May screamed like nothing he had ever heard. He hit the end of the rope, the wrap he had taken twisting hard around his right hand, clamping down on it like a vise.

Short of breath, Clarence kicked his feet, searching for a foothold, finding none. His strength was almost sapped, his chest racked in one great excruciating throb. He was going to have to pull himself up, hand over hand. He had done it before. Rope-climbing had been part of his exercise routine back home. But never while wearing twenty-five extra pounds of gold. Never while suffering an impact to the chest like a mule's kick.

"Pull yourself up, Clarence!" May was near hysteria. "Pull yourself back up to the ledge, damn it!"

He couldn't imagine her cussing like that. He pulled up with both arms, the rope feeling as if it would pinch his right hand in two. He didn't have the strength to raise himself more than an inch. He was going to have to do something quick. He was growing weaker by the breath, and breath was short.

It was the gold! Damn his father's gold! It had weighed on him his life long, and now it was killing him, literally, as it had slowly suffocated him since he was a boy.

It was time to shed the burden, if it wasn't too late. Clarence released his left hand, letting his whole weight hang from the right hand with the rope wrapped around it. May yodeled in terror, thinking he had lost his grip, and the pain from the rope twisting his right hand made a tear cloud Clarence's eye. Clumsily, fighting the searing agony in his chest, he flopped his left arm until the heavy sleeve slid off.

He paused, for the next move seemed impossible. He had to take the rope in his left hand, release his right, and let the death jacket fall. How could he hold on with his left hand, with the pain concentrated in the left side of his chest? Feeling weaker, he knew he must act. The pain of the rope crushing his right hand was unbearable, anyway. Death on the rocks below could not possibly be more painful.

A sore ache and a knife-edged pang collided in the Vermonter's chest as he took hold of the rope with his left hand. The twist snapped away from his right hand, and the rope burned his left palm as it plowed past all the grip he could muster.

"Clarence!" May screamed, her voice a demanding censure.

Quickly he let his right arm drop and felt the sleeve slip over his wrist. He looked down to see the oilskin jacket snag but a short distance below on a sharp rock that might have broken his back had he fallen on it. He saw the bullet hole near the left lapel, a singular glint of gold metal glowing from it.

With his right hand on the hemp again, Clarence achieved enough purchase to stop slipping down the rope. But now what? Dropping the gold had helped, but he couldn't hang here long. He still couldn't pull himself up, exhausted as he was, weakened by the blow to the chest.

Now something crept into the Vermonter's mind. He had learned a few basic mountaineering skills from a college friend who liked to scale rocky places in the White Mountains. There was a way to hang here almost effortlessly, and a way to move across the face of this cliff to safer ground.

He felt the rope against his left knee, ran it first between his legs, then under his left thigh. Taking the dangling end of the rope in his left hand, he ran it across his chest, lifted it over his head, and let it fall over his right shoulder. Now he took a firm grip with his left hand on the loose end of the rope hanging down his back.

Clarence felt the familiar bite of the rope under his thigh and over his shoulder. *Abseil.* That was the name of this maneuver. Used in descending steep grades. The friction of the rope running under his thigh and over his shoulder took a share of his weight, easing the task on his hands. His palms served only as brakes now, to keep the rope from slipping around his body.

"Good!" May was saying. "You're thinking now."

He turned his eyes upward, feeling lighter, stronger, free of his father's weight, his father's intimidating success. He spoke something silently to himself that was stronger than a vow. He would be independent from here to death. He would rely on his own energies, his own abilities. His father's wealth could sink to the pits of hell for all he cared. Clarence Philbrick was his own man.

"Do something!" May shouted. "You can't just hang there!" She didn't see how he had managed this much. Hadn't a bullet bowled him off this ledge?

She was right, Clarence thought. Now, before his last stores of energy failed him. He looked to both sides, found a place to the left and below him where he could stand. From there, his eyes found a series of crags and ledges that would give him toeholds, handholds, all the way up to the brink where May and the others could pull him to safety.

He hadn't done it in a few years, but the method reeled from his trained muscles like second nature. He let himself slip cautiously downward, the rope smarting where it cut under his thigh and over the opposite shoulder. Now he remembered the drawback of the abseil method. It hurt! Here the cliff face sloped outward, and he managed to get his feet situated squarely on it. His legs pressing against the rock took still more weight, and the grip required of his hands lessened.

Still, he had to remember. His grip was the only thing that kept him from falling hundreds of feet. The wind was cool around him in this strange place, so high and wild. Sweat braced his brow. He looked below, saw the jacket just ten feet under him, his own rope lying over it. He disregarded it. It was the last thing he needed.

"What are you doing?" May said, for he had slipped beyond her sight over the ledges.

Good question, he thought. Why put it off longer? He took a few steps to his left along the cliff face, then swung like a pendulum back to center and beyond. He repeated the maneuver, each time swinging farther, until he was able to drop onto the flat ledge he had spotted from above.

The relief was instant. Pain ebbed from his palms, his shoulder, the underpart of his thigh. Only the left side of his chest still smarted, and even that had loosened up with the exercise.

Tying the rope around his waist as a safety line, Clarence began climbing up the series of handgrips and footholds he had located before. May scrambled along the cliff face to meet him, Mary Whitepath and Elder Hopewell close behind her.

When he got near the ledge, they reached down to grab his shirt and raised him up. They dragged him onto the rock, and May fell on him crying, searching him for wounds, finding only a little blood caused by the fall.

"It's a miracle," Hopewell said. "The shot hit him in the chest. I saw his left shoulder jerk back when Hassard fired." With his long fingers, he probed the area where the bullet should have hit.

May was sobbing on top of him now, feeling warm. "It's a miracle, all right," Clarence managed to say, though every word hurt.

Clarence was on his feet when the two strangers came down from the divide. One was a tall man in a dusty black suit. He wore a revolver that had seen much service, and a visage of utter fatigue and failure mixed on his face.

The boy was sad and quiet and looked as if his faculties were not all with him. He looked like Clarence felt, and Clarence wanted to know what had happened.

"Let's get down to the timber first," Moncrief said, "and make a camp for you folks before dark. Then we'll sort this out."

They built a fire in the timber, divvied a meager supply of jerked venison. Elder Hopewell began, telling Moncrief about the Church of the Weeping Virgin, from the first days.

"What now?" the reverend asked, after he had heard the fantastic story.

Hopewell shook his head and looked sadly into the fire, drained, exhausted. "It's over for me. Something went wrong, and I don't even know when or where. We're not a church anymore. We're lost. I knew that when I saw the Snowy Cross. That cross has been there thousands of years, I guess. It will last. The Church of the Weeping Virgin won't."

The boy's story was the hardest to get clear. He seemed dazed, unwilling to speak. But Mary Whitepath was Comanche, and knew Spanish better than she knew English. At length, she got the boy started, and it became a glory for Ramon to recount his journey with Sister Petra.

May noticed a peculiar look on Clarence's face when the boy mentioned the village of Guajolote and the Ojo de los Brazos land grant that Sister Petra had sought to save. The more she watched him, the more astounded he seemed, and she hoped the fall hadn't rattled something in his head.

"He says they came into this valley south of here," Mary Whitepath interpreted, "and they found a big red mule with hobbles on, so they camped there."

Moncrief's interest peaked. He squinted his eyes and turned one ear to May. "Didn't Hassard claim a big red mule threw him somewhere up the trail?"

"Yes, but if that's true, what would the mule be doing wearing hobbles?"

Mary Whitepath broke in: "The boy says an old man came to get the mule, and this old man told him and the sister where to find the cross on the mountain. Then the old man took the mule away."

"Ask him what the old man's name was," Moncrief ordered.

"He does not know the name, but he says it was the old man the people talked about in Buena Vista. The one who got lost and found the cross so high on the mountain."

"Sounds like the same old prospector we saw down at Tigiwon," Clarence added. "Didn't get his name. Hassard was the only one who talked to him."

"Did he have a mule with him then?" Moncrief said.

"No," the Vermonter said. "He carried a pack on his back."

Carrol grinned at the ground. It sounded for all the world as if old Jules Billings had come to take Hassard's big red mule away. Jules was in the ground on the banks of the Blue River, but it was a happy thought, however impossible. No telling how many played-out prospectors there were tramping around in these hills, looking for another 'forty-nine.

Ramon tugged Mary Whitepath's sleeve, for he wasn't through. "We did everything we were supposed to do," he told her. "We found the cross. We even found the money to save the village. And then that man came and shot Sister Petra and took the money away from us." He covered his face with a hand. "I couldn't do anything. The man had a gun, and it happened before I could do anything."

They sat in silence after Mary Whitepath translated for them.

"Tell him to keep the faith," Clarence said suddenly to the translator. Then he looked right at the boy. "Your Sister Petra would want you to keep the faith, boy. If you do, I guarantee you'll get the money you need to carry out what she wanted."

"I wouldn't make promises I can't keep," Moncrief warned. "Even if I manage to catch up to Hassard, all the money he's got belongs to other people."

Clarence shot a sure glance at him. "I can keep my promises, Reverend. Sister Mary, tell that boy he'll have the money he needs."

The parson's brow wrinkled, but he didn't have time for

argument. "I'm goin' back down to the big camp," he said, rising. "Maybe there's a chance that old miner you all ran into took Hassard's red mule up the valley." He chuckled. "The Lord works in ways like that sometimes. You never know. Maybe I can catch up to him."

"You can take my horse when you get to Tigiwon," Clarence said.

Carrol dipped his hat brim. "Obliged. Walk with me a little ways down the trail," he said. "I want to talk to you."

Clarence rose and followed the big reverend out of camp.

"Tell that Mexican boy to stay with the pilgrims," Moncrief ordered. "After I get Hassard, I'll come back for him and take him to his village in New Mexico."

Clarence nodded.

Moncrief reached into the breast pocket of his coat and pulled out the certificate Edgar Dreyer had given him in Frisco. "You'll take this in payment for your horse. Don't argue with me, because I don't even know that it's worth the paper it's printed on."

"What is it?" Clarence asked, unfolding the certificate.

"Mining claim over near Frisco. I got it in payment for a funeral I preached there. I've got no use for it. I ain't no miner."

Clarence nodded and tucked the claim into his pants pocket.

"One other thing," Moncrief said. "I ought to know better than to stick my nose into another man's business, but if you don't marry that girl over there, you're a blasted idiot. God intended some couples to pair off, and if they can't see it, well, somebody ought to have sense enough to tell 'em. I'm duly vested by the Territory of Colorado to perform the rites of matrimony, and if Dee Hassard doesn't sneak a bullet through my skull, I'd consider it an honor to conduct the ceremony myself."

Clarence bristled a little at first, for he was his own man, but he saw Carrol Moncrief's intentions for good ones and nodded with a smile on his face. "Good luck," he said, shaking the big man's hand.

It was like a dream that May would remember at odd moments as long as she lived, and it would move her more each time she thought of it.

She woke in the night when she sensed some movement in camp and found Clarence adding wood to the fire. He smiled at her to let her know everything was all right. Later she woke again; the fire was flickering nicely, but Clarence was gone. She slept quite a while before waking a third time, and found him kneeling at the fire again, probing it with a stick. She was curious now, so she sat up, but he cautioned her with his open palm and held a finger to his lips, glancing at the boy, Ramon, who slept nearby.

In the morning Clarence woke them and told Ramon to stoke the fire. As the boy went to gather wood, May found the coil of rope on the ground near Clarence's bedroll. She was sure she had left that rope trailing over the ledge yesterday after rescuing Clarence. When she questioned him with a look, he answered her with a wry smile—a smile that would lodge in her mind's eye and mean more to her every day.

It was only a few minutes later that Ramon was on his hands and knees, fanning the embers of the fire with his hat. He was feeling lonely, mourning Petra, missing Gua-jolote. The Indian woman had gone off into the woods somewhere, so he didn't even have anybody to talk to.

Then the ashes flew away from something, and Ramon cried out.

THIRTY-ONE

Carrol was no expert tracker, but he knew enough to read the desperation in Dee Hassard's trail. He had found the camp at daylight—seen the nun's diminutive tracks, the boy's, the large curve of the big red mule's.

The old miner who had taken the mule left no tracks at all. Maybe he wore moccasins, Carrol thought. Maybe he had learned some Indian trick. Maybe. It didn't matter. He had to keep his mind focused on Hassard.

The swindler's tracks had come down from Notch Mountain and were falling on top of the mule's prints now. The trail was easy enough to read from the back of Clarence Philbrick's horse. Hassard had made no attempt to cover his trail. He was in too much of a hurry. He was short, the parson recalled. Maybe five-foot-seven. But this was the stride of a six-footer. Dee Hassard had been running for his life when he left these prints, trying to catch that mule.

But by now he had to know it was too late. The mule had headed into a small creek valley whose slopes had grown steeper, evolving gradually into a box canyon. Hassard was trapped here. Even if he managed to catch the mule, his only way out would be back down the mouth of the canyon.

Carrol passed over a spot where Hassard had stopped to rest. He made out the place where the heavy bag of gold and money had plastered a cool patch of green grass to the ground. He let his mount's head bob three times, then pulled up, looking back at the place.

He had caught an inkling of something. Hassard never stopped to rest. He had stopped here to think. He had known by this time that he would not get away clean. He had stopped to plan something, like the gun he had planted at the South Platte camp to kill Frank.

It would be something different for Carrol, of course. Ambush? Probably not. Carrol would be expecting that. He knew how to move into a possible ambush, keeping to cover. He had learned that in his old rustling days, when the vigilantes had marked him for execution. He would be able to read an ambush here. Besides, Hassard was more of a back shooter than a sharp-shooter.

It would be trickier than a mere ambush. That was Hassard's style. His guile beat all. He had thought way ahead of Frank, and Frank had been the most thorough of lawmen. It was going to be something unexpected.

While Carrol was trying to guess ahead, Dee Hassard suddenly came walking into view with his hands in the air. The preacher turned the horse, drew his revolver.

"Easy, Moncrief," the redhead cried, stopping in his tracks. "I'm givin' up. You've got me cornered. I'd rather take my chances with the hangman later than have you shoot me in this godforsaken place."

Carrol rode forward, his sights trained on the murderer.

His jaw muscles tensed so hard they hurt. He noticed Hassard's empty holster. *Tricky bastard thinks I won't shoot him unarmed.* He came within a few paces of the swindler and swung down from the horse. "Where's your gun?" he said.

"I lost it," Hassard said.

Carrol smirked.

"I wouldn't believe it if I was you either, but it's true. Anyway, you can see I don't have it on me." He turned around with his hands in the air.

Carrol knew he was lying. May Tremaine had told him that Hassard carried two pistols. How could a man lose two? The funny thing was that he knew Hassard didn't expect him to believe the story. Dealing with this swindler was like wresting with a man's mind. Well, there was only one thing to do. Teach Hassard a new hold. Do something unexpected. Throw him off guard.

There was a rope tied to Carrol's saddle. "So, you'd rather face the hangman?" He took the rope down and tossed it to Hassard. "Build yourself a loop."

"You're not gonna hang me. That's murder, Moncrief."

"What jury would convict me for hangin' a nun killer?"

"Nun?" Hassard said, as if insulted. "What nun?"

"Sister Petra of the Snowy Cross. You killed her yesterday up on the divide."

"I didn't know she was a nun! What in the hell would a nun be doin' a way out here?"

Carrol shook his head. "Just put the noose on. I'd as soon shoot you if you don't."

"You're forgettin' something," Hassard said. "The money!"

"I don't give a damn about the money."

"I hid it good," Hassard said. "You won't find it without me."

"I said I don't give a damn about the money. I just want to free the world of your stench, and the quicker the better."

"But there's thousands!" Hassard cried, dropping to his knees. "Please, let me take you to it! Let me live just that much longer!" Real tears poured from his eyes.

Carrol laughed. "All right, you can get up now, that's all I wanted to know."

Hassard stared.

"Well, get up! You didn't really think I'd lynch you, did you? You didn't really think you could fool me with all that whimperin' after what you pulled on me in Denver, did you?"

Hassard sniffed and got to his feet. A cold pit began to form in his stomach. Yes, he had thought Moncrief really was going to lynch him. He had been taken in. He couldn't believe he had fallen for that part about the nun. He had lost the edge, and he knew it. Worse yet, he knew Moncrief knew it.

"Show me where the money is," Moncrief ordered. "But don't go grabbin' at it real quick, because I know what you'll pull out." He grinned and twisted his revolver in the air.

Reluctantly, Hassard turned back up the canyon, his hands above his head. Carrol followed, anxiously watching every move. He couldn't help remembering how Frank had let his guard down. How he himself had been so readily taken in that night in Denver. Was Dee Hassard ever finished conniving?

They came into a grove of aspens—a pleasant place

within earshot of running water, with summer-green leaves filtering the sun onto the white tree trunks. It was an older grove with bigger trees, well spaced. The two men wound their way among the trees, and Hassard rested his palms on top of his hat, for the lowest limbs swept just over his head, and his arms were tired.

"It's there," Hassard said, thrusting his chin toward a hollow log. It had been a large pine tree, long dead now, still showing vestiges of charcoal from some prehistoric forest fire. Aspens grew up on both sides of it like and-irons holding it in place.

Carrol was taking no chances. He kept thinking about what Clarence Philbrick and May Tremaine had told him. Hassard had waited until the last moment to kill Charlie Holt. He trusted no move the little man made. He wasn't even willing to reach into the hollow log for the saddle-bags. Maybe that was what Hassard wanted. A trap of some kind in there? Something to break his arm? Maybe Hassard was still thinking ahead of him.

Putting his muzzle against the back of Hassard's neck, he said, "Reach in there real slow. One hand. Any move you make too quick will get you killed."

Hassard trembled, and it was with real fear now. Moncrief had him as turned around as old Jules Billings before he found the Snowy Cross. He had never had a game turn this bad on him, and it made his senses swim. What Moncrief would do with him next was a terror and a mystery. Maybe the big preacher really would hang him. Maybe that woman on the mountain really was a nun. He couldn't say. He didn't know. He just reached into the log slowly, slipped his palm carefully under the leather, and drew the saddlebags out.

"Put it down and back away over yonder," Carrol ordered. He kept his sights trained on the vest buttons as the little sneak shrank away in small, timid steps.

"Don't kill me," Hassard blurted. "For the love of God, Moncrief, don't kill me here." Tears burst from his eyes like a flood.

"Shut your trap," the preacher growled, disgusted. He looked down at the saddlebags and turned back the flap of the near pouch. Inside he found the .36-caliber Smith & Wesson, rust pitted, cocked, lying on top of a stack of paper money.

Frank's Colt must be in the other pouch, he thought. Or . . .

Frank had gotten him almost to Cañon City. Almost to the penitentiary. He had let his guard down.

The thought shot at him like a lightning bolt, and from the corner of his eye, he saw that Hassard was still backing away, timidly, in little shuffling steps. Even before his eyes could glance up, the notion was in his head, and he remembered a low limb behind the crown of Hassard's hat. Backing toward it now, his hands in the air, pleading, blubbering, conniving.

Carrol's eyes came up, wild and alert, and saw Hassard's desperation. It was already happening. Dee Hassard was pretending to trip backward over a rotten limb in the grass. His hands were reaching for the low-hanging limb above him, as if to catch himself from the fall. Frank's pistol was up there. Lodged in a fork or something. It wasn't in the saddlebags at all. Hassard was one beat ahead, and there was no time to think.

Carrol let the barrel find its mark, tightened his grip on the trigger. He saw the murdering little swindler hump in midair, the blast whipping him to the ground as the rotten limb in the grass caught his heel.

The parson sprang, cocked the revolver for another shot. He looked down at Hassard and found the pale blue eyes open, reflecting flickers of light on fluttering aspen leaves. He kicked him once or twice, just to be sure. He checked for warm breath, pausing long.

Finally, Carrol Moncrief let the hammer spring rest on his revolver and slipped the weapon back into its holster. He sighed, trying to exhale the ball of nausea in his gut.

He looked now at the tree limb above the dead man, but found no revolver there. No knife. Nothing.

Stepping slowly to the saddlebags, he knelt, and shot yet another reassuring glance at the body. He opened the leather flap of the second pouch and found Frank's .45-caliber Colt inside, cocked, resting on a pouch of gold dust.

Dee Hassard had finally connived himself to death.

THIRTY-TWO

In years to come, Ramon would tell it often to the children of Guajolote: how the gold Sister Petra had prayed for appeared in the coals of that high mountain campfire in the country of the Snowy Cross. And the children's parents and grandparents would tell them it was true, for they had been there the day Ramon returned to Guajolote with the gold coins, back when he was just a boy.

"Why Guajolote?" the incredulous young ones would ask, crowding around the good father in the shade of a cottonwood that grew between the two arms of the Ojo de los Brazos. "Why would God want to save this village?"

"*¿Quien sabe?*" Ramon would tell them, shrugging his shoulders. "One never knows. Perhaps in a thousand years, this place will amount to something." He would laugh and stroke his fingers through the black hair of one of the children. "That is God's business."

"Padre Ramon, tell us about Sister Petra."

His heart would throb and he would reply: "What do you want to know about her?"

"What did she look like?"

"*Ay, muchachos,*" he would say, turning his palms to the brilliant New Mexican skies, his eyes sparkling like an ax against a grindstone. "She was the most beautiful woman you ever did see."

THE LAST
CHANCE

For Eric Allen "Brick" Blakely,
with whom I am well pleased.

ACKNOWLEDGMENTS

Thanks to my editor, Bob Gleason, a literary survivor out of the old rock.

A special thanks to Joe Vallely of the Flaming Star for riding points on the long trail.

ONE

They called her Chug. Ross wondered why, but he didn't ask. You kept your mouth shut in this man's army. You followed your orders and you didn't bother anybody with questions. When your sergeant said, "Private, you'll ride Ol' Chug today," you saddled Ol' Chug and awaited your order to mount.

She was the smoothest-riding horse Ross Caldwell had straddled since taking the Union oath. The other troopers bounced all around him on swaybacked nags, but he rode at a glide on Chug. He had covered hundreds of miles on stiff-legged cavalry cobs rough enough to split you in two from the crotch up, but this big gray mare could waltz.

You and your rump ought to be grateful, he thought. But he was not. Good fortune in the cavalry service tended to rouse Ross's suspicions. There was something wrong with all this. The other troopers should be grousing more. They should be coveting this mare. Ross hardly knew this Sergeant Parkhill, or any of the other men in this detachment. Why had he been given the privilege of riding Chug today?

And why "Chug"? It wasn't unusual that a horse like this should have a name. She stood out—a hand taller than any other mount in the string, sleek, well muscled, alert. He had heard that she came from the regimental band at Fort Laramie. But why "Ol' Chug"?

He pulled the brim of his campaign hat down low over his brow and squinted through the dust and the glare of summer sun on the dry plains. The valley of the North Platte fell away to his right, but his eyes kept drifting away to the left, where the Laramie Mountains rose. There were trees up on that near ridge. He could see rows of them sticking up like hackles on a dog's back. Trees meant shade. No shade down here.

Damn, these blue coats were hot. The grays had never seemed this stifling. Not even in Georgia. No cause to complain, though. This was still freedom, after all. Open territory as far as a man could see. A chance to start over in a young country. A chance to be with Julia. Sure, it was dusty. Hot, too. Cold last winter. Hard under the hailstones and lightning and sheets of pounding rain. But any common hell beat that prisoner of war camp in Chicago.

The telegraph wire stretched ahead of the riders, sagging between crooked posts as if it would melt in the sunshine. They had strung this section tight last winter, Ross recalled, after the blizzard winds had flattened four miles of it, snapping posts like toothpicks. Now the line drooped like strings of taffy in the heat.

It was broken somewhere west, and Ross had been riding with Sergeant Parkhill's detachment since dawn, looking for the break, wondering what had caused it this time. Probably Indians again. Ross fully expected to fight Indians today. If there were fewer than fifty, the detachment could hold them off. If there were more, he hoped Ol' Chug could run. Up to now, he hadn't let her go faster than a trot.

"The missus could ride her," a voice said to his right.

Ross looked, recognized the face, but couldn't place a name with it. "Pardon?" he said. The plains had murmured with Southern drawls since they rode out this morning, but this was the first to speak to him.

"Ain't she your wife? The laundry gal?"

"Yeah."

The corporal grinned. "Shore is nice to have a lady to talk to now and then. She's a fine lady. Your name's Caldwell, ain't it?"

Ross nodded. He saw Sergeant Parkhill look back at him, the dark pupil hard against the corner of the eye, the stubbled cheek bulging with tobacco.

"My name's Gene Dillon." The corporal thrust a tattered leather glove over the fork of his McClellan saddle.

Ross shook it. "Pleasure," he said. This Corporal Dillon had about six teeth missing from his smile. He had seen that gapped smile a time or two at Fort Laramie. Several times at Camp Douglas, Chicago. And even that day in Ohio. The day of the battle at Buffington Island. Two years ago. The day he threw down his weapons and became a prisoner of war.

"How'd you end up in this outfit?" Dillon said.

"Been down with the grippe. My squad rode to Platte Bridge without me and I got reassigned."

"Lucky for us you got sick," said a high-pitched voice. A blond-haired private reined his horse closer.

"What do you mean?" Ross said.

"I reckon your wife would have gone to Platte Bridge with you."

Ross nodded. "I reckon you're right."

"That would have left us shy of women around camp."

Ross smirked down at the private. The first sergeant at Camp Marshall kept a Cheyenne wife. One of the civilian scouts lived with a Sioux woman whose sister also stayed with them. A couple of privates and the camp sutler had also taken Indian wives. "There's half a dozen women there yet," he said.

Dillon and the yellow-haired private laughed at Ross from both sides.

"I ain't talkin' about no half-assed squaw brevet-wife," the girlish voice said. "I mean the genuine thing—a Southern white gal. We ain't got but one of them."

Ross didn't like the way he said "we," but he let it go. In a way, Julia did belong to everybody in K Company, 11th Ohio Cavalry. She was its inspiration. A heroine to every man in uniform. In that way, Ross knew he had to share her. "Maybe when the new captain gets to camp, he'll bring a wife with him," Ross suggested.

"Wouldn't be a Southern gal," the blond-haired private said. "Better not be, anyway. No damned Yankee captain better not marry a Southern gal while I'm still a Rebel."

Sergeant Parkhill tightened his reins and let his mount fall back between Chug and the mount of the blond-haired private. "He ain't married, anyway," Parkhill said.

"Who?" Dillon asked.

"The new company commander we're fixin' to get. Captain Jasper Jones. Now, ain't that a name for a Yankee greenhorn?" He drilled Ross with a squint, craned his neck, spit on his mount's rump, adding to the brown streak that trickled down the horse's leg, collecting dust.

For a bunch of soldiers in Union fatigues, these men sure threw that term "Yankee" around freely enough, Ross thought. Every man in this detachment, though a former Rebel, wore Yankee blue now. Galvanized Yankees, as the newspapers called them, although Ross couldn't figure why. To galvanize meant to coat with zinc—at least that's what it had meant back in his father's hardware store in Georgia. He couldn't see that he had been galvanized. A Georgia Rebel-turned-Yankee coated with zinc? What kind of sense did that make?

"I said, ain't that a name for a Yankee greenhorn?" Sergeant Parkhill growled. He rode a shorter horse, but his own height made up for it, and he looked square at Ross.

"Sounds like it," Ross said. This big sergeant seemed to be testing him for something. Ross didn't really know Parkhill, but remembered him wearing the tattered rags of a prisoner in Camp Douglas, Chicago. It was still strange to see him wearing blue, though he wore it with no great pride—his jacket and shirt both missing buttons, revealing a patch of chest hair under his sweaty civilian bandanna.

"How do you know this Jasper ain't married, Park?" Corporal Dillon asked.

"I've studied up on him. They kicked him out of West Point for sneakin' out to meet girls. Went through some academy for his commission. Only fought one battle before the war ended. Kennesaw Mountain. Got his arm shot off. Don't know a damn thing about Indians. He'll get us all killed if we give him a chance." The dark pupil drilled

Ross again. "Of course, we won't give him a chance, will we, Private?"

Ross squirmed in the saddle. He couldn't tell if Parkhill was joking, or what. "I don't guess that would do us much good," he said.

"Riders comin' back!" a voice shouted.

Ross saw the two plumes of dust slanting against the sky, like twin whirlwinds. Behind them, something he hadn't noticed before. A haze in the air, hanging low—a reddish blur under the crisp blue of the big sky.

Parkhill spurred ahead to meet the advance patrol. As the riders reported, the big sergeant sat hunched in his saddle, turning once to splatter tobacco juice on the rump of his horse. He was an intimidating specimen, Ross thought. Shoulders like a bull, legs like whiskey kegs, a trim waist, a jaw like a block of granite and fists to match. Crafty, too. The only Galvanized Yankee Ross knew of who had managed to climb to the rank of sergeant. He hated Yankees, yet could get whatever he wanted from them. The upper echelon considered him a model soldier.

When the detachment caught up to its sergeant and scouts, Parkhill was drawing his Colt revolver from his cavalry holster. "Get ready, boys," he said. "They're over the next divide."

"Who?" Dillon asked.

"The bastards that busted our telegraph wire. Hundreds of 'em."

"Hundreds!" the yellow-haired private said. "Then let's turn tail and git!"

"You do and I'll shoot you in the back, Lloyd. No coward deserves any better than that."

Ross glanced at the other faces, felt the familiar throb of sick fear in his stomach. Time after time he had held it down and charged into ridiculous dangers. He had never taken worse than a scratch from bullet or bayonet, but this looked like the final charge. Hundreds of Indians over the divide and a sergeant crazy for battle.

"Park, there ain't but seventeen of us," Dillon argued. "Why the hell should we go attackin' 'em?"

"They ain't carryin' no guns. Just pointy things to stick you with. We'll stampede 'em before they figure out what the hell hit 'em. Form a skirmish line and draw your weapons!"

Ross groped at the flap of his holster. Were they really going to do this? Outnumbered—what—ten to one? Twenty to one?

As they trotted toward the divide, he began to figure out why he was riding Ol' Chug. His head stuck up higher than any other—a tempting target. And which horse would the Indians want most? He could already feel their arrowheads and spear points. He remembered the bodies of horribly tortured settlers he had come across on the plains. Staked to the ground, burned, slashed, scalped, butchered.

He felt the initials, *RWC,* that he had carved into his pistol butt, slipped his hand around the wooden grip, and drew the Remington from his holster.

The war was over. Everybody else had gone home. But Ross Caldwell had switched armies, found new enemies. Oh, how could this be happening? Why now? Why here? What would become of Julia?

He sensed something in the air besides dust. A hum, like voices at a crowded ball, but different. It came from over the divide, through the rattle of the detachment. Ross thought he heard a cough, a moan, maybe the collective chaw of a great herd grazing.

He glanced down the line, saw Parkhill grinning around the quid in his cheek. This army life galled a reasonable man. He could not fathom why maniacs so readily made rank.

They approached the telegraph pole planted at the top of the divide, the cursed wire dragging the ground under it. A spiderweb stood a better chance of lasting in this hostile wilderness. Ross reckoned a million splices must have been made by now between Missouri and California—all so the newspapers could spread rumor and the army could issue its ridiculous orders. Might as well dig a ditch and fill it with the blood of soldiers and Indians who had killed each other along this route. Send messages down that. They said the railroad would follow the telegraph line. The railroad was a damn fool if it did.

He held his Remington revolver at his shoulder. Chug smelled something, her nostrils flaring, ears angling forward. She wanted to lope, but Ross held her back. Maybe his luck would hold. It had to be hard to aim those bows. He wondered what an arrow felt like piercing one's skin, slicing through muscle, slamming into bone.

One thing for sure. The moment Sergeant Parkhill gave

up his scalp, Ross was going to turn tail and see how fast
Ol' Chug could run.

Riding a head taller on the big mare, he saw first over
the rise—a sight he could scarcely gather. The sallow
plains had grown dark and rippled now like windblown
waters. Sunlight struggled through the haze of dust overhead and glinted against curves of black horns. Something twitching violently a quarter mile away caught his
eye. A telegraph pole: a scratching post for a woolly buffalo bull. It cracked and fell across the back of a cow,
sending a shock wave through the herd as a stone tossed
into a pond.

"God A'mighty!" Dillon said under his breath, wheezing with relieved laughter. "It's buffler!"

"You expect Indians?" Parkhill said. "You think I'd risk
my ass for a damn piece of Yankee wire?"

"No, but I 'spected you might risk mine."

The herd found the riders on the divide and started moving away.

"They're fixin' to git," Lloyd said, pressing his hat down
tight over his blond hair.

"And we're fixin' to git after 'em," Parkhill said, speaking loudly. "Give 'em a Rebel yell, boys, and lay 'em low!"

Ross gouged with his spurs as the voices rattled and
whooped like a whole battalion. His fear lifted like a bank
of steam, and joy rushed into his heart. Ol' Chug surged
ahead, and he gave rein. Within two leaps she had the lead.
Yes, Ol' Chug could run!

The muzzle of his carbine slipped out of the socket on
the saddle ring and began to bounce on his right thigh, so
he held it down with his elbow. If it went to flailing just

right on the strap slung across his shoulder, it would raise knots all over him.

He saw heels and bristly tails appear through the dust ahead. He heard—no, *felt* a rumble that must be shaking Georgia now. He spotted a hump higher than the others—a big bull. He cocked his revolver as he faintly heard Gene Dillon's voice:

"Hold on, Ross!"

He couldn't find his gun sights for the dust and the rollicking gallop, but he aimed by instinct, pointing his weapon at the bull. He almost had to hit something in the mass of woolly flesh ahead of him.

His pistol bucked and he rode instantly through the pungent black smoke. All at once he saw the buffalo butt the ground and roll, heard a concerted volley behind him, and felt Chug leap forward under him.

He cocked his feet outward to keep his toes in the stirrups, felt the cantle rising hard against his rear. The mare hadn't even begun to use her steam! Ross groped for leather, managed to pull himself back into the seat. His heels found the stirrups. Now he leaned back on the reins, but Chug charged headlong among the galloping buffalo. She had taken the bridle bit in her teeth. Ross jerked. The bit was lodged! Like trying to rein in a locomotive or a riverboat chugging downstream.

Didn't they call her Ol' Chug?

Ross saw a tongue lolling out against his right knee, an eye rolling back in a mass of dark curls, a blunt black horn crusted with dried mud and hair. He heard another volley, and Chug angled in front of the bison, bumping it aside as she streaked deeper into the herd, gun-shy and cold-jawed.

He jerked the reins, felt them jerk back as Chug stretched her neck through the stampeding bison. He smelled a hundred cuds. His carbine bounced off his knee, whirled on its swivel, slammed its barrel against his shoulder, came down on his thigh, sprang up to his cheek. It beat him like a living nightmare on a tether until he managed to knock it down and pin it with his elbow.

He felt for his holster with his pistol barrel and glanced back, as if help might be coming. He saw galloping bison, three rows deep, billows of dust rising behind them. He had to make Chug stop, or they would tell stories about how he disappeared in the stampede, never again to be seen.

He pulled the right rein, hard and wide. Chug ran cockeyed, head sideways, but veered a little to the right. He wrapped the rein once around his hand and pulled wide again, looking over his right shoulder. He saw an opening behind him—a gap in the stampede.

His shoulder muscles were burning with the strain when he saw the hooves of the cavalry mounts cutting the dust behind him. A corridor had appeared in the buffalo herd, but it wouldn't last long. He took a wrap with the left rein, pulled with everything he had as he flung the leather from his right. Swinging his right leg over the cantle, he jumped clear, taking up slack on the rein as he sailed through acres of dust.

The rein jerked tight, stretching him out to bounce hard on the ground. Chug bowed her head, touched her nose to the dirt, and somersaulted as Ross burrowed into dirt, slid, hit a clump of grass, rolled.

He saw the belly of a horse pass over him, then dirt

clogged his eyes. His ears rang. The ground quivered under him.

"You all right?" Dillon's voice said.

Ross wheezed, choking on lingering clouds of soil, but he nodded at the trooper.

"Knocked his wind out," Dillon said.

Ross heard the yellow-haired private laughing over him.

"Bet you wondered how come us let you ride Ol' Chug!"

"Stand back!" Parkhill said, casting his shadow on Ross's face. He put his palms on his knees and peered down, the bulge in his cheek like a grotesque goiter in silhouette. "You're all right. Give me your hand."

Ross reached upward, felt the sergeant's big hand grasp his like a vise. Parkhill lifted him to his feet, but as he rose, he felt something in the grip of the sergeant—two deliberate points of pressure, alternating, from the little finger to the index finger. Ross belonged to the brotherhood. He knew a secret grip when he felt one. But this was not the Masonic grip. It was something else. Parkhill was testing him out. Did he belong? Belong to what? He stared at the sergeant, coughed, squinted dust from his eyes.

Parkhill released his grip. He wrenched his thick neck to spit over his right shoulder, a dismounted private dodging to avoid the brown stream. The sergeant shook his head. "I don't know about you, Caldwell. I just don't know."

Ross took a sudden idea. He squeezed one eye shut and looked sideways, at just the left side of Parkhill's face. Yes, now he remembered. The huge bulge of tobacco had been throwing him off. There had been no tobacco inside Camp

Douglas. That was where he knew the sergeant from. They had spent a year behind the walls of the same prisoner of war camp in Chicago.

Gene Dillon's tooth-shy smile and Lloyd's pale yellow hair came together now, too. They had always been a trio—Parkhill their leader. The memories he had forced aside were surfacing again. This big Union sergeant had commissioned himself a Confederate captain in Camp Douglas, created a secret troop of Rebel cavalry. They had all looked different then—half-starved and sickly—but it was them. The Knights of the Golden Circle. And now he knew their secret grip.

"Mount up!" Parkhill shouted. "Take the humps and tongues, then we'll have to go back to camp for more wire and poles."

Ross caught Chug, backed her up to test the bridle bit. She was fine now: a model of equestrian discipline. He mounted and began checking his gear as he rode toward the nearest kill. He seemed engaged with his equipage, but his mind was drifting back, trying to remember how he had landed so far west with this bunch of Confederates in Union dress.

THREE

Ross had wanted no part of the Rebellion when it began. He had never owned slaves. He wasn't mad at any Yankees. He had friends in the North, in fact, and did business with them through his father's hardware store in Athens. And he had just married Julia Lynn Porter, daughter of a town councilman. This was no time for running off to get shot at.

The conscription law gave him no choice. He donned the gray, kissed his bride good-bye, left Athens. He owned a horse, so he wound up in the cavalry under General John Morgan. He learned to mask his fear in a Rebel yell. He did his duty. He was, he thought, neither hero nor coward.

Then one day he and another trooper, looking for forage, spotted a cornfield and crossed a creek to get to it. As they came out of the creek bed, a squadron of Union infantry opened fire on them from the rail fence across the field.

Ross's partner took a rifle ball in the chest and gouged his mount with his spurs as he fell back. The horse bolted, carrying the wounded rider into the center of the cornfield, dropping him there, as Ross managed to rein his horse back into the creek bed for cover.

He could have ridden back to his company. He knew his partner only well enough to know that he didn't like the man very much. He didn't even know if the man was still alive, but he lay alone out there in that cornfield between Ross and a squadron of enemy foot soldiers.

Thinking about it took only a fragment of a moment, then Ross was off his horse, tying the reins to a switch. He knew the Union boys would detect his approach through the field. He had plowed across only three furrows when the fusillade began.

What had only been an idea a second before was happening now. He was charging a superior force to rescue a man that might well be already dead. Between the rifle reports, he heard bullets clipping the broad leaves of the green corn plants. An ear exploded beside his head. He kept running, following the path the horse had half trampled into the field.

When he got there, he found the man heaving strangely for breath, blood spurting from his wound. The Union men were shouting, rattling ramrods down their barrels. The soldier looked up and smiled as Ross reached for him.

Bullets cut the corn like sickles again as Ross struggled to run under the weight of his fellow Rebel. When he reached the creek, he had a dead man on his back, and the Union boys were cheering him—cheering as if he were General William Tecumseh Sherman.

He mounted and rode up the creek bed, never telling anyone what he had done, not understanding it himself. Was he fool or hero? He couldn't say. But the image of that smiling Rebel stayed with him in glory.

He did not, of course, tell Julia. She would have felt more rage than pride. He wrote letters to her daily, telling her about camp life, the boredom, how he missed her cooking, her embrace. He did not mention the casualties. That would only have upset her. He knew she wrote back every day, but her replies only occasionally found him in camp.

Then came Indiana, Ohio, invasion of the North. Total defeat at Buffington Island, he and hundreds of his fellow Rebels swarmed under by bluecoats. A hard march to Chicago. Camp Douglas—a greater hell than battle.

He found walking corpses there. The men were sick, dirty, ragged, covered with fleas and lice. Some of them could only wallow in their own filth along the latrine ditches, too weak with dysentery to crawl back and forth to the barracks. The dead left daily, wrapped in blankets.

Ross stopped to help a fellow prisoner one day, the man delirious with fever, writhing on the ground, cursing. "Let the son of a bitches take me!" he said. "God, let 'em have me!" His shredded clothes were alive with fleas. His skin hung across his bones like soiled white linen. Ross rolled the man over to help him up and found maggots crawling in open sores on his knees.

"Oh, they've got me!" he screamed. "They're all over me!"

One morning, his third month there, he walked to the edge of camp, stopped at the line of lime wash on the ground—the dead line, the guards called it. The plank wall of the prison camp stood fifty feet away. He looked up at the sentry house, the guard looking back at him, the rifle barrel jutting over the wooden rail. He could step over and end it. Wasn't it better to die trying to escape than to rot by degrees?

But what if the war ended tomorrow? What if Julia came next week?

He turned away from the line while he could still walk. When he came crawling, consumed by vermin and maggots, he would cross it.

He stole scraps of paper, hid his stub of a pencil, begged the Union clerks to mail his letters. A single page from Julia found him, lifting him higher than the prison walls. He saw Georgia that day. The page said she was trying to borrow money to get to Chicago.

He was shivering in his blanket one day, sitting on the floor of the barracks, methodically picking lice from his hair, pinching them between his fingernails.

"You Rebels get up!" a guard shouted, bursting in. "It's your turn in the house."

As he shuffled across the frozen yard on bare feet, Ross mulled over the rumors he had heard. Some called it an interrogation. Others said it was an interview, a survey. A wild-eyed man from another barracks had said it was a way out. He was a big man who called himself Captain Parkhill, though he wore a sergeant's stripes. This Parkhill was always whispering and plotting with a clutch of hardened men. Two in particular seemed always at hand. One with a bunch of teeth missing, the other yellow-haired.

"It ain't treason if you don't mean it," Parkhill had said. "An oath can't change allegiance. The idea is to get out of here and finish the Rebellion."

Ross waited, shivering, outside the guardhouse until the prisoner before him had left. Then he entered to find a one-armed lieutenant sitting behind a desk, the empty left sleeve folded up and pinned short.

The young officer glanced at Ross's bare feet, his hatless head. "Sit down," he said.

"I'd rather stand at the stove," Ross replied.

"Very well. State your rank, name, and native state."

He saw a pen in the lieutenant's hand, a large ledger book open in front of him. "Private Rossiter Caldwell, Georgia."

"What is your age?"

"Twenty-three."

The lieutenant made an entry in the book, dipped the pen in his inkwell. "I have a few questions to ask you, Private Caldwell. They are all hypothetical and independent of one another. Do you understand?"

Ross rubbed his hands above the stove. He nodded. His whole body suddenly convulsed with a short-lived shiver.

With the heel of his one hand, the lieutenant adjusted a leaf of paper over his book and read from it. "Given the opportunity, would you desire to go South as a prisoner of war for exchange?"

Ross's eyes widened. "Yes, sir," he said. He watched as the one-armed officer made a mark in the book.

The little finger of the clean white hand moved down the page to point to the next question. "Given the opportunity, would you desire to take the oath of allegiance to the United States of America, and be paroled from this camp, under penalty of death if found in the South before the end of the war?"

His eyes shifted, and he took a moment to interpret the language. "Yes," he answered, coming now to the chair the officer had offered. Yes, to get out of this prison, he would speak a damned oath.

"Given the same opportunities and penalties, would you desire to be sent North to construct public works?"

Ross sank to the hardwood surface of the chair. "What kind of public works? Forts? Breastworks?"

The officer tapped the page of questions with the point of his pen, leaving an ink spot. "I'm not sure," he said.

"Then neither am I, sir." He sniffed, rubbed a tattered sleeve under his nose.

The officer scrawled a note in his book. "Given the same opportunities and penalties, would you take up arms against the Southern Rebels?"

Ross sneered at the book. "I believe I am a Southern Rebel."

"What is your answer?"

"Of course not."

The one-armed lieutenant put a mark in its column, then looked up from the book, into the sunken eyes of the prisoner. "If given the opportunity, would you take the oath of allegiance to the Union and enlist in the Army of the U.S. to be sent to the western territories?"

Ross stared at the officer for several seconds. This was the real question. He could sense it. The officer had committed the words to memory and was looking back at him to judge his response.

"For what purpose?" Ross said.

The lieutenant lay his pen aside and fell back in his chair. He shrugged, causing the empty sleeve to flap. "I would presume to protect travelers and settlers from hostile Indians."

He's only a couple of years older than me, Ross thought. I could have been an officer. This one's brass buttons are tarnished, his hair unkempt, jacket wrinkled. I guess it's hard to press a jacket with just one arm, though. How will I look in Union blue?

"What is your answer, Private?"

"Well, sir. West ain't South, and West ain't North. Yes, I'd take the oath and go West. I'd rather fight Indians than tribes of vermin."

Several weeks passed before Ross heard his name on a muster roll for the 1st U.S. Volunteer Infantry. He was allowed outside the walls of Camp Douglas, given a uniform, fed decent rations.

The regimental surgeon interviewed him one day in a hospital tent. "Have you ever been sick?" he asked.

"No, sir," Ross answered, lying straight-faced. He only thought the words he wanted to say: Yes, sir. Sick of your lousy Camp Douglas.

"Have you ever had fits?"

"No, sir." But I expect I might have if I hadn't gotten out of Camp Douglas.

"Ever received an injury or wound upon the head? A fracture, dislocation, or sprain?"

"No, sir." What if I have? There's a war going on, you damned fool.

"Are you in the habit of drinking?"

"No, sir." Except when I'm thirsty.

"Have you ever had the horrors?"

"No, sir." Except for Camp Douglas.

"Are you subject to piles?"

"No, sir." Except for those piles of unthinkables I was subject to inside.

"Do you have any difficulty urinating?"

"No, sir." Would you like a demonstration?

A dozen desertions occurred after word came that they would travel west to Fort Laramie, in the Dakota Territory. Ross feared the army would send all the converted Rebels back behind the prison walls, but nothing of the kind happened.

The day before they were to board the train west, he still hadn't heard from Julia. He had to wonder if he would ever see her again. He had tried to explain in his letters why he had joined the Yankee army. For all he knew, she considered him a traitor. He might go back to Georgia after the war to find a lynch rope waiting for him, Julia ready to fix it around his neck.

It was the self-commissioned Captain Parkhill who provided him with a patriotic argument. Parkhill was a Union corporal now, having already convinced the company commander to promote him from private.

"Hey, soldier," he said, catching Ross alone in a four-man tent the last day in Chicago. "Have you heard there's a meeting of the Golden Circle tonight?"

"The what?" Ross said.

"The Knights of the Golden Circle. Ain't you ever heard of 'em?"

"No."

"Are you true to the South?"

"I'm from Georgia!" Ross said, lifting his chin.

Parkhill glanced both ways down the row of tents. "The Knights mean to carry the war west. There's a secret meeting tonight in the woodlot, after taps."

Ross caught Parkhill looking at the letter he was writing to Julia and put his forearm across the fresh ink. "Are you a member?"

"I'm just tellin' you what I've heard, soldier." And he withdrew from the tent, his shoulders almost pulling it down as he left.

Ross turned back to the letter, picked up his pen.

. . . You must understand, my dearest Julia, that even in this, the army of my recent enemy, I cause no harm to my beloved Georgia. Perhaps I may even serve the

South in the Army of the Potomac, or serve the causes of Southerners in the West. I take not lightly my allegiance to the Confederacy, but how shall I serve her rotting to death in prison?

Oh, Julia, that this war might end, and I might enfold my trembling arms again about you. I fear neither battle nor death, only life without you . . .

FOUR

The dry wind blew hot across her hands, cupped as they were around the hewn points of the timbers at the top of the watch tower. Another minute here and her hands would dry, crack, bleed. It was better to go back down the ladder and plunge them into the laundry barrel again, into the harsh lye soap and wads of dirty woolen uniforms.

Behind her, and below the guard tower on which she stood, Camp Marshall writhed with rare energy. The new company commander, Captain Jasper Jones, had arrived, and every soldier was making his first impression count. The sentry on duty beside her stood at attention on his post, glaring across the valley, trying hard not to blink.

Julia lifted the chestnut hair from the back of her neck, the hot wind cooling her sweat there, feeling good. She put the other hand on the small of her back, arched the kinks out of her spine, twisting her hips. She caught herself and snapped to attention, her hands falling on the points of the timbers again. It wasn't wise to provoke all these men with too much bodily undulation. A woman had to remember her military bearing here.

East of camp, La Bonte Creek twined through the valley like a long spangled snake lazily taking in sunshine on its way to the North Platte. Greenery only feathered its flanks, hard-pressed by shortgrass and sage-covered slopes. Ross had looked magnificent riding up them this morning on the big gray mare, his crisp, clean uniform sitting ramrod-straight in the saddle.

Julia was bone-weary of war and Indian campaigns. She longed for days of peaceful civilian pursuits. But she still admired the way her husband looked in his cavalry outfit—the dark blue blouse over the azure britches, the shine of polished black leather from knee boots and the rifle strap slung across one shoulder, the hat cocked forward on Ross's head. He had the legs of a horseman, the dash of a cavalry soldier, and she would always remember him that way, even after he traded his uniform for a store clerk's apron and went back to hawking hardware.

He had looked as well in the Confederate grays she had tailored for him before he left her in Georgia. She had watched him ride away in them, too. She was a silly young bride then, weeping because she figured she was supposed to. Now she knew a cry was not a thing to waste; now she had wept genuine tears and somehow cherished every one as a pearl.

She had had her first real cry when she learned the truth about Camp Douglas, Chicago. News of Ross's capture had actually relieved her until then. She had assumed he would be safe there, removed from combat. But a letter from another Camp Douglas inmate, to his wife in Athens, found its way to her, and the horror occurred to her all at once. In his one letter that had gotten through, Ross had said nothing of the sickness, the filth, the death. But he was like that, never one to worry another with his own trials.

Julia knew she would have to go to Chicago, but there was no money, no reliable transportation. When she received his letter saying—almost apologetically—that he would rather take the Union oath and go west than endure another year in prison, she left Athens on foot with food for only two days. She would never see him again if she didn't. He would not come back to Georgia after wearing Union blue.

She slept in a barn the first night, under a wagon the second. The third day north, she heard distant gunfire. It lasted all day. At dusk she reached the tents, soaked by the rains that seemed to follow all big artillery battles. She thought the soldiers might feed her.

As she spoke to one of the pickets, a soldier staggered aimlessly by her, bleeding from a terrible wound that had taken one ear off. She steered him back toward camp, asking for the hospital tent. As she sat the man among other bloody, moaning uniforms, a harsh voice called out:

"You, girl! Come here! I need you!"

Julia looked up to see a heavyset woman standing in the opening of the tent. The front of her dress was covered with blood, and she held a pair of scissors in her hand.

"Well, come on! Hurry up!" The big woman turned back into the tent.

Julia saw two men staring at her, one with a ball of bloody bandages around the stump of a leg, the other with an empty sleeve dangling. She swallowed and went into the tent.

"Put these limbs out," the big woman said. "They're piling up."

Julia stood over the arms and legs, mounded randomly like branches on a beaver dam.

"Buck up, girl, and make us some room. Boys are dying!"

She picked up a leg, warm and limp, cut off above the knee. Carrying it outside, she found a patch of muddy ground to drop it on. She thought of running, but a soldier inside was screaming, and she did not care to think herself a coward.

She stacked the limbs like cordwood. They were cold and stiff on the bottom of the pile. "What do you need now?" she asked the woman.

The big bloody matron glanced at her pale face, looked closely at her for the first time. "You can't be more than nineteen. How long have you been a nurse?"

"I'm not a nurse," Julia said.

"Then who are you?"

"Just a wayfarer," she said, her Southern voice smoothing the edges from the words. "My husband's been taken prisoner and sent north."

"When was the last time you ate?"

"Yesterday, but I'm not hungry now."

A surgeon was calling for a saw.

"Go out and find the ones we can save," the nurse said, turning to the table. It was a common kitchen table, strewn with bloody cutting instruments. "Get the worst ones first, but if they're dying, let them lie in peace."

Two days later, Julia rode a supply wagon north, the horrors of the hospital tent lingering, oozing among her thoughts. She felt a lasting pity for the dead and wounded, but none had disgusted her, no matter how terrible the wound, how mangled the flesh. She surprised herself in this, and set her jaw as she rode north. Things would turn out all right. The West could be no worse than that battle-field.

She came out of the green grass to a field of mud—a vast mire stamped by thousands of marching feet. Over the sagging canvas ridges of the troop tents she saw the plank walls of Camp Douglas. She smelled beans cooking, heard the swearing Southern voices. The four men at the first tent sprang as if to attention when she approached.

"I'm looking for my husband," she said. "His name is Ross Caldwell."

The men looked at each other.

"I don't know him, ma'am," said one.

"You can find the lieutenant and check the roll," said another, "but some of the boys are changin' their names. Don't want their real names to go down on Union rolls."

"Where is the lieutenant?"

"The big tent up the row," a private said, pointing.

Julia quickened her step. Oh, for a bath. But she had freshened up some at the creek a few miles back, crushed some wild rose petals for perfume.

She rapped on the tent post, saw the surprise in the lieu-tenant's eyes as he looked out through the open flaps. "I'm looking for my husband. His name is Ross Caldwell." She glanced at the men standing all around, staring at her, but none was Ross.

The officer sprang from his stool. "Please, come in. I'll check the rolls."

"I'll wait out here," she said, searching a new face among the tents.

The lieutenant came out with the muster roll. "Rossiter Caldwell?"

Her heart vaulted into her throat. "Yes."

"He's assigned to Company B right now. Tented on the next row over, at the end. If you wish, I can send someone . . ."

Julia had already turned. Her foot slipped as she mounted a trot. She sprang over a guy rope, reached the next row of tents. Toward the end, she slowed her pace, peered into a couple of tents, catching one soldier shirtless. She turned her eyes quickly, pursed her lips in frustration. He was here. Ross was right here. She couldn't stand this.

"Ross!" Her own voice surprised her, squeaking down the row, silencing the low voices of men. "Ross Caldwell!" She turned, saw heads poking out of tents. "It's Julia, Ross! Where are you?" She came around, full circle, found him standing four tents down, paper in one hand, pen in the other. Thin, drawn, nearly beaten, but it was him.

He dropped the letter on the mud as she ran toward him. He lifted her from her feet, pressed his stubbled face against her neck as three other men poured from the tiny tent.

"God forgive me, Julia," he murmured, his voice breaking.

"Hush, Ross."

A Galvanized Yankee looked at the sky and nudged one of his comrades. "No rain tonight, boys. We'd best quarter outside."

FIVE

They were hurting now—all those places that had taken blows from the flailing carbine and the trembling ground. But Camp Marshall was in sight and Ross was thinking more of Julia. Soon he would be alone with her inside their little log cubicle, and he could forget about his bruises, Sergeant Parkhill, and the Knights of the Golden Circle.

Suddenly she appeared in the guard tower, her faded print dress setting her apart from the uniforms on sentry duty. He saw her hand raise and wave, and he waved back, unable to keep his face from grinning.

"Look at him, Gene," said the yellow-haired private named Lloyd. "Looks like a damn possum."

"Hell, I'd grin, too, if I was him," Gene replied.

Ross paid them little heed. He was squinting ahead, the grin melting from his face. Julia was saying something. Her signs were subtle, but he knew her every move. She was like a signalman to him. She stood at attention, then looked purposefully down into the fort.

Ross saw Sergeant Parkhill's mount turn. The big man twisted in the saddle, spit on the horse's rump, and drilled

Ross with a glare. "She tryin' to tell you somethin', Caldwell?"

The sergeant might as well have stepped between them in a dance. He had no business intruding like that, and it galled Ross more than his bruises, more than the fatigue of the hard day's ride.

It alarmed him, too. This Parkhill missed nothing. Not even signals sent unspoken between a wife and husband. Yet, Ross enjoyed his leverage. Only he could interpret Julia this way. He knew what was going on in the fort. He might have gloated over it, and kept the intelligence to himself, but he wanted to make a good first impression. He would stand out on Chug. Better to warn the whole party.

"I think the new captain's here," Ross said, glancing up at Julia's faraway outline against the graying sky.

"Oh, hell," Parkhill grumbled, slumping for a moment in the saddle, glowering at Ross as if it were his fault. "All right, shape up, you sorry-lookin' sacks of shit. Dust yourself off, Caldwell. You look like hell."

The moment the column rode into Camp Marshall, Ross found Julia near the laundry tubs. He winked, then looked toward the officers' quarters. He spotted the new commander, recognizing him almost instantly. It was the one-armed lieutenant from Camp Douglas, now wearing twin bars of silver.

Captain Jasper Jones was leaning against a post on the porch of his quarters, pulling at the collar of his rather disheveled uniform. The empty sleeve was bunched haphazardly below the stump of his left arm. There was little dash about the man, but Ross remembered him well for germinating his release from the prisoner of war camp. It made sense now, the interest this officer had shown in sending captured Confederates west. It was probably his project, his idea. Now he was here to make it work.

"Sergeant!" Captain Jones said, stepping down from the porch. "Report!"

Parkhill sniffed, raised his hand to stop the detachment. He jumped down in front of the captain and cocked his thick arm in a salute. "Sergeant Parkhill reporting as ordered, sir."

Jones returned the salute as if swatting at a fly. "The wire, Sergeant, the wire."

"Busted. Over the mountains in the Platte Valley. Big herd of buffalo took out a stretch almost a half mile long. We'll take a wagon load of poles and wire tomorrow and fix it."

Jones squinted at the big sergeant. "You from Mississippi, Parkhill?"

"Before the war, sir."

"Northeastern Mississippi, I'd say."

Parkhill's eyes widened. "Yes, sir."

"I thought I recognized that strain in your dialect. Did I interview you at Camp Douglas?"

"Yes, sir."

"You've made good rank." The captain frowned as he looked over the men, his eyes finally landing on Ross, perched high atop the big gray. "What happened to you, Private?"

His answer was ready. "The buffalo stampeded me, sir."

Jones snickered. "Get any meat?"

"As much as we could pack, sir."

"Georgia, right?"

"Yes, sir."

"Make sure you clean every speck of dirt out of those weapons tonight."

"Yes, sir."

"Sergeant, you've got two minutes to care for your animals and get your men in formation. Lieutenant Deihl! Any more detachments out?"

"No, sir," the lieutenant said.

"Then call a general assembly. I want three sides of a hollow square around the flagpole."

The post flew into instant pandemonium as all troops save those on sentry duty rushed to find their places, the lieutenant screaming, sergeants cussing. The wire detachment was the last to fall in, after hastily stripping mounts at the corral.

As the last boot shuffled into position, Captain Jones cleared his throat and looked over his new command. "My name is Captain Jasper G. Jones," he began, his sharp tenor voice easily reaching the back rows. "The first man who considers that name amusing will find himself on the sorriest duty this camp has to offer for the duration of his enlistment." He paced in front of one prong of the formation, stopping to glare at a corporal who refused to make eye contact with him.

"Those of you who are former secessionists will remember me from Camp Douglas. It was my idea to have you rot here instead of there, so you can thank me if you want to—I really don't care either way. Don't expect me to thank you back, though, because you've all but ruined my military career. I put my trust in the idea that a Southern man could serve the Union as well as a Northern man, and that has been my undoing."

Jones turned the corner of the hollow square and strode in front of the second row of troops. "Your primary mission here, gentlemen, in this garden spot of civilization, is to keep the telegraph line intact between Platte Bridge and Bridger's Ferry. One damned skinny piece of wire, and all you have to do is keep it spliced together. So far, you have failed miserably."

He stopped in front of Sergeant Parkhill, stood facing the big man, inches away, staring at the missing buttons on his blouse. "Like most of you, I don't give a *damn* whether or not some Californian can wire Washington, D.C., or New York City. I don't give a *damn* whether or not the United States Army can telegraph its orders across the continent—most of them contradict each other, anyway. What I give a damn about is *this!*"

He whipped a folded sheet of ink-smeared newsprint from his pocket and waved it in the air. He turned away from Parkhill and walked to the middle of the square. "Sergeant Parkhill, what is this?"

"It's a newspaper, sir."

The captain rolled his eyes. "Not just a newspaper, Sergeant, a *western* newspaper. No self-respecting eastern rag could fold up in a man's breast pocket without making a bulge! This is a copy of the San Francisco *Daily Alta California*. Allow me to quote from one of its editorial columns."

He shook the paper open with a flourish, struggling to arrange a page with his one hand. Clearing his throat, he began.

" 'The telegraph wire was cut by Indians between Platte Bridge and Bridger's Ferry again, and as such we have no news from the East. Repairs are commencing with the usual dedication to lethargy and disinterestedness along that section. We have recently learned the reason for this weak link in the transcontinental telegraph system. Several companies of Galvanized Yankees are stationed in that region. We must not expect any finer level of service from captured secessionists and defeated Rebels.' "

The captain threw the newspaper to the ground and let it blow away on an evening breeze that plastered it against a private's shin.

"If I ever want to wear an oak-leaf cluster," Jones continued, "I must make liars of the editors of the *Daily Alta California*. I must keep telegraph communications open from the Atlantic to the Pacific with a mixed force of Southern and Northern men. I must repair promptly all breaks. To rescue my military career, I must prove what I still suspect to be true: that former enemies can put aside their old differences and splice a nation back together. I ask you to do nothing I am unwilling to do myself. I buried my left arm at Kennesaw Mountain!"

He paused to let his echo resound across the parade ground. "But I buried my bitterness and enmity with it." Captain Jones began slowly to approach Sergeant Parkhill, moving like a stalking wolf.

"The war is over, gentlemen, but the states are still divided. Their only common ground lies here, in the West. The reparation of a nation begins with us, men. And it starts with a piece of wire."

He stopped in front of Parkhill, looking the big sergeant

in the eye. "From this moment forward, no wire inspection detail will take the field without a supply wagon loaded with the materials needed to repair one mile of line.

"Sergeant Parkhill! You will mount your detachment on fresh horses, harness a buckboard, load it with posts and wire, and leave immediately to repair the break you found to the west today. I want communications restored by dawn. The rest of you men report to your lieutenants for inventory duty. We will count every post, every foot of wire, every peg, clamp, insulator, posthole digger, and pliers before breakfast.

"Dismissed!"

Ross felt the company surge against him as the sergeants barked. He groaned, looking for Julia. She was there, shrugging at him from her laundry barrels. He took a step toward her, felt a hand clamp his shoulder.

"Where the hell do you think you're goin', Caldwell? The corral's that way!" It was Parkhill, fuming like a mad dog. He shoved Ross toward the horses and went to rant at another private.

Ross gestured helplessly to his wife. She put her cracked fingers to her lips and blew him a kiss.

SIX

The invitation came as a complete surprise, and almost terrified Ross. Dinner with the captain in his quarters? That kind of fraternization was against regulations, wasn't it? But Ross had learned in the three weeks since Jones had arrived that the camp commander abhorred regulations. The man had a knack for getting things done on his own terms, regulations be damned.

Ross shined his boots as Julia buttoned herself into her finest gown. They stood at the door and inspected each other in the lantern light before they left.

"You're beautiful," Ross said.

"Oh, hush," she answered. "And stop worrying. It's just dinner."

They felt the eyes on them as they walked across the parade ground to the captain's quarters. When Jones opened the door, he was wearing an apron over civilian garb, holding the handle of a large wooden spoon between his teeth.

He took the spoon in his hand and kicked the door shut behind his guests. "Welcome, Mrs. Caldwell, Private Caldwell. Hope you like antelope stew. It's almost ready, and I've made enough to feed the regiment."

Julia inhaled the aromas as she entered, and let Ross take her shawl from her shoulders. "Are you baking bread?" she asked.

Captain Jones was on his way back to the kitchen. "Sourdough biscuits," he shouted. "I'll give you a starter if you'll use it."

"Thank you, I will," she answered, standing uncertainly in the dining room. She gestured at Ross. "Say something," she whispered.

"What?"

"Anything."

Ross frowned. "Beg your pardon, sir, but you do your own cookin'?"

"Always have," the captain answered, clacking his

spoon against the rim of his stewpot. "Learned from my mother. She runs the best boardinghouse kitchen in Boston. Simple fare, but it sticks to your ribs." He jutted his head from the kitchen. "Set the table, Private. Silver's in that drawer. Mrs. Caldwell, you're not to lift a finger."

When it was ready, the captain banged the pot of stew on the table and whipped the lid away with a flourish. "The only way to cook this wild game is to boil the devil out of it! Do the two of you indulge?" He raised a bottle.

Ross looked at Julia. "Whenever we can get it, sir. If it's affordable."

The captain put the bottle between his knees and pulled the cork stopper. "It's just some porter I borrowed from the surgeon," he said, filling three glasses. "Not much spirit to it, but I've got plenty. Sit down."

The captain blessed the meal and attacked it, sopping his biscuits, slurping broth from his spoon. He was still wearing his apron and used the tail of it as his napkin. "Private Caldwell," he said, "I'm told that Mrs. Caldwell is an inspiration to the entire regiment. What has she done? Killed an Indian or something?"

Ross laughed, feeling more at ease after a few glasses of porter and a feed of hot stew. "No, sir." He beamed at his wife. "She just does what has to be done, that's all."

"That so?"

"Yes, sir. When I was in the infantry, 1st U.S. Volunteers, she marched with the regiment all the way from Leavenworth to Laramie, step for step."

"Did she?"

"Yes, sir. Then we got reassigned to the 11th Ohio for some reason . . ."

"A mysterious quirk of military logic," the captain injected.

"Yes, sir. And even then she wouldn't ride a wagon when we dismounted to lead our horses. She'd jump off the wagon and walk with the men."

Julia put her hand against her throat and felt herself blushing.

"Mrs. Caldwell," Jones said, raising his glass, "you are of more value to this company than my entire corps of officers. No general can command inspiration."

Ross lifted his porter and clinked it against Julia's.

"I'm told we nearly lost the two of you to Platte Bridge recently."

"Yes, sir. I was sick when my squad rode out. Just before you took command."

"How did you come to be reassigned to Sergeant Parkhill's squad?"

Ross shrugged. "Mysterious quirk of army logic, I guess."

"There's something mysterious about that squad, all right," Jones said, wringing his hand in a wad of his apron tail. "I've been studying the muster rolls, and there are supposed to be quite a few Northern men in that unit, but they all speak with a Southern drawl. How do you explain that?"

Ross's chair squeaked like a new saddle as he squirmed in it.

"If I may, sir," Julia said. "Some of the men are reluctant to use their real names and their home states on the muster rolls. Afraid they may suffer some bad treatment when they return to their homes in the South if it was discovered that they served the Union Army."

"They've lied about their native states?"

"They've chosen new homes in the North," Julia said.

"Yes, though they don't intend ever living there," Jones said. "And the false names?"

Julia turned her glass between her toughened fingers. "General Grant changed his name when he entered West Point."

Jasper Jones smiled, chuckled. "So he did. *Noms de guerre.* Perhaps I should have chosen one." He looked at Ross. "What am I to think of Sergeant Parkhill?"

Ross raised his eyebrows and glanced about the room. "He's tough. Not afraid of anything. Smart."

"How smart?"

"Sir?"

The captain sighed as he refilled his glass with porter. "Private, I'm going to put you in a very delicate position. I'm going to ask you to watch and listen for signs of unrest in your squad. I've looked into Sergeant Parkhill's background and found that he's managed to keep the same clutch of men with him since he was active in the Confederate cavalry. They're apparently quite loyal to him, and perhaps to the Confederacy. If you overhear anything, I want you to inform me through Mrs. Caldwell. Have her deliver a note in the pocket of my uniform when she does my laundry."

Ross looked at Julia, found her face showing a mixture of pride and surprise. "Why me, sir? I'm just a private."

"I wired your former lieutenant at Platte Bridge. Asked him to recommend an enlisted man at Camp Marshall I could trust. He suggested you. I tend to agree with him now. Any man who could convince a woman like Mrs.

Caldwell to follow him out to this ten acres of perdition must be worthy of trust."

Ross was beginning to suspect Captain Jones's flattery. "What is it you expect me to find out about Sergeant Parkhill?"

"Nothing that isn't there. Hopefully nothing at all. But I fear he may be planning either a mass desertion or a mutiny. As you said, he fears nothing, and he has a rumored history of involvement in groups like the Knights of the Golden Circle and the so-called Sons of Liberty. If you hear anything, report to me through the laundry. For obvious reasons I won't invite you back to my quarters."

Ross pushed his half-full glass of porter away.

"I trust I'm not asking too much."

Ross looked at Julia. "No, sir. Not of me."

"Mrs. Caldwell?"

"No, sir," Julia said, concealing her excitement. I am a spy, she was thinking.

The captain rose and his guests sensed it was time for them to go.

"Private, tell your squad that I am the most high-handed, obnoxious, arrogant personage you have ever had the misfortune of dining with. I'll invite the other married couples at the post to dinner in the future so no one will suspect our arrangement.

"Yes, sir," Ross said, draping Julia's shawl over her shoulders.

Jones opened the door, then grasped his chin and studied the young couple. "The two of you come from the same hometown, don't you?"

Ross nodded.

"East of Atlanta, I would guess. Maybe near Monroe or Athens or Jackson."

"Yes," Julia said, quite surprised. "Athens."

The captain's eyes glittered. "Dialects fascinate me. I remember you from Camp Douglas, Private Caldwell. You were the one who said you would rather fight Indians than tribes of vermin."

Ross smiled, this time surely impressed. "Yes, sir. But here you have to fight both. I think we're winnin' against the vermin, but the Indians haven't showed us their strength yet."

"Indeed they haven't, Private. Good night, Mrs. Caldwell. Thank you both for coming."

Later, alone in their little room, curled together on the narrow bed, Ross whispered to Julia about Sergeant Parkhill and the Knights of the Golden Circle.

"Why haven't you told me before?" she asked.

"I didn't want to worry you. This is dangerous business."

"Oh, hush," she said, dragging her rough hands across his skin. "I'll show you dangerous business."

SEVEN

Sweat ran from him like a river. It was ninety-five degrees to begin with, and Ross was making wagon tires red-hot in a big bank of coals. He could grasp his shirt, unbuttoned down the front, and pump some air across his sweaty skin for a moment of coolness, but he longed to douse himself with the bucket of creek water he knew Julia would have waiting for him.

The post's blacksmith grunted at him, and Ross put his tongs on the iron wheel rim in the coals, lifting one side as the smithy raised the other. Wordlessly, they moved the smoking iron ring to the wagon wheel mounted horizontally near the fire, tapping it down around the perimeter of the wheel where it would cool and draw tight. It was between taps of the smithy's hammer that Ross heard the first shot.

"Indians!" a sentry shouted. "Damn! A hundred of 'em!"

Captain Jones burst out of his quarters as if they were on fire, and the crackle of distant gunshots reached into the fort. "Saddle thirty mounts!" he shouted as he scrambled up a ladder to look over the rim of the sentry box.

Ross looked toward Julia's laundry barrels, relieved to find her there. She might have been trapped at the creek. He ducked under a corral rail and caught a horse as other soldiers grabbed blankets and saddles.

"They got the horses!" the sentry shouted as the captain sprang to the platform beside him. "Three men pinned down."

Jones leaned over the hewn points of the timbers, squinting at the struggle taking place almost a mile up the creek to the south. The three herders had shot their horses to use as cover and were fighting back a circling ring of Cheyenne warriors.

Jones all but grinned at the beauty of the sight, the men staggering their fire to keep the enemy at bay. Since taking command, he had refused to let the entire herd out to graze at one time, though it meant extra grazing details for the men. Now his precautions would pay off. He had plenty of horses in the fort to mount a rescue party and recover the stolen herd.

"Thirty volunteers!" he shouted as he hurried down the ladder. "Mount up!"

Ross drew a saddle cinch tight and stepped up on a stirrup to find Gene Dillon mounted beside him. He glanced about and found the yellow-haired Lloyd. He spotted another of Sergeant Parkhill's squad, then another, then Parkhill himself, the big man leading two horses. One was a lean sorrel. The other was Ol' Chug.

Captain Jones jumped from the fourth rung and took the reins of the big gray as Sergeant Parkhill handed them to him. "Form a skirmish line on the south perimeter and prepare to charge!" he shouted, vaulting into the saddle. "Lieutenant Deihl, you have command of the fort in my absence. Defend it!" He spurred Chug and led the men southward.

Ross wanted to warn the captain about the big gray mare, but the rumble of hooves rose like an explosion around him. He could only rein his mount into the current of horseflesh and head for the battle. Then Julia's shrill voice knifed through the noise and he found her running toward him, his gun belt in her hand, and realized he would have charged the enemy unarmed if not for her.

He held his horse back and veered toward her at the rear of the rescue party, catching the leather as she lobbed it to him. He put his head and one arm through the belt and kicked his pony's ribs to catch up.

Clearing the barracks, he found an uneven skirmish line forming, but before Ross could fall in behind Chug, Captain Jones had given the order to charge and the rescue party was galloping south for the three surrounded soldiers.

Wind filled his shirt, cooling the sweat he had been working up all day. He fixed his hat more firmly on his head and gave his pony rein, preparing to catch Ol' Chug when she bolted.

The Indians fired a few long-range shots at the rescue party, then withdrew up the creek with their stolen horses. Fifty of them stopped on a slanting ridge that angled toward the creek, and watched to see what the bluecoats had in mind.

As the rescue party arrived, two of the three herdsmen stood to greet it. Through the dust, Ross saw the third sitting on the ground, grasping an arrow shaft in his thigh. Captain Jones tightened his reins as he approached the three herdsmen, and started to say something, but Parkhill moved in behind Chug, drew his revolver, and fired a shot toward the distant raiders.

Chug leaped as if slapped on the rump with a razor strop, and a dozen other revolvers opened up. Captain Jones pulled leather, but the big gray took the bit between her teeth and gained momentum, running toward the Indians on the slanting ridge.

Soldiers milled in the confusion, the men from Parkhill's squad staying back, the other volunteers halfheartedly following Captain Jones. Only Ross rode with a purpose. He dodged the faltering mounts ahead of him and took second position in the charge.

"Turn her, Captain!" he shouted, but he was too far back yet. He saw the Indians regrouping on the ridge, their battle feathers whipping in the breeze. He figured he had about a minute to catch Chug before she carried Captain Jones within reach of the raiders.

He looked over his shoulder, saw the other troopers falling back, reluctant to charge fifty braves on high ground. Finding the flap of his holster, he opened it, drawing the big Remington, gripping it surely. He would come alongside and shoot Chug if he had to. The air-chilled sweat around his torso braced him, shivered him with confidence.

"Turn her, Captain!" he shouted again, and this time he knew Jones heard him, for the commander held one rein wide and pulled with everything he had, bowing the gray's strong neck to the right.

Ross began to make up ground, but a flutter on the horizon caught his eye, and he saw fifty braves streaking down the slanted ridge like cloud shadows, each anxious to count the first coup on the two foolish soldiers who had charged too near. Jones saw, too, and pulled so hard on the right rein that he almost fell out of the saddle.

Ross closed in on Chug in seconds. "Let her go, Captain! Jump on with me!"

Jasper Jones hit the ground, rolled, found his footing, raised his arm. He had ordered the men to practice this drill—the mounted trooper picking up the man on foot. He had made a contest of it and felt it pay off now as he landed solidly behind Private Caldwell with war cries stabbing his ears. This soldier was strong, sure of himself. God bless Georgia, he thought. But he wasn't safe yet. The

Indians would descend on them like diving hawks. They had to reach the rest of the rescue party.

Looking over the private's shoulder, he saw the nearest soldiers following the appropriate procedure, every fourth man holding the horses while the others formed a firing line. The carbines hurled the first volley at the Indians, and Jones looked back to see a horse drop from under a warrior.

The rest of the raiders, however, remained eager for battle. They chanced a few long shots, having ridden within reach of the two bluecoats. Jones saw an arrow go by, hit the ground in front of him, then pass under him.

The second volley came from the soldiers on foot, half of them reloading as the others stepped up and took aim. The warriors heard the bullets whistle. They scattered, spreading the carbine fire, turning back to the slanted ridge.

"Well done, men!" Jones said as Ross reined in behind the riflemen. "Get down, Private, and let me have your mount."

Ross slid from the sorrel as Sergeant Parkhill and the rest of the rescue party rode up from the rear.

"Sergeant Parkhill!" Jones shouted. "Form a detail of the men from your squad and get that wounded man to the surgeon."

"Yes, sir!" Parkhill growled.

"The rest of you men will come with me to recover the herd. Private Caldwell, tell Sergeant Webber to mount his squad and follow my trail."

"Yes, sir," Ross said as the captain led the party away, leaving him with Parkhill, Gene Dillon, yellow-haired

Lloyd, and several other Southerners from his squad—all of them glaring down at him from their horses.

"Caldwell, are you sweet on that captain?" Parkhill said. "His ass was good as scalped till you rode him down."

Ross shrugged. "I know what it feels like to ride that cold-jawed runaway."

"We could have gotten shed of the son of a bitch," Parkhill replied.

Ross snickered as if the idea were ridiculous. "What's the use? They'd just send some West Pointer to take his place. I'd rather keep Jones."

Parkhill spewed a brown stream of spit onto his mount's rump, then turned back to Ross. "We could all be in the Montana gold fields by the time the next Yankee gets here," he said.

The smile slid from Ross's face. "I haven't heard any talk of such."

"That's because you keep yourself to your wife too much," Gene Dillon said, smiling. "Get out of the house now and then of an evenin', and you'd learn somethin'."

Ross nodded, playing the spy all the way now. "I'll do that. About damn time you boys let me know what was goin' on."

Parkhill turned toward the wounded soldier, lying a hundred yards away among the dead horses, and Ross followed on foot, his legs feeling weak under him. This spy business was more frightening than battle. It was impulse, quick and resistless, that caused him to run stupidly into cornfields after wounded comrades, or rescue his captain from a Cheyenne charge. But this was a calculated march into a hostile stronghold.

And now Ross knew. He wasn't a hero. He was a damned fool.

Late that night, Captain Jones returned to Camp Marshall, having recaptured only twenty-seven of the more than one hundred horses stolen by the Cheyenne. When he got to his quarters, he found a freshly laundered uniform folded on his dining room table, and in its left breast pocket, a note from his company spy.

EIGHT

D amn it!" captain Jones shouted, wadding the piece of paper and throwing it across the room.

The telegraph clerk flinched. "You want me to reply?"

"Yes, tell Colonel Kulp he can . . ." Jones fumed, searching for words.

Lieutenant Deihl bounded into the captain's office, eyes wide with curiosity.

"Tell Colonel Kulp he can rely on me to follow his orders," Jones said, composing himself.

"What's happened?" the lieutenant asked as the telegraph operator left the office.

"I've been ordered to take half my command north to the Crazy Woman River and rendezvous with Colonel Kulp in two weeks."

"For what purpose?"

"Campaigning, of course."

Deihl clapped his hands, rubbed them together. "It's about damn time!"

"Like hell it is! We can't keep the telegraph line open with half our force off hunting Indians. Our scouts don't know a damned thing about the Crazy Woman country. And on top of that, I've got a mutiny to put down."

"What mutiny?"

"You'll know about it soon enough. Why does the army always choose the worst possible timing?"

"You could allow me to make the rendezvous with Colonel Kulp while you continue to command the post," Deihl offered.

"You know I can't do that. The orders are for me. You'll have to take over things here."

Deihl's mouth opened in astonishment. "You can't leave me here. I'm second-in-command!"

"Exactly why I must leave you here, Lieutenant, and you will have your hands full! Now, call a general assembly and let me address the men. And arm a police detail from Sergeant Webber's squad. Six men, and make them ready to fight!"

When Camp Marshall had drawn itself into a formation, Captain Jones ordered his police detail to present arms. "Sergeant Parkhill!" he shouted. "Front and center!"

The burly sergeant obeyed, marching forward from the ranks.

"Sergeant, you are under arrest for attempting to incite the men to mutiny. You will reside in the stockade until such time as you will stand court-martial. Detail, take custody of the prisoner."

Parkhill's face became an instant contortion as he

lunged for the captain's throat with both hands, knocking the commander onto his back. The police detail grabbed the big arms, but Parkhill kicked two of the soldiers off their feet and continued to strangle Jones until a rifle butt clubbed him on the back of the head.

The captain coughed as Lieutenant Deihl helped him to his feet. He rubbed his throat and sopped the tears from his eyes with his sleeve. He tried to speak, but only croaked, then coughed again. Finally catching his breath, the commander stepped up on the board porch of his quarters to watch with satisfaction as the detail dragged Sergeant Parkhill in through the door of the tiny stockade.

"Corporal Dillon, you are now in charge of your squad," the captain ordered hoarsely. "Prepare your men immediately for an extended campaign. Rations for thirty days. Be ready to march at fourteen hundred hours. Lieutenant Deihl, wire Horseshoe Station and Deer Creek. Have each send a squad to rendezvous with me at Bridger's Ferry. Lieutenant Redding will accompany me from there. Dismissed!"

Ross heard the men grumble around him, felt somebody bump him. He turned to see Lloyd glaring at him through pale blue eyes.

"What?" Ross said.

"Nothin'," the high voice said, Lloyd sneering as he turned away.

Ross walked toward his quarters and found Julia waiting there, the door latch in her hand. She let him in, closed the door, bolted it.

"Do they suspect you?" she asked.

"I don't know. I think maybe Lloyd does, but he never liked me, anyway."

She put her arms around his waist. "They won't do anything out there without Parkhill. The captain was wise to order them on the campaign."

"Yeah," Ross said, his hand finding the back of her neck under her hair. "I wonder if he'll want me to testify against Parkhill."

"It doesn't matter. We'll get through it one way or the other." She pulled his shirttail out of his trousers and put her hands on his back. They were cool and soft, having just come out of the washtub. "You've got this campaign to worry about first. What have you heard?"

"No more than you just did. Rations for thirty days. I'll be gone awhile this time."

"Yes, but when you come back it will be almost time to muster out. Then we can go anywhere. Back to Athens if you want to. Or Denver. Even California. We'll be free then."

It was the first time she had talked of what would happen after the army, and he was glad to find her agreeable to staying in the West. When he thought of them growing old, he saw plains and mountains around them. When he thought of his children playing, he saw them riding like Dakota whirlwinds.

"We can start our family," he said, and he kissed her, his dry lips pushing hard on hers.

"We have three hours before you have to go," she said, her hands reaching under his shirt. "Let me have one. The army can have the other two."

t had been eleven days, and still he could not clear his mind of their parting. She had run at him across the parade ground of Camp Marshall, grasping his knee as he rode away. He had reached down to touch her face and felt her tears run across his fingers. It was in his heart, before his eyes, around his empty stomach.

He was lonely in the wildest country he had ever known. They were camped at the confluence of the Crazy Woman and its south fork, waiting for Colonel Kulp. Since leaving Fort Marshall, they had seen no Indians and little game. About half the salt pork had gone bad for some reason—not cured properly, Ross suspected. Bugs had gotten into the hardtack. At least they had plenty of fresh water from the river. It flowed eastward, out of the Bighorn Mountains, which loomed seductively in the west.

There were grassy hills all around, some rolling, some rather pointed. The summer had given the plains more rainfall here than at Camp Marshall, and the ground undulated with waves of greenery. You could watch that grass ripple for hours, almost hypnotizing yourself, Ross had learned. There wasn't much to do here besides watch the grass and wait.

He sat on his blanket, spread evenly across the ground, a rock on each corner. The pieces of his Remington revolver lay in front of him on the blanket. Meticulously, he cleaned them of dirt, grain by grain. He had to make each task last. Idleness only made him pine for Julia.

The sun burned through the scant shade of the small cottonwood at his back, and what little breeze there was blew hot. The gurgle of the Crazy Woman—a mere brook by Georgia standards—was a mockery. Even the water ran warm today.

He sensed a group of soldiers approaching, but was too intent on his weapon to look up, until a spray of sand rained on his blanket, peppering his gunmetal with grit.

"Oh, damn, how clumsy can I git?" Lloyd said, his ugly mouth set in a grin.

It had been like this every day since Parkhill's arrest, and Ross had taken enough. It swept him up—an impulse of the sort that seemed to dog him when he was away from Julia—and he sprang from the blanket to stagger Lloyd with a shove. Before the yellow-haired private could strike back, Gene Dillon had stepped between them.

"What the hell's wrong with you two? The captain'll put a lash to your back for fightin'."

"I just want to stick a knife in that damn Yankee-lover, that's all," Lloyd said.

"I've told you he couldn't have had nothin' to do with it," Gene said.

"With what?" Ross asked.

"You know what you done." Lloyd sneered.

Gene held Lloyd back with one arm. "He thinks you got Parkhill arrested."

Ross scoffed. "How could I have had a damn thing to do with that?"

"You told the captain about Park's plan."

"I never even speak to the captain."

Lloyd sniffed, and looked Ross over from boots to hat.

"Your wife does, and she's a damn Yankee-lover, too. She sure likes that captain. You ought to see her with him when you're out on detail, Caldwell. I'm surprised she's got any left for you."

"Shut your filthy mouth." Ross lunged, swinging a fist, but the blow missed as Gene Dillon caught him around the waist and slung him aside.

"Don't do it, Ross." He stood between the two soldiers. "Damn, Lloyd, are you hell-bent on trouble? Let's git." He turned the yellow-haired Southerner away from Ross and pushed him along the riverbank. "I'm not gonna break you two up again, Lloyd. Next time, you'll get whatever's co-min'."

"Next time I'll kill the son of a bitch. I swear to God I'll kill him."

Jasper Jones was sitting in his tent, smelling the moldy canvas, drumming his fingers on a yellowed map. He hated being here. Hated it so much he wanted to rant and pull hair. This campaign was lunacy to the last detail. Colonel Kulp had actually ordered him to bring two howitzers along. Imagine, fighting the world's finest light cavalry with artillery in a roadless country. It would be like fighting off bumblebees with bricks.

Where is Colonel Kulp, anyway? Lost, probably. Does he know we will soon be starving here? Does he care that my men are restless? Does he realize half my force consists of former Rebels who would just as soon desert as stay another day in this wasteland?

Twilight was coming on, and the heat was lifting. He was wondering if Indians would attack at night. He thought they preferred daylight combat, but he wasn't sure. He would have to call for the civilian scout and inquire. But he hated talking to that damned smart-mouthed scout. Full of himself and his frontier savvy, which didn't impress Captain Jones as being extensive.

If I were an Indian, I would attack now. This force is weak, low on morale, short on rations. The attack is coming. I know it is coming. I must prepare my men. I must . . .

A knock on his tent pole brought him back to the moment. He rose and slung the tent flap aside to find Corporal Dillon. "What are you doing here? Did I send for you?"

"No, sir, but . . ."

"But what, soldier? What do you think you're doing?"

Dillon glanced nervously over his shoulder, hoping no one would see him. "Can I come in, sir?"

"In my tent?"

"Yes, sir. I've got my reasons. Somethin' you ought to know."

Irritated, Jones stepped back so the corporal could come in. "Very well. What is it? It had better be important."

Dillon stood uncomfortably in the tent, his service cap in his hand. "Can I speak my mind, sir?"

"Yes, get it over with."

"Do you know a Private Caldwell, sir? The one married to the laundry gal?"

"Of course I know him. He saved my life. What of him?"

Dillon lowered his voice. "I heard some of the Southern boys talkin', sir. They say they're gonna kill him. They think he's been spyin' on 'em for you. They're gonna kill him and desert."

A pang of remorse struck Jones in the heart. He had brought this on Caldwell. But he showed the corporal no emotion. "Some of the Southern boys? Which ones?"

"It was dark and I couldn't see their faces, sir. I just heard 'em. I don't know none of them Southern boys, anyway. I'm from Indiana."

Jones sneered. "Corporal, you are from Montgomery County, Alabama, as sure as I'm born and bred Boston. Now, which ones said they'd kill Caldwell?"

"As God watches over me, Captain, I swear I don't know."

"Then your intelligence is worthless to me." He glared, and Dillon looked at his feet. "You're sure it's not just talk?"

"It's more than talk, sir. They're gonna do it tonight when Caldwell's on picket duty. They planned it down to particulars."

Jones sat down. He wanted to snap something, tear something to pieces. He might have, if he had had two arms. He rested his head in his palm and thought for a few seconds. "Find Caldwell," he said, getting up. "Tell him to come to my tent at nightfall. Don't let anybody see you talking to him, and don't let anybody see you leave here." He stepped outside for a look across the camp. "Come on, the way is clear. Don't fail me, Corporal."

Ross knocked on the pole and made his salute ready. "Private Caldwell reporting as ordered, sir."

The captain grabbed him by the sleeve and pulled him into the tent. "Forget the damned protocol, Caldwell, just sit down."

Ross took a seat on a three-legged stool.

"Now, listen carefully. You're in danger, Caldwell, and seeing as how I got you into it, I intend to get you out. Some of these Knights of the Golden Circle have figured out that you informed on Sergeant Parkhill and they mean to kill you for it."

Ross nodded. "I know, sir." It was a relief to know the captain actually gave a damn. "But what can I do about it?"

"You're going to desert."

"Sir?"

"You heard me. Saddle a good horse and ride like hell."

"But, sir. What about my wife? What about . . . ? I don't want to be a deserter."

"Look here, Private, I'm ordering you to desert. It won't be a real desertion. I won't report it. Your name won't go down in infamy or anything. Hell, you're due to muster out in a few months, anyway. You've done your service."

"But what about Julia?"

"You'll ride up the Crazy Woman to the Bighorn Mountains. Cross them and you'll strike the Bridger Trail. Follow it to Virginia City and wait there. Get a job at a gold mine or something. When I get back to Camp Marshall, I'll tell your wife where to find you and send her with the first wagon train headed that way."

A hundred thoughts stirred in Ross, but he had known calamity for so long that nothing showed on his face. "When do I go?"

"Immediately. The damned Knights of the Golden Circle have ordered your murder tonight. Take your service revolver and some rations. And keep your eyes peeled for

Indians. Colonel Kulp has probably stirred them up like a nest of hornets by now." Jones stood and offered Ross his hand. "Good luck, Mr. Caldwell."

Ross shook the captain's hand. "Just make sure Julia knows," he said, risking a flagrant insubordination. "Sir," he added.

When the private left, Captain Jones sat down at his writing table and lingered over his diary. Something should be set down in writing, he thought. Some record should exist. Finally, he dipped his pen into the inkwell and wrote:

Pvt. Caldwell left at dusk, assigned to special duty for duration of his enlistment.

TEN

Two days had passed since Private Caldwell left, and Jasper Jones had all but forgotten him. He had other worries. Still no sign of Colonel Kulp. No game to kill. Food running low. Morale sinking.

This place had not been wisely chosen as a rendezvous point. It was difficult to defend with such a small force as Captain Jones had at his disposal. Too much low ground. Too many hills for the Indians to reconnoiter among. This was the enemy's native soil. He would know it like Jones knew the streets and alleys of Boston.

Yesterday he had drilled the men, and he felt good about that. The camp had regained some semblance of discipline. The pickets looked alert this morning through his field glasses. Today he would put them to work digging rifle pits. Maybe he would send scouts out to look for Colonel Kulp.

One thing about these plains—dawn here made a man feel small. Never had Captain Jones imagined such an expanse of quietude. His clamorous urban culture had ill prepared him for this.

He swept the glasses across the hills once more, balancing them on the fingertips of his one hand. He sighed and let them dangle from the strap around his neck. Nothing out there. These false instincts could be damned. Nerves. Cowardice—that was what it was. Nothing more. No formidable force could possibly sneak near enough to completely surprise him, Indian or not.

He rose, dusted the dirt from the seat of his pants. He was about to turn back toward his tent for breakfast when he saw three pickets running toward camp from the east. He knew instantly in his heart that something horrible would follow those terrified soldiers over the near hill, but on its surface he could merely note what an oddly stirring sight it was to see those men sprinting through the grass.

When it came over the hill, he simply stared for the first second, for it enthralled more than it quailed him. Then the terror struck deep and he ran for his tent. He saw the three pickets overwhelmed by a solid line of mounted warriors, a quarter of a mile long. The hill had become a huge canvas for painted faces and horses; fringed shirts and leggings; eagle feathers that groped skyward like fingers.

The yelping voices made him cringe as the Rebel yells had at Kennesaw Mountain, and he felt the old minnie ball shatter his missing left arm again. He suffered the shameful stab of failure and remembered his guns lying on his cot. The first rifle shot came from his camp of surprised men, too late to give adequate warning.

Plunging into his tent, he found his revolver and cartridge belt. An arrow popped twice through the canvas as he charged back outside and added his gunfire to the meager resistance his men had raised. The first wave of warriors swarmed past him now, circling the camp. He saw their faces alive with glory and anger. They were men his own age and younger, but infinitely wiser than he about warfare on these plains.

His soldiers were stampeding toward him in a chaotic retreat. "The wagons!" he shouted, trying to turn them. "Hold the wagons!" As fast as he could shout at them, their bodies sprouted feathered shafts, but a few lucky survivors read his strategy, turned on the attackers, and began blasting painted riders from horses.

The counterattack grew around Captain Jones—a core of resistance in the massacre—and it moved with strange ease toward the wagons.

"Turn 'em over!" Jones shouted. He felt an unseen projectile pierce the right side of his body below the rib cage. Whether it had come from front or back, he could not say, but it hurt like hell.

A wagon box landed beside him and he fell against it between a sergeant and a private. He held his revolver between his knees and reloaded it as the screams and shouts engulfed him. Looking up, he saw Lieutenant Redding leading a small clot of men across the Crazy Woman to the artillery.

"No! Not the damned cannon! Lieutenant!" But his shouts were lost and he watched the Indians cut the artillerymen down one by one as they tried to turn a howitzer on its carriage. His trembling fingers were trying to slip a primer cap over the last nipple of his revolver when an arrow pinned the stump of his left arm to the wagon box. He grunted, felt the nausea grip his empty stomach.

The sergeant beside him broke the arrow in the middle and yanked the captain's stump off the shaft. Jones looked up as a bullet blew away a chunk of the sergeant's head. The Indians had surrounded the wagon box, rendering it virtually useless as cover. They had captured army weapons. Bullets splintered the wagon bed by the second.

Jones cocked his pistol, found a brave aiming his way, fired, cocked the weapon again, looked for his next target. He mourned a great political career that would never come. He thought of his mother in her kitchen in Boston. The pistol bucked in his grip again as he remembered an old friend, a place he wanted to go, a woman he should have married. Something like a horse kicking him took his breath away, and a thousand notions crossed his mind in an instant.

The battle blurred as he fired again, and he thought of times he had known, aromas he would miss. He relived his old thrills, sorrows, and terrors, tasted flavors bitter and sweet. And for a fleet splinter of a moment, Captain Jasper Jones wondered who would tell Julia Caldwell that her husband awaited her in Virginia City. But gradually, like sunlight flooding the new day, it ceased to matter.

ELEVEN

The monotony of the work and the sounds of rushing water had all but drawn him into a trance. Machine-like, he dumped his shovelload of gravel into the sluice box and stepped back into the shallow prospect hole. He slid the shovel along bedrock and scooped up another load of gold-dusted gravel, lifting it without thought or feeling.

Then it happened again. The wave of dread consumed him, sucking him back through the weeks and the miles. Had he forgotten something? What was he doing here? Where was Julia?

Alder Gulch writhed with human enterprise around him. He doubted it had ever been much of a place to look at, but now it rivaled a battlefield in its devastation. Every available stick of wood had long since been hacked and burned. Every stretch of ground along the creek had been staked, claimed, and burrowed into. The once crystalline rivulet of water in the bed of the gulch ran thick and brown with silt.

He beat the wave of dread down to a shudder in his heart and fixed his grip around the shovel handle once more. He had done everything he could do. It was all beyond his control. He would just have to wait for Captain Jones to get back to Camp Marshall. Then wait longer as Julia made her way here. Then they would make yet another start.

One realization had sprung from all the thought he had

given his predicament. He was here without Julia because of Sergeant Parkhill and the Knights of the Golden Circle. How stupid he had been to fear them and their visionary scheme. How cowardly he had been for not exposing them like a man, instead of as a sneaking spy. He swore he would never again turn a blind eye to any secret society trying to undermine the law of the land. A man had to learn his lessons, and this one had come hard. His sentence for complicity and complacency was hard labor without Julia.

As he stepped out of the prospect hole and poured his load of gravel into the sluice box, he heard the jingle of trace chains up the gulch, and the crunch of metal wagon tires on the rocks. He glanced, spotted the Summit Short-line coming up from Virginia City, dropped his shovel, and ran to the rutted road. He fell in beside the stagecoach and trotted along beside. "Any women today?" he asked the driver, a familiar face behind a cascade of mustache hairs.

"Two," the driver said. "One just a whore, but the other one might be your'n. Good-lookin' dark-haired gal."

"Get her name?"

"Nope."

"Where'd she go?"

"Didn't ask." He let the coils play out of his whip and split air over the team as the coach lurched forward.

Ross went back to his prospect hole to find his boss standing there—an old man, veteran of many rushes.

"She here?" the old miner asked.

"Maybe," Ross said. "A woman got out in town."

The old man scooped up some gravel to wash in his prospecting pan. He climbed out of the hole to the sluice

box. "Well," he said, filling his pan with water, "it bein'
Saturday evenin', you might as well go on down to town."

Ross smiled. "It's a little early to quit."

The old man pulled a small pouch from his pocket. "I'll
dock you a little pay, then." He loosened the drawstrings
and took a pinch of gold dust from the pouch, flicking it
into the air.

Ross caught his week's pay in the pouch as the old man
tossed it. "Thanks," he said, turning down the gulch. "See
you Monday."

The old-timer stared into his pan of swirling gravel. "I
don't look that far ahead."

He hiked past sluices, trenches, rockers, and odd piles
of gravel as the music of steel against stone rang from
every bend of Alder Gulch. He came to the reservoir above
Virginia City and paused briefly in the shade of a lone
tree to wipe the sweat from his brow with his bandanna.
The clamor of the boomtown reached him here: the ham-
merblows of workmen punctuating the music from the
hurdy-gurdy dance houses.

High rolls of green grass and sagebrush climbed all
around the city. Beyond them, the high and distant timber
of the Tobacco Root Mountains rose like a crown. An odd
setting for a town of ten thousand, but the town showed
no inclination toward going away.

Striding down on Main Street, he turned right onto Wallace and went straight to the overland stagecoach office.
He asked where the woman had gone who had gotten off
the coach earlier.

"You don't mean the whore, do you?" the ticket teller
said.

"The lady."

"I believe she went to the newspaper."

"You believe?"

"She came in and asked me where she could find it. I guess she might have gone to get a room first."

Ross continued down Wallace Street, trotting in the dirt to avoid pedestrians on the boardwalks, looking for the offices of the Virginia City *Post*. It was just like Julia to take care of business first. She would ask the editors about her husband, and if they didn't know, she would get them to help with an article or an ad or something. Wouldn't she be surprised when he walked in!

He saw the sign hanging over the doorway and barged in, pausing to catch his breath. Three men were gathered around a dark-haired woman, chatting with excitement.

"What are we going to cut?" a young reporter said.

"My column," a big man in suspenders replied.

"You sure? What's it about?"

"Same old thing: shut down the hurdy-gurdies; clean out the brothels. Wasted ink. Give me an uppercase *C*. Mary, are you sure it was an entire column?"

"It says a detachment here," the woman replied. "About forty-five men."

Ross took his hat off, curled the brim in his hand. "Excuse me. I'm looking for someone."

The three men turned to stare at him, one stepping aside to reveal the woman's face. It wasn't Julia, of course. Ross already knew from her voice. But he had so convinced himself Julia would be here that seeing this lady didn't make any difference.

"Who?" the reporter said.

"My wife."

"You've come to the wrong place," the big editor said. "This is a newspaper. Now, we're busy getting an issue out, if you don't mind."

"A lady came here from the Wells Fargo office," Ross continued. "I think it was my wife."

"And I think I told you you're mistaken," the editor replied, never looking up from his printing plate. "This young lady is my cousin. She's just arrived from the East, and she's brought important news. Now, get out and leave us be."

"Oh, Ed!" the woman scolded. "Can't you see he's asking for help?" She approached Ross, holding a folded newspaper page in her hand. "I rode in on the stagecoach, sir, and there was just one other woman on it with me. I'm sure she was no one's wife."

"Oh," Ross replied, the wave of dread trying to gush up from his chest again. "Sorry, but they said she was a pretty dark-haired lady, and I . . . I see now they meant you."

The woman smiled sympathetically. "I'm sure your wife will be along in time. How long have you been waiting?"

Ross shrugged. "Only a couple of weeks."

The editor turned from his printing plate. "What kind of Indians were they, Mary? Did it say what tribe?"

She glanced at the newspaper in her hand. "Cheyenne, they think. Possibly with some Sioux warriors." She put her hand on Ross's elbow. "Give her more time. It's a long trip here from anywhere."

"Yes," Ross said. "You're right."

"What was that captain's name?" the editor said, situating a lead block in his plate.

Mary handed the newspaper to a reporter. "It's right here," she said. "See for yourself." She turned back to Ross. "Tell me your wife's name. I'll watch for her arrival and contact you when she gets here."

"Captain Jasper Jones," the reporter said.

"Jasper Jones!" the editor bellowed. "No wonder he got massacred—greenhorn name like that!"

The newsmen burst into laughter, but Ross merely stood with his mouth open.

"Your wife's name," Mary said, ignoring the outburst, "what is it?"

Ross stormed across the room and snatched the newspaper from the young reporter's hand.

"Hey, what's the idea?" the reporter said, but Ross swatted him aside.

As he read, the wave burst from his heart. Colonel Kulp had attacked a village of Indians and driven them west—directly into the camp of Captain Jasper Jones and a detachment of K Company, 11th Ohio Cavalry. Every last man in the column had been killed, stripped, mutilated.

This was the dread that had lived in his heart for weeks, and now it overwhelmed him as he came to understand it. Julia wasn't coming at all. He had no idea where she might be, and no way of communicating with her.

"I'll take that, if you don't mind," the editor said, yanking the newspaper from Ross's hand. "What's wrong with you, mister? Have you lost your mind? What did you say your name was?"

"Never mind," Ross answered. "It doesn't matter now." He felt his pocket for the pouch of gold dust and turned for the door.

TWELVE

Julia waited in the parlor, sitting primly on a sofa, her back straight, feet together on the floor, hands clasped in her lap. The house included some of the finest appointments she had seen anywhere in the West, but it was obvious that Colonel Kulp didn't know what to do with them. There was no flow in this room. No theme, no pattern. Just furniture bunched together. Oh, well, the man was a soldier, not an interior decorator.

How much longer would he keep her waiting? Was he really that busy or just hoping she would go away? She would not go away, of course. She had questions to ask. The official report had failed to satisfy her.

She had refused to cry the day Lieutenant Deihl came to her room at Camp Marshall and told her the news. Ross could not have been killed. She would have had a dream or something, felt his soul's embrace. It was true that something had overwhelmed her the day Ross left, but that was just sorrow in seeing him ride away again. She didn't care if there was a massacre. They had not proven to her that Ross was dead.

"Mrs. Caldwell," a bespectacled corporal said, "the colonel will see you now."

Julia smiled and rose, her heart beating crazily, as if she would enter the office and find Ross there. She found, instead, a fat, aging, oily-haired man in crisp uniform.

"How do you do, Mrs. Caldwell?" he said, coming around his desk to meet her. He was a big man and he looked down on her with a smile and sad eyes, his head cocked to one side. "I wish we could have met under happier circumstances."

Julia took his hand. She hadn't expected him to behave like an undertaker, and she didn't like it. Why did everybody act this way? She was here for answers, not sympathy.

The colonel gestured toward a chair as he lumbered back to his seat behind the desk. "If it is any consolation at all, I can assure you that the savages who murdered your husband will be punished most severely." He put a pair of grimy lenses on his face and shuffled a few papers. "I've arranged for you to collect your late husband's pay." He pushed a voucher across the desk, followed by a small brown envelope. "And the men took a collection for the widows' fund. It's not much, but it will help you get back East."

"I'm not going back East," Julia said. "And I don't want any part of any widows' fund." She shoved the envelope back at the officer. "I want to know what makes you so sure my husband was killed."

Kulp's mouth gaped for a moment, then he took in a long, rattling breath. He removed his glasses. He had encountered this kind of widow before. The angry kind. What did she expect? Her husband had joined the army. "The entire detachment was wiped out. Your husband's name was on the roster."

"Show me his personal effects."

"Ma'am?"

"I want his wedding ring, his watch, his revolver. Where is his uniform?"

"I don't mean to upset you, Mrs. Caldwell, but you must understand that the Indians leave nothing behind. They take all weapons. They cut off fingers to get rings. They strip their victims of everything."

The colonel's tone was making her mad. "Do you know what my husband looks like?"

"I cannot know every soldier in my command."

"Then no one recognized him on the battlefield?"

"Even if I had remembered his face, Mrs. Caldwell . . ." He looked down at his paperwork.

"What?"

"The Indians scalped them. They cut out tongues, slashed faces, mutilated arms and legs. Opened . . . opened the body cavities and took the organs out. It was plain that Captain Jones offered some resistance, but he was hopelessly outnumbered. It was a total defeat, Mrs. Caldwell. No one could have survived. Every last officer and man was killed, I assure you."

"How many?"

"The entire detachment."

Julia clenched her fists and glared across the desk. "How many dead bodies did you find on the battleground?"

The colonel scowled for a moment, then yanked at a desk drawer. He removed a file, opened it, put on his glasses. Licking his fingers, he thumbed through leaves of hand script, finally pausing to peruse one. "Forty-two by one account. Forty-four by another."

Julia gasped. "You didn't count them yourself?"

"I did not."

"Which count is accurate? Forty-two or forty-four? Or shall we average them and call it forty-three?"

The colonel's jowls trembled. "You weren't there. Men wept as they buried the dead. The stench was horrible. You have no idea what a battlefield looks like, Mrs. Caldwell. You wouldn't have had the stomach to count, either."

"I once worked as a nurse on a battlefield, Colonel, and I placed exactly fifteen legs and twenty-two arms in a pile outside the hospital tent. I would have counted."

The colonel's eyes twitched with surprise. "You would have wasted your time. It's quite possible that wolves dragged some of the corpses away. The Indians themselves might have taken live prisoners to torture. An exact count would have meant nothing."

Julia scoffed. "It means a great deal to me. How many men were assigned to Captain Jones's detachment? Do you have an exact count on that?"

Kulp's face reddened as he leafed through his file again. "Two officers and forty-four men."

"That makes forty-six total. If an *average* of forty-three were killed in the massacre, wouldn't that leave three unaccounted for? Hasn't that occurred to you? Three soldiers could be in the hands of the Indians as we sit here!"

"They are all dead, Mrs. Caldwell."

"Let me see the reports," she demanded, holding her hand across the desk.

"I don't have the authority to allow that."

"Damn your authority!" She sprang from her chair and lunged for the files.

"Corporal!" Kulp shouted, retreating with his documents.

Julia heard the door open behind her and knew the corporal was there. "May I ask one more question?" she said.

"There are some questions I cannot answer."

"Did you know Captain Jones would be bivouacked on the Crazy Woman?"

"Captain Jones followed his orders."

"Then why in the name of God did you drive hundreds of enemy warriors directly into his camp?"

"Corporal, see Mrs. Caldwell out."

"You should be court-martialed," Julia said, her voice scathing.

"You are impertinent, Mrs. Caldwell."

"*You* are incompetent!" She felt the corporal's hand on her arm, wrenched herself free of his grasp. She snatched the pay voucher from the colonel's desk, leaving the envelope from the widows' fund.

When she had collected Ross's pay, she left the fort and went to the stage stop to wait for the next coach west. She sat on a bench in front of the whitewashed board building, her bags at her feet. The day was pleasant and the sunshine felt good on her legs. A cool snap had blown down from the north. The long summer was over. She put her hands on her stomach and fought back the urge to cry.

If he had died like that, she would have felt something. She refused to mourn him until she knew for certain. She had followed him before and found him. She could do it again.

It was different this time, of course. Finding him would be fraught with difficulties. This time she had lost him beyond the frontier. This time she was pregnant. She was going to have Ross's baby. He could not have died out there on the Crazy Woman.

THIRTEEN

Ross wore a beard ten months old the day he rode back into Virginia City. The horse he straddled was not much to look at, hell to ride, but bent on getting there. Ross called him Ol' Whitey. He was the color of milk spilled on the barn floor.

Against his saddle bounced his sack of possessions, around his hips a gun belt, in his boot a bag of Colorado gold dust. As he approached town, he realized that Virginia City was where he had last put a razor to his face. Even if anyone here remembered him, they wouldn't recognize him. The beard had covered his jaw. The soldier's haircut had come bristling out under his dusty hat. Tons of ore had left scars and calluses on his face and hands.

Julia, if he found her here, would not know him. But he had learned to moderate his hopes of finding her. He would never stop looking, of course, but a disappointment in every town had tempered his expectations.

He heard Virginia City coming two miles down the mountain: brass horns, gunshots. It was July 4, a rare miner's holiday. For Ross it was a day to change strategies. No more drifting from town to town, searching, writing letters, sending wires. He was going to stay put for a while. Maybe he and Julia had missed each other coming and going. Maybe she would find out somehow that Captain Jones had sent him to Virginia City and would turn up here if he gave her time.

As he reached the edge of town, he slowed his horse to

a walk and began habitually shooting glances at the faces of women. Most of them on this side of town were harlots, and they returned his looks with calculated glances of their own. But Ross hadn't touched a woman since he reached down to brush the tears from Julia's face at Camp Marshall.

He rode past two blocks of hurdy-gurdies, an occasional dollar-a-dance girl attracting his attention. He had to wonder if time had exaggerated Julia's beauty in his memory, for none of these women even remotely compared.

When he turned the corner onto Wallace Street, the full force of the celebration hit him, and even his tired horse perked up. A boxing ring had been erected in front of the Virginia City *Post,* and two men were sparring in it, barechested and bare-fisted. As he rode closer, he recognized the larger man as the editor of the *Post.*

He rode up behind a band uniform at ringside and stopped. The man in the uniform had a trumpet slung over his shoulder on a string and held a mug of beer in one hand. "What's this all about, partner?" he asked.

The man looked up, misty-eyed, and saw Ross for fellow pick and shovel man. "You just ride in?"

Ross nodded.

"Welcome to Sin City, friend."

Ross reached down for a handshake.

The trumpet player gestured toward the ring with his mug. "The big fellow puts out the newspaper. Name's Ed Johnson. The little dried-up fellow's Bob Hodges. Runs the Break o' Day Saloon." He pointed down the street.

"I take it the editor's against wet goods." Ross seemed to remember a puritanical streak in some editorials he had read here ten months and more ago.

The crowd roared as the pugilists came together, the editor snapping the saloon man's head back, and the saloon man burying a fist in the editor's flab.

"Against it wholesale, but particular at the Break o' Day. He wrote in the paper that Bob's been waterin' down drinks and short-weightin' his scales."

Ross leaned across his saddle horn. "Looks like that riled ol' Bob."

"No, Bob let that much go. Laughed about it, in fact, and said you could pan that editor out clear down to bedrock and not raise a color. Now, when Johnson got a earful of that, he dared Bob to fight him boxin' rules come the Fourth, and there they stand."

The saloon owner whipped a sudden uppercut into Johnson's chin and the big man hung on the ropes for a second, then hit the rough-sawn floor. Someone at ringside struck a brass bell with a mallet and Bob went to his corner for a shot of whiskey while a reporter for the *Post* poured a bucket of water on Johnson.

"How many rounds is that?" Ross asked.

"Eight or ten," the musician said. "They're just gettin' started good."

"Who'd you put your money on?"

The happy miner raised his mug. "My heart's with Bob, but my dust is on the big fellow."

Ross grinned and reined his mount around the spectators as he saw the editor getting up. He didn't wish any loss of dust on the trumpet player, but he was hoping the newspaperman would take a good whipping today. He remembered the editor's ill temper ten months back, the day he went looking for Julia.

He had left Virginia City that day, the very hour he heard about the massacre on the Crazy Woman. The stage took him south to Fort Bridger, the nearest telegraph station by his reckoning. He sent a wire for a Mrs. Caldwell at Camp Marshall, receiving an almost immediate reply. Mrs. Caldwell had gone away.

He didn't go to Camp Marshall. They would recognize him there, wonder why he hadn't been massacred, suspect him of desertion. In fact, he became so worried about getting arrested for desertion that he invented an alias: R.W. Colby. It matched the initials carved into his pistol grip. He himself didn't know what the *R.W.* in his alias might stand for, but it didn't matter. It wasn't considered polite out here to ask.

He let his beard grow out as a disguise as he headed for Denver. He and Julia had talked about going there, but he found no trace of her. When he ran out of gold dust, he went to work in the Gregory Gulch diggings, replenished his funds, drifted farther south.

He wasted part of the fall on a virgin farm near Pueblo, helping get the harvest in, then drove a bull train to Julesburg. From there he sent a wire to the folks back in Athens, thinking Julia may have gone home.

"Ross!" the reply read. "Army claims you were killed! No word from Julia. What goes on?"

His only answer was to say that he would find her. Somehow he didn't feel the need to explain it all to his folks, or Julia's. They had never lived out here. They wouldn't understand the difficulties.

He returned to Denver through a blizzard. He found the name of a Mrs. Caldwell in a hotel register there, but it wasn't written in Julia's hand. It didn't make sense. He was the one who was supposed to be lost, but it was Julia who had vanished without a trace.

Winter in Boulder was miserable. He got out as soon as the weather broke and started heading for Montana again.

When he reached Fort Laramie, he worked up the nerve to enter the post and ask Colonel Kulp's clerk if anyone had heard from Julia Caldwell.

"Who are you?" the corporal said.

"Name's R.W. Colby. I'm a friend of her folks back in Georgia. They haven't heard from her in a long time and asked me to look around for her."

The corporal nodded. "She was here last September to collect her husband's pay. He was killed with Captain Jones on the Crazy Woman."

Ross merely nodded. "Where did she go?"

The corporal shrugged.

It was the first lead he had turned up, and it had grown cold as an ice-clogged river over the winter. There was nothing to do but go back to Virginia City and hope.

The brass bell rang as he dismounted in front of the Break o' Day Saloon, and the boxers began stalking each other again. He had a notion to go in for a drink, but knew he should case the town for Julia first, so he walked to the first hotel down the street and began his search.

"Can I see the register? I'm lookin' for somebody."

The hotelier turned the book around so Ross could read it.

He ran his finger down the list of current guests and curled his mouth in a practiced frown. "I'll be in town a while. If I don't find who I'm lookin' for at some other hotel, do you mind if I come back and look through the back pages of your register?"

The hotelier shrugged. "All right with me."

By the time Ross had inquired at every hotel and boardinghouse in town, Ed Johnson's left eye was swollen shut, and Bob Hodges had a stream of blood running from his nose.

"How many rounds?" Ross asked, stepping up beside the trumpet player at ringside.

"Must be twenty-five or thirty. I think Bob would whip him in another couple of rounds if he'd lay off the panther sweat."

Ross chuckled as he watched the fighting saloon man throw back a shot of liquor. "Well, he's got to prove his point his own way."

He walked back to the Break o' Day Saloon, pushed his way inside, and stood at the bar until the bartender found time to glance at him.

"What's the whiskey like?"

"Got three kegs of valley tan fresh from Salt Lake."

"I'll have a taste of that and a cigar," Ross said, reaching into his boot for his pouch of dust. He traded the pouch for his drink and a long cigar, watched the bartender sprinkle dust until the scales leveled out at two bits' worth.

"Torch?" the bartender said, handing Ross a box of matches with the return of his gold pouch.

Ross nodded and lit his smoke. He had taken to smoking an occasional cigar in Boulder after hearing a drunken mule skinner recite a line of barroom verse:

When weary I are,
I smokes my cigar:
And when the smoke rises
Up into my eyeses,
I thinks of my true love,
And, oh, how I sighses.

He had laughed when he heard it. Then, having a few drinks under his belt, he had almost cried. Now the smoke was in his eyes again, the sigh on his lips. He was weary indeed, and thinking of Julia. The valley tan had a scalding edge to it, and he heard the brass bell ring outside.

FOURTEEN

He clenched the stub of his cigar in his teeth as he stepped outside to see how the fighters fared. The clean mountain air carried smoke into his lungs, and his head droned with a whiskey hum. The pugilists had to have gone fifty rounds by now. Each staggered, leaning on the other. Johnson was hurt, his face swollen and bloody. Hodges was merely drunk and a little tired.

A volley of gunshots drew Ross's attention up the street, beyond the fighting ring. He saw a freight wagon coming, bristling with gun barrels. A dozen voices sang, hollered oaths. As the wagon rumbled nearer, he sensed the fight spectators dispersing. A pistol round shattered a second-floor window and Ross recognized the familiar drawl of Dixie in the rough voices.

His instinct, though whiskey-clouded, told him this was a good time to take his horse to a livery. But he looked a little closer at the wagon and saw a familiar figure holding the reins. He didn't have to wonder. Men like Parkhill didn't come in pairs. He was wearing an old Confederate cavalry cap. His shoulders sprawled against his shotgun riders, and he sat spraddle-legged on a whiskey keg, driving his team of four wantonly into the throng at ringside.

"Hey!" he yelled, drawing rein and nudging one of his men. "Don't I see that Yankee editor?"

A lean, squint-eyed rake steadied himself on Parkhill's shoulder from behind. "What's left of him."

"What was that he said about me in his paper?"

"Said the way you treat them poor Chinee bastards, you might as well have resurrected the slave trade of the wretched Old South in the Rockies."

"Now, Wink, are you sure he said 'wretched Old South'?"

Wink whipped a newspaper from behind his back and pointed out the line for Parkhill as the men in the wagon began an ominous moaning.

"I believe that calls for an ass-whippin'," Parkhill said, jumping down from the wagon. Wink tripped out behind him, catching a boot heel on a sideboard and landing on his shoulder. Several other men jumped from the wagon, picked Wink up, and followed Parkhill to the boxing ring.

As Parkhill started to climb through the ropes, someone grabbed him by the arm.

"Wait a minute, Parkhill," the trumpet player said. "This here's a prizefight. We've got side bets. You can't git in there."

Parkhill shook the man off, but the feisty miner only grabbed him again. Two of Parkhill's men pulled the musician back by the trumpet looped around his shoulder while a third clubbed him over the head with the barrel of a Navy Colt.

Ross sank his teeth into his cigar and stepped off the boardwalk as Parkhill climbed into the ring.

"I'll finish him off for you, Bob," he said, pushing the saloon man aside.

Johnson was scarcely coherent, smearing blood around his eyes with the backs of his fist, searching for his opponent. Parkhill pushed up his right sleeve as the editor staggered. He wound his arm a few times as if cranking a mill. Then he slammed a fist into Johnson's nose and watched the editor stumble back into the ropes and bounce on the floor.

Ross pushed his way among the laughing Parkhill men, picked up the trumpet player, and helped him to the boardwalk, where he could sit down. When he turned back to the ring, he saw Parkhill stomping the unconscious editor in the ribs, forcing him under the ropes and out of the ring. The saloon owner was standing in the far corner, looking suddenly sober.

Parkhill grabbed the prize purse full of gold dust as he stepped between the ropes. "Drinks for Dixie at the Break o' Day!" he shouted, waving the pouch, and his men stormed the saloon.

"You all right?" Ross asked.

"Yeah," the musician said, rubbing the back of his head, checking his fingers for blood.

"What's the deal with that big Reb?"

The musician blew some dust from his trumpet valves. "Name's Parkhill. He owns the hydraulic works up the gulch. Only hires Chinese, except for his overseers, and they're all Sesech. He also freights some. Owns another claim up at Last Chance Gulch and runs a weekly stage-coach up there. Says the road's his and he'll whip anybody who won't pay his toll."

"Looks like he means it."

"One fellow thought he didn't," Fritz said. "Pennsylvania boy tried runnin' freight to Last Chance and wouldn't pay the toll on Parkhill's road. They found that boy dead. Had three numbers painted on his freight outfit."

"Numbers?"

"Three, seven, seventy-seven."

"What's that mean?"

"Vigilante code they used to use in California. Nobody knows what it means for sure, but a grave is about three foot wide, seven foot long, and seventy-seven inches deep, ain't it?"

Ross threw the stub of his cigar down in the street and watched the reporter for the *Post* trying to revive Johnson. "So Parkhill's a vigilante?"

"Make up your own mind about that," the trumpet player said. "Once was the time we had to have vigilantes around here for the likes of road agents, but now what we need is law for the likes of the vigilantes. I believe in checks and balances, and the damned vigilantes have gone too far."

Ross looked toward the Break o' Day and saw a steady stream of men coming out. "What's your name, friend?"

"Fritz."

"Pleasure to meet you. I'm R.W. Colby. You better have somebody look at that head. Clean it out or you'll get the lockjaw."

"I know a gal across town that'll look at it," Fritz said, getting up. "But if she cleans anything out, she'll start with my pockets." He slapped Ross on the back and headed up the street.

The laughter of the Parkhill men rang from the saloon, and Ross felt a strange urge to join them. He had cursed Sergeant Parkhill and the Knights of the Golden Circle a thousand times over the past months. If not for them, he would never have lost Julia. Of course, he might have been massacred on the Crazy Woman instead, but Parkhill deserved no credit for that chance stroke of luck.

Right now Ross had just enough whiskey in his stomach and felt just enough frustration in his soul to desire some retribution. It was like that day in the cornfield. Like riding after Chug with Captain Jones on her back. It was as good as done, foolhardy or not.

"Hey!" Parkhill shouted as Ross entered the saloon. "Let's drink to the Sons of Liberty!"

Their voices rallied, then died for a second as the liquor poured down their throats.

"To the Knights of the Golden Circle!" Wink said, lifting his drink again. He threw the last of it past his teeth as his squint searched the room. "Hey, Bob," he said to the saloon owner. "Come on and have a drink with us."

Hodges was looking in the mirror of his back-bar, cleaning blood from his swollen face with a wet cloth. He merely glanced at Wink's reflection.

Parkhill's lieutenant strutted to the bar. "I said drink to Dixie, Bob."

"I'm all drinked out," Bob answered.

"You're still standin'. Ain't you from Dixieland?"

"Maryland."

"Hell, that's Dixie! Drink up, Bob, I'm buyin'!"

Bob turned around to look at the drunken mine foreman. "I didn't fight for the Confederacy. I ain't no rich plantation owner."

Wink turned his head and sneered. "You didn't turn Yankee, did you?"

"No. Came out here to stay neutral. Couldn't fight against my home state." He filled Wink's glass, hoping he would take it and go away.

"Neutral, hell," Wink said. "You're a Southerner, boy. Let me hear you whistle 'Dixie.'"

"My lip's busted."

"Hum it."

Bob glanced at Parkhill, as if for help, only to find the big man grinning. "I can't carry a tune in sack, Wink. Leave me alone."

Wink shoved the drink back at Bob. "Then drink to Dixie, damn it."

"No."

Wink's bloodshot eyes widened and glared. He pulled a small revolver from his belt, cocked it, and pointed it at the saloon owner. "Drink!"

"Go to hell," Bob said.

The revolver erupted, knocking Bob against the back-bar. He sank to the floor, holding his left side.

"Goddamn, Wink," Parkhill said, coming to look over the bar, his boots thundering across the floor in the midst of the sudden silence. "You better run for a doctor. Then just keep runnin'. Hide out till things settle down."

Ross let out the breath he had been holding since the gun fired. He saw Wink put the revolver in his pants and stroke his stubbled face nervously.

"I said git," Parkhill ordered, leaning over the bar. "He ain't dyin'. Don't worry about it. Just git."

Wink staggered toward the door, staring blankly at the light of day through the open doors.

Before Ross could contemplate, he felt his Remington in his right palm. He reached under Wink's left arm as the foreman passed him, grabbed the little revolver from the top of Wink's pants, and put its muzzle under Wink's chin. His Remington rose smoothly and covered the rest of the saloon as he pulled the foreman in front of him as a shield.

Every eye in the smoky room turned to stare. Then Bob Hodges rose from behind the bar, holding his rib cage.

"Put your hands behind you," Ross said to Wink. He paused to swallow, to breathe, to think. "Now stick them through your belt. That's right, now clasp them together. You try to get those hands loose, and I'll put a bullet right through your head."

"Who the hell are you?" Parkhill demanded. "Turn that man loose before you get hurt."

Ross covered the big man with his revolver, looking right over the sights, amazed to find them so steady. "Send an unarmed man for the doctor."

"If you don't stop givin' orders, you're gonna need the goddamn doctor."

Ross watched his pistol sights float to the high ridge of Parkhill's cavalry cap. Send a shot over his head, he thought. Let him know you mean business. He squeezed his trigger, felt the satisfying recoil, saw Parkhill standing wide-eyed and hatless. Damn, Ross thought, didn't mean to get that close!

"Frank," said Parkhill. "Take your guns off and fetch a doc."

Bob Hodges climbed onto the bar and lay down as if waiting to be examined.

With a jab of the pistol barrel under Wink's chin, Ross pulled him backward toward the door. "We're goin' to the jailhouse," he said.

"All right," Wink answered. "Careful with that piece, it's got a hair trigger."

They backed out of the bar and into the street, Ross's boots scuffing against Wink's. He kept his Remington trained on the door of the Break o' Day and saw Parkhill appear there, his hand on the revolver at his gun belt.

As he stumbled over ruts, Ross watched the Parkhill men follow at a distance. He risked only glances in the direction of the jailhouse, trusting Wink to lead the way. He knew he was there when he saw the wall at his shoulder. The jailhouse had been built of sawmill lumber laid flat, each layer overlapping at the corners. The walls stood eight inches thick, solid wood, bulletproof.

The stale smell of dust greeted him when he entered with his prisoner. He slid his Remington into its holster as he closed the door behind him and bolted it. He shoved

Wink toward a cell, grabbing a key on an iron ring from the sheriff's desk. Before he pushed the foreman in, he took the time to frisk him, finding a knife in a boot scabbard. The iron door made a solid sound when it slammed, and the key slipped into the hole as if it knew the way. He tested the door: locked tight.

Ross put Wink's revolver on the sheriff's desk and sat down. Whirlwinds of dust swirled in the sunlight beaming through the tiny window. He glanced at the gun rack: empty. He raked a finger across the desk, leaving a trail. He felt something unusual on his right palm and found his initials raised in reverse from the flesh.

Boots scuffled outside. Parkhill's fist pounded on the door and a shadow filled the window.

"How long's Sheriff Jackson been gone?" Ross asked.

"Jackson?" Wink said from the cell. "He's been dead two months."

Ross shot a glance into the cell. "What happened to him?"

"Somebody killed him on the road to Last Chance Gulch."

The fist pounded on the door again, harder this time.

"Who's the law around here now?" Ross asked.

Wink stared at him through the iron grating. "You mean, it ain't you?"

Parkhill's voice bellowed from outside: "Open up, lawman, and let's talk this over!"

FIFTEEN

The whiskey hum had left his head, and a dull ache had taken its place. Ross was sitting in a lawman's chair, trying to figure out what to do next. His only consolation was the fact that Parkhill had finally quit pounding on the door and gone away.

He stared at the dust suspended in the sunlight until he heard another pair of boots on the boardwalk.

"Open up!" a slurred voice said.

"Who is it?"

"The Virginia City *Post*."

Ross lifted the bolt and cracked the door to find the swollen face of Ed Johnson. The editor held a pencil and a pad of paper in his hands.

"What do you want?" Ross asked.

"I want to know what happened."

Seeing as how he needed information worse than Johnson right now, he figured he might as well let the editor in. "This man shot the owner of the Break o' Day Saloon," he said, opening the door, "so I put him in jail. How's the wounded man?"

"Unconscious right now, but the doc stopped the bleeding and says he'll pull through all right."

"It was an accident," Wink said from his cell. "My gun went off."

"It'll do that when you pull the trigger," Ross replied.

"What's your name?" the editor asked.

"R.W. Colby," Ross replied.

"You the deputy marshal we've been waiting on?"

"No."

"What kind of lawman are you?"

"I'm not a lawman at all. At the moment."

Johnson cocked his head back to see through his left eye—the one that wasn't quite swollen shut. "But you've heard we've got no law here."

"I heard your sheriff got killed a couple of months back."

"So that's what you're after," Johnson mumbled. "You sure know how to start a campaign, but there's no need for one. Nobody will run against you. Nobody wants the job."

"What job?"

"Sheriff."

"I'm not so sure I want it." Ross rubbed his temples as the whiskey throb grew.

"It's a good job for a lawman. You get a cabin on the edge of town, good pay, and support from the county and the city."

"I'll think about it."

"If you want the job, I can print ballots tonight, announce a special election in tomorrow's issue, and have you in office in a couple of days."

"What am I supposed to do until then?"

"Guard your prisoner, I guess. I imagine the mayor will be by directly to appoint you town marshal until we can arrange the county election. That will give you jurisdiction in Virginia City for the time being. Where did you say you were from?"

"I've been on the drift."

Johnson shrugged. "Doesn't matter. Talk's all over town already. You sure know how to make an entrance."

"It just happened, that's all."

"What's the charge against Wink?"

Ross kept a straight face while his mind scrambled for some kind of legalism. "Attempted murder."

"I've got to get this story on the press," Johnson said, looking up at Ross as his hand continued to scribble notes. "I'll come back for a more detailed profile on you tomorrow. Anything I can do for you till then?"

Ross rubbed his stomach. "See that my horse gets to a livery, if you would. Bring me my bedroll and something to eat."

"You bet," Johnson said through his swollen lips, and he took his leave.

"I wasn't tryin' to shoot him, Colby," Wink said. "Honest."

"I wasn't tryin' to arrest anybody today, Wink. But these things happen."

Ross heard a fist beating on the jailhouse door and woke up staring at the bottom of the sheriff's desk. It would have been almost impossible to get a bullet under the desk from the little window, so he had slept there for the night. It seemed a little ridiculous now, and he decided he had been overly cautious.

"Who is it?" he said.

"Fritz."

Ross opened the door to find the trumpet-playing miner holding a tray of steaming food and drink.

"Thought you and Wink might want a little breakfast."

"Obliged," Ross said, inhaling the fragrances of coffee and biscuits. When he allowed Wink a share of the food, he noticed the prisoner's right eye twitching uncontrollably. "Got somethin' in your eye?"

"Nervous twitch. Runs in my family."

"I didn't see any twitchin' yesterday."

"I was drunk yesterday. It quits when I'm drunk."

"It don't quit," Fritz said. "It goes to your trigger finger."

Ross chuckled. He took his share of the breakfast and ate at the desk.

"You had me fooled yesterday," Fritz said. "I thought for all the world you were a prospector."

"What about you?" Ross said. "Not workin' your claim today?"

"Sold it."

"Worked out?"

"No, there's plenty of color left in it."

"Then why'd you sell?"

"I was thinkin' of runnin' for sheriff till you showed up. I'd settle for deputy."

Ross slurped coffee and wiped his mouth with a napkin. "What's your last name, Fritz?"

"Green."

"Where you from?"

"New York City. I was a police officer there for a year."

All night Ross had been feeling like a prisoner of his own impulses, locked up in a musty jail-house on account of a hasty decision. He had slept cowering under the desk, for heaven's sake, afraid to step outside even to relieve himself.

But this Fritz Green—this new friend of his—had brought the light of dawn back into his thinking. This was no way to live. He got up, flung the door aside, and stood in the open portal. Nobody shot him dead, so he turned back to Fritz.

"Deputy Green, guard the prisoner. I have business to attend to."

SIXTEEN

With a hard snap, Hector Beauchamp tested the horsehair rope he had just twisted. It was sound, as usual, from end to end—a stout measure of bristling line long enough for making a bosal or a set of reins. He was in no hurry to make anything of it right now, though. He had to kill his time wisely. Maybe he would take a nap first.

"When we were stealin' ideas from the Mexicans," he said aloud to himself, "who was the dumb-ass who left out the siesta?" He stretched the rope again. "We got horsehair ropes, but we forgot the siesta. And tortillas. Why the hell didn't we get tortillas?"

He coiled the rope and looked southward down the street. "Beats the hell out of me," he said, answering himself. Denver was hot today; most folks staying in the shade. Only a few people moving around out of necessity. There went Tim Elliot in his lumber wagon, dragging a cloud of dust down the dirt street.

"I'd hate that. Every day, drive the damn wagon up the

street, down the street." He looked north. "Load it, unload it." He waved at a friend turning into a log-walled saloon with a canvas roof. "Son of a bitch," he said. "Probably just sobered up."

Things were mighty dull today, but Heck wasn't complaining. He considered his job the best a lawman could have. A lot of benefits came with being a sheriff in a wide-open town like Denver. People tended to take care of you when they needed you as bad as Denver needed Heck Beauchamp.

He had two good permanent deputies and half a dozen reservists he could call on anytime trouble arose. He also carried a deputy U.S. Marshal badge, which gave him jurisdiction outside of his county. This allowed him to hire out as a detective to anyone who could afford his fee when he occasionally got bored with town life. Yes, this would be quite a setup if outlaws would quit shooting at him, and drunks would quit vomiting in his jail.

A woman came around a corner two blocks away. Carrying something. A baby? "Who the hell is that?" He watched her walk a block, her auburn hair bouncing on her shoulders. "She don't waste no time, do she? Got a stride, by golly."

When she angled across the street for his office, Heck Beauchamp rose from his chair, tucked his shirt in, stomped his pant legs down inside his boots, repositioned his hat, and twisted the handlebars of his mustache.

He could see her face now, and she was pretty. Her look of determination concerned him a little. Whose baby was that? She wasn't a sporting girl, was she? Didn't look like one, now, but he had seen some of them clean up almost proper. But, no, he would have remembered her, even painted up in some dim social parlor. He breathed a sigh of relief.

"Afternoon, ma'am," he said.

She walked up the steps, uncovering the baby's face under the shade of the gallery roof. "Are you Sheriff Beauchamp?"

He brushed his finger across her baby's cheek and made dovelike noises. "Hector Beauchamp, ma'am. My friends call me Heck."

"I'm Mrs. Rossiter Caldwell. I need help finding my husband. I was told to come to you."

Heck tickled the baby under the earlobe. "I'm not generally in the business of trackin' down runaway husbands, Mrs. Caldwell."

"He didn't run away. He's lost. The army says he's dead."

Heck pulled the horsehair rope across his palm. "And you don't believe the army?"

"They have shown me no proof."

He stood back to admire the mother and child. "How old is she? It is a she, ain't it?"

"Yes. Her name's Fay. She's two months old."

He made baby noises at the infant again, then turned adult to address the mother. "How long has Mr. Rossiter Caldwell been lost?"

"He doesn't know he's a father."

Heck put his hand on his chin and pretended to contemplate. He was not at all in the business of tracking down husbands, whether they were lost or dead or whatever. But he had gone a long time without having a conversation with a woman like Mrs. Rossiter Caldwell. "Come in and let's talk about it," he said. "Maybe I can help."

Heck came to one conclusion rather easily as Mrs. Caldwell told her story. The poor woman's husband was dead and she just didn't want to admit it. She wanted her baby to have a father. The whole thing was a little sad, but it had the ring of opportunity. Hector Beauchamp was thirty-one years old, and at the present time enjoyed no prospects for lifelong female companionship.

"You have to know how to put a ring in the army's nose," he said, twirling one end of the horsehair rope. "Shouldn't take much sniffin' around to find out what they know. It usually ain't much. If the army doesn't know anything, the Indians will."

"What Indians?" Julia said.

"The ones that massacred that column on the Crazy Woman."

"But you can't just go out there and talk to them."

"Why not? I get on famous with Indians. I know the hand signs."

"But they're hostile."

"Oh, they tend to get a little bloodthirsty when the army rouses 'em from their pallets with a bugle charge and tramples their papooses into the ground. But they'll calm down after they take a few scalps to even the score. I hear they've been quiet this summer on the reservation."

Julia stared at his face, glanced at the twirling rope end. "The same Indians who massacred Captain Jones's column are now on a reservation?"

Heck nodded. "Eatin' government rations. That's Indian policy, ma'am. Don't make much sense, do it?"

Julia pursed her lips and looked down at the baby in her arms. "We should discuss your fee," she said. "I might be a while in raising it."

Heck slapped his hands against his knees. "Mrs. Caldwell, you happen to be in luck. I have to go up through Fort Laramie and the Sioux country on another investigation. Seein' as how your case won't require much pokin' around, I'll just take it on as a favor to you and little Fay. Why, come to think of it, I wouldn't take a fee from such a good-lookin' pair if you were rich as you are pretty."

"I can raise the money in time," Julia said. "I don't expect any favors."

"We've already settled that. Now, where are you stayin'?"

"Mrs. Masterson has been kind enough to give me the use of a room until she gets a paying boarder. I've been helping her with the cooking and cleaning."

Heck shook his head. "I'm glad you came to me, Mrs. Caldwell, because one of my deputies, Elliot McDaniels, is married and lives in a house with an extra room."

"Oh, no, I couldn't," Julia said.

"They're expectin' a baby of their own in a couple of months and Elliot was telling me just the other day how he wished he had a woman around who could help his wife with her chores, and I said, 'Elliot, why don't you help her yourself?' And you know what he said? He said, 'Heck, you won't find no biscuit dough on my pistol grip.' But that's just the way Elliot is." He got up and urged Julia toward the door.

"This really isn't necessary," she said. "I didn't come here to beg charity."

"You'll be doin' 'em a favor. I'll borrow a buggy and we'll drive up there together. You'll like Elliot's wife. She's a Southern gal, too."

Julia felt the baby squirm in her arms. Well, if they were nice people, and if she could stay for a while, what was the harm? She had to have a place to live until she found Ross.

"At least meet 'em, for heaven's sake," Heck said.

She sighed. "Oh, all right. I suppose it wouldn't hurt to meet them."

SEVENTEEN

"Y   ou see him?" Ross shouted over the roar of the spray.

"He ain't here," Fritz answered. "I don't see him nowhere."

A rainbow hung over the Parkhill Hydraulic Works—the only pretty thing about the place. Ross had seen streams and gullies pretty well carved up by placer miners, but this hydraulicking ate at the world like a locust. There had been a hillside here last year, he recalled. A gentle slope covered with high grass and studded with young pines. Now there was a ragged bluff seventy feet high and a gaping void where tons of gravel had lain for eons.

Three men were operating artillerylike nozzles, spraying jets of water onto the exposed hillside. The lawmen had hoped Wink might be among them, but he was nowhere to be seen.

"Where are all the Chinamen, Fritz?"

"They work the sluices below and the reservoirs above."

"The hard work," Ross suggested.

"Yeah, and dangerous. Four of 'em's been killed."

Ross watched the jets undercut the raw bluff. "Avalanche?"

"Two were killed in an avalanche. One drowned when he was sucked into a pipe. The fourth was cut damn near half in two by that hydraulic spray."

Ross shot a glare at Fritz. "How the hell could that happen?"

"Talk was that Parkhill executed him with that nozzle for tryin' to lead a wage strike. I saw the body. It was a damn hell of a sight."

Ross's lip curled and he spotted Parkhill riding toward him across a ridge. "Here comes the big bastard now." As he watched, the mine owner twisted quickly in the saddle, spitting on his horse's rump. It drove Ross's thoughts back twelve months and more, and he suddenly felt himself riding Chug in Parkhill's repair detachment. He had to grin, feeling the advantage he had. Parkhill still hadn't recognized him, though he could tell the big man had been trying to place him.

"What brings you out here, Sheriff?" Parkhill asked, drawing rein in front of the mounted lawmen.

"Checkin' on Wink. Makin' sure he hasn't jumped bail." Ross caught himself putting gravel in his voice, subconsciously disguising it.

"Hell, if he jumped bail, I'd be after him before you. I was the one put the money up. Besides that, I can't do without him. He's my chief engineer. Wink's the one brought the pipes and nozzles and all the Chinamen from California."

"So where the hell is he?" Fritz said.

"He's got a work gang on a new flume around the bend. Come see for yourself if you want."

Ross nodded at his deputy and they nudged their horses up the gulch.

"Sheriff," Parkhill said as they rode, "I keep gettin' the feelin' I know you from somewhere. Have we met before?"

"I'm a stranger out here."

"Where do you come from?"

"Nowhere."

They rode in silence for a minute.

"Some operation you've got here," Ross said. "Where'd you get the capital for it?"

Parkhill turned to spit. "Where do you think? It's root, hog, or die out here, Colby. I staked a claim in Last Chance Gulch that paid six dollars to the pan, and diggin's was shallow. Then I made some improvements on the road between here and Last Chance, so the legislature awarded me a franchise for the toll road."

"What kind of improvements did you make?"

"Cut down trees, dug up rocks, blasted. I even put in some corduroy road where it washes out regular."

"Fritz tells me this road of yours is plagued by outlaws."

"Nothin' you can do about that," Parkhill said. "Them road agents are gonna steal from you out here. Course, they don't bother me, because I take precautions. I send a shotgun rider with every stage and freight outfit I put on the road. Out here you take care of those things yourself, Colby. No offense, but lawmen ain't much use in this country, except maybe for collectin' fines from whorehouses."

Ross smirked. "When did you start this hydraulickin'?"

"Just this spring. When Wink showed up with all the trappin's, I bought him out and hired him as engineer. He's a good man."

"His gun goes off easy," Fritz said.

"Nobody can help accidents," Parkhill replied. "Part of life."

As they rounded the bend, Ross spotted the work gang wielding picks, carving a notch in a hillside for a flume. The Chinamen wore their distinctive hats and ragged work clothes. A couple of them went barefoot. Wink was looking down on them from his horse, his leg hitched lazily over the saddle horn.

Ross reined in his mount. "What do you pay those poor devils?"

"They get a fair wage. They don't complain."

"Wouldn't be healthy for 'em if they did," Fritz added.

"Shit, if it wasn't for my payroll, they'd starve. Every damn one of 'em's just glad to have a job."

"I've seen enough," Ross said. "Let's go."

"Don't you want to say howdy to Wink?" Parkhill asked.

"Yes," Ross replied. "In court."

The lawmen spurred their horses to a trot and put the bend between themselves and Parkhill.

"Fritz, I want to have a look at those Chinamen's living quarters."

"All right, but I hope your horse is gentle."

"Why?"

"Because, if he ain't, the rats and mice are liable to spook him clean to Idaho."

Ross sat staring, his eyes squinted, nostrils pinched. Even from the edge of the shantytown he could see rodents crawling among the hovels in broad daylight.

"The hell of it is that they're spreadin' up into Virginia City," Fritz said. "We'll be overrun by the damn things by the time summer's over."

"Aren't there any cats in town?"

"There's three toms that I know of, and Lester Shinn has one old she-cat over at his livery barn."

"Why don't they breed a litter?"

"They tried," Fritz explained. "That ol' she-cat whipped every one of them toms. Mort Frawley trapped a bobcat and tried to breed that to her, but she whipped him, too. Course he was missin' one foot where the trap got him."

They rode in among the first of the shacks and Ross shook his head. The Chinamen had used old boards, logs, brush, pieces of wagon sheets. They had tried to establish winding streets, but rains had turned them into gullies on the hillside. A child sat in one of them, playing with rocks. The mother worked nearby, scrubbing clothes in tubs made of whiskey barrels sawed in half.

A sudden pang knifed at his heart as he remembered Julia laboring over the laundry barrels at Camp Marshall, and he knew he had to do something. "How come they don't fix these places up a little?" he asked.

"Parkhill works the men long hours at the hydraulic

works. They don't have no time for fixin' up their houses. Even if they had the time, they don't have the money to buy lumber. They gotta pay their rent first."

"Rent?" Ross scanned the hovels again. "Parkhill?"

"Takes it out of their wages before they ever see it. Nobody wants 'em here, anyway, R.W. They work too damn cheap. Any more of 'em, and they'd put all the American miners out of a job. But, damn, nobody ought to have to live like this."

Ross reined his horse back toward town. "I've seen enough. Let's go."

They were three blocks from the jail when Ed Johnson burst out of the barbershop with the towel still around his face. "Sheriff! You better get down to the Break o' Day!"

"What for?" Ross said.

"Bob Hodges is leaving town!"

Ross and his deputy loped to the saloon, only to find it deserted. Across the open door, just under the etched-glass window, they found three numbers scrawled in red paint:

3-7-77

"Bob!" Ross shouted, entering the barroom. He found Hodges coming down the stairs from his room above the saloon, carrying a bag stuffed to bulging. "Where do you think you're going?"

"Salt Lake City."

"The grand jury expects you to testify next week."

"No, it don't. I dropped the charges against Wink. Decided it was just an accident."

"What the hell did you do that for?"

"You seen the numbers!" Hodges shouted, jutting a finger toward the front door. "I'm a dead man if I stay in this town."

Ross's eyes followed the saloon owner behind the bar. "I'll put you under guard at the jail where nobody can get you," he offered.

"So you can be a dead man, too? Forget it, Sheriff. We're whipped. It was an accident."

"But what about your saloon?" Fritz asked.

Hodges was lining the bar with pouches of gold dust, tying them together. "I sold it."

"Let me guess," Fritz said. "Parkhill."

Hodges nodded.

"How much did he give you for the place?"

"None of your damn business." The saloon man stuffed the gold dust in his traveling bag and turned toward the door.

"Think about what you're doin'!" Ross pleaded.

Hodges stopped on the threshold and slung his bag on his back. "The only thing I have to think about is catchin' that stage to Salt Lake. You don't know these vigilantes, Colby. If you're smart, you'll let the matter rest and go back to collectin' fines from whorehouses and hurdy-gurdies." He glanced at the numbers painted on the door of his former saloon. "Virginia City ain't ready for no law yet."

Hodges left, his heavy boots clogging against the board-walk.

"Well," Fritz said, slapping his hat against the bar. "We might as well have us a drink on Parkhill." He reached for a whiskey jug.

Ross felt the anger boil up in him until he could no longer hold it back. He lashed out, kicking a table, flipping it onto its side.

"Hey," Fritz said, "take it easy, R.W."

But Ross didn't hear; didn't even feel the deputy's presence anymore. Parkhill's secret societies and contempt for everything just had taken him again from a blind side and swept him up in a whirlwind of anger. Was Parkhill following him in life, or what? Maybe that was it. Maybe God was throwing obstacles in his way to test him. Do something about Parkhill, and you can have Julia back.

"R.W. R.W.!"

Ross blinked and found Lester Shinn standing next to Fritz. "Huh?" he said. "What is it, Lester?" He hadn't even seen the livery man enter.

Lester fumbled with the hat in his hands and looked at the floor. "Well, you know this mornin', when I loaned you that bay mare, so your old white horse could rest?"

"Yeah." He was hardly listening to Lester. Something else was trying to speak to him.

"Well, I didn't tell you at the time, because I thought maybe he'd get over it."

"Over what?" How do you hurt a man like Parkhill? he was thinking.

Lester glanced sheepishly at Fritz. "Well, I must have left his stall unlatched last night, and Ol' Whitey got into a pile of green alfalfa hay I had stacked in the barn. Colicked hisself. I didn't want to tell you this mornin', so I loaned you the bay. Thought maybe I could walk it out of Whitey, but he sat down and wouldn't get back up."

"What are you sayin', Lester?" Ross asked.

Lester forced himself to look the sheriff in the eye. "He's deader than hell, Sheriff. I'm sorry. I'll give you any mount in my stable in trade."

Ross sighed and looked at his bearded, weathered face in the mirror behind the bar. "Ol' Whitey's dead, huh?" He could feel himself on the verge of a wild idea. "Guess I better drag him out of town and burn him."

"I'll take care of it," Lester said. "It was my fault."

Ross put his hand on Lester's shoulder. "He was my horse, Lester. You understand. I'd better do it myself."

EIGHTEEN

Ross pulled his pocket watch out to check the time. Four-thirty in the afternoon, and still no sign of the Parkhill stagecoach. It should have passed here by this time. This waiting was torture.

A woodpecker drummed suddenly against a hollow tree behind him, making him flinch. He liked this high country: the cool pine-scented air, the long views. These Tobacco Root ranges along Parkhill's toll road to Last Chance reminded him of the Bighorn Mountains Jasper Jones had ordered him to cross. Hard to enjoy them today, though. Other things on his mind.

He wasn't sure he was going to go through with it now. He could always go back to town and let the Parkhill men drive by unmolested as if he had never come up with the idea in the first place.

The white horsehair beard he wore was starting to make him sweat and itch, but he didn't dare scratch at it for fear he would pull it out of place and show his real whiskers. The disguise was the most important part of the scheme. If it failed, he was ruined.

Maybe the gold shipment from Parkhill's diggings at Last Chance Gulch wasn't coming today, after all. That would be both a relief and a disappointment. Maybe he hadn't thought about this thing long enough. It might be well to go home and sleep on it a few more nights.

He sighed and tucked his watch back into his pocket. It's just as well, he thought. You never could have gone through with it, anyway. You're good on a whim, boy, but premeditation never was your strong point.

Just as he was getting up to leave, he heard the crack of a whip and the crunch of wagon wheels on rocks below. His heart jumped like a startled animal trying to burst from his chest. Looking down the grade, he saw the coach coming up the road, a passenger's elbow jutting from one of the windows.

The vehicle slowed as it mounted the steep grade. The driver cracked his whip over the six mules, turned to his partner to continue some story he was in the middle of. The shotgun rider bounced on the seat, listening, grinning, his weapon across his lap.

Let them go by, Ross thought. You can't do this. It was a ridiculous idea in the first place.

But when the stage neared the top of the grade, he felt his body surge ahead through the trees. He put the stoop in his shoulders, the gravel in his throat, and—in a moment of invention—a limp in one leg. He stepped into the road just as the lead mule prepared to drop down the next slope, and the big animal balked when it saw him there. The coach stopped, rolled back a foot as the mules tossed their heads.

"Git your lazy asses up!" the driver roared, drawing his whip back. Then he saw the old man in the road pointing the double barrel at him, and the strength left his arm. The burly old highwayman's tattered hat covered the top of his face, and the long white beard hid the front of his dirty vest.

"Set the brake!" Ross ordered, scarcely recognizing his own voice. "Don't lift that scattergun, boy!" He saw a head jut momentarily from a window.

The shotgun rider put his hands in the air, leaving his weapon on his lap.

"What do you want, old man?" the driver said. "Git the hell out of the road!"

"Shut your mouth, you scrawny little pup. You boys work for Parkhill?"

"Yeah."

"Good. Throw down the strongbox."

The stagecoach men looked at each other.

"Now!"

The driver glanced down the twin barrels of the old bandit's shotgun, then reached for the box behind him. He had to put one knee on the seat to heft it. He slid it over the edge of the coach roof and let it drop to the ground.

"Now, git!" Ross ordered. "Anybody looks back'll see buckshot comin'."

The whip cracked and the coach dropped quickly down the grade, leaving Ross alone with the silence of the high country, and the strongbox, a small wooden trunk braced with iron straps. He felt suddenly sick, but stuck to his plan, dragging the box into the trees. He put a steel bar in the padlock and twisted, popping the latch off the box. He threw back the lid and found rows of white sacks. Lifting one, he knew it contained gold dust.

Dizzily, Ross began stuffing the bags of dust into his saddlebags, but there was too much to carry. He couldn't seem to catch his breath. He left half the gold in the broken box and ran back to the road.

Looking to make sure no one was coming, he crossed to the other side and ducked into the timber. He ran a hundred yards with his shotgun in one hand and the saddlebag slung over his shoulder until he reached the buckskin horse Lester Shinn had traded him for Ol' Whitey. He flung the heavy bags on behind the cantle and tied them down. He stripped his costume off, revealing his own clothes underneath. He dropped the fake beard, the garments, and the sawed-off shotgun onto the waiting blanket and made a bedroll of them.

After securing his things, he mounted and took a high trail across the mountainside. The way he had it figured, the coach was just now arriving at the dead tree he had pulled across the road. The coachmen would have to unhitch a mule to clear it out of the way. He could push his horse hard and arrive at his cabin fifteen minutes before the coach got to town.

"God, you've done it now," he said to himself as he whipped his horse with the ends of his reins. But he felt a grin crawling under his whiskers as he imagined the look on Parkhill's face.

He stopped to look across the gulch before he approached his cabin. It was almost dark now, and his place stood at the far corner of town, so he would probably not be seen. Even if someone heard him riding, they would think nothing of it. Darkness tended to bring a lot of activity to Virginia City.

He trotted his tired horse across the gulch and up to his shed. The bay horse he had borrowed from Lester this morning waited inside. He stripped his saddle from the buckskin, then hustled to his house carrying his saddlebags and bedroll, leading the fresh bay. He tied the bay to his rickety picket fence and hurried into the cabin.

Locking the door behind him, he pushed a heavy table aside and pulled up a floorboard he had loosened. He dropped the bedroll and the stolen gold into the hole and covered it again, positioning a table leg over the loose plank.

Walk, he told himself. Act natural. He stepped casually outside, trying to whistle through his dry lips. He led the borrowed bay horse down Cover Street, tipping his hat to the occasional greeting along the way.

"Lester," he called, sticking his head into the barn. "I brought your horse back."

"Howdy, Sheriff," Lester said, coming out of the feed room. "You do any good prospectin'?"

Ross smirked. "I found a little color."

"Where'bouts?"

"I ain't tellin' you, Lester. You'll stake it before I can pan it out."

"You didn't go far, judgin' by this horse."

"Oh, it's handy," Ross said.

"How's that lame hoof on that buckskin?"

"It wasn't as bad as I thought. He'll be all right in a day or two." He listened for the whip of the Parkhill stage driver. "Anything happen while I was gone?"

"Couple of fights is all. Fritz broke 'em up. Nobody hurt bad."

The sheriff nodded approvingly. "Well, thanks for the loan of the horse, Lester."

"Anytime."

He went to the jail to find Fritz turning the key in the front door.

"Evenin', R.W. Didn't expect to see you till tomorrow."

"I had forgotten how dull prospectin' could get. Any trouble while I was gone?"

"Not a lick. I was just fixin' to make a round and go home."

"I'll walk with you."

They strolled down the street, checking locked doors, eyeballing thirsty miners on their way to favorite saloons. As they passed in front of the bakery, the Parkhill stagecoach suddenly thundered around the curve onto Wallace Street, Parkhill himself holding the reins.

"Colby!" Parkhill bellowed, stopping the team. "Saddle up! My stage got robbed!"

Ross looked at his deputy, then back at Parkhill. "Robbed? Where?"

Shaken passengers began pouring out of the coach.

"Comin' up Bear Pass," the driver said. "An old man held us up and got the strongbox full of dust."

Ross crossed his arms over his chest and cocked his head. "I thought you took precautions against road agents, Parkhill. Why didn't you take care of it yourself?"

"Because I wasn't there!" Parkhill roared. "These chickenshits just picked me up at my wagon yard on the way into town!" He elbowed the two stage men flanking him. "Now, you saddle up and go out there and catch the bastard! What kind of a lawman are you?"

Ross pulled a cigar out of his pocket and rolled it between his fingers. "Didn't you tell me just a few days ago that lawmen weren't much use in this country? Except for collectin' whorehouse fines?" He bit the end from the smoke, spit it toward Parkhill.

"I've *found* a use for you!" Parkhill shouted. "Go out there and find that road agent!"

Ross took a match from his pocket, struck it on the brick wall of the bakery, touched its flame to the end of his cigar. "Bear Pass, huh? That's across the county line, ain't it, Fritz? That's out of our jurisdiction."

"Since when do we have a county line?" Parkhill snapped.

Ross laughed smoke into the breeze. "Settle down, Parkhill. I'm just needlin' you a little for gettin' yourself robbed. I'll go have a look in the mornin'."

"You'll go right now!"

"What good would it do? Maybe spook that bandit into the high country is all. I'll have a look in the morning when I can see something, but I doubt it'll do any good. Like you told me the other day, Parkhill, outlaws are gonna steal from you out here. That's just all there is to it."

Parkhill spit a stream of tobacco juice in front of his shotgun rider. "You're worthless, Colby. How the hell did you ever get elected sheriff?"

Ross shrugged, fighting to keep the laughter down inside him. This was better than he had ever imagined. "I guess I was just in the right place at the right time. Sort of like that fellow who robbed your stage."

Parkhill hissed and shook his reins, driving the coach down the street.

"Damn," Ross said, turning to Fritz. "You'd have thought I robbed the damned stage myself."

NINETEEN

"You know he's dead," Heck said to himself as he trotted his horse past the rows of troop tents outside of Fort Laramie. "Would you let a wife like that run loose if you wasn't dead?" He bounced along in silence until he was almost to the sutler's store. "If he ain't dead, he's about the sorriest outfit I ever heard tell of."

"Hold it, mister," a soldier on sentry duty ordered. "What do you want?"

"Government business. I'm Deputy U.S. Marshal Hector Beauchamp here to see Colonel Kulp." He peeled back his vest to reveal his badge.

"Come with me," the soldier ordered.

Heck followed the private around the sutler's store and along the borders of the parade ground. They stopped in front of "Old Bedlam," the building that housed the bachelor officers and served as post headquarters. The private ordered him to wait outside as he stepped into the commander's office. He got down and gave his mount some breathing room in the cinch. He tipped his hat back, enjoying the breeze that cooled the sweat on his forehead.

Three lieutenants rode up to Old Bedlam and jumped down from their mounts, leaving their horses at the rail. After they went inside, Heck walked to the horse nearest to him, patting it on the rump to let it know he was there. He grasped the top of the horse's tail with both hands and, in one smooth stroke, ran a tight grip all the way down the tail, harvesting a single horsehair. He went to the second mount and got another hair. As he was pulling his hands down the third horse's tail, the sentry came out of the headquarters building.

"What the hell are you doin'?" the private said.

Heck wrapped the tail hairs around his fingers, making a small coil. "Buildin' a horsehair bridle for a lady friend of mine." He tucked the coil into his vest pocket. "You ain't gonna tell the President I took these, are you?"

The private smirked. "The colonel's clerk wants to see you."

Heck walked in, holding his hat. "Howdy," he said.

The clerk glanced up and down at him. "Howdy yourself. What's this official business you have with the colonel?"

Heck pulled up a chair and fanned himself with his hat. "Well, to tell you the truth, it ain't all that official or anything. You can probably take care of it yourself without even botherin' the old man."

"That's usually the way. Now, what brings you here?"

"I was first cousins with Captain Jasper Jones, the fellow who got hisself scalped last summer."

"I know who he was."

"Figured you did. Well, his mother—my aunt—wired me from Boston and said she never did get Jasper's personal things from the army. Asked me if I'd find 'em and send 'em to her."

"That's all?"

Heck shrugged. "That's about it."

The clerk leaned his chair back on its hind legs. "Captain Jones's things were held here until after the investigation. I think they're still in the warehouse."

"Can I look?"

"No, but I can."

"Can I go with you?"

He rocked forward in his chair as he got up. "I guess so. Let's see if the stuff is still there."

They left Old Bedlam, walked across the parade grounds, passed the infantry barracks, and proceeded to the warehouse. After inquiring with a few soldiers, the clerk located Captain Jones's personal effects stacked in a dusty corner.

"I'll see that it gets sent out today," the clerk promised. "My apologies to the family for the delay. You know the army."

Heck's eye caught a splinter jutting from a small portable writing desk. "This looks like a bullet hole," he said.

"That was found in Captain Jones's tent on the battleground."

Heck sighed and shook his head. "Poor old Jasper. Do you mind?" he asked, removing a stack of folded uniforms from the desk so he could open its top. He scanned a few leaves of paper in the desk, then his hand touched a leather-bound book with a buckle on it. "What's this?" He opened it and found a dated notation on the first page. "Why, it's Jasper's diary."

"Is it?" the clerk said.

"Corporal, do you mind if I express this one item to Boston and let Jasper's mother know the rest of his things will be comin' soon?"

"I guess that would be all right."

He clasped the corporal's shoulder in his hand. "The family'll be grateful to you, Corporal."

Heck sat down in the shade of the sutler's store and began with the last entry in the diary, something about drilling the men today and feeling good about the restored discipline. After turning just two pages back, the name of a Private Caldwell leaped up at him from the diary.

He read aloud to himself: "Private Caldwell left at dusk, assigned to special duty for duration of his enlistment." He looked up at his horse. "What the hell kind of order is that?" He looked down at the diary, then back up at his horse. "Damn, that sorry outfit didn't git massacred, after all. He might still be alive somewhere."

He tore the page from the diary and stuffed it into his pocket. "If he's alive, he ain't worth spit," he said as he got up. "If she was my wife, I'd find my way back to her, by God."

TWENTY

The band was playing a waltz when Ross entered. He stood for a moment to let his eyes adjust from the glare of the afternoon to the dim smokiness of the hurdy-gurdy house. The dance floor came into focus first: only three couples waltzing, but it was early.

He focused on the orchestra next: five men sitting in a corner, each with an instrument or two and a glass of something within reach. A rail separated the band from the dance floor, and it led Ross's eyes all the way around the room. Near the bar he saw two miners standing inside the rail, ogling something against the wall. He sauntered that way and finally made out a row of women sitting against the wall on a bench. They paid little attention to the two miners judging them from across the rail.

"You. Hey, you, darlin'!" one of the miners said. "You and your friend care to dance?"

Two girls got up to speak to the men. They wore fine gowns from back East and really looked quite proper in the gloomy light. After a moment of conversation, they directed the miners to the scales where the bartender measured out a dollar per man in dust, then they stood waiting for the next song to begin.

"How about you, Sheriff?" a giggling voice said.

Ross found a young blonde emerging from the dark. "Pardon?" he said.

"I'll dance with you. Dances are on the house for you."

She wasn't more than seventeen, he thought. "No, thank you, miss. I'm here to see the proprietress."

"Oh," the girl said, her enthusiasm wilting. "I'll tell her."

The waltz ended and one of the hurdies had to fight off her dance partner, who insisted on kissing her.

"Let her alone," Ross warned, his voice rasping across the dance floor. "Kissin' ain't part of the deal."

The miner left grousing, and the band struck up another number.

"She'll see you now," the young blonde said, appearing at Ross's shoulder. "This way."

He followed her to a dark corner, the wooden floor creaking under his feet. She opened a door, blinding Ross with daylight that streamed in through lace curtains, falling like spray on the form of a woman sitting at a small desk. She seemed to glow, as if the light were hers and not the sun's. He squinted, shaded his eyes, glanced through another door to see a canopy bed draped with lace, silk ropes, and tassels. The blonde girl closed the door behind him, shutting the music out.

"Sheriff Colby," the woman said, getting up from her desk to approach him. "I finally meet you."

For a moment he thought she was smiling, but it was just that the corners of her mouth turned upward in a misleading way, like dangerous barbs to her full painted lips. Her eyes sparkled through fronds of darkened lashes. Curls of reddish-black hair strayed onto her round cheeks, her shoulders, her bare throat. The eyes were . . . What color *were* they?

"Can I get you something to drink?" she asked, placing her right hand in his.

"No, thanks."

She gestured toward a chair and Ross nodded. He sat down, put his leather case on his lap, and removed a ledger book. "I don't believe I know your name," he said. Looking up, he noticed a small safe on the floor beside her writing desk.

She turned to a small mirrored bar and watched him in the glass as she pulled the top on a decanter of amber drink. "Sage."

Ross smirked. "Sage what?" He was expecting something like "Lovejoy" or "Darling." Already today he had collected fines from hurdies and sporting women with names such as Ranche Belle, Scarlet Valentine, Goldie Rush.

"Just Sage," she said, filling a second glass with liquor. She turned back to Ross, offering the drink to him.

"This is a business call," he insisted.

"A short whiskey's good for business." She swirled the drink seductively in front of his eyes.

Ross looked past the liquor to find her looming over him, standing uncomfortably close. She was smaller than average, but her presence overwhelmed him. The enticing curve and swirl of the whiskey in the glass seemed to flow from her, through her fingertips.

He took the drink, his eyes following the contours of her dress to her lips. Was she smiling, or was that just the way her mouth turned? Her face seemed to say that she just really did not give a damn about anything.

"Thanks," he said, and she turned away, giving him room to breathe. "Now, what's the name of your establishment?"

"It doesn't have one." She sat upright at her desk chair, crossed her legs, and clasped both hands over a knee.

"All I have here is a description of your place," he said. "I have to put in a name for the business."

"Then make one up."

He sipped the whiskey. It was good smooth stock: not some cheap valley tan or flash of lightning. He put it on a glass-topped lamp table at his elbow and opened his ledger book. "I'll just call it Sage's Place."

She locked her elbows and inhaled a sigh that pushed swells of white flesh up from her neckline. "That's really not very imaginative. Why not call it the Golden Sage?"

She turned her head to look across the room at nothing and he noticed a small black beauty mark under the curve of her jaw. "All right," he said. "The Golden Sage." He wrote it down, then paused for another sip of whiskey. "Now, Miss Sage, I suppose you've heard that the city has an ordinance against dance-for-pay places, or hurdy-gurdies, or whatever you want to call 'em."

"Are you going to shut me down?"

"No, but the town is charging you the annual four-hundred-dollar fine for operating."

"That's ridiculous. If you're not going to shut me down, then it's not a fine. It's a license to operate."

He looked for indignation in her eyes, but found only that hollow indifference. When he concentrated on the corners of her mouth, he could almost convince himself that she was enjoying his company. "Call it what you like, but if you don't pay it, I *will* shut you down. That's the way the ordinance works."

"It's ridiculous, and you know it. I can see it in your

face. You detest it, don't you? It's not as if I were operating a brothel or something."

"Are you going to pay it or not?"

She rose and smoothed the fabric hugging her waist. "Of course I'm going to pay it."

He picked up the whiskey and watched her kneel in front of the little iron safe. As he watched her work the combination, he inhaled the aroma of whiskey and enjoyed a sip. He put the glass on the table again and looked up to find Sage standing there—just standing—as if waiting for him to watch her. She approached and handed him a pouch of gold dust.

"I already weighed it," she said. "I've been expecting you."

Ross put the dust in his leather bag and made the entry in his ledger book.

"I'll have a receipt," she said, taking her seat at the desk. "And since I'm purchasing this license to operate, I feel entitled to say that a portion of that revenue should be used for relief instead of all of it going into the pockets of the town bureaucrats."

"Relief?" Ross said.

"Men sleeping on saloon floors because they have no homes, mothers and children begging for food, and those Chinese people living in those shacks outside of town. It's all a disgrace. The city should establish a relief fund."

Ross closed his book, tucked it slowly into his leather bag. He could feel his eyebrows hunching up on his forehead. She was right. He had thought of it often. There was enough gold dust blowing down these streets to feed every empty stomach in town. He had enough under the floorboards of his cabin to put roofs over every miserable soul. The question, up to this moment, had been how to distribute it.

"What?" she said, reading the look on his face.

He took up the whiskey glass. "I have a better idea. Establish your own relief fund. If the city did it, the bureaucrats would just bleed it to death, anyway. A private charity would be much more effective."

Her eyes angled away. "Where would I get the money?"

"I'll collect it. You distribute it."

Until now, she had prophesied his every move and word. He was just a man, after all. A lawman at that—one of the easiest breeds for a woman in her profession to predict. But this suggestion was extraordinary, and she caught herself feeling suddenly unaware of what message her features were sending back to him.

"How about it?" he said. "Do you want to help those unfortunate wretches out there or not?"

"You can use my safe." She turned in her chair and kicked the door of the iron box shut. "I'll contribute the first hundred dollars myself." She shrugged. "Maybe the publicity will be good for business."

He poured the last swallow of whiskey down his throat, buckled his leather bag, and got up. The thought of Parkhill's money buying food and shelter for his Chinese laborers tickled him so much that a grin formed on his face. He took a step toward Sage and held his open hand out to her. "Congratulations, partner. You and I just became philanthropists."

She looked at his palm for a second, then put her left hand against it and used it to steady herself as she rose.

Strange handshake, Ross thought. Why does she stand so close? How old is she? Twenty-five? Thirty-five? She seems childlike and innocent in a way. Is that smile genuine? He caught himself staring at her lips, felt Julia over his shoulder.

The band stopped playing and a girl screamed outside. Ross yanked his hand from Sage's and rushed to the dance floor to find a group of miners laughing, one of them holding a girl on his back.

"Here, now, put her down!" he ordered.

"Hell, Sheriff, I would if I could shake her off. She jumped on me."

"What for?"

"A big ol' rat ran across the dance floor!"

Sage came to Ross's side. "The vermin situation in this town is deplorable. The City Council should do something."

TWENTY-ONE

Sage juggled the figures a dozen ways, and still came up short. That orphan Turner boy had to be sent back to Iowa before winter came on. Men were still sleeping on the bare floor in the relief barracks. The hospital needed a new shipment of medicine and supplies. And those Chinese families in Parkhill's tenement town still didn't have enough food to go around.

Sheriff Colby had raised more than she expected, but it was already gone. Now she would have to test his commitment. She wasn't at all certain she had him figured out yet.

Deputy Green had delivered all the contributions. Sage hadn't seen the sheriff since the day he sold her the license to operate her place. She had expected to work directly with him in this relief fund, but he was obviously avoiding her. She knew she had gotten to him that afternoon in her office, so why hadn't he come back around? Shy? She didn't think so. Probably had something to do with another woman. Women were always ruining men before she could get her hands on them.

She smiled and stuck her pen in the stand. She should meet with the sheriff personally on this budgetary matter, she thought, and there was no better time than now. Evening was coming on and he would soon be stopping at his favorite saloon for a whiskey on his way home. Maybe he would like to sample some more of the Golden Sage's reserve stock.

She got a shawl from her bedroom, paused to apply a drop of perfume to her throat, and set out for Wallace Street. As she passed the *Post,* she heard a knuckle wrapping on the inside of the glass. Glancing, she saw Johnson trying to wave her into the office. She ignored him, and kept walking, but heard him storm through the door behind her.

"Miss Sage, I need some clarification," the editor said. "Is that Turner boy going to make it back to Iowa or not?"

"He will be among his relatives before the first snow."

"Do you have enough in the relief fund for the Turner boy *and* the cots in the relief barracks? The public has a right to know where their contributions are going."

"We'll manage to meet all the needs of this community somehow, and the public can come look at the books if they wish."

"Just wondering," Johnson said, pacing with her down the boardwalk. "What kind of salary do you take for managing the funds?"

"The kind that brings business into my dance hall."

"So you admit that your philanthropy is motivated by personal gain."

Sage stopped and turned on the editor. "How much have you contributed to our fund?" she asked.

He straightened and tugged his vest down over his stomach. "What I contribute is more valuable than gold dust."

"And what might that be?"

"Publicity. To your cause I contribute my lexicon."

She smirked. "Not everyone in town has learned to eat words as well as you." She turned her back on him, stepping down to the street.

She crossed to the other side so she wouldn't have to walk in front of Parkhill's Break o' Day Saloon. But even across the street, one of the drunks spotted her through the open door.

"Miss Sage!"

She didn't have to look to know it was the voice of Parkhill himself.

"I've got some boys in here need some charity."

She set her jaw to the burst of laughter and continued to the jailhouse.

"Evenin', Miss Sage," Fritz said, springing from his chair. "What brings you here? Trouble at your place?"

"No," she said, not bothering to look at him. "Where is Sheriff Colby?"

Fritz was trying to shape his hair to its best advantage. "He went fishin' this mornin'."

"When will he be back?"

"Well," Fritz said, coming around the desk to approach her, "if he catches a mess of trout, he might come on back tonight. Otherwise, he'll probably stay out another day. Can I help you with anything?"

"No. I need to meet with him regarding the relief fund."

"Well, I've been helping him with the collections," Fritz said. "If it's anything I can help you with . . ."

Sage was already halfway through the door. "No, thank you." She shut Fritz inside and stood for a moment. She could go back to the Golden Sage and try again tomorrow. Or she could check the sheriff's cabin on the edge of town. Maybe he was back from fishing. Maybe he would feel more comfortable on his own ground.

She turned for the cabin, snugging the shawl around her neck against the evening chill. The light faded as she made her way through town, ignoring the dozens of miners who tipped their tattered hats on their way to the saloons. It was almost dark when she saw the cabin. The tiny window revealed no light from inside. Still, she had come this far. Why not wait a few minutes?

As she walked through the fading dusk toward the cabin, she heard hooves clacking against rocks in the gulch. She stopped and listened. A rider was approaching the cabin; she heard the squeak of saddle leather. She stepped behind the woodpile to watch. In the low light she could just barely make out the form of the rider entering the shed.

She smiled and loosened the shawl to reveal her throat. Sheriff Colby was in for a surprise. Tiptoeing, she made her way to the cabin porch. She sat on the steps and waited. Within a minute she heard the sheriff's boots scuffing the ground as he approached. She sat perfectly still as he came quickly around the corner, carrying a bedroll under one arm, his saddlebags slung over his shoulder.

Ross's foot was almost on the step before he noticed her. He jumped back and reached for his Remington, but recognized her shape, even in the twilight, and took his hand from the pistol butt.

"I didn't mean to startle you," she said.

"Miss Sage." He panted, his heart pounding against his ribs. "What are you doin' here?"

She stood, making his path up the steps a narrow one. "I came to discuss the relief fund."

He adjusted the saddlebags on his shoulder, forced the rising wave of panic back down his throat. "I was thinking about that when I was out fishin' today," he said. "I'm gonna start a new campaign for contributions. Can you come to my office tomorrow and talk about it?"

"That will be difficult," she said. "I'm busy tomorrow. Why not right now?"

He shuffled for a second or two. "Let me put my things away and we'll walk to my office."

"No need to go all the way down there. We can talk here."

He stood in silence. "Wait here, if you don't mind." He brushed past her and disappeared in the darkness of the cabin.

Sage waited, listening. She heard the heavy saddlebag hit the floor, recognized the rattle of the coal-oil lantern. The light wavered through the window and the sheriff opened the door.

"It's a nice evening," he said, closing the door behind

him. "Let's talk out here." He hung the lantern on a stob and gestured to the bench against the log wall. "Now, what did you have in mind for the fund?"

She fought off a shiver as she sat down, but she wouldn't think of covering her bare skin with the shawl now that the light was on her. "The problem is the irregularity of the contributions. I realize that you and your deputy have just so much time to collect for charity."

"We'll redouble our efforts," Ross said, glancing toward town as he sat a safe distance from her on the bench.

"I believe I've thought of an alternative. A system to keep the contributions coming in regularly."

Ross looked at her face for the first time, the lantern light sparkling in her eyes and glowing along the curve of her fair cheek. "What do you mean?" He saw that hint of a smile still lingering at the corner of her mouth.

"We've had a problem with certain businesses in this town short-weighting their customers," she explained. "They use loaded counterweights on their scales and over-charge for every purchase. The amount is usually so small that no one notices, but it adds up."

"I'm familiar with the trick," Ross said. "What does it have to do with our relief fund?"

"What if we *encouraged* businesses to short-weight their scales—openly and deliberately? But instead of pouring the extra gold into their pockets, they would contribute it to our fund. We could get the newspaper to list the participating businesses, so it would be free advertising for them."

The idea made him smile, in spite of the whirlwind of nerves spinning in his stomach. He leaned toward her, resting his elbows on his knees. "Short-weighting for charity."

"In my business, for example, every time a gentleman purchased a dance with one of my girls, he would contribute a few pennies to help his fellows, and he would scarcely notice the loss."

"I like it," Ross said. "Are you willing to give it a trial run at the Golden Sage?" He saw her eyes narrow at something on his shoulder.

"Yes," she said. "I think it will be good for business." She scooted toward him on the bench and reached for his lapel.

Ross straightened, craned his neck nervously as her fingers closed on nothing and withdrew. Then he saw it: a long hair shining yellow in the lantern light, blowing on the chilly breeze.

"What's this?" she said, a tease in her voice.

"Must be a horsehair," he said, brushing his shoulders for anything else she might find. A knot tightened in his stomach.

"Your horse is a buckskin." Her smile became genuine now, a taunting flare of red lips. "This looks rather blond."

"Yes, but . . ." He looked toward town. "My horse was lame a while back and I borrowed a paint from Lester. I must have been wearing this coat."

She let the hair slip from her fingers and blow away on the breeze. "You should be careful of what you pick up while you're out . . . fishing. I don't suppose you caught anything. I would hope not, anyway."

Ross squinted and scooted an inch away from her. "I'm not sure what you're . . ."

A rumble of hooves interrupted him, erupting like an avalanche as the riders rounded the corner of a warehouse down the street. Four men galloped to the cabin, drawing rein in the light of the lantern hung on the porch.

"Colby!" Parkhill shouted. "The damn stage got robbed again!"

"What!" Ross said. "Where? Same place?"

"No," the stage driver said. "It was at the top of the corduroy road this side of Rebel Creek. The same old bastard with the long white beard!"

Sage looked away from the men and found the pale hair snagged on a log end at the corner of the cabin, waving lazily on the breeze. She saw through the yellow coal-oil light now and found the whiteness in the sheen. It streamed like a banner in the sunlight for a sharp eye.

"I want something done this time, Colby," Parkhill was saying.

When she looked back, Sage caught Parkhill following her eyes into the night, trying to find what she had been looking at beyond the end of the porch. She drew his attention with a subtle flourish of her skirt, and stepped to the edge of the porch to sit on the rail, moving between the lantern and the corner of the cabin, casting her shadow on the long white hair.

TWENTY-TWO

Just like last time," Ross said, staring down at the open strongbox. "Looks like he left more than he took."

"He got thousands," Parkhill growled. "Anyway, I don't care if he just took a handful, it's stealin'."

"Wonder who he is," the sheriff muttered. "If he was a pro, he'd take it all. The old codger must have it in for you, Parkhill. You must have jumped his claim or somethin', and now he's gettin' even."

"Wonder why he pulls that tree onto the road?" Wink said.

"Probably wants to slow the coach down," Ross said, "make sure it's dark before the law gets the word. He's picked the dark of the moon for both robberies. Doesn't want a posse chasin' him in the night. I wouldn't send any more gold shipments on the dark of the moon if I was you, Parkhill."

Parkhill spit over his shoulder, splattering a brown stream against his horse's rump. "It ain't your job to tell me how to run my business, Colby. Just find the old fart."

"It's not gonna be easy," Ross said. "If it's like last time, he'll pick a hard mountain trail and lose us in the rocks. He knows these mountains."

"He's gonna make a mistake sooner or later," Parkhill said. "And when he does, I don't care how old he is, I'm gonna stretch his goddamn old neck."

"You do, and I'll have you in jail on murder charges," Ross snapped. "Everybody gets a fair trial in this county."

Parkhill glared at the sheriff until he heard hoofbeats coming.

"We found where he mounted!" Fritz hollered. "This way, R.W."

Ross spurred his horse in front of Parkhill's and followed Fritz back across the corduroy road and into a ravine where several Parkhill men were waiting. The deputy jumped down to point at the sign on the ground.

"Here's a boot heel in the dirt," Fritz said. "Looks like he rolled his blankets into a bedroll over there where the grass is pressed down. The horse tracks lead down the coulee."

Ross squinted at the sign on the ground as if he intended to follow it. Fritz made a pretty good tracker for a former city cop, he was thinking. "Comb every inch of this area for evidence." He frowned and shook his head. "Parkhill, I wish you'd keep your men out of the way when I'm conducting an investigation. They've trampled more sign than they'll ever find." He nudged his horse along the trail, leaning to his off side as if he had to read sign to know where he had ridden the day before.

As the sheriff followed the trail down the ravine, Wink leaned toward his boss and spoke low. "I'll say one thing for that Colby. He sure reads sign good. Follows a trail faster'n anybody I ever seen."

Ross didn't have to look when he rode past the *Post*. He knew Johnson would be watching for him. He heard the door fly open and ignored the editor's call except to point toward the jailhouse. Johnson was there before Ross could shut the door behind him.

"Any clues?" the editor asked.

"If I had any, I wouldn't tell you. You'd print 'em and scare the old man off."

"You have a suspect?"

"Not exactly."

"Now, Sheriff, I don't want to have to make my speech again."

"What speech?" Ross said, putting a Henry repeater on the rack.

"The one about you being a servant of the public, and the public having a right to know what you are doing about lawlessness in this region, and . . ."

"Oh, that speech," Ross said, tipping his hat back to rub his forehead. "All right, Johnson, sit down. Give me a second to collect my thoughts, and I'll give you something you can print." He skidded his chair back and plopped down behind his desk as the editor clutched his pencil in anticipation.

"We've got two robberies," Ross said, heaving with indignation. "We don't have a suspect yet, but we're startin' to get an idea of who the bandit is. He's an old man, of course. Probably a prospector, judging from his description. Both times he's struck just before nightfall, on the dark of the moon. He picks a spot where the stage has to move slow and robs it on foot with a scattergun."

Johnson scribbled furiously on his notepad.

"Both times he's left more gold than he's taken. Leads me to believe he's not in it for the gold. I think he's got a grudge against Parkhill. He's crafty and careful. Plans everything to the last step. Both times his trail has led to a dead end. He knows all the creek beds and rocky places where his tracks won't show. I'm guessin' he's a loner or a hermit. Lives up in the high country."

Johnson's pencil scratched along the bottom of the page. He tapped a period and flung a fresh sheet into play. "That's it?" he asked, looking up at the lawman.

Ross shrugged. "Except to say that I've advised Parkhill

to send a double guard with his gold shipments and be wary of places where the coach has to slow down. And of course, I've told him not to ship any gold on the dark of the moon."

"But what about the manhunt? How close are you to the bandit?"

Ross smiled knowingly. "Closer than you might think, Johnson."

"What does that mean? Do you know his whereabouts?"

"Maybe."

Johnson sighed and rolled his eyes. "Is there *anything* else?"

"Yes, as a matter of fact." Ross leaned his chair back and propped his feet on his desk. "There is one other thing I want to talk to you about. We need some publicity."

"For what?"

"Miss Sage has come up with a new moneymaking idea for the relief fund. She calls it short-weighting for charity . . ."

TWENTY-THREE

Most of 'em's drifted into the Black Hills for the winter," the translator said. "But ol' Bad Wound was too weak to go, so he come here."

Hector Beauchamp had his horsehair reins in his hands, leading his mount away from Fort Reno, walking toward the lone tepee on the plains. "Was he there?"

The translator nodded his greasy head in a succession

of jerks. "Oh, yeah. He knows the massacre good. Been paintin' pictures about it since the day."

Heck flipped the collar of his wool coat up around his ears to turn the sharp north wind funneling along the eastern slopes of the Bighorns. A gray blanket of clouds hung overhead, but he could sense no rain. "Will he talk about it?"

"If he's of a mind to. Don't let him gall you. He's not liable to like you."

When they reached the tepee, Heck dropped his reins and let his pony stand. The translator rapped his rifle barrel on the lodgepole, then flung the skin aside and stepped in, muttering something in the Cheyenne tongue. "Come on in, Heck," he said, his head emerging from the oval.

Heck ducked into the hide lodge, his nostrils instantly flaring at the familiar scent of the nomadic people. Some called it a stench. Heck knew better. It was not exactly his favorite aroma, but he had been raised with houses and towns. Even a dog had sense enough to know that every tribe of people God had ever put on this earth reeked of its own culture. Heck knew he smelled like a horse most of the time himself.

He found the eyes of an aged warrior looking up at him, set deep among sagging pockets of flesh. A single eagle feather stood above his head, its dark tip almost invisible against the shadowy interior of the lodge. White hair hung across a blackened buckskin shirt, parting to reveal a necklace of bear claws and elk teeth.

Heck nodded and smiled, but Bad Wound just looked back at the hide spread across his lap. The gnarled fingers gripped a feather he was using as a paintbrush. As Heck watched, the old artist moistened the tip of the feather in a tin of water, then dipped it into a small buckskin bag filled with red powder.

As the translator spoke to Bad Wound, Heck squatted and took his hat off, noticing piles of soft hides around him, different sizes, all painted. The horses caught his eye first. Dark horses, pale horses, paints, and Appaloosas. They had thick bodies and stiff legs. Each carried a rider.

He dragged a small hide from a pile and studied it closer. In the scene, the rider of a spotted horse wore long braids, carried a bow in one hand, and had a fringed quiver on his back. In front of the Indian pony, a soldier lay flat, an arrow standing on its point on the bluecoat, blood streaming across the ground.

The old Cheyenne spoke softly as he lay his feather aside. He moistened a finger on his tongue and stuck it into a buckskin bag of blue powder.

"Says they're all dead and that's all there is to tell," the translator reported.

Heck grunted. "I wouldn't answer you no questions, either, if you just busted into my place and started wantin' to know things." He held the hide painting up to catch a beam of light coming down from the smoke hole. "Warm up to him. Ask him what he makes this paint out of."

The translator asked, and as Bad Wound replied, he thrust the blue finger toward Heck before applying it to his painting.

"Says the colors all come from different things. The red's made out of clay and roots. The green's made out of plants and dirt. That blue he's got on his finger is made out of mud, boiled rotten wood, and duck shit."

"Ask him who this is," Heck said. Then, catching the old man's eye, he signed the question himself, pointing at the figure in the painting, waving his right palm, flicking his index finger forward in front of his mouth.

Bad Wound muttered something as he touched his blue finger to a soldier's uniform on the large hide spread across his lap.

"Says that's Crazy Thunder killin' a bluecoat that tried to get away."

Bad Wound pulled the folds out of the robe he was painting, spread it out, and pointed to a pair of figures along one edge. It was Crazy Thunder again, riding the same horse, wearing the same identifying design on his leggings, looking down on the same dead soldier.

Heck pulled another small painting from a pile: a mounted warrior teetering in his saddle, blood gushing from his chest. "And this feller?"

Bad Wound shifted the hide on his lap, pointed to the same figure near the middle of the scene, and spoke in a wheezing voice.

"Says it's Circlin' Dog where the White Captain shot him."

"Looks like he listened to all the stories of the battle," Heck said, "and painted each warrior's part on a little piece of hide. Now he's puttin' it all together in one big scene."

"I don't believe I'd stick my finger in duck shit," the translator said.

Heck rocked forward onto his knees and pulled the last folds out of the big hide the old man was painting. The simple figures of Indians, soldiers, and horses took breath and he sensed the wind streaming through braids and war bonnets as the braves attacked. He heard war whoops, rifle shots; smelled powder; and actually felt the rumble of the ground under the hooves. Blood streaked the Crazy Woman.

"He ain't much of a artist, is he?" the translator said, rasping a laugh.

The battle shrank back into the hide, but its echoes circled Heck in the lodge as he glanced his disapproval at the white man. He turned to the old warrior and signed a question: where is Bad Wound?

A gnarled finger straightened slowly and pointed. In the vortex of the carnage, Heck made out a rider holding a rifle. A line led from the barrel to a blue-coated figure pressed against a box with spoked wheels. The old veteran muttered as his steady finger hovered over the painting.

"Says he killed the captain hisself. First time he'd ever shot a gun. Says he shouted Good Medicine out of that gun barrel and chanted it home, whatever the hell that means."

Heck only nodded, absorbed as he was with the battle scene. Then Julia entered his mind. "Ask him if anybody left the soldiers' camp a day or two before the battle."

The translator spoke haltingly and the chief dipped his feather in the tin of water and swirled it. Placing the feather across the top of the tin, he signed with both hands:

Tracks. West. One rider. Two sleeps. Catch the Eagle follows. Soldier ride much in river. Bighorn Mountains. Big wind. Dirt hide tracks.

Heck stared into the steady old eyes for a moment, almost able to see Ross Caldwell riding for his life up the Crazy Woman. He usually saw Ross as sort of a dried-up, rat-faced character, although he doubted Julia would fall for that sort. No, he was probably a silver-tongued rake blessed with a bit of good looks.

Either way, he was a sorry excuse for a husband, if he wasn't dead. Any man who wouldn't fight off a whole tribe of Indians to get back to a wife like Julia didn't deserve her, anyway. He may have gotten away from Bad Wound's Cheyenne, but there were other bands out there, other tribes. Not to mention outlaws and grizzlies.

"What's that?" the translator said. "You're mumblin' to yourself."

"Huh?" Heck focused on the squinted face of the translator. "Tell him I want to buy one of these pictures from him." He shuffled through the hides until he found one representing four warriors surrounding a dead soldier, the bluecoat stuck with half a dozen arrows. "This one here."

"He wants to know what you're gonna pay him with."

Heck stepped out of the tepee, returning with a coiled length of horsehair rope. He let it play out in front of Bad Wound's eyes so the old man could inspect his workmanship. Bad Wound took it in his hand, pulled on it, looked up at the white man, and nodded.

Heck put his hat on, rolled the painting and tucked it inside his vest. He didn't know a farewell sign—didn't think there was one—so he touched his hat brim before he stepped out of the lodge.

"He took to you," the translator said outside. "Never seen him talk sign to a white man before."

Heck gripped the horn and rose on the stirrup.

"What are you gonna do with that picture you swapped him out of?"

"Keep it," he said, patting the roll flat against his chest. "That's history, sure as our books."

"Shit. Damn stick figures. You'd have got more use out of the rope."

"When he dies, you ought to see that those pictures get in a museum somewhere. That big one's as good as a photograph of the Crazy Woman massacre."

"I'll see what I can git for 'em."

Heck frowned, suddenly feeling as lonely as old Bad Wound. He pulled his coat collar tight around his neck and spurred his horse south for Denver.

TWENTY-FOUR

F ritz drew a breath to steady his nerves and let it out as a cloud of vapor. Frost had come to the high country. Some of the seasonal miners had already gone south. The owners of the best claims would stay until ice choked their sluices, but they would be drifting soon, too. Fritz knew that if he was going to impress Miss Sage, he would have to do it before winter froze the flow of revenue.

He stepped into the Break o' Day and felt the silence spread from his feet to the far walls. He walked briskly to the end of the saloon, turned his back to the corner, and hefted the wooden box to the surface of the bar.

"Get out from behind there," he said to the bartender.

"What the hell do you think you're doin'?" the Southern voice drawled.

"Investigating a fraud. Move."

"Like hell I will."

Fritz put his hand on his revolver. "I'll give you one more chance to get out of my way, then I'll arrest you for interfering with an investigation."

The bartender snarled and threw a rag down on the bar. "All right, have it your way, Deputy. You want me to move, I'll move right upstairs and get Park out of his office."

"I'd appreciate that." Fritz let the bartender squeeze by and watched him stomp up the first few steps of the staircase. He slid the dovetailed box to the Break o' Day's scales, opened the brass-hinged lid, and removed a set of measured weights, checking the bar patrons occasionally for signs of trouble.

"What are you lookin' for, Deputy?" somebody asked.

"Got a tip about some short-weighting going on here." He opened the saloon's box of weights, put twenty ounces in one pan and twenty ounces of his own in the other. He waited for the needle on the scale to settle, then shook his head in disapproval. Some of the drinkers began to grumble as Fritz added smaller weights, one by one, until he made the scales balance. "How 'bout that," he said. "Twenty Parkhill ounces is equal to twenty-one of the genuine article."

Two pairs of boots stomped down the stairs.

"Get the hell away from my scales!" Parkhill roared.

Fritz quickly looked the saloon man over for weapons as he descended into view. "Do your customers know they're paying a nickel on the dollar more than you advertise?"

The murmur of voices grew.

"Those are the same scales Bob Hodges left when he sold me the saloon. If they're short-weighted, it's his fault."

"You're responsible for checkin' 'em," Fritz said.

Parkhill sauntered toward the scales. "Who made you inspector? Where's Sheriff Colby?"

"He went deer huntin' today."

Parkhill sneered. "He oughta be huntin' that old bandit. You both oughta be huntin' my stolen gold instead of comin' in here to take more."

"Don't change the subject, Parkhill."

"You oughta be out there guardin' my stagecoach. I can't afford to pay all them extra guards. They cost me more than the damned old bandit did."

"I wouldn't worry about it today," Fritz said. "The new moon's a week off yet. I'd worry about these scales if I was you."

"You sure that lead is weighed right?" Parkhill stepped up to the scale and squinted at the weights.

"To the grain."

"Well, I'll be damned. You're right, Deputy Green. Ol' Bob Hodges short-weighted these scales. I thank you for pointin' it out to me. Jim, give the deputy a drink on the house."

"You can't buy me off with a drink," Fritz said. "You're going to have to make restitution one way or the other."

"What do you mean? You're not gonna try to charge me with anything illegal, are you?" Parkhill swaggered back a step or two from the bar and stood defiantly.

Fritz put his weights back in the wooden box. "I could, according to city ordinances. Then, again, I might assume you've been short-weighting for charity, like every other business in town. If that's the case, I'll just take your contribution and go."

Parkhill smiled and turned to his customers. "Now, that's reasonable, ain't it, boys? What'll I give? Fifty? Sixty?"

"Seventy-five!" somebody said.

"That's mighty low," Fritz said. "I figure you take in a couple of hundred a night average. At a nickel on the dollar, that would come out to ten dollars a night, and short-weighting for charity's been runnin' a month now. Let's call it three hundred and be done with it."

Parkhill couldn't hold the smile up any longer. "Three hundred! How the hell can a man make a livin', givin' that much to bums and drunks?"

Fritz shrugged. "The fine's five hundred, if you'd rather pay that."

"Shit!" Parkhill blurted. "Jim, give him three hundred."

The bartender reached under the counter and produced three sacks of dust. Fritz lined them on his box of weights and headed for the end of the bar. "Miss Sage will be grateful to you, Parkhill."

"Don't come back for any more. I'm gettin' those scales fixed. And don't give any of my gold to those Chinamen. You've spoilt 'em bad enough as it is!"

Fritz sidled out of the saloon, his right hand hovering over his revolver. He was anxious to put his weights back in the jailhouse so he could deliver the gold to Miss Sage. This was bound to impress her. Not even Sheriff Colby had brought in three hundred in one lump. And from Parkhill, at that!

He flung the door of the jailhouse open to find Ross putting his Henry repeater in the rack.

Ross jerked the rifle nervously from the rack before he recognized his deputy. "Damn, Fritz. You're liable to get shot bustin' in here like that."

"I thought you went huntin'."

"Nothin' was movin'," Ross said. "I didn't even get a shot at anything." He noticed the bags of dust and the box of calibrated weights. "Whose scales you been checkin'?"

Fritz grinned. "The Break o' Day's. And look what I collected for the relief fund." He dropped the three pouches of dust on the desk.

"Son of a gun, Fritz. It's a wonder you didn't collect a bunch of knots all over your head at the same time. Why didn't you wait for me?"

The deputy tugged at his gun belt and puffed his chest out. "Parkhill didn't even put up a fight. I'm gonna take this over to the Golden Sage right now."

"I'll do it," Ross said. "I need to discuss some charity business with Sage, anyway. Looks like we might get through the winter all right with what we've got, thanks to Parkhill's contribution."

"You sure you don't want me to go?" Fritz said, each word taking a little wind out of his chest. "I don't mind."

Ross chuckled. "I don't guess you would, the way those hurdies fall all over you in there. Walk over with me, if you want to."

Fritz stared longingly at the three bags of gold for a moment. "Well, if you're goin', there's no need for me to go. I'll lock up and make the rounds before I walk home."

"Good man." Ross slapped Fritz on the back, put the three bags of dust in his coat pockets, and struck out for the Golden Sage.

TWENTY-FIVE

The smell of burned wood and hot stovepipes drifted in and out of the streets and alleys as he kept an ear tuned for the Parkhill stage. He nodded to the passersby who greeted him, reasoned that the coachmen must have run into trouble moving the dead pine he had pushed down on the road. He heard the Golden Sage orchestra playing a quadrille and paused at the door to light a cigar.

It seemed the publicity generated by her charity work had done wonders for Sage's business. Even with Virginia City's population falling off as fast as the temperatures, the Golden Sage continued to attract crowds. Ross stepped inside, stayed to the outside of the rail to avoid the dancers. He tipped his hat to the ladies as he made his way to the corner. He knocked on Sage's door, took the cigar from his mouth, and blew smoke rings at the wall lamp.

Sage opened the door, and he saw her lips tell him to come in, though the band drowned out her voice. She shut the noise behind them and slid her hand across his lapel, petrifying him.

"May I take your coat?" she said.

"Let me get the gold out of it first."

She hung the coat on a brass hook and poured him a drink as he put the three sacks of dust on her writing desk. She was wearing lavender tonight, and it warmed the glow of her pale skin. He had never seen her wear the same gown twice. She must have a closet stuffed full somewhere.

Suddenly he realized he was staring at her through his cigar smoke. He glanced at her face in the mirror, saw her looking back, and knew she knew.

"This is a surprise," she said, handing him the whiskey, taunting him with that perpetual smile. "But I'm glad you stopped by. I went looking for you earlier. Your deputy told me you were out for the day."

"What was on your mind?" He inhaled the aroma and took a sip.

"The relief fund. Revenues are up, but it's going to be a long winter." Her sleepy eyes glanced languidly at the three sacks of dust on her desk. "Those will help."

"Deputy Green just collected that from the Break o' Day." He smiled, imagining the looks that must have crossed Parkhill's face. "Caught Parkhill short-weighting his customers."

"Still," she said, "it's going to be a long winter."

"Don't worry. I've been doin' some fund-raisin' of my own. We'll have enough to get us through."

Sage questioned him with a tilt of her head as she glided to the sofa facing his chair. She sat down, kicked her shoes off, and stretched her legs out on the seat. "You don't mind my getting comfortable, do you?"

Ross glanced at his glass, thought about guzzling it and getting out of there. But the whiskey was too good. "Why should I mind?"

They sat in silence for a moment, Ross looking vacantly at her. He thought about Julia, remembered her wholesome beauty, contrasted it to the soft paleness of this dance hall siren. What would Julia think if she saw him sitting here? Some people in town already had the wrong idea. But Ross trusted himself. He came here for business purposes only, though Sage tempted him in her silent way.

Julia . . . The image of Sage blurred as he thought of her. Where was she now? With whom would she be sitting tonight? If he didn't hear from her soon, he would hear nothing until spring. He had to find her. Without her, life would continue to ricochet like a bullet among the rocks. She was the one constant that could keep things from . . .

"Are you going to tell me about it?" Sage said.

Ross snorted, as if waking suddenly. "About what?"

"Your fund-raising."

He took a sip of the whiskey, tapped the ashes from his cigar. "That's what I came here for." He shifted in his chair. "I've managed to get pledges from a number of businesses to contribute so much a month through the winter. So, I'll be sending small amounts of gold to you at regular intervals until spring."

"Sending?" She toyed with a curl that brushed against her neck. "Why don't you deliver the goods yourself?"

Ross chuckled. "I wouldn't deprive Deputy Green of the pleasure. I think he's got a sweetheart among your girls. Every time he comes back from the Golden Sage, his eyes look like marbles in a moose head."

Sage seemed irritated. "I've seen the same look in your eyes."

Ross felt the smile slip from his face as his grip tightened on the glass of whiskey. He was getting anxious to leave now. Why didn't he just get up and go?

"Deputy Green said you went hunting today. Did you catch anything?"

"Catch?" he said. "You don't catch anything when you go huntin'; you shoot to kill. You're thinkin' of trapping. Trappers catch their game."

"Are you a trapper as well as a hunter?"

Ross looked into his glass and felt her eyes on him. They were whiskey-colored, he realized: intoxicating. "I've done some of both."

Layers of petticoats rustled as she pulled her legs into them. "What kind of animal would you like to catch, Sheriff Colby?"

Ross looked up at her, sifting for suggestion in her voice, trying to think of a reply. He was about to attempt something clever when the door flew open, letting a blast of dance music in.

Ross sprang from his chair, sloshing the good whiskey as he whirled and reached for his Remington.

Parkhill kicked the door shut behind him as he brought a scattergun out of his coat. "Take your hand off that pistol, Colby. You've got some questions to answer."

"What is this?" Sage said, scrambling off the sofa. Her eyes flashed a frenzy. "Get out of my place!"

"Not until the sheriff tells me where he was this afternoon. And I mean *exactly* where he was."

"It's none of your damn business where I was," Ross said, his thoughts racing, wondering what he had left undone. Nerves wrenched his stomach into a bundle. "Get out before I arrest you for trespassing."

Parkhill latched a hammer back on the double-barrel. "Talk Colby. Your deputy said you were huntin'. I want to know where and you'd better convince me."

"South of town, if it's any concern of yours."

"Where's your game? What'd you kill?"

"I didn't see anything to shoot at. What's this all about?"

"My stage was robbed by the old man again today, and somethin' dawned on me. Where were you the day of the first robbery?"

"Hell, I don't remember."

"Prospectin'. Where were you during the second robbery?"

Ross stiffened as if he were getting mad. "What's your point, Parkhill?"

"You were fishin'. Where were you today? Huntin'. Looks like you're out of town every time the old bandit robs me."

"So what?"

"Who knows when the shipments come? You do. I've been a damn fool enough to tell you myself."

"Half the hard cases that work for you know when you ship gold. Ever think of that? Any one of them could have leaked the information in some saloon."

"Who told me to double my guard on the dark of the moon?" Parkhill's eyes glanced around the room, found the three bags of gold from his saloon.

"What's that got to do with it?"

"It ain't the dark of the moon today. How'd that old road agent know to change his game?"

"If I could read his mind, I'd have caught him by now."

Parkhill set his jaw, showed his teeth. "I think you know somethin', Colby. I think you know who the bandit is. I think you're in it with him."

"Then you're a bigger fool than I expected."

"Where did you go huntin' today? And I'd better be able to find your tracks there tomorrow."

Ross glanced at the twin muzzles. Now what? Bluff? Yes, bluff, and you'll have the night to think of something. "Well, let's see," he said, stalling. "Hard to say exactly where I was. I was huntin', not blazin' a damn wagon trace." He rubbed his head, tried to get his mind to come up with something.

"You might as well tell him the truth," Sage said. She stepped to his side and stood with him in the path of the buckshot.

"What?" Ross said.

"He's caught you. You might as well tell him where you were."

"What are you talkin' about?" His innards throbbed with terror.

"Sheriff Colby wasn't hunting today." She put her arm around Ross's waist and ran a hand across his chest as if smoothing his shirt. "He was here with me."

Ross held his breath as he let her words sink in. She knew. Sage had known since the night she found the long white hair on his coat. She could have turned him in a month ago, but now she was offering him an alibi.

"With you?" Parkhill said, his eyebrows gathering. "Doin' what?"

"Running his trapline, what do you think? Do I have to spell it out to you?" She looked up at the sheriff. "I know you wanted to wait, darling, but this is as good a time as any to let it out."

Ross put his arm around her shoulder. With her heels off, she was smaller than he had realized.

"What about the first two times?" Parkhill said, his suspicions giving way to intrigue.

"Are you an idiot?" Sage said. "You found us together at his cabin the day he was supposed to be fishing. It doesn't take a detective to figure it out."

Parkhill lowered his shotgun and grinned. "Huntin' today huh? Huntin' the wildcat!" His laughter erupted like gunfire. "The newspaper's gonna have a fit with this one." His grin turned quickly to a scowl and he put his hand on the doorknob. "It don't change the fact that my stage was robbed again, Colby. You'd better get on the trail of that old outlaw pretty damn quick or you'll be huntin' a trail out of Montana."

The band music burst in on them, and then Parkhill was gone.

Ross tried to step away from her, but she held on.

She turned to face him, looked up at him with flashing eyes. "I don't like lying for a man," she said, "but I'll make an exception in your case."

He felt her hands interlock at the small of his back. "What do you want from me?" he asked.

She faked a look of astonishment. "Nothing. That is, nothing any other woman wouldn't want. Just a little gratitude and devotion."

He shook his head. "There are things you don't know about me."

"I know you've got some woman on your mind. I can make you forget her."

"It's not that simple." He tried to pull her arms away, but she locked her hands together tighter. He felt like a weakling.

"Now, listen," she said, a vicious new note in her voice, "I just told a lie for you. I think you owe me something."

He had thought about what it would be like with Sage in that adjoining room. "Owe you something? Like what?"

Her painted lips lifted in a true smile—not the false look of indifferent bliss she usually wore, but a visage of wicked amusement. "Let's start with tonight."

His voice came wheezing up his throat. "And what if I told you I already had plans for tonight."

She released him and went to her safe to open it, looking back at Ross as she picked up the bags of gold dust and threw them into the iron box. "That would be risky. I might have to tell Parkhill the truth. Otherwise, what would be in it for me?" She kicked the safe shut, walked to the doorway leading to her bedroom, and waited for him to decide which way he would turn.

Ross faltered for a moment, trapped in her snare. He felt smothered with foolishness, consumed by guilt for the base desires he held for her. Finally he approached her, stood over her whiskey eyes.

She grabbed a handful of his shirt and pulled him in. "It's going to be a long winter," she said.

TWENTY-SIX

Julia winced at the board creaking under her foot. She looked over her shoulder to make sure she hadn't wakened Fay, or Hanna McDaniels—who was sick in bed with some mysterious ailment that to Julia looked suspiciously like laziness—or Hanna's baby, Elliot, Jr. To her relief, they all continued to sleep.

She took her shawl from a peg and turned the brass knob quietly, opening the door by degrees until it was wide enough for her to get outside. She felt her fatigue as she tiptoed to the porch step, pulling the shawl tighter around her shoulders.

The mixture of cool air and warm afternoon sun felt good where she sat. She looked down on the crooked little city of Denver as she relished the first break from labor she had had all day. What a strange, barren spot to locate a home, she thought. The winter wind would surely freeze them all through the cracks in the thin board walls of the McDaniels house. She hated staying here.

Deputy Elliot McDaniels grumbled from the moment he woke up in the morning until he went to sleep at night. His wife, Hanna, was worse, because she was there all day. "If you're gonna stay with us, you'll be expected to pull your weight," she had told Julia the day they met. Since then, Hanna had apparently decided that Julia was to pull most of her weight, too. She took sick on a regular basis and thought nothing of ordering Julia around like a house servant.

This was a miserable existence. Hector Beauchamp had been gone for weeks and she was beginning to think he would never come back. A thousand calamities could have befallen him between here and the Sioux country. Would she ever find out what had happened to Ross?

She thought often now, in her moments of rationality, that Ross must be dead. The chances of his escaping the massacre seemed slimmer every day. And yet she still experienced a moment now and then that made her look over her shoulder to see if he was standing there. A mind could play tricks on a tortured soul.

She glanced back toward the smoke trails of Denver and saw a rider trotting up the hill toward the McDaniels homestead. Hector Beauchamp had been gone so long she thought she had forgotten what he looked like, but she recognized him instantly. The hope and dread clashed in her stomach again as she rose unconsciously and started to walk toward him.

They met on the treeless hillside, a few dried tufts of grass whistling, bending in the wind. Heck got down from his saddle and let his horsehair reins dangle. He smiled, but he did not look happy.

"Hello, Julia."

"Sheriff Beauchamp. What did you find?"

Heck sighed, reached into his pocket, and pulled out a folded scrap of paper. "I tore this out of Captain Jones's diary. He wrote it two days before the massacre."

Julia had only seen the captain's handwriting a couple of times, but she recognized the heavy pen strokes. She read the words, gathered their meaning. "He wasn't there," she said. "Ross wasn't at the Crazy Woman." Her eyes grew wide with hope, but she saw something in Heck's face that kept her joy from leaping.

"No," Heck said. "If he had been, there would probably be no way to ever prove how he died. But he was on the prairie alone when it happened."

"When what happened?" she said. "What are you talking about?"

"My guess is that Captain Jones sent your husband out to find Colonel Kulp. You know he relied on Ross."

"Yes, but if he wasn't at the Crazy Woman, he wasn't killed in the massacre."

Heck turned to his saddlebag, opened the flap. "No, he wasn't at the Crazy Woman. He was a day's ride east when a Cheyenne scouting party found him." He pulled a rolled piece of tanned hide from his saddlebag.

Julia felt a cold lump in her stomach pressing hard against her heart. "How could you know that?"

"I talked to the leader of that scouting party. An old warrior named Bad Wound. He described Ross perfect. Said Ross gave 'em one hell of a chase before he finally holed up in a buffalo wallow. They charged him several times, but he held 'em off. He ran low on ammunition, Julia. He knew it was over. Bad Wound said it was the bravest thing he ever saw. Ross came out of the buffalo wallow and charged the whole Cheyenne scouting party. They shot him full of arrows, and he died quick."

Julia shook her head, slinging a tear across her cheek. "No. I don't believe it. It could have been any soldier."

Heck bit his lip to steady himself. "Bad Wound showed me his gun, Julia. The old Remington revolver with his initials carved on the grip. It was him."

Her mouth opened, and her eyes darted helplessly.

He hated doing this to her. He had dreaded it for days. But he was sure of himself. There was no doubt that it was the best thing for *him*. And he had also decided it was best for Julia. He unrolled the painting he had bought from Bad Wound and gave it to her.

"When the Cheyenne have a great battle, they paint a picture about it. This is Bad Wound's picture about the death of Ross Caldwell. I've never seen such a thing done for a single white man. I know it doesn't help any now. But in time you'll be grateful you know how it happened."

Julia threw the painted hide back at Heck. "No!" she shouted, almost doubling over with sobs. "I don't believe it!"

Heck took her by the arm but she shook free. He grabbed her again, and she pummeled him with her fists, but he held on, pulling her closer. He took a pretty good beating from her until she gave up and buried her face in his shoulder.

He held her for a long time as his horse wandered a short way off to graze on a tall clump of grass. He had to squint hard to keep tears from coming out of his own eyes, and he felt a nagging guilt for the lies he had told her. But he knew he would get over it in time. And he knew Julia would get over Ross. It wouldn't take her long. They had already been separated for over a year.

Right now this felt like the worst thing he had ever done. But he knew in the long run it would be the best thing that had ever happened to him. And he would prove to Julia that it was the best thing for her and little Fay, too. He was holding her now in her moment of greatest sorrow. He would hold her someday in rapture.

Heck heard the front door of the McDaniels house slam and looked up to see Hanna standing there shielding her eyes against the afternoon glare. He heard the raspy voice rattle down the hill:

"Julia! Where the devil did you go? The baby's cryin'!"

TWENTY-SEVEN

SENSATIONAL CRIME!

PARKHILL STAGE
ROBBED AT GUNPOINT!

HERMIT HIGHWAYMAN COMMITS
FOURTH DARING HOLDUP!

Ed Johnson trembled with excitement as he positioned exclamation points. It had been a long, dull winter, but now news was busting out everywhere. He had been putting together a good issue even before the robbery. Now he was looking at the biggest edition ever.

His ink-stained fingers groped for capitals in the tray as he composed the headline for his second front-page story:

TELEGRAPH SERVICE REACHES
VIRGINIA CITY

He had waited two years to print this story. To editor Johnson it meant access to national news almost as it occurred. The *Post* would flourish. He might even go daily.

In fact, the telegraph had been his lead story until yesterday, when he heard Parkhill roaring in the street about the robbery. He had sprinted with Parkhill and Deputy Green to the sheriff's cabin. They had knocked furiously on the door until it opened to reveal the infamous Miss Sage standing there in her dressing gown—one thin layer of silk between her curvaceous skin and editor Johnson's bulging eyes.

He shook his head and put his mind back on business. He might have printed something about catching Sheriff Colby in a tryst with the most notorious woman of soiled virtue in town, but that was hardly news. It had been going on all winter.

The important news about the sheriff concerned the shoot-out at the Golden Sage three nights ago, told here at the bottom of page one:

SHERIFF WOUNDED IN GUNFIGHT WITH DRUNKEN BANDIT

Something like this happened about this time every year. Some miscreant would get cabin fever just before the ice began to thaw, get drunk, and commit some absurd crime.

This particular culprit was a mule packer from Idaho who had decided to rob the relief fund in Sage's office. She had caught him trying to throw her safe through the window, and he had forced her to open it at gunpoint. When he reached in for the gold, she slammed the door on his hand and he had shot at her as she ran from the office.

Sheriff Colby, who happened to be in the Golden Sage, charged the office and exchanged gunfire with the bandit, disabling him with a bullet that hit him in the face, shattering his jaw. A piece of flying glass from a shattered lantern globe had cut Colby on the cheek. It wasn't much of a wound, but it made for a compelling headline.

And there was still more sensational news to print, spilling right on over to page two:

PARKHILL LINE LOSES MONOPOLY
ON LAST CHANCE ROAD

Oh, this was a fine piece of reporting! Rumors of corruption in the territorial legislature had led to an investigation of so-called road franchises granted to certain freight line operators who just happened to hail from Dixie, as did most of the legislators.

The executive branch, made solely of Union men, had now declared the roads public property, but Parkhill—and this was deliciously inflammatory—had vowed to continue operating the Last Chance Road as a tollway in clear defiance of the territorial government.

And there was still more!

RODENT POPULATION EXPLODES!
CHINESE INFANT BITTEN BY RABID RAT!

Well, nobody was sure it was rabid, but Johnson was relatively certain it was a rat, although it could have been a big brother who slept with the infant. The point was that Virginia City had a serious vermin problem, and nowhere was it worse than in Parkhill's Chinatown.

Oh, mercy! What a week for news!

The brass bell on the door clattered and Johnson looked up to see Mary.

"Hurry, cousin," she said, "the ceremony's about to start!"

Johnson glanced at the clock. "Where has the morning gone?" He grabbed his overcoat and hat and escorted Mary toward the new Western Union office on Main Street.

The Virginia City Marching Band was there, Fritz blaring on his trumpet. To one side of the band, the townspeople stood dressed in fluff and finery. To the other side, the telegraph line construction crew waited in dirty work clothes and bearded faces. Among them, a few miners and prospectors stood to witness the ceremony.

Under the canvas awning of the telegraph office, Sheriff Colby stood with the mayor and a Western Union representative. Behind the telegraph key a boy of about nineteen years sat wearing full telegrapher's uniform—eye visor, white shirt, black sleeve garters, bow tie.

Johnson pushed his way through the crowd with Mary and whipped out a notepad and pencil. His searching eyes caught sight of the notorious Miss Sage standing near the band, her white skin like porcelain in the light of day. She stared longingly at the sheriff, seemingly aware of little else. Scandalous, he thought.

As the band finished honking its march, the crowd applauded and the mayor stepped to the edge of the board-walk.

"That's enough speeches and fanfare, ladies and gentlemen. Now the moment we have all been waiting for. Time for Virginia City to join the age of modern communications. I have been asked to choose someone to send the first telegram to the Western Union offices in St. Louis. For this honor, I have chosen someone with an appreciation for the language, a person who is well known and highly regarded in our community. Reporter for the Virginia City *Post* and president of the Virginia City Literary Society, Miss Mary Johnson!"

The editor smirked as his young cousin gasped beside him. The mayor, that lecherous old bachelor, had been after Mary for months. She took the mayor's hand and sprang up to the boardwalk, so excited that she could scarcely speak.

"This is such a surprise," she finally said. "I have no idea what to say."

Ross took the cigar from his mouth, put his hand around Mary's arm, and whispered something in her ear.

She giggled. "How shall I compose it?" She pondered a moment, then began writing on a sheet of paper at the telegrapher's elbow. She shook her head, scratched something out, scrawled another line.

The crowd raised a common grumble, and Ross looked on as Mary scribbled. When she was done, she showed the message to the sheriff, and he nodded in approval. She handed the note to the young telegrapher. The boy shrugged, and began tapping the key.

"Well, what the devil does it say?" a miner yelled.

The telegrapher paused, looked at the mayor. The mayor gestured approval. Haltingly the key operator read the message aloud as he sent it east, his voice breaking as he began:

"Greetings . . . St. Louis . . . from Virginia City . . . Montana Territory . . . Gem of the Northern Rockies . . ." The boy paused as the crowd applauded. "Help! Our city . . . has been . . . invaded by . . . tribes of natives . . . Save us . . . Send cats."

Laughter sprang from the crowd, the bandleader brought the musicians to attention, and a brassy waltz began to plod from the bandstand. Johnson looked up from his notepad to see his cousin offering her hand to the sheriff. The sheriff gallantly threw his cigar aside. The editor felt himself flush with embarrassment as Mary began to dance with the famous philanderer of the Golden Sage.

The girl was so ridiculously naive, he thought. Really, she didn't have the sense of a goose. The crowd, however, was loving it—raising quite a round of applause. All except for Miss Sage. Her hands were clenched in little fists. Her lips seemed to smile, but her eyes glared.

When the waltz ended, the crowd began to break up, most of the celebrants drifting off to various saloons. Johnson saw Sheriff Colby pull the young telegrapher aside for some sort of serious conversation. The editor put his notepad in his pocket and grumbled to himself. Nothing of interest to add to the telegraph story. Except maybe the message Mary had composed. That was rather ingenious, even if Colby had helped her think of it.

He looked for his cousin, anxious to escort her back to the office and get back to work on the paper. He spotted her stepping down from the boardwalk, but as she reached the bottom step she stopped. Sage was standing in her path. Mary smiled. Sage drew an arm back and hit Mary across the cheek with a roundhouse blow that knocked her flat on her back on the boardwalk.

As Mary tried to get to her feet, Sage sprang on her, smiling wickedly as she pummeled the president of the literary society with her fists. Mary shrieked, kicked Sage away, and sprang to her feet.

The crowd surged. Ross tried to push his way through spectators. Fritz jumped over the bandstand rail with his trumpet. Johnson rushed forward to protect his cousin, but Sage had grabbed her by the ankle and pulled her off her feet. The smiling wench was on Mary again, pulling her hair viciously. Wild-eyed, Mary threw an elbow in Sage's stomach and leaped free.

Sage lunged again, but Sheriff Colby caught her around the waist and lifted her from the boardwalk. Fritz leaped in between the two women, protecting Mary. Johnson tried to catch his cousin as she stumbled backward, but she fell on the cracker barrel at the general store, scattering a nest of mice living within it.

"My God!" Johnson shouted.

The miners and construction crewmen laughed, the townspeople gasped, and Ross struggled to control Sage. She continued to scratch and kick in Mary's direction, her face contorted with insensible anger—except for the smiling corners of her paradoxical mouth.

"Arrest that woman!" Johnson shouted. "She should be thrown in jail!"

The sheriff appeared mortified with it all, unable to respond.

Fritz helped Mary to her feet among the cracker crumbs and rodent droppings.

"No," Mary said, composing herself, smoothing her dress, and raking her hair back from her face. "She didn't hurt me."

"But she attacked you!" Johnson roared. "Something has to be done!"

"I said no!" Mary snapped. "It's not worth the trouble. I'm going home." She nodded at Fritz. "Thank you, Deputy Green," she said, and walked away with all the dignity she could muster as some of the miners, for some reason, awarded her a round of applause.

Johnson glared back at Sage. She was hanging from the sheriff's arms like a rag doll now, and she still had that idiotic smile on her face.

"This does not bode well for you, Miss Sage," the editor declared, drawing himself to his full height. "Nor for you, Sheriff Colby." He straightened his top hat and turned for his office, relishing the befuddled look on Colby's face. He could already feel the lexicon boiling inside him, aching to burst out and splatter all over the editorial page.

The telegraph key began to tap wildly and the young operator reached for his pencil. Fritz lost his view of Mary as she entered her boardinghouse down the street, so he sauntered toward the telegraph operator and looked over his shoulder.

"Well, what does it say?" the mayor asked.

"They misunderstood," Fritz said. "They think we're really under attack. Says, 'Clarify. Message reads *cats*. Do you mean caps? Firing caps?'"

Sage suddenly wrenched away from Ross, smiled defiantly up at him, and strode away toward the Golden Sage.

Ross sighed. "Better clear it up or we'll have the damned army marching up here. Tell 'em *felines* this time."

TWENTY-EIGHT

Ross spread the *Post* to its full width in front of his face and stared dumbfounded at the editorial page. Johnson had vented a journalistic thunderclap over yesterday's brawl between "Sheriff Colby's depraved concubine" and "Virginia City's quintessence of female purity."

He read one passage aloud: ". . . but behind the facade of their vaunted relief fund lurks a union so perverse and scandalous that it would shock even the vilest class of humanity, nay, even the rats that propagate under our houses . . ."

And this Ross could not deny. He had once been a devoted husband. Now he robbed stagecoaches and consorted with lewd women. This was life after Julia.

But he was trapped. Sage held a noose around his neck that she threatened to tighten every time he tried to distance himself from her. If he had known how possessive she would become, he would never have used her alibi. He would have taken his chances with Parkhill. But now he had lost all control.

It had started enjoyable enough—except for the guilt, and even that could be explained to almost nothing. He was being blackmailed, after all. Sage had shown him pleasures he had never conceived. But when the veneer of her charms began to fall off, Ross saw their true nature. She used her sensuality as leverage to lodge him where she wanted him; as reward for behavior she expected. She trained him like a dog, taking no pleasure from him in return, feeling nothing for him but a desire to control.

He had only heard about the first attack. Sage had fired one of her girls, run her off to another hurdy-gurdy. Ross had heard she roughed the little thing up pretty bad, but figured the hurdies must have exaggerated the beating. Now, after seeing Sage tear into Mary Johnson, he realized how bad it must have been.

All winter he had kept his sanity by consoling himself with the same rationale. This had started as a way to punish Parkhill, and Parkhill deserved it. If Ross hadn't robbed the stagecoaches and spread the gold around, people would have starved and frozen to death this winter—particularly the Chinese. Parkhill had been so preoccupied with the Hermit Bandit that vigilante activity had practically ceased around Virginia City.

He couldn't have foreseen Sage finding out, Sage blackmailing him, Sage going berserk with jealousy.

The jailhouse door opened and Ross let the newspaper collapse in front of him. He saw Johnny Tibbits, the young telegraph operator, stepping in.

"That editor let you have it pretty good," the boy said.

Ross forced one side of his mouth into a smile. "Nobody takes Johnson too seriously."

Johnny glanced at the jail cells. "Is that the robber you

shot in the Golden Sage?" he asked, seeing the man with the bandaged face sleeping on a cot.

"That's him. The doc says he's gonna pull through to stand trial."

The young man sat down in front of Ross's desk. "Is it true what the paper says? Is that lady, Sage, your . . . concubine?"

Ross folded the paper with a flourish. "Don't believe everything you read in the newspaper. And don't ask so many damned questions. What have you got for me?"

Johnny drew a Western Union envelope from his pocket. "A telegram came in your code name. A reply to the one I sent to Georgia for you yesterday."

Ross straightened suddenly and glanced at the prisoner in the cell. He put his finger over his lips to caution the boy. He took the envelope handed to him and opened it hastily.

Ross! Heard from Julia recently. Wrote from Denver to say you were killed on Crazy Woman. What has happened? Reply!

"You all right, Sheriff Colby?" the boy said. The sheriff had stared at the telegram long enough to read it three times. Then he had looked blankly at the wall. Then he had read the telegram again.

"Huh?" Ross said, springing to his feet. He paced to the gun rack, put his hand on his Henry rifle, walked to the jail cell, looked at the wounded prisoner.

"What's it mean?" Johnny asked.

Ross felt Julia's warmth in the telegram pressed against

his palm. The boy's words got to him as he moved aimlessly to the window to look toward Denver. "It's all in code," he said. "It has to do with some outlaws I've been after a long time. You don't tell anybody about this, you understand?"

"Yes, sir," Johnny replied. "You want to make a reply?"

"Does Denver have telegraph service yet?"

"No, sir."

"No reply, then." He could scarcely think for the wild fluttering in his stomach.

"Anything else?"

"No, that's all." He heard the boy get up and open the door. "Wait, Johnny. Has the Wells Fargo stage left yet?"

"No, sir."

"Tell the driver to wait for me. Tell him I'll be there in ten minutes."

"Yes, sir."

"And, Johnny. After I leave, deliver a couple of messages for me. Deputy Green's out on the road to Last Chance today, scouting for sign of the Hermit Bandit. When he comes in, tell him I had to go to Denver on urgent business. Tell him somebody's tryin' to jump my mining claims up Gregory Gulch. And give the same message to Miss Sage. Tell her she'll have to start the spring charity drive without me."

"Yes, sir," Johnny said.

Ross grabbed his gun belt and slung it around his hips. "Hurry! Hold that stage for me!"

Johnny tried to bound through the doorway, but ran into the barrel chest of Parkhill and bounced back into the jailhouse.

"Sorry, sir. Excuse me."

"Watch where you're goin', boy," Parkhill said as Johnny skulked past him and ran out of the jailhouse. Wink came in behind him, his eye twitching like a bug in an ant bed.

"What do you want, Parkhill?"

"I want to know what in the hell you're doin' about that damned old bandit."

"Got Fritz out lookin' for sign right now."

Wink laughed and went to the jail cell to look at the wounded prisoner.

"Hell, Fritz couldn't track a stuck pig to the butcher. You're the one reads sign so damn good. You ought to be out there yourself."

Ross slapped his hat on. "There's more than one kind of sign to read." He forced his arm through a sleeve of his coat.

"What the hell is that supposed to mean?" Wink said.

Ross grabbed the door handle.

"Where are you goin'?" Parkhill said. "I ain't done talkin' to you."

The sheriff looked back and forth at the two men. "All right, I guess I'd better tell you what's goin' on, just in case I don't make it back alive." He glanced at the man in the cell and motioned for Parkhill and Wink to step outside.

The sheriff looked up and down the street before he started talking. "There's been a stage robbery in Colorado that sounds like the work of our old hermit."

"How the hell would you know what's goin' on in Colorado?"

"The wire, Parkhill. Don't you know anything about telegraphs?"

"I used to ride guard on the telegraph. Hell, I used to fix the damn thing."

"I'm sure you did," Ross said sarcastically. "The point is, I just got a telegram from a Colorado lawman about this stage robbery and he thinks he has a lead on the bandit. I'm goin' down there to help catch the old codger."

"Colorado?" Parkhill said.

"Makes sense. Our road agent probably went to spend your gold down there and couldn't resist doin' a little business while he was at it. Now, if you'll excuse me, I have to grab a few things and catch the stage."

He could barely keep from grinning as he turned his back on Parkhill and headed for his cabin. The long winter was over and he was heading south into spring and summer. Julia was waiting for him down there. Poor thing. She had been grieving for him almost two years now. Oh, to see the look on her face when he found her. He could almost feel her now. They would start over again. Head for California. And he would never see Parkhill, Sage, or Virginia City again as long as he lived.

TWENTY-NINE

When Ross arrived at Denver, he felt every mile he had traveled in the small of his back. For day after solid day he had ridden the rollicking stagecoach, stopping only to eat and change teams. He had slept with his feet on someone's shoulder, someone else's head on his knee, one arm dangling out of the window.

But Julia was near. He knew it. There was no time to rest now. He had to find her.

"Hey, partner," he said to the man unhitching the mule team. "Who's the law here?"

"That'd be Sheriff Hector Beauchamp. Everybody calls him Heck."

"Where can I find him?"

The harness man pointed. "His office is on Broadway."

There had been more than enough time to think on the trip south, and Ross had decided to go to the local law first. He knew virtually every permanent resident in Virginia City, so he figured the lawman here would know his town equally well. If this Heck Beauchamp could tell him where to find Julia, it would save him a lot of snooping around in hotels and boardinghouses.

He felt dizzy walking down Broadway, passing the slower pedestrians, listening to the rattle of buckboards and buggies. He wondered if it was the long trip or the prospect of finally finding his wife that made him so light-headed. Passing a dry-goods store, he glanced at his reflection in a large plate-glass window. God, what a sight. Would Julia recognize him? Maybe he should clean up before he actually approached her. Get a bath and put on a clean suit of clothes.

He saw the sign over the sheriff's office and broke into a trot. He angled across the street, dodging traffic. He stomped up the steps and reached for the knob before he saw the scrap of paper closed in the crack of the door: "Out to Lunch."

He pulled his watch from his vest pocket. Sheriff Beauchamp employed rather liberal luncheon hours. It was almost two o'clock. His eyes spotted a barbershop across the street. There was an option. Trim the hair and beard, watch for the sheriff's return. Why not? If Beauchamp had not returned by the time he left the barbershop, he would find Julia on his own.

Ross ran in front of a milk wagon and leaped to the barbershop door. "Howdy," he said, looking over the shop as he stepped in. A one-chair outfit. The barber's hand hovered around the head of a dandified customer, scissors snipping like some chirping bird.

"Have a seat," the barber said. "Be with you in a minute."

He took off his coat, sat in a chair that gave him a view of the jailhouse. He picked up a copy of the *Police Gazette*.

"You gonna take a little more off over the ears?" the customer said.

The barber sighed. "I ought to charge you double every time you come in. You take twice as long."

"I look twice as good when I leave," the customer replied.

The scissors snipped, then paused. "You mean half as ugly."

Ross glanced through the window. Busy out there. A man in a big hat approached the sheriff's office, but walked on by. Ross turned the page as if he had read it.

The scissors chirped for a while, then clattered against the counter. The barber picked up his hand mirror to give the customer an all-around view. "How's that?" he asked.

The customer craned his neck, inspecting every angle. "Put some of that oil on," he said. "The smelly stuff."

"Smelly stuff, huh? Where you goin'?" He rubbed a splash of tonic between his soft palms and stroked it onto the customer's hair.

Through the glass, a man stepped into Ross's view and seized his attention as if in a hawk's talon. He knew the look of a lawman. A glimpse told him that was Hector Beauchamp.

With a grin, the customer yanked the apron from his neck. "Someplace where the service is more cordial than here and you get more for your money."

Like a flash of blinding light, Julia appeared at the lawman's side. Ross froze, the newspaper lurching with every mighty throb of his heart. He wanted to call to her, but his breath was stuck in his chest. For a moment he floated in halcyon bliss. Then an unnamed panic began to grow.

"Not if you complain as much there as you do here." The barber laughed and took the customer's money. "You're next, mister."

Ross stood, but he hadn't heard the barber. Heck Beauchamp had his arm around Julia's waist. Julia was carrying a child. A little squirming toddler. The customer passed in front of him, disrupting his view.

"You're next, mister," the barber repeated.

"Who is that?" Ross asked, pointing.

The barber looked past the painted letters on his window. "That's Sheriff Beauchamp."

"I mean the woman," Ross said.

"His wife," the dandy replied, easing a derby down over his new haircut. "Julia Beauchamp."

The couple stood at the door to the office as Beauchamp

put his key in the lock. Julia smiled at something he said, carried the baby inside as he opened the door for her.

"Hey, you're next," the barber said. "You gonna sit down or not?"

Ross grabbed his coat and stepped outside, bumping the smelly dandy out of his way. He stepped into the street, heard someone holler, saw a horse veer from him. He stopped, traffic passing in front of him, behind him. Through the sheriff's office window, beyond the reflections of false fronts across the street, he saw Julia move as he had seen her in a thousand dreams. He walked blindly into the path of a delivery wagon, hardly noticing the horse that balked to keep from running into him.

"Watch where you're goin' there!" a voice shouted.

He stepped onto the boardwalk and peered breathless through the window. Beauchamp's back was turned. His arms were around Julia. She was turning her cheek, pushing against his chest. Ross felt his hand move to the pistol grip of his Remington as his anger reached an instant boil.

Her smile shined through the dusty windowpane. She moved the baby to her other arm, slipped a hand behind Beauchamp's neck. She kissed him.

His grip felt feeble on the revolver. She hadn't waited. She hadn't searched. She hadn't mourned or grieved or cried. She had taken up with a lawman. No wonder he had found no trace of a Mrs. Ross Caldwell. She was Mrs. Hector Beauchamp now. Judging from the size of that child, she had been Mrs. Beauchamp for quite some time.

The door opened, and he turned away, standing at the street as if waiting to cross. He gathered his shoulders and hunched his back, partly to disguise his build, partly to ease the stranglehold in his stomach.

"What time is supper?"

"About six o'clock."

Her voice brought a tear to his eye.

"What are we havin'?"

"Oh, hush. We just ate lunch. You just be home on time."

Ross heard her shoes tap down the boardwalk, and they seemed to slow for a stride or two as she passed behind him.

"*Adiós,* honey," Heck said.

THIRTY

He woke not knowing where he was. For long minutes he stared at the strange ceiling above him. Oh, yeah, Denver. The dim light of day shone through the window. Had he slept a night, or a night and a day? Was it dawn or dusk?

Rolling out of bed, he sat up for a few minutes, then walked to the window. He saw bright sunlight on the mountains west of town. It was morning. He tasted paste in his mouth, remembered the saloon and the things he had learned about Hector Beauchamp from his drinking companions.

What a nightmare. In his dream he had killed this Beauchamp, the tall sheriff with the handlebar mustache. Shot him in the back. But when the sheriff fell, Julia was standing there with the baby. The bullet had gone through the man, hit the baby, the mother. He had killed them all. What a horrible dream.

But as the dream haze lifted from his thoughts, the reality struck. He remembered the barber and his customer talking. He hadn't heard them at the time, but he recalled every word now. The customer was talking about going to a whorehouse. He wanted scented hair tonic. He and the barber had joked with each other as if there were nothing wrong.

But something had gone terribly wrong. Julia was kissing the sheriff. Heck Beauchamp: man hunter, tracker, detective, county sheriff, deputy U.S. Marshal.

He got dressed, left the hotel. He had no appetite. Maybe because he could smell himself. He hadn't bathed since Montana. He stopped to look at himself in a shop window. The mining camp beard put ten years on him. His clothes held a cloud of trail dust.

He didn't know where he was. The sun was high. He smelled leather, looked at the lettering on the window: "High Plains Saddlery." His eyes focused on something beyond. An angry face looking back at him. He barely heard the voice through the glass:

"Go on, git out of here. Move on, you tramp!"

He must have stood there longer than he thought. He looked for the mountains, got his bearings, wandered back toward the middle of town. He recognized the stagecoach office and remembered that he had left his bag there yesterday. He checked. It was still there.

He should buy a ticket to somewhere, he thought. But where? Virginia City? Why? What did he have there besides a job and a lot of trouble? California? No. Not without Julia. Texas? New Mexico? Georgia? Remember Georgia? Before the war? The honeymoon, the simple plans they had made.

There was a saloon across the street. A whole row of saloons. Maybe a drink or two would help him decide.

From his table at the window, he saw the stagecoaches come and go. Black Hawk, Dodge City, Santa Fe. He had to go somewhere. He couldn't stay in Denver. A hazy thought had dogged him all day. He saw himself shooting Hector Beauchamp dead right in his own office. The foggier this saloon grew, the clearer the image became. If he didn't get out of Denver he would get one of those impulses that always got him into trouble.

He poured another shot into his glass. No one had come near him since he came in. Must be smelling pretty fierce. They probably wouldn't let him on a coach until he cleaned up. A bath and a meal were what he needed. He'd rather sit here and drink. Finish the bottle. Hell, you paid for it.

The muffled rattle of another coach came through the pane, and he glanced to see where it had come from. What the hell?

Cage upon cage rode atop the coach. Poultry cages four tiers high. Ross had seen that kind of shipping crate on trains and farm wagons back East, each one carrying a live turkey or chicken. But wait. Those weren't birds in those cages. Those were . . . Cats!

And there were more cages inside the coach! Cats to the

ceiling! Cats in the boot! Through the dust he saw graceful waves of red and yellow lettering on the coach door:

Fort Worth and Jacksboro Shortline

Two cats were squalling. Fort Worth? Wasn't that in
Texas? A crowd of boys appeared in the dust of the coach
as the team of six came to a stop.

Only now did Ross look at the driver's face. If it wasn't
a black man! The driver set the brake and jumped down
from the seat, the tails and cape of his long blue coat flying behind him, affording a glimpse of a side arm holstered butt-forward on his left hip. He coiled a rawhide
whip as he turned to smile at the boys running up from
behind.

Ross left his whiskey on the table and stepped through
a crowd of onlookers on the boardwalk.

"Sorry, boys," the black man was saying. "These cats
is headin' north. No, I ain't got no dogs!" He laughed.
"Don't want none, either." His ambling felt brim shaded a
close-cropped beard and two sharp eyes.

"Where did you get all those cats?" Ross asked.

"Caught 'em in Dallas and Fort Worth. Strays. They
got more cats than they knows what to do with down
there."

"Where are you takin' 'em?"

"Virginia City, Montana Territory. Folks up there got
rats like a dog got fleas." He laughed again.

"How did you find out?" Ross said.

"It was in the newspaper. Virginia City got 'em a telegraph while back and the first telegram they sent says

'Send cats!' God have mercy! Must be rats up there like dust on ol' Brownie!" He slapped the rump of his wheel-horse, raising a cloud of alkali.

"Mice, too," Ross said. "You can get fifteen dollars a head for those cats. Maybe more for the toms."

"You been to Virginia City?" the driver asked, taking a more discriminating look at this stranger.

"I'm the law there. Sheriff R.W. Colby."

The driver narrowed one eye, glanced Ross up and down.

Ross brushed his lapel. "I've been on the trail some time after a road agent."

"Cyrus Rose." He jutted a hand toward Ross. "Call me Cy. When you goin' back to Montana?"

"Directly, I guess."

"Be happy to have you ride with me." He swept his arm toward the high seat overlooking the team. "Be obliged, in fact. I don't know the trail."

"Hey, boy."

Ross and Cyrus Rose looked back at the coach to see a burly red-haired man poking a finger into one of the cages. A pearl gun butt gleamed inside his coat.

"Give me this big ol' tom."

Cyrus put his hands on his hips, casually sweeping the blue coat back. "Sorry, mister. Them cats ain't for free. Fifteen dollars a head."

The redhead sneered. "Like hell." He drew back to strike, smashed the poultry crate open with a forearm and fist.

Ross saw Cyrus square himself with the redhead and put a hand on his Colt revolver. As the redhead reached into the cage, the big tomcat hissed, wrapped both fore-paws around the hand, and sank its teeth into the thumb.

The Colt sprang from Cyrus Rose's holster as the big redhead hollered and slung the tomcat to the ground. The animal hit on all fours and kicked dirt in its first leap for freedom, but the stage driver's Colt sprayed fire and black smoke, rolling the tomcat in a bloody heap.

"You'll pay me for that cat," Cyrus said, covering the man with his Colt.

The redhead clutched his bitten thumb in his left hand and glared at the muzzle of the pistol.

"What's the trouble here?"

Ross looked through the gun smoke to see Heck Beau-champ trotting toward the coach. He felt his muscles tense, yearned for the grip of his Remington.

"This man just bought hisself a dead cat," Cyrus said.

Heck looked at the redhead. "Buck?"

Buck snorted with hatred, whistling his breath through his nostrils like a maddened bull. "The son of a bitch's got mad cats, Heck. That one bit me."

Heck looked at the dead cat on the ground. "Stranger, you can't expect a man to pay for a cat if you shot it dead. What's a man gonna do with a dead cat?"

Ross found his voice, took a big step forward. "Either he pays for it, or you arrest him for tryin' to steal it." He felt his eyes glaring at the lawman.

"Now, who the hell are you?" Heck said.

"Sheriff R.W. Colby. I'm here to escort these cats to Vir-ginia City, Montana."

Looking over his sights at the redheaded Buck, Cyrus could not keep himself from grinning.

"Escort for a load of goddamn cats?" Buck yelled.

"Well, Buck," Heck said, "Montana tends to breed peculiar folks, but they generally mean what they say. Now, you've got a lawman here who can testify you stole a cat if you won't pay for it. The choice is yours. I'd just as soon you paid for it and get it over with."

Buck heaved a sigh that made his lips flap. "Oh, goddamn it, all right, Heck. Goddamn catfreightin' black-assed son of a bitch, anyway." He pushed his bleeding hand into his pants pocket and pulled out a handful of coins. Sorting out three five-dollar pieces, he tossed them onto the dirt at Cyrus's feet.

"Pick 'em up!" Ross ordered. "Pick 'em up and hand 'em over proper."

"Now, that's all right, Sheriff," Cyrus said, resting the hammer on his Colt. "I don't mind stoopin' to pick up my pay." He slid his Colt into the holster and bent at the knees to reach for the coins.

As the coach driver's eyes turned to the ground, Ross saw the redhead reach into his coat for the pearl handle. He brushed his own coattail aside and groped for his Remington.

Beauchamp's big fist snapped upward and slammed into Buck's nose, then opened as it swept down and slapped against his pistol grip.

Ross began to pull, but found Beauchamp's muzzle swinging up on him as Buck hit the ground on his back and Cyrus's coach whip played out behind him in his left hand.

"Easy, men," Heck said. He glanced between them.

Trembling, Ross took his hand off his pistol grip and

pulled his coat over it. He was stunned by the fast draw, enraged and shamed.

Heck put his gun away. "You two headin' for Montana anytime soon?"

Cyrus began coiling the whip. "I got to dope the axles, trade for a fresh team, and get some meat to feed this livestock, but then we'll be gittin' out of here faster than a rooster with socks on."

Heck looked at the Montana sheriff. If eyes could damn a man to hell, he thought . . . Hello, Satan! That was one lawman who didn't like to have a gun pulled on him. "I'll keep Buck locked up until you're on the trail." He glanced at the cats and shook his head. "Good luck."

Fighting an urge to test the nightmare he had dreamed last night, Ross watched the big sheriff lift the redhead to his feet and lead him away from the coach.

"I'd like to get a bath and a change of clothes before we leave," he said after Heck had gone.

Cy nodded. "Like the preacher told me, 'Cleanliness is next to godliness, because that devil's one dirty son of a bitch!'"

THIRTY-ONE

Ross didn't mention it for three days on the trail, and Cyrus Rose, not knowing this sheriff well, avoided stirring him up with a lot of talk. Cy had been teaching the lawman to drive the team, and Ross had the reins in his hands when the subject finally came up.

"Whatever possessed you to shoot that cat?" he asked.

Cy laughed loud above the jingling chains and crunching wheels. "That cat was gone, anyway. Figured I might as well make him talk."

"I didn't hear him say anything."

"Ol' redheaded peckerwood Buck sure did. Cat say, 'Look here, Buck! Brother Cy don't go that route. Brother Cy don't give up nothin' that easy!' "

"Brother Cy sure shoots straight."

The coachman laughed as he whistled his whip through the air and cracked it over the team. "See, you heard that dead cat talk!" The stage approached the top of a long grade. "Don't nobody take something I call mine that easy. If it's worth me havin', it's worth me fightin' for it. That's one thing, Sheriff. Brother Cy ain't afraid of no fight."

Ross shook the reins as the divide passed under the wheels. "That Sheriff Beauchamp sure pulled that gun out quick."

Cy whistled, remembering. "Punched the man in the nose and grabbed his gun before the man hit the ground!" He braced his boot heels on the footboard as the coach rocked down a hill. "Now, that's a lawman!" He glanced at Ross, saw the eyes flashing, and decided to speak no more on the subject. Professional jealousy, he assumed. This R.W. Colby didn't like being beat to the draw.

Two days later, they came down from the Medicine Bows and camped on the North Platte. Cy was cleaning cat cages in the river when he looked up the bank and saw Ross standing on top of the coach, waving a handkerchief, looking out over the vast grasslands of North Park.

"Oh, shut your mouth," Cy said to a cat protesting the

water running across the bottom of the crate. He looked up again and saw Ross kneeling on top of the coach now, holding his Henry repeater, still waving the handkerchief. Curiosity got to him, so he crept up the bank to see what the white man had in mind.

Between the wheels of his coach, Cy spotted a white patch of fur standing above the grass, and focused his eyes on a pronghorn buck approaching cautiously, still a couple of hundred yards away. The crooks of the black horns stood above a set of bulging eyes that seemed fixed on the waving handkerchief. Cy knelt and watched as the creature came nearer. Then the Henry erupted and the antelope dropped from view.

"There's dinner," Ross said, tossing the repeater down to Cy.

"How'd you know he'd come up?"

Ross stepped from the seat to the rim of the front wheel and sprang to the ground. "I hunted 'em when I was in the army at Fort Laramie. One fellow I knew there used to bring 'em up by standin' on his head and wavin' his feet. They're curious devils."

Cy walked with the white man toward the downed pronghorn, anxious to try a fresh antelope steak. "You was in the Union Army?"

"For a while."

"You sound like you come from down South."

"I do. Georgia. It's a long story."

Cy wanted to hear it, but he had just seen where curiosity had gotten the antelope.

"How 'bout you?" Ross said. "How'd a black man from Texas come by his own stagecoach?"

"Bought it from old Boss Rose. I was born a slave in Louisiana. Boss Rose bought me when I was a boy and told me he'd let me buy myself free for a thousand dollars. He paid me a little on his farm there, where I worked, and I made extra money fixin' harnesses and stuff."

Ross was stretching his neck to see the dead antelope in the grass. "If he wanted you to be free, how come he didn't just let you go?"

"I asked him that one day. He said, 'Cyrus, ain't nobody gonna give you nothin' in this ol' world, now you might as well learn how to work for it.' I was free five years before the war."

They came to the carcass of the antelope and stood over it for a moment. Ross pulled his knife from his gun belt scabbard.

Cy knelt and grabbed the rough black horn of the buck, the first he had lain his hands on. "Well, it ain't like a deer, and it ain't like a sheep," he said. "It's somethin' like a goat, I guess." He looked over the sleek coat of the animal. "No, it ain't no goat, either. He just is what he is." He helped Ross roll the animal on its back and held two legs up so Ross could make the cut up the belly.

"You didn't say how you came by the coach," Ross said.

"Ol' Boss Rose had him that stagecoach. Had him a store and a freight line and a farm, too, but I wanted to drive that stagecoach. So I asked him, after I bought myself free, if he'd hire me on to drive it. He said I could earn my way up to it if I tried, and he started me driving a freight wagon. Little buckboard. Well, that was all right, but them mules was slow, and I wanted to sit up high and pop that whip at them horses, you see. So I stayed with it, and kept pesterin' ol' Boss Rose, and after three or four years, he let me try it."

"You must have liked it," Ross said.

"Sheriff, I thought I was God's reason for wheels. When I felt them six horses get up, I knew what I wanted. I bought that stagecoach when the war started and moved it west. Made the run from Fort Worth to the Butterfield Line in Jacksboro twice a week. Did all right, too, but I got tired of driving that same ol' road. I hear there're lots of new roads in Montana and lots of miners headin' up 'em, so here I am."

"With a load of cats," Ross said, groping through the viscera of the dead antelope. "You want these innards to feed 'em?"

"Just the choice pieces. I don't want to ride with no gut eaters." He watched as Ross cut the heart out of the antelope. "You don't eat no chitlins, do you, Sheriff?"

Ross looked up at him and chuckled. "I haven't yet," he said. "But you never know what life will serve up for you next, Brother Cy."

The next day they came over a roll in the prairie to find a mounted Ute warrior waiting near the road. As they passed, the warrior paced them, slowly closing. Ross glanced at his rifle once, but kept his hands away from it. The warrior had a bow case and an arrow quiver slung across his shoulder, but the bow wasn't strung and the Indian merely seemed curious about the strange cargo lashed to the top of the coach.

It wasn't until the warrior veered away and disappeared that Ross noticed the look set on Cy's face. "What's wrong, Brother Cy? Haven't you ever seen an Indian before?"

Cy glared. "I can show you places where Comanche arrows hit this coach. Hell, I can show you where one hit me." He handed the reins to Ross and pulled his trouser leg up over his left calf to reveal a jagged scar. "Iron point stuck in the bone. The doctor in Jacksboro had to get the blacksmith to pull it out with a pair of tongs."

"Comanches bad down there?"

"They sure was during the war. The Union Army pulled out, you see, and the Comanches took back a lot of land they'd been beat out of. Raided Jacksboro so much that half the people left. Didn't hurt my business none, though, because most of the other shortlines out of Fort Worth quit runnin'."

Ross shook the reins and crooked his left wrist to steer the lead horse back into the wallowed-out ruts. "Well, these aren't Comanches up here, they're Northern Utes. As long as we don't go shootin' at 'em, they'll probably let us be."

"I don't want no trouble with 'em," Cy said, sweeping his eyes across the vastness of the park. "Ain't no place to hide out here, and we ain't got that much ammunition."

"We could always stampede the cats over 'em," Ross said. He smiled, then chuckled, the laughter easing for a moment the hollow sickness of Denver in his stomach.

An hour before sundown, they saw the Indians coming. The dust trail in the sky clearly showed their path out of the Park Range.

"Looks like a bunch of 'em," Ross said.

"I'd say twenty or twenty-five," Cy replied. "How far is the next stage stop?"

"It's up on the Muddy. Too far to outrun 'em. We'll just have to take our chances."

As the riders closed on the stage road, Ross handed the reins to Cy and picked up his Henry, resting the butt on his thigh so the barrel would stand in the air as a warning. "Is your shotgun loaded?"

"Always."

The Indians cut across the grasslands and waited on the road in front of the coach.

"You're the coachman," Ross said. "What do we do?"

"Stop. If it comes to shootin', we can aim better standin' still. We can't drive through that many Indians, anyway. Too easy for them to take a horse down." As he approached the warriors, he reached under the seat for his scattergun and let the team slow to a trot. "Be friendly, but don't give 'em nothin'. If they want somethin', make 'em trade."

As the coach rolled up to them, the warriors spread out and engulfed it. Ross noticed that their bows were strung, but none had taken an arrow from a quiver. He pressed his back against the poultry crates and guarded his side of the coach as Cy watched the other.

"I don't know too much about these Utes," Cy said. "But if they're anything like Comanches, I'd say they ain't lookin' for scalps today. They ain't painted much. Their horses, either."

"Maybe they're just curious. We are a strange-lookin' outfit."

The warriors had been circling the coach, speaking freely to one another, and studying the cats. One poked at a cat with the end of his bow. A bunch at the back of the coach burst into a short fit of laughter over some mumbled joke. Ross recognized the rider they had seen earlier in the day, caught his eye, and nodded to him.

The warrior nodded back and said something.

"What?" Ross said, shrugging.

The warrior pointed at the cats, spoke again, made an eating sign, pointed at the men on the coach.

Ross and Cy glanced at each other, grimaced.

The brave smiled, gestured at the cats again, and tossed his head in an inquiring gesture.

"He wants to know what we're gonna do with 'em," Cy said. He handed the reins to Ross and slowly put his shotgun back under the seat. "You watch 'em. I'm gonna try to get along with 'em."

He climbed down from the coach as the Indians gathered on his side. Ross started to complain, but felt more comfortable with all the warriors bunched together, so he let Cy handle it his way.

"Now, there's a big town," Cy said, pointing down the

stagecoach road. Some of the braves looked down the road, but none of them understood. Cy used the same finger he had pointed with to make a line in the dust on the side of his coach.

"What are you doin'?" Ross asked.

"Drawin' Virginia City," he said, finishing the roofline and front door of a cabin. Next to it, he drew another cabin, and behind them, more rooftops and chimneys. He pointed again down the road. One of the braves nodded and spoke to the others.

"Now we're gittin' somewhere," Cy said. Beside the town he made a drawing of a rat: a big rump, two small ears, a pointed nose, a long tapering tail. He looked back at the Indians and they grunted, nodding at him.

Cy pointed at the rat drawing, then pointed at the ground, his eyes bulging. He charged the point of ground, began stomping in circles as the Indian ponies withdrew nervously. Finally he ground his heel in the dirt and grinned at the warriors, swelling with pride.

The Indians chuckled at him, spoke loudly to each other.

Cy picked up his invisible dead rat by the tail, flung it over the coach, and dusted his hands against each other. Suddenly he flinched, his eyes locking onto another point of ground. He charged the spot, stomped it to death. Then he spotted another, pointed at it. Another under an Indian pony. Another between the coach wheels. More rats overhead, underfoot, everywhere. He stomped crazily as the Indians laughed. He tore at his hair, threw his hat, and finally gave out in exhaustion.

But his eyes brightened as he conceived an idea. He

pointed at a cat in a cage, and with his next breath, became the animal himself, hunching over, prowling. He was hunting—taking several quick steps, then crouching, his eyes riveted to the picture of the rat he had drawn on the side of the coach. When he was close enough, he sprang, flinging himself against the side of the coach. He scuffled for a few seconds, then made out like he was eating something. When he stepped away, the Indians could see that his rat drawing had been wiped out.

"Now I got 'em with me," Cy said, looking up at Ross. He gestured toward his coach loaded with cats and beamed with pride. Now he was a coach driver again, bouncing on the seat, cracking his whip over the team, shaking the reins. He spotted something ahead and pointed. He broke character just long enough to point to his drawing of Virginia City, then he was with the coach again, driving into town.

"Whoa!" he said, pulling back the reins.

The Utes found this hilarious, saying, "Whoa," to one another, and mocking Cy's exaggerated motion with the reins.

But Cy was into the next scene, waving at townspeople, shouting voicelessly for them to come out of the houses and stores, showing them his cats. He had to stop somebody who got too close, however, and he held out his hand, pointing at his open palm with a finger of his other hand. He smiled, closed the fist, and stuck it in his pocket. Now he took an invisible crate off the coach and handed it to the customer.

He sold another cat, and another, continued to stuff money into his pocket until his pocket would hold no more.

He filled up both front pockets, both hip pockets, and began stuffing money in his shirt.

Finally he sold the last cat, waved at his customers as they left. He breathed a sigh of exhaustion, fanned himself with his hat. He smacked his lips as he surveyed the street. He spotted something, pointed, and smiled wide.

Swaggering, he strode without moving. He pushed open a pair of double doors, nodded, shook hands, talked, laughed. He took some money out of his pocket and slapped it down. His hand cupped and lifted something. He raised it to his friends. It seared his nostrils when he smelled it, but he threw it down his throat, anyway.

The Indians yelped as Cy's eyes widened and his tongue lolled out. He gripped his throat as he gasped for air. He pounded a fist against his chest, placed a palm gingerly upon his stomach. Finally he squinted, shook his face with a growling kind of moan, and grinned glassy-eyed. He snatched another handful of money from his pocket, slapped it against the bar, and held his glass out for a refill.

The Ute raised their bows and ripped the prairie air with a war whoop that shivered Ross's spine and tightened his grip on the reins. Then something came over him and he reverted to battle. The Rebel yell growled somewhere deep, began to come up with a rattle, breaking into a squeal.

The Indians stared up at him as Brother Cy climbed up to the seat. In the silence, Ross looked around and saw the vast grasslands in spring green. Not a tree in sight, save for the vague darkness of the forests on the distant mountains. The wind whipped a feather on top of a warrior's head.

Cy took the reins. "Do it again, Sheriff. You got 'em!"

Ross stood and raised his Henry overhead. He sucked in an intoxicating breath of sage-scented air and let the Rebel yell tear at his windpipe again. He screamed his defiance at the world; at life, fate, and at the whole damned West.

A chorus of Ute squalls rose to join him and he fell back against the cat cages as Cy cracked his whip between the horses. The warriors rode as escort for a mile, then turned for the Park Range and rode away as if mounted on antelopes.

Cy let his worries go on a breath. "Them Indians know firewater," he shouted over the rattle of the cargo.

Ross nodded, his rifle bouncing on his thighs. He felt as if he were driving a hundred miles an hour back into Virginia City. Cy was saying something else to him, but he wasn't listening. What was he going to do about Sage, about Parkhill, about Heck Beauchamp? Oh, what on earth was he going to do about Julia?

Do I remember holding her? Yes, I do, but it means almost nothing now. I remember her skin, her scent, her vital embrace. Remembering isn't enough. A man who holds just a memory holds less than thin air.

THIRTY-THREE

This might be a good road for you," Ross said. "Virginia City to Butte." They were only a couple of hours from town, passing troops of miners returning on foot to the Alder Gulch diggings.

Cy waved at the men who stopped on the side of the road to stare up at his strange cargo. "I thought the placer mines was playin' out up at Butte."

"Not really," Ross said. "There's still some traffic up that way."

"I've heard good things about Last Chance Gulch," Cy said. "Ain't that the biggest strike in Montana now?"

"The Parkhill Line already runs to Last Chance. Twice a week."

"Then I'll go every three days," Cy said.

Ross shook his head. "You don't want to mess with Parkhill. He's mean, and he's Old South. He wouldn't take well to you competing with him."

"I don't care," Cy said. "The man can't be no meaner than a Comanche."

Ross rode a quarter mile in silence. He caught himself inspecting the telegraph line as they flanked it, as if he were still a Galvanized Yankee charged with keeping it intact. "It's different up here," he finally said. "Parkhill had a franchise on the Last Chance Road. The government did away with the franchises, but he still treats the Last Chance route as his private toll road. He's trouble and everybody knows it. Folks pretty much stay out of his way."

"Well, Sheriff, Brother Cy don't step out of nobody's way—Old South, Northwest, or in between. If the best diggin's is in Last Chance Gulch, that's where I mean to run my line."

"The diggin's are just as good at Butte. Leave Last Chance alone."

"Say!" Cy shouted to a clot of miners taking a break alongside the road. "Where you gentlemen headin'?"

"Last Chance!" they shouted as the coach passed.

"Good luck!" Cy yelled, then turned to grin at Ross as his whip cracked like a rifle shot. "I ain't the kind to let no Parkhill back me down, Sheriff. You ain't, either. Not the way I saw you stand against the lawman in Denver." He laughed. "You got mad right quick when he come up, Sheriff. Brother Cy got a temper, too. I go after what I want. Damn a man who tries to stop me."

"Even if it gets you killed?"

"I ain't afraid of dyin'. I'm afraid of not livin'."

"Ain't that the same thing?"

"I'm talkin' about not livin' while I'm alive. Ain't no Parkhill or nobody else gonna keep me from goin' after what I want long as I'm breathin'."

Ross wasn't big on philosophies, but he found he could grasp this one. What did he want out of life? Julia. She was the only thing he had ever worked or planned for, and now she belonged to somebody else while he rode shotgun for a load of damned cats. He had let Hector Beauchamp stand between him and the only thing that made life worth living. Cy was right. A man could die years before he stopped breathing.

The coach hit a rock in the road and almost lurched Ross over the side. When he clawed back onto the seat he had made up his mind. He was going to do something. He would not let Julia forget him so conveniently. He wasn't afraid of dying. Not now that he had lost everything worth living for. The only thing left in his life was to get Julia back, or die trying.

When they reached town, an instant throng formed behind them and followed, cheering, down Wallace Street.

Ross had sent a wire about the cats to Fritz from Salt Lake City. Apparently, Deputy Green had alerted the town.

"Well, Sheriff," Cy said as he pulled the reins in at the jailhouse. "You got us here, and we only lost one head of livestock. I'm obliged to you."

Ross smiled, shook the coachman's hand, and climbed down to the ground.

"Where did they come from?" Johnson asked, having just lumbered up with his notepad. "Did they come all the way from Texas?"

Cyrus began hawking his cats on the spot, but the sight didn't compare to the show he had put on for the Ute near the Park Range.

"Ask the cat-wrangler," Ross said, turning away. "His name's Cyrus Rose."

"Welcome back, Sheriff!" somebody said.

Ross nodded as he pulled his bag out of the carriage boot. He found Fritz Green standing at the door to the jailhouse. "Howdy, Fritz," he said. "Any trouble?"

"The usual," Fritz said. "A lot of drunks. A few fights. One of 'em was at the Golden Sage."

Ross felt the burden of Sage again. "What happened?"

"One of the girls quit. Said she was movin' to Last Chance. Miss Sage accused her of sneakin' off to meet you in Colorado, and she tore into the poor little thing like a bulldog. I thought I was gonna have to throw her in jail."

Ross entered his office, sighed, and dropped his bag on the floor. He put his rifle on the rack. That did it. This had gone on long enough. He was tired of having his life run by Parkhills and Sages and Beauchamps.

"How'd your trip to Colorado go?" Fritz asked. "I heard

you were goin' to check on some mines, then I heard you were goin' to investigate a stage robbery. Now you come back with a load of cats. What happened?"

"Let's just say the trip was a total loss," Ross said. "Except for the cats." He looked through the window, saw Cy exchanging a caged cat for a pouch of gold dust. Then a shadow covered the glass and Parkhill's face appeared.

"Colby!" the big man said, stepping into the jailhouse. "Did you catch the bandit?" Wink stepped in behind him, his afflicted eye under the calming influence of valley tan.

Ross smirked and plopped down on his desk chair. "Damnedest thing. Turned out it wasn't the same bandit. This was a young fella tryin' to copy our hermit. He wore a white beard made of horsehair. Ain't that the craziest scheme you ever heard tell of?"

Parkhill spit on the floor. "You mean you didn't do me one damn bit of good?"

The way suddenly became clear for Ross, like sunlight bursting through a cloud bank. Sage wasn't going to be happy with him. Hector Beauchamp was likely to murder him. And Julia was either going to hate his guts or love him more than ever. But Ross was ripe for a desperate course. "I wouldn't say the trip was a total loss."

Fritz smirked. Sheriff Colby hadn't made sense to him in months.

"What's that supposed to mean?" Wink said, slurring.

Ross propped his feet on his desk. He could hear laughter outside, and knew Cy had his customers where he wanted them. "Parkhill, I'm at the end of my rope over this Hermit Bandit. What you need to do is hire an expert. You need a detective. And I found one for you down in Denver."

Parkhill angled his eyes to look through the window. He sneered and shook his head. "It's a sorry damn day when a man has to go clean out of the territory to find a decent lawman. Who is this detective you're talkin' about?"

"Name's Hector Beauchamp. He's sheriff there, and a deputy U.S. Marshal. He's the best tracker and investigator in the Rockies. If you really want to catch this Hermit Bandit, I'd try and hire him."

Parkhill looked at Wink. "Ain't it a pity, Wink? Man can't do his own damn job."

Wink belched.

"If I get robbed again, I'll damn sure contact this Beauchamp," Parkhill said. "Hope he's better than you."

"There's just one problem," Ross said. "Beauchamp don't like to leave his wife and baby on any extended trips. So, I suggest you invite the whole family up here. Put 'em up in a nice hotel like a summer vacation. I doubt he'll come without his wife."

Parkhill's indifference showed as he grabbed the door handle. "What the hell are lawmen comin' to, when they won't travel without their wives." He hissed as he opened the door and looked out on the street. "I hope that boy you brought back with them cats ain't plannin' on runnin' that coach to Last Chance Gulch. That's still my road."

"He's been advised of your claim on the road," Ross answered.

"That's all we need is a bunch of free niggras up here runnin' white men out of work. Come on, Wink."

Wink bumped into the edge of the open door on the way out and cussed the carpenter who had hung it there.

When they were gone, Fritz Green went to the door and watched the black man hawk his cats. "Sounds like you had more of a trip than you're lettin' on," he said.

Ross nodded apologetically. "I don't mean to be mysterious about it, Fritz, but it was mostly personal business."

"Well, it would help if you could keep me a little better informed," the deputy said.

Ross stood and picked up his bag. "I'll try to do that. In the meantime, just stay on your toes." He looked out at the crowd milling around Cy. They were bidding on cats by the head now. "I have a feelin' all hell's gonna break loose around here this spring."

THIRTY-FOUR

Hands up, driver!" Ross waved his double-barrel threateningly, saw the shotgun rider reaching for his weapon behind the seat. "Double-aught comin', less'n you git them hands up, boy!"

Reluctantly, the two Parkhill men raised their hands.

"Throw the box down!"

"Ain't hardly nothin' in it, old-timer," the driver said. "You picked the wrong coach to rob."

"Ain't gonna be hardly nothin' left of your head if'n you don't throw it down!" Ross growled. He could tell the driver was right when he lifted one end of the box with one hand and tipped it over the edge of the coach. It didn't matter. He wasn't after gold this time. He just wanted to goad Parkhill into summoning Hector Beauchamp.

"That's all there is," the shotgun rider said. "Just let us go now, and we'll leave you be with it."

"Pick up them reins!" Ross ordered. "Now, git, and don't look back less'n you want to meet the devil!"

The driver reached for the leather, whistled at the team, and started off down the slope.

When they had gone far enough, Ross dragged the box into the trees and picked up the pry bar he had left there. A twist or two popped the latch off, and he threw the lid back to find a mere half dozen pouches of gold dust and some mail. Not much of a haul, but it had served its purpose. He was putting the first pouch in his pocket when he heard the running gear rattle.

They were coming back! Panic roared through him like a fireball. Where in the hell had they turned around? He grabbed the last two pouches as he sprang to his feet and sprinted across the road. He made it just before the team came into view at the top of the pass. He slid behind a clump of sumac and turned to get a glimpse of the coach.

A large patch of bright red paint glistened through the underbrush. That was no Parkhill coach!

"Whoa, team!" the baritone voice sang. "Which way did he go?"

That was Brother Cy's voice! What the hell was he doing on Parkhill's road?

"He dragged the box over here!" the Parkhill driver shouted.

Cy leaped down from the seat. "See if you can pick up his trail. I'll take my lead horse loose and try to chase him down."

Ross's breath burned his throat and his heart throbbed

against his stomach. He craned his neck to read the yellow scroll lettering through the underbrush. What did it say? The Last something. The Last Chance . . .

THE LAST CHANCE EXPRESS

"He left his shotgun!" the Parkhill man yelled.

Ross looked at his empty hands. Damn!

"Son of a bitch! It ain't even loaded!"

A couple of passengers got out of the Last Chance Express and began helping Cy with the lead horse.

"The footprints go across the road!" the Parkhill driver yelled.

Ross turned away and picked a quiet path on the pine needles. He had moments to get to his horse. Then what? He knew Brother Cy. That man would come after him hard. He broke into a sprint as he pulled off the old jacket. He tore the horsehair beard from his face and stuffed it into a sleeve. He could see his horse grazing in the clearing below.

He dropped the suspenders from his shoulders and collapsed as he reached the blanket he had spread on the ground earlier. The boots came off none too quickly and he wriggled out of his oversized pants like a man in an ant bed. He slipped the boots back on and yanked the laces tight, neglecting to tie them, stuffing them into the boot tops. He rolled the blanket sloppily around the fake beard and hermit costume.

He heard Cy's big lead horse coming as he tied the roll on behind the cantle. Glancing across the clearing, he sprang into the saddle, kicked his horse. No time to check for evidence left behind. Brother Cy was almost in sight.

Ross rode recklessly down the slope, weaving among trunks of young pines, bowing his hat brim to whipping branches. His mount would have the advantage in speed over Cy's, but what if Cy could read sign? He had to think of something. And quick.

The glint of water caught his eye below, and Ross remembered the stream. An idea began to form. He charged downward, his mount leaping rocks and dead trees. Yes, it might work. He had maybe two minutes to smooth out the details.

Pulling leather at the stream, he made his horse step in. He rode downstream a few yards. No, better to ride the other way. He turned upstream and flogged the hesitant horse with his boot heels, watching his back trail for signs of Cy.

After charging a hundred yards up the stream, he turned back toward the road. He hadn't ridden thirty seconds when he heard Cy's big draft horse crashing through the forest, and angled across the slope to catch him. His first glimpse revealed Cy riding bareback on the draft horse, reaching for the Colt at his hip as he wheeled.

"Hold it, Brother Cy. It's just me!"

Cy eased up on the hemp reins he had tied. "Sheriff! Where'd you come from?"

"I had him, Cy! Damn it, you came along at the wrong time!"

"What the hell are you talkin' about, Sheriff? How'd you get here so quick?"

"I got a tip on the robbery. Somebody left a note at my

cabin. Didn't credit it much, but decided to follow the coach a little ways just in case, and sure 'nough, I saw the whole thing!"

Cy slid forward on the broad bare back of the horse. "Why didn't you stop him, then?"

"Hell, I didn't want him to shoot nobody. I let him rob the coach, then I started slippin' up on him through the trees. That's when you came over the pass in that big red coach and spooked him. I saw him cross the road just before you came over the rise. I angled across to catch him, heard you ridin', and thought you were him."

"He ain't far ahead," Cy answered. "I was on him just before you caught up to me. I heard him crashin' through the trees this way."

"Come on," Ross said, spurring his mount in front of the draft horse. "Maybe it's not too late."

They galloped downhill, Ross leading the way to the stream, stopping at its edge to study the water.

"Looks like he riled the water ridin' in the creek. Cy, you go downstream and look for him. I'll go upstream. If you don't find anything, meet me back at your coach."

"Yes, sir, Sheriff!" He kicked his lead horse and lumbered away down the creek bed.

By the time Ross and Cy got back to the Last Chance Express, Parkhill's men had abandoned it and gone on to Virginia City. Ross sent Cy on to Last Chance Gulch, then lay tracks in the woods to bolster his story. It was dark when he finally got back to town, and he found Parkhill and Wink waiting for him when he rode down Wallace Street.

"Did you get him?" Parkhill asked, turning convulsively to spit over his shoulder.

"No. He gave me the slip somewhere up a creek."

Parkhill stomped his feet like a five-year-old. "Goddamn, Colby! You had him in sight, on foot, and you still let him get away!"

"He got mounted and got away. I would have had him if Cyrus hadn't come along."

"Who the hell is Cyrus? You mean the colored boy? What the hell was he doin' there, anyway? I thought you warned him about my road."

Ross resisted looking back at his bedroll. He wanted to check it to make sure no white horsehair was sticking out of it, but it was better not to draw attention to it. "It's called competition, Parkhill. You'd better get used to it."

"Used to it, hell. I'll get rid of it. Anyway, don't change the subject. What about this note you got on the robbery?"

"Somebody slipped it under my door."

"Where is it?"

"In a safe place. It's evidence. So's this." He patted the sawed-off shotgun tied to his saddle strings.

"What else did you find?" Parkhill said, his thin eyes searching the horse. "What's in the bedroll?"

"Blankets. Camp gear. What do you think?"

"What did you carry that for?" Wink said, his eyes blinking on every word.

"I was ready to stay on the bandit's trail for days if I had to. But, like I said, he lost me up a creek. I was that close, too." He put this thumb and forefinger almost together in the air.

"Shit," Parkhill muttered. "I doubt you even seen him.

If you can't catch the old bastard with somebody tippin' you off, Colby, you're worthless. I'm gonna bring in that Marshal Beauchamp from Colorado."

Ross shrugged. "If he'll come. He might not want to leave his wife and baby."

"Then I'll tell him to bring 'em, damn it. Anybody's better than you."

Ross frowned. "Look, Parkhill, I want this bandit caught just as bad as you do. That's why I recommended Beauchamp. He's a specialist. In fact, I'll tell you what I'll do. I'll contact him for you. He knows me."

"You sure you can handle it?" Wink drawled.

Parkhill smirked. "All right, Colby, you take care of it. It's the least you could do."

Ross nudged his horse up the street. He had to get to his cabin. Sage was waiting for him. He had to hide the gold, manufacture the note he had told everybody about. Then he had to get rid of Sage and compose a dispatch to Hector Beauchamp. What might happen after that was anybody's guess.

Parkhill put his hand on Wink's shoulder when the sheriff had ridden out of earshot. "Wink, how would you like to get stinkin' drunk tonight?"

"Planned on it."

"I want you to hit every saloon in town. Spread the word that the Vigilance Committee has met and issued a warning."

"About what?"

"About the Last Chance Express. Anybody caught ridin' it's liable to get lynched right alongside its black-assed driver."

THIRTY-FIVE

Heck had been so considerate on this trip, Julia thought. Stopping a full three days in Salt Lake City for her and Fay to rest. She kept telling him that it wasn't really necessary; that she could travel just as hard as he could and keep going till they got there. She thought of telling him about how she had ridden and marched with the 11th Ohio Cavalry from Leavenworth to Laramie, but talk of her days with Ross always made Heck grind his teeth.

Those memories were hers to cherish in silence. Of course, when Fay got older, she was going to tell her all about her daddy, and Heck would just have to take it. She wasn't going to pretend Ross had never existed.

It was raining and the coach was stuffy with the canvas covers rolled down over the windows. They flapped a little when the coach rocked, letting in a gust or two of fresh air with the raindrops. The mud had slowed them down some, but they would make it to Virginia City soon. Heck had insisted it was going to be as much of a holiday as a job. Julia couldn't remember the last time she had had a holiday.

She wondered if this would be a regular part of life with Heck. She hoped so. Denver could get dreary at times, and she tended to get mired in memories. She liked seeing new places. In fact, it was she who had talked Heck into coming here.

"I don't really know this R.W. Colby," Heck had said. "Met him one day in town with a load of cats headin' for

Virginia City. He was a little testy that day. I'm surprised he wants me in his territory."

"I say we should go," Julia had answered. "It doesn't sound dangerous. The bandit's an old man. Anyway, it's going to get hot here, and I'd rather stay cool in the mountains."

The whip cracked outside, and the driver forced a rattling yell up his throat. Julia nudged Heck, who was snoring on her shoulder. "We're almost there," she said.

Heck pulled himself up on the coach seat, curled his handlebar mustache. "Already?"

Julia rolled the canvas. She didn't care if she got wet, she was going to have a look at this town. The first thing she caught sight of was a collection of ramshackle huts with floodwaters coursing among them. My Lord, she thought, say this isn't the town. But the people looked different, dressed in unfamiliar garb. One wore a hat like a dish. Why, if they weren't Chinese.

A row of log cabins swept by, then a frame building. Now a brick store. This was more like it. The coach sloshed mud as it rounded a curve and rolled between rows of two-stories. She saw a laundry, a drug emporium, a photographic gallery. The team slowed as it passed the newspaper office, then stopped near the portico of a large hotel.

The driver jumped down and threw a board between the coach and the hotel steps. Heck squeezed past Julia and jumped out into the mud. He steadied her as she climbed out with her child and walked along the board to the shelter of the portico.

"I'll get your bags," the driver said. "You folks can stay dry."

It was chilly here. Crisp and clean-smelling. She had never been this high, and she noticed a peculiar shortness of breath. It made her slightly dizzy.

"You Hector Beauchamp?"

Julia turned with a start. She knew that voice. Looking into the darkness of the hotel lobby, she saw a big man emerging. Camp Marshall came rushing back at her through the months. She retreated a step, felt Heck's strong arm against the small of her back, held Fay closer to her breast. She hoped her daughter wouldn't wake now to see the likes of Sergeant Parkhill.

"I am," Heck said. "Who are you?"

"Name's Parkhill. It's my stage line the old bandit's been robbin'." As he reached for Heck's hand, his eyes angled to Julia and locked on her.

"This is my wife, Julia Beauchamp," Heck said.

"*Your* wife?" He glared at her. "Lady, I know you. Camp Marshall. You was that boy's wife." He snapped his fingers, trying to remember the name. "You washed uniforms."

"That boy's dead," Heck said, sounding perturbed. "The Cheyenne got him. She's Mrs. Beauchamp now."

Julia felt faint. Her mind had long since pushed thoughts of Parkhill aside. But seeing the big conspirator here now made Ross come alive again.

"Howdy, Sheriff Beauchamp."

My God! She was hearing his voice! Blinking as she gaped into the lobby, she saw the familiar cut of his shoulders materialize from the shadows. She was seeing him now, in this bearded lawman! That was his face in the mass of whiskers! His swagger! Her dead husband's hand reached for her live husband's, and they shook.

"Mrs. Beauchamp," he said, looking right at her, glowering, touching his hat brim.

That was him! Her knees trembled. Ross's eyes cut angrily from her, to Heck, to the baby. She felt Heck's arm tighten around her waist as she saw the ghostly-white woman appear at Ross's side. A grin parted the black beard and Ross's arm took in the corseted waistline. He pulled the woman hard against him, and the woman put a familiar hand on his shoulder, smiling eerily for no reason.

"I'd like y'all to meet a lady friend of mine," Ross said. "This is Sage. Sage, this is Heck Beauchamp, and his wife . . . Julia."

She glanced at the red lips against the pale cheeks, the full bosom heaving from the fancy low-cut gown.

"Miss Sage," she heard Heck saying vaguely, as if far down a canyon. Parkhill's suspicious glare rushed by her as if she were back in the coach and rolling past him. She felt Fay squirm, tried to lock her elbows under Ross's daughter. She glimpsed the side of Heck's face, a dark curl against that woman's bare neck, a brown stain at the corner of Parkhill's mouth.

It all began to whirl, and her knees buckled under her. Ross's black beard grew like a powder blast, engulfing everything in its ugly darkness as she felt herself falling.

THIRTY-SIX

The smug grin dropped from Ross's face when he saw Julia's eyes flutter, and he scrambled to catch her as she fell. She reeled back, protecting the baby even as she collapsed, and Ross caught her inches from the floor on one knee, bumping Sage aside.

"Take the baby," he said to Beauchamp, turning Julia's limp body in his arms. He remembered carrying her across the threshold on their honeymoon. It was different then, her body full of life and clinging to him. Now it was all he could do to keep her from slipping through his arms.

He carried her up the stairs and lay her on the bed in her room, though he didn't want to let go of her. Looking over her peaceful face, he felt a wonderful moment of hope. Then Sage pressed herself against him.

"Miss Sage," Heck said, shoving Fay into Sage's arms. The baby had slept through it all, but was opening her eyes now, shedding nameless dreams.

Sage held the child awkwardly as Heck sat on the bed and patted Julia's face.

"Here," Sage said, abruptly handing the little girl to Ross. "I'll get some water."

Fay looked at Ross and began to cry, trying to push herself away from him. Somehow, he knew to cradle her upright, to give her arms and legs freedom, to let her see her mother lying on the bed. He pulled the soft white blanket back from Fay's face, bounced her in his arms, felt her tiny hand grasp his finger.

"There, now, honey," he said, speaking smooth as silk. Her large round eyes looked up at him and he smiled. She had a lot of her mother in her, and he liked her, in spite of who her father was.

Julia gasped and looked at the ceiling. Ross carried Fay around the side of the bed and let her crawl to her mother. Julia looked at him, astonished.

"You all right, honey?" Heck said, patting her hand.

"We better go," Ross said. "We can talk in my office later, Beauchamp."

Sage put a glass of water on the table beside the bed and followed Ross from the room. At the door, he stopped and looked back, and he stared at Julia for a moment, suddenly consumed with guilt. Then Sage closed the door in his face.

"Who is she?" Sage said, starting down the stairs.

Ross stopped, looked down on Parkhill in the lobby. "What do you mean?"

"She fainted dead away when she saw you."

"Well, it ain't my fault. Maybe it was Parkhill. He's a damn sight uglier than me. She said she knew him from Camp Marshall."

"She was looking at you," Sage insisted, her eyes contradicting the perpetual smile.

"For God's sake," Ross said, taking her by the arm and leading her down the stairs. "If you ain't jealous of your own shadow. Now, I've got business to take care of over at the jailhouse, so I'll see you later."

"You'd better," Sage warned.

Parkhill joined Ross at the front door of the hotel, where Sage turned for her side of town.

"Is he comin' down?" Parkhill asked.

"As soon as she's feelin' better." He stepped into the rain and ran across the street, feeling the muddy water in his boots. As he reached the opposite boardwalk and turned for the jailhouse, he heard Parkhill splashing behind him.

"I knew this was a bad idea," Parkhill said, "him packin' women and babies with him."

"Once they're settled in, they won't slow him down any." He stomped his feet a couple of times and entered the jailhouse.

"You don't know that woman," Parkhill said, coming in behind the sheriff. "If I'd have known he was married to her, I'd have never hired him."

"What difference does it make," Ross said, feeling irritated, "as long as he gets the job done?"

"She got me thrown in the stockade back at Camp Marshall. Her and the damn Georgia cracker son of a bitch she was married to then. They was spyin' on us old Rebels for the camp commander. Little Yankee-lovin' slut."

Ross's fist clenched quick as a snakebite. He saw Parkhill's square jaw as a target, the big man turning toward him now from the door. His arm was coming around before he could think, the knuckles landing solid against the bulge of tobacco.

The thick neck wrenched to the right, the well-packed quid flying out and bouncing off the jailhouse wall. Parkhill fell against the door he had just shut. His eyes bulged with surprise and reflex anger as his fists came up.

Ross felt the burst of realization, but it was too late now. He tried to follow his first punch with a left. But Parkhill stopped the amateurish roundhouse blow with his right forearm and buried his left fist in the sheriff's stomach. Lunging, he rammed Ross with a shoulder, staggering him back to his desk.

Ross rolled, gasping for breath as he got the desk between himself and Parkhill. He read the warning in Parkhill's eyes as he scrambled around the desk to keep out of the big man's reach.

"What the hell did you hit me for?" Parkhill growled, grabbing across the piece of furniture.

"You shouldn't talk about ladies with that kind of language," he groaned, putting his hand over his stomach.

Parkhill put one knee on the desk. "And you shouldn't try stoppin' me." He sprang onto the desk and leaped like a panther, scattering paperwork.

Ross grabbed the bill of Parkhill's Confederate cavalry cap and pulled down with everything he had, rolling the big man headlong to the floor. Then he backed off, his mind racing. He could run, but Parkhill was mad enough now to shoot him in the back. He could shoot, but he hadn't resorted to murder yet. Or he could stand up and take a whipping.

As Parkhill found his footing, he came after the sheriff, who he found waiting, fists up, in the middle of the office. Parkhill stepped right into a punch that made his ears ring a little, but otherwise failed to phase him. He snapped a meaty row of knuckles into Ross's eye and felt the instant satisfaction as the sheriff backpedaled into a jail cell door.

Ross kept from falling by holding on to the iron grating.

When Parkhill approached, he grabbed the iron bars with both hands, lifted his feet from the floor, and kicked, two-footed, like a mule. One boot heel missed, but the other landed squarely on Parkhill's nose.

Ross saw the blood gushing as the Alabaman staggered back, and knew he'd better follow with something quick. He rushed Parkhill, threw a punch. But the big man blocked it, and Ross found himself stumbling senselessly back again. He felt the grating hit him in the head and the floor hit him in the rear.

The next thing he knew, he was rising, his shirt cutting into his armpits. He felt the blow to his stomach take his wind. He bit his tongue when the fist caught him under the jaw. He tried to fight back, but could see only blurs.

Panic surged through his limbs. He brought a knee up violently and heard a muffled groan. The floor jolted him again, and he knew he was in for it now. He blinked and saw Parkhill doubled over, just a few feet away. He heard a growl like that of a surly grizzly bear and saw Parkhill's glare appear under the bill of his cavalry cap.

A line of gray light appeared behind Parkhill as the big man took one step and kicked hard. Ross moved his head fast, and the boot only clipped his ear. The line of light widened, and Ross focused on it long enough to make out Heck Beauchamp reaching for a side arm.

"Hold it, Parkhill!" the deputy marshal yelled, cocking his revolver. "Back up, or I'll shoot."

"This ain't got nothin' to do with you, Beauchamp."

"I said back up!" Heck ordered.

Ross rolled to all fours and pulled himself up on the grating.

"What's this all about, Colby? You want to make an arrest?"

"Like the man said," Ross answered, his tongue swelling in his mouth, "it ain't none of your business."

Heck looked the two men over and glanced around the office. "Somethin's goin' on here," he said. "I don't like this. You don't act much like a lawman to me, Colby, brawlin' like this."

Ross staggered toward the door. "Don't you Colorado boys ever enjoy a good ol' fight?" He opened the door, stepped outside, and stuck his head under the eave of the jailhouse roof, letting the cold rainwater pour onto his head.

"Not to the point of stovin' each other's heads in." Heck put his revolver in the holster. "Parkhill, do you have an office in town?"

"Over the Break o' Day Saloon."

"Wait for me there, and we'll talk about this bandit you've had trouble with. I want to talk to Colby first."

Ross heard Parkhill's big boots scuffing the floor as he left for his saloon.

"You up to some detective talk?" Beauchamp asked.

Ross shook the water from his hair and squinted at the deputy marshal through his one open eye. "Yeah, I guess so. How's . . ." He knew better than to call her by her first name, but he couldn't bear to call her Mrs. Beauchamp again. "How's the lady?"

"Well enough to run me out of the room. And a damn sight better off than you."

Ross raked his wet hair back over his head and took a good look at Beauchamp. His knuckles were still throbbing where they had connected with Parkhill's jaw. He had waited a long time to take a jab at the big man, and it had felt good. He almost wanted to laugh.

He caught himself smiling as something peculiar occurred to him. He was beginning to like Heck Beauchamp. The man had a way about him. Ross might have wanted to kill him, but damned if he didn't see things he admired in Julia's new husband.

"I hope we'll all be a damn sight better off when this thing is over," Ross said. "But I'm afraid it may not come that easy. Somebody's liable to get hurt."

THIRTY-SEVEN

Deputy green will show you," Ross said. "I've got things to do in town today."

Fritz looked up from the shotgun he was cleaning. This was the first he had heard of it. What had happened to Sheriff Colby's promise to keep him better informed?

"Well, let's get goin'," Heck replied. "I want to see where every robbery happened." He jammed his hat down and walked outside.

"Go borrow a horse at the livery, Fritz," Ross ordered.

Fritz put his tools down and grabbed his hat on the way out. Parkhill followed. Ross stood in the jailhouse door and waited for them to mount.

Stepping down from the boardwalk, Heck walked around the back of Parkhill's mount and paused to pull a long stroke down the horse's tail with both hands. He got two long hairs for his trouble and wound them around three fingers as he moved to his own horse. As he passed between the two horses, he noticed a brown streak of something, glistening in the sunlight on the rump of Parkhill's mount.

Turning away, he put the hairs in his pocket and began tightening his cinch. He didn't hold much respect for a man who would spit on his own horse. The horse didn't know better, but the man ought to.

Ross stood at the door until they had mounted and ridden away. He saw Fritz come out of the livery on a little black. He watched them ride down Wallace Street and drop from sight on the road out of town. He waited a minute, then crossed the street and walked down to the Virginia City Hotel. He breezed through the lobby without speaking to the desk clerk, went upstairs, and knocked on Julia's door.

The door opened and Julia's face peered out. She looked so beautiful that he could hardly breathe. Finally she opened the door wider and let him come in.

When he heard the door click, he turned, and blinked in reflex to the open palm rushing at his cheek. He drew a startled breath when he felt the sting, and started to speak.

Julia put her finger over her lips and glanced at the child on the bed. "Shh! Fay's asleep."

"Then what the hell did you slap me for?" he whispered hoarsely.

She gasped. "I don't believe your gall! I know all about you, Ross Caldwell, alias R.W. Colby. I had a long talk with the newspaper reporter, Miss Mary Johnson. She told me all about your scandalous affair with that woman!"

Ross nodded for a moment and shuffled his feet. "Well, I'll tell you one thing. I dang sure ain't *married* to her!" he hissed.

Her eyes sparkled. "If you hadn't deserted me, I wouldn't have gotten married. I thought you were dead!"

"I never deserted you."

"You certain never came back!"

"I did!" he said, taking her arm. "But it was too late."

She yanked her arm away. "I thought I knew you."

He took a deep breath. "Listen. Give me a chance, and I'll explain. That's all I ask."

She crossed her arms and tapped her foot. "Oh, I wouldn't miss hearing it for the world."

He paused to group his thoughts. He wasn't sure he could explain it all to himself anymore, much less to Julia. Start at the beginning, he told himself. One step at a time. "We were at the mouth of the Crazy Woman. Parkhill's men were gonna kill me, and Captain Jones found out about it, so he ordered me to desert and wait in Virginia City. He was gonna tell you where to find me, but the Indians got him."

"Why didn't you come back?" she said, sneering, her hands propped on her hips.

"There was no telegraph here then. By the time I heard about the massacre and got to a telegraph station, you had already left Fort Marshall. I wired back home, but they hadn't heard a thing from you." He paused, narrowed his eyes, and came to something that had nagged him through the seasons without her. "Why didn't you bother to tell the folks back home what had happened? Didn't you care?"

"Oh, hush!" she gasped. "I cared so much I couldn't

bear to think of you dead. I refused to admit it, and I refused to write home until I had proof."

Ross glanced around the room in frustration. "What proof? I'm not dead, damn it. What proof did you have?"

"I hired Heck to search for you, and he found some Indians who said they had killed you. They had your weapons."

"What weapons?"

"The Spencer carbine, and the Remington revolver with your initials on it."

Ross's eyes shifted. "Why, that sorry liar. He never found diddly, Julia. I never lost my weapons." He pulled his old Remington from his holster. "Here's my pistol, right here, and there's my initials. I bet you described my guns to him before he went lookin', didn't you?"

Julia stared at the gun grip as if it were a lost memory come alive. "Yes," she said. "But I never thought he'd . . . I mean, I never dreamed."

"He lied through his teeth. He wanted you for his own. That explains everything."

She was confused now, angry at them both. They were liars. All men were liars. "It doesn't explain your relationship with that woman."

Ross dropped the Remington into his holster and raised his hands. "She tricked me," he said. "She trapped me just as sure as Beauchamp trapped you."

"How?"

"She's blackmailin' me. She won't hardly let me out of her sight. She gets jealous enough to fight every time some other woman speaks to me. She's off her rocker, Julia."

"She's blackmailing you?" Julia said. This had the smell

of another lie, and her face showed her suspicion. "What's she going to do? Tell everybody who you really are? Turn you in to the army as a deserter?"

"No, she doesn't even know my real name."

"What, then? What has she got to blackmail you with?"

Ross's mouth moved, but he couldn't find words to spit out. "I can't tell you that," he finally said.

"Why not?" she blurted.

"I can't tell you why not, either." He stood in front of her, gesturing uncertainly, knowing she didn't believe him.

She reached for the doorknob. "Then get out. I don't want to look at you anymore."

"But you don't understand."

"That's the honest truth." She opened the door and stood glaring at him. "I don't understand how I could have been so wrong about you."

"But what are we gonna do?" he whispered.

"About what?"

"About us. About Beauchamp. Are you just gonna forget we ever married?"

"I don't know, Ross. God help me, I don't know what to do. Just get out!"

A stranger passed by the open door and glanced at the couple. Ross stepped out, turned back, started to say something. But the door closed in his face. He stood there for some time, considered bursting back in. Then he heard her sobbing through the door, and he turned toward the stairs.

THIRTY-EIGHT

Heck shifted in the chair, making it squeak something awful. He looked over his shoulder to see if he had wakened Julia or Fay. They both slept like angels. He turned back to the window overlooking Wallace Street and stared down at the town.

"Don't make a damn bit of sense," he muttered to himself, wrapping three white horsehairs around his fingers.

The light of early dawn revealed three drunken miners staggering arm in arm down the street, singing. Heck turned his ear to the thin pane of glass, trying to make out the words. Ah, yes, "Gypsy Davy." He found their place in the song and sang along under his breath.

> "Yes, I've forsaken my house and home
> To go with the Gypsy Davy,
> And I'll forsake my husband dear
> But not my blue-eyed baby,
> Not my blue-eyed babe."

"Why are you singing that?" Julia said.

Heck flinched so hard that the horsehairs cut into his tough fingers. "Dang, woman," he said. She had a way of sneaking silently up on a body. "You give me a start."

"Why were you singing that song?" She stood at his shoulder and looked down on the street.

"Just singin' along with the boys," he said, pointing at

the trio winding its way down the street. "Didn't mean to wake you up." She had been downright cantankerous ever since he brought her to this town, and he was trying not to rile her.

"You've been muttering to yourself for an hour," Julia said. "What's wrong?"

Maybe this would help, he thought. She liked to talk about investigations. "Oh, it's this Hermit Bandit case. It don't make no sense." He turned his chair toward her.

"What doesn't make sense?" she said, sitting on the edge of the bed.

"For starters, this Sheriff R.W. Colby. He's the one called me in on this investigation for Parkhill, right? Well, you'd think he'd want to help me solve it, but so far he hasn't lifted a finger. Every time I go to talkin' about the bandit, he changes the subject around to Parkhill. Keeps tellin' me Parkhill is a vigilante boss in these parts, suspected of killin' the last sheriff and lynchin' a boy who was tryin' to compete with him on the road to Last Chance."

"Knowing Parkhill, I wouldn't doubt it," Julia said. "He was jailed at Camp Marshall for conspiring to lead the Knights of the Golden Circle in a mutiny."

Heck grunted and nodded. "Him and Colby don't get on good at all. I caught 'em in the jailhouse the other day tryin' to break each other's necks. Parkhill says at first he suspected Colby of bein' in on the stagecoach robberies."

"What?" Julia said. "Why?"

"Because on the days of the first three robberies, Colby was either fishin', huntin', or prospectin', but he never brought back no fish, game, or gold. Then Parkhill found out he'd been carryin' on with this woman, Sage, over at that hurdy-gurdy house. Parkhill figures that's a good enough alibi, but I ain't so sure."

"Why not?"

Heck rubbed the stubble on his chin. "During the first four robberies, the only person who could place Colby was this Miss Sage. So I went to talk to her. Well, she got to carryin' on about how much of a good fella Sheriff Colby is and how her and him have been collectin' money for charity since last year. She showed me the books she keeps for the relief fund, and I'll tell you, Julia, either this is the biggest gold strike since forty-nine or this town is made up of the most generous people God ever put on earth."

"Why do you say that?"

"Sage's books says they've spread thousands of dollars of gold dust around this town to poor folks. I asked a few saloons how much they give to the relief fund a month, and they told me, and I sort of averaged it out and multiplied by the number of saloons and other places in town, and it don't even come close!"

"What does that prove?"

"Could mean Sheriff Colby and Miss Sage have got another source of gold somewhere."

Julia began to see Heck's logic. "You think he's in on the robberies?"

Heck shrugged innocently. "He hates Parkhill's guts. Wouldn't surprise me to find out he's been playin' Robin Hood. And there's somethin' else, too. What was Colby doin' in Denver when I met him the first time? He says he went there to escort that load of cats to Virginia City. But the colored fella, Cyrus Rose, says that ain't so, that he just happened to meet Colby there by accident. Deputy Green says Colby went to Denver to check on some mines he owns down there. Parkhill says Colby went to Denver to investigate a stagecoach robbery by the Hermit Bandit."

"I don't remember any such robbery," Julia said.

"That's because there wasn't one. But Colby told Parkhill they caught that bandit in Colorado and he was a young fella tryin' to pin it on the Hermit Bandit by wearin' a fake beard made out of white horsehairs."

Julia was worried, but she had to smile. Ross could come up with some wild notions. "That's preposterous."

"I ain't so sure," Heck said. "I went out to all the robbery sites. Studied 'em pretty good. I found these in three different places." He unwound the long white hairs from his fingers and gave them to Julia.

She studied them in the light a few seconds. "From the hermit's beard?"

"Them ain't human hairs, Julia. I reckon I ought to know a horsehair when I see one. I've pulled enough of 'em between my fingers."

Julia's heart broke into a gallop. What had that damn fool husband of hers done? "But if Sheriff Colby's the Hermit Bandit, why would he invite an investigator to come up here and catch him?"

"That's the thing that don't make sense." Heck got up and paced the floor in his stocking feet. "He had some other reason for wantin' me here, and I can't figure it out. It must be right in front of my nose, but I can't smell it."

Julia squirmed on the edge of the bed. She knew that look in Heck's eye. He was close. He would figure it out in a day or two if not sooner. "Are you going to arrest him?"

"Not yet. All I have is a lot of talk and three horsehairs. Juries like solid proof."

Julia winced at the mention of juries. "What are you going to do?"

"I've got two angles left. The first is this scattergun Parkhill's men found after the last robbery. If I can link that scattergun someway to Colby, I'll have him."

"What's the other angle?"

"If I can't get anything on the scattergun, I'm gonna go ahead and search Colby's cabin. If he's the bandit, or if he's in with the bandit, I'll find somethin' there. I got a gut feelin' about this Colby, Julia. When a man starts spreadin' a bunch of different stories around, that means you can't believe any of 'em. I think he's lawman and outlaw rolled into one. And he's something else, too, but dang it . . ." He scuffed his foot across an elkskin throw rug. "I just can't quite figure out what it is."

THIRTY-NINE

Julia didn't know what she would say when she got to Ross's cabin. There was no clear way ahead of her; no obviously right thing to do. Everything had been twisted. Her first husband was a stagecoach robber. Her second husband was a liar. She, herself, was a fool. Maybe it wasn't her fault that she had been made a fool, but she was a fool nonetheless.

She tried to behave as if she were out for a stroll as she passed the prospectors and townspeople on Cover Street.

She just vaguely knew where Ross's cabin stood, from Mary Johnson's offhand descriptions and from seeing Ross walk that way from the jailhouse.

When she found a likely cabin near the gulch, she stopped across the street from it, looked both ways, pretended to scrape mud from her shoes as she waited for the street to clear. She walked calmly to the cabin, trying not to attract attention.

She rapped on the door. Ross opened it. He gasped with surprise to see her there, coughing on a cloud of cigar smoke.

"May I come in?" she said, trying to sound civil.

"Of course." He stepped aside and held the door open for her.

"When did you start smoking cigars?" she asked, fanning the sharp odor away from her nose. She felt very awkward here.

"A couple of winters back, in Boulder," he replied, snuffing the ember from the end of his stogie.

They stood in silence for a moment, looking at each other.

"Where's the baby?" Ross said.

"I left her with Mary Johnson."

Ross nodded and shuffled his feet. "Do you want to sit down?" he said, gesturing toward his finest chair.

"No."

"What did you come here for? A couple of days ago you said you never wanted to look at me again."

Julia held her tears back. She had changed her mind about that. She had wanted only to look at him ever since she figured out how Sage had blackmailed him, and how

Heck had tricked her into marriage. They had both been played for fools. It still made her sick to her stomach to think of Ross with that other woman, but she knew he had to feel the same way about her and Heck.

"I came to warn you," she said.

"About what?"

"Heck traced the hermit's sawed-off shotgun back to Sheriff Jackson. He knows it had to come from the jail-house or this cabin. He knows you're the bandit, Ross."

"What? That's the craziest nonsense I ever heard," Ross said. "I'm the law here. I couldn't have . . ."

"Oh, hush, Ross. Heck found white horsehairs from your fake beard at the robbery sites. He's going to search your cabin for more evidence in the morning."

Ross stared at her, put his palms on his face, and rubbed his eyes.

"Why, Ross? Why did you steal all that gold?"

He let his arms fall to his sides. "I didn't keep any of it. I spread it around to the poor folks. That damned Parkhill was runnin' things around here with his secret societies just like he did back at Camp Marshall. I had to do somethin'. I couldn't let him get away with it again. If it hadn't been for him and his Knights of the Golden Circle, I'd have stayed at the Crazy Woman, and I'd be dead and happy right now."

"It's not that bad," Julia said, taking a step toward him.

"It's worse. Every minute I've spent away from you, I've just been diggin' a deeper hole for myself. Now you're married to another man who's gonna arrest me tomorrow. How could it possibly be worse?"

Julia bowed her head to hide a tear she felt on the verge

of escape. "There's only one thing to do," she said. It had just come to her, like a reflex.

"Run like a scalded cat?"

"Yes." When she nodded, the tear came rolling down her cheek. "We'll leave tonight. No, we'll leave immediately." The tears came like a flood current, and she stepped closer to Ross. "I'll get Fay and we'll leave right now."

Ross was stunned, and he wanted badly to go along with her plan, but it wasn't that simple. "I didn't mean you and Fay," he said, taking her uncertainly by the arms. "I meant me. If you and Fay come, Beauchamp will come after us."

"We'll cross the border into Canada," she said, sobbing.

"That won't stop him. He'll go anywhere to get his wife and daughter back."

Julia inhaled a tear, tasted it on her tongue, held her breath as if her windpipe had closed. She wiped the blur of tears away from her eyes and gawked at Ross. "*His* daughter? My God, don't you know?"

Ross glanced around the cabin. "Know what?"

"Fay is *your* child. I didn't even meet Heck until after she was born." She saw wonder and astonishment sweep his face. He might have been a boy looking at a pony or a sinner finding salvation. His eyes moistened. His mouth dropped open, then grinned.

"Mine?" he said. He could see it now. Yes, she did look like him. Or at least like he used to look before the beard and the hard living.

"I thought you knew," Julia said.

Ross wrapped his arms around her, almost crushing the breath from her in his excitement. His whole body crawled with fire. "All right, then," he said. "We'll all go together.

The three of us." He released her, took her shoulders in his hands, slipped one rough palm behind her neck. He kissed her, and everything that had happened since Camp Marshall sank into oblivion.

Suddenly Julia wrenched free and pushed herself away. "I hate you for sleeping with that woman, Ross Caldwell."

"I couldn't help that," he said, dazed by the sudden turn. "She would have turned me in if I hadn't done it."

"I hate it."

He remembered Denver. "Well, I'm not real happy about you marryin' another man, either."

She rushed at him again, wrapping her arms around him. "I swear I never loved Hector Beauchamp. I'm sorry, Ross. I've made mistakes."

Ross felt his anger subsiding, an avalanche of cares falling away. "If you've made one mistake, God knows I've made a hundred." He closed his eyes and held her, only now remembering how good it felt.

"How will we get away?" she said, her voice muffled against his vest. "We'll have to leave right now. But . . . How?"

"It's Tuesday, ain't it?"

"Yes," she said, looking up at him. "What has that got to do with it?"

"The Last Chance Express runs today. We can head north and keep goin' to Canada."

"Can we get a seat this late?"

He chuckled. "On the Last Chance Express? We'll get a seat. Cy hasn't had a single passenger since Parkhill started spreadin' rumors about lynchin' anybody who rode his stage. It's the best chance we've got to get out of town unnoticed and get a jump on Beauchamp."

Julia stepped away from him and pulled her shawl back up around her shoulders. "I'll get Fay and meet you on the coach," she said. She grabbed him by the face and placed a quick kiss on his lips before she turned to the door. Cracking it, she looked out to see if the way was clear. She stepped out, but before she closed him inside, she turned back to him. "If we can get through this, Ross, we can get through anything." She saw him smile, and she closed the door.

She wanted to sprint back to Mary Johnson's boarding-house room to get Fay, but she restricted herself to a brisk walk. Everything was all right, she insisted. Heck wouldn't miss her till after dark. He wouldn't figure out what had happened until morning. By then it would be too late for him to catch up. It would serve him right. He had been only slightly less devious than that woman—that Sage.

As she approached the corner of Wallace Street, an arm reached from an alley and pulled her in. She gasped, stumbled between the buildings off balance, and caught herself against a wall. Wheeling, she found the emotionless stare of the infamous Miss Sage piercing her.

"What were you doing in there with my man?" Sage said.

Julia felt her heart throb fear. Mary Johnson had mentioned the beating Sage had dealt her for dancing with Ross. She steeled herself, refusing to look intimidated. "None of your business. Get out of my way."

She started out of the alley, thinking how odd it was that

this strange woman should smile so serenely at her as she left. She looked toward the street, but saw the sky rush down, felt the hair pulling at the back of her head. She hit the ground, saw a swirl of Sage's skirt over her, and felt the pointed shoe kick her ribs.

Fury flooded into her and she scrambled like a wild animal, lashing out as she found her footing. But Sage somehow reached through her flailing arms, grabbed another handful of hair, and pulled Julia off her feet. She had done this before. She knew tricks. Julia kicked at Sage's shins and caught a glimpse of the doll-like face still smiling eerily down at her.

Suddenly her hand bumped something cool on the ground. As she kicked, her fingers groped for it, wrapped around it. She hurled it, and saw it—a green bottle— bounce off the pale brow.

Julia found a split second to leap, rising to face the dance hall mistress. She stomped on a toe, slapped away a hand reaching for her hair, and punched Sage hard in the ribs. She heard herself growling as she leaned into the woman and shoved, sending Sage tripping backward. She pursued, feeling an advantage, sensing time slipping away. When Sage stopped, she was there, ready, balanced, and certain. She aimed her hard fist at a painted eye and saw Sage buckle under the blow.

Sage sat against the wall, stunned. She put her hand over her eye. Looking up, she saw Julia dusting herself off, walking toward the street. Then Julia stopped, turned toward her, and glared down at her with hatred.

"He never was your man, you *dog,*" Julia said. Then she was gone.

FORTY

Cy dragged open the sagging double doors of the barn he had rented and let the evening sunlight swell inside. He was determined to stay on schedule, even if he didn't have any passengers. He had managed to keep running by charging low rates for freight, but even that trade had dwindled since Parkhill began spreading rumors.

He turned back into the barn to inspect his coach, and the sight made him hold a breath. What a vehicle. He cleaned it thoroughly after every run, and it gleamed now in the rays of sunlight slanting through the open doors. Behind six strong horses, it all but came to life.

Reality clouded the bright paint a little as he went about his inspection of wheels and running gear. If he didn't start attracting some passengers soon, he would be out of business in Virginia City. He had stretched the cat profits about as far as they would go. He hated to let Parkhill get the better of him, but what could he do? He was thinking now of moving his operation to Idaho before it was too late.

He walked around the back of the coach and inspected the luggage boot. The leather was getting a little cracked around the edges. It would have to be replaced before too long. He sighed as he ran his fingers over a pitted iron wagon tire. They were expensive up here. He had never planned on it being easy, but making a living in Montana Territory had proved harder than he had thought.

As he walked past the right-hand passenger door, something unfamiliar caught his eye, leaping from the intricate paint job like a wounded squirrel or something. There, scrawled across his beautiful yellow lettering, painted sloppily in bloodred paint, were three numbers obliterating the word "Chance" on the side of his coach:

3-7-77

"What in the hell," he groaned. He stood back, put his hands on his hips, and stared at the eyesore. "Don't even make no damn sense."

"Brother Cyrus!" The voice rang clearly through the barn.

Cy walked to the front of the coach to find Sheriff Colby standing across the tongue. "Howdy, Sheriff. Say, what do you know about arithmetic?" He gestured toward the right side of the coach.

"Enough to know I'm gonna make it worth your while to run me to Last Chance Gulch." He tossed a pouch of gold dust to the stage driver. "I'll take every seat if we can leave as soon as you get the horses hitched."

Cyrus caught the heavy leather pouch and forgot all about the nonsensical formula on the side of his coach. "You got yourself a deal, Sheriff."

"Bring your wheelhorses, and I'll start hitchin' 'em while you get the others."

Cyrus left at a trot for his corral, and Ross pulled the doors halfway shut for some privacy. As he lay out the rigging, he kept a watch for Julia and Fay between the weathered boards of the barn doors.

His family came into view finally as Cy was fixing the blinders on his lead horse. Ross felt a current of joy mix with his desperation, and he glanced both ways for trouble through the cracks in the doors. He saw a few people in the street, but nobody seemed to notice anything out of the ordinary.

When she walked in front of the barn doors, Ross pulled Julia in and took Fay from her arms. He couldn't keep himself from chuckling as he bounced his daughter in his arms and grinned at his wife. "How come you named her Fay?" he asked.

Julia shrugged. "I liked the way it sounded with Caldwell. Her middle name's Alice."

"My mother's name," Ross said.

Julia nodded, smiling.

It suddenly occurred to Ross that Julia had a few hairs out of place, and a lot of dirt ground into her clothing. "What happened to you? Did you fall down somewhere?"

"With a little help from your Miss Sage." Her face hardened as she brushed a wispy hair back from Fay's eyes.

Ross looked up to find Cy staring back at him from the front of the team. He handed his daughter back to Julia and coughed a warning. "Tell me about it later," he said to his wife. "Right now I think you better get in the coach."

"Afternoon, Mrs. Beauchamp," Cy said, catching Julia's eye. "What brings you around this side of town?"

"She's coming with me," Ross said.

Cy watched Ross as he helped the mother and child in through the left-hand door of the coach. "Is Heck comin', too?"

"No," Ross said. "Trust me, Cy. It's best that you don't ask a whole lot of questions on this one."

The stage driver shrugged, and checked the reins running through the rings in the horse collars. "All right. We'll be headin' out directly, Sheriff. Better git yourself in."

Ross climbed in with Julia and sat across from her so he could look at his wife and child. "Where do you reckon we'll end up?" he said. He heard Cy climbing up to the driver's seat.

"It doesn't matter," Julia answered. She felt the team take the slack out of the rigging.

"We don't have much of a choice, do we?"

Julia smiled. "No, we don't. Like the sign says. This is the Last Chance Express."

Light began to fill the coach as it pulled out of the barn.

"We'd better let the shades down till we get out of town," Ross said.

Julia untied the straps around the rolls of canvas on the right side of the coach and let them fall over the windows. Ross turned to the left side and watched the open barn door pass by him as he yanked the slipknot out of the strap holding the canvas up. The roll fell, unwinding, covering the window to the outside world.

Only a glimpse of the street made it to Ross's eyes as the coach cleared the barn door, but with it came the face of Sage. The perfect curls had burst into wads of fluff. The paint had been smeared around one swollen eye. But the born smile, still hinting false serenity, passed by the window just as the canvas darkened the interior of the coach.

Ross slid away from the window, as if from a nightmare, and heard the whip crack as the coach made the turn into the street.

"Did she see us?" Julia asked.

"I don't know."

"What if she followed me here?"

Cyrus was putting on his usual show outside, cracking pistol shots with the whip, hollering at the team.

"Don't worry," Ross said. "She won't tell Heck. She's in it too deep herself now." He moved to Julia's seat, sat beside her, and peeked through the gap between the canvas and the edge of the window. He saw Sage standing in the street, watching the coach pull out of town. He chuckled.

"What could you possibly find amusing?" Julia said.

"You must have used her head for a mop," Ross replied. "She looks like somethin' Brother Cy's cats dragged in."

FORTY-ONE

She couldn't think of a way to hurt him enough. This was nothing. This would probably just get him kicked out of the territory. Even if he got sent to prison, he would get out someday. She thought about telling Parkhill, but then it would be over too quick, and R.W. would just be dead. She needed to think of something that would torture him through the years.

"Well," she said. "Aren't you going to do something?"

Heck looked down on Wallace Street from his hotel window. "You're sure you saw 'em both in the coach?"

"Yes, I've told you, I'm sure. It was them. They were together. They had the baby with them. Are you going after them or not?"

Heck nodded, looked at the sky. "I'll catch 'em before dusk." He took his gun belt from the bedpost and strapped it around his hips.

"Who is she to him, anyway?" Sage said, leaning casually back against the dresser.

Heck jammed his hat down on his head. "She used to be married to him, till he ran out on her."

Sage nodded vaguely. Now he's running out on me, too, she thought, but he won't get far. She wasn't going to let him have that woman, or the baby, or his freedom. That would hurt him, but it was still not enough. She had to think of something more.

"Here's what I want you to do," Heck said, putting his hand on the doorknob. "Go to the sheriff's cabin and pull up the floorboards where he's been hidin' the fake beard and the gold and all. I'll have Deputy Green meet you there to collect the evidence. He'll arrest you and put you in your own custody, then he'll follow me on the road to Last Chance and help me bring Colby in."

Sage nodded and left through the door Heck held open for her. She walked with him down the stairs and through the hotel lobby, quite aware that they were being stared at.

Heck stopped her before he turned for the livery stable. "You're lucky you turned yourself in, Miss Sage. I was plannin' on arrestin' you and Colby both tomorrow. I'll put in a good word for you with the judge."

She walked away unimpressed. All she could think of was hitting R.W. Colby where it hurt. She would have done anything for him. She would have fought off every woman in town, catered to his every desire, lied for him with her dying breath. But he had proven no more worthy than any other man she had ever made the mistake of claiming.

Still, it was different with R.W. He had been kind to her. He had never hit her, or cussed her, or ridiculed her. In a strange way, it made her hate him more than she had hated all the others put together. After that woman came to town, he had brushed her aside like an insect.

Oh, that woman's words had echoed around her since the moment they were spoken: "He never was your man, you *dog*."

She knew how to hurt most men. If they were gamblers, you traded some ruffian a few pleasures for breaking a few fingers. If they were swindlers, you went for the face. Nobody trusted a scar or a broken nose. But how did you hurt a gentleman sheriff? How could you make it stay with him as long as he lived?

She found herself at the cabin, opening the door, walking in. She could smell him. She remembered every moment they had shared here. Looking back, she realized that he had been one step from bolting the whole time. She had been a fool to think she could hold on to him, though she had tried every way she knew.

"He never was your man . . ."

She lifted one end of the heavy table and swung it

aside. Kneeling, she caught the edge of the loose board with her fingernails and flipped it over, revealing the bedroll below the floor. She picked it up, dropped it on the table.

She was getting ready to untie the rope around the bedroll when a glint in the light from the window caught her eye. He had left his lawman's trappings in a pile on the chair. Leg irons, handcuffs, jailhouse keys, and his shiny sheriff's badge. She remembered fogging the badge with her breath, polishing it with a lacy cuff.

". . . you *dog* . . ."

The hemp rope around the bedroll was a new one, and its stiff bristles pricked at her tender fingers like thorns. She unwound it from the blanket, slipped the noose off, and spread the blanket roll across the table, revealing the evidence. She leaned over the hermit costume, clutched it in her hands. She settled facedown on the table, her cheek against the fake beard, her breast upon a half dozen pouches of gold. She had made him put the outfit on one night, almost laughing at the way he looked in it.

And where was he now? She pushed herself away from the table, taking the rope in her hand as she stepped back. How did you hurt a man who risked his life to rob money for poor people? What was his weakness?

She slipped the noose of the rope around her wrist and drew it tight. Something he had said one night spoke to her, as if he were floating above her.

"I never wanted to drag you into this. I don't want any-body gettin' hurt on account of me. I couldn't live with that."

She looked up for the voice, saw the log rafters overhead. Now, that might work. She saw his soft spot now: his conscience. Poor tortured soul. It would destroy him. She would have to do it right, though. No backing out. No second thoughts. And she would have to do it now, before Fritz Green got here.

She stepped over the hole in the floor to snatch the handcuffs from the chair. Glancing through the small window, she saw no sign of Deputy Green coming, but knew she might have no more than a minute to pull it off. She snapped the cuffs around one wrist and climbed onto the table.

She took the noose from her wrist, pulled one end of the rope over a rafter spanning the hole in the cabin floor. She tied a knot and left the noose dangling six feet above the floor. She climbed down from the table to move it a foot away from the hole in the floor. She wasn't going to leave herself a way out. She might change her mind, try to step back up on the table. But now it would be too far away.

"He never was your man, you *dog*."

She hissed at the echo. "Go to hell," she said, wishing she had said it when Julia was standing over her.

Glancing through the window one last time, she still saw no sign of Deputy Green. She put her knee on the table, climbed back on. She was glad it was built sturdy. She pulled the noose toward her, stepped to the very corner of the table. She had to lean out over thin air to get the loop around her neck.

Groping blindly behind her back, she closed the open

ring of the cuffs around her free wrist. Now everything was set. She looked at the sheriff's star gleaming in the sunlight.

"I'm so sorry," she said aloud. "But you deserve it." Closing her eyes, she stepped off of the table and felt the stiff bristles rake her tender skin.

FORTY-TWO

We're comin' up on Bear Pass," Ross said, looking ahead through the window as the coach slowed. "This is where I robbed Parkhill the first time."

"Hush," Julia said, covering Fay's ears. "Don't talk about it anymore. You don't know what your daughter will remember."

"Sorry," he said. "I won't bring it up again. We can put it all behind us now."

They stared at each other as the team fell to a walk up the steep grade. Fay reached for Ross's hat and he handed it to her, chuckling as she bit the brim.

Suddenly Cyrus shouted something from the driver's seat and cracked his whip. Ross sensed a shadow filling the window and turned to see a man opening the right-hand door of the coach as it jerked to a stop.

"Colby!" Wink shouted, waving his revolver as he stepped into the coach. "What in the hell are you doin' here?"

"What is this?" Ross demanded.

"Is Colby in there?" Parkhill said, riding up next to the coach to look inside.

"And a woman!" Wink said. "That marshal's wife. Her baby, too."

Ross ignored the gun and backed Wink out of the coach. He found three Parkhill men holding guns on Cyrus, Cyrus with his hands in the air.

"What are you doin' in there with Beauchamp's wife?" Parkhill said.

"What are you doin' here wavin' guns at this coach?" Ross demanded.

"Park, you didn't say nothin' about no passengers," one of the men complained. "Especially not no women and babies."

"Shut up!" Parkhill shouted. "If they can't read the sign, that's their own damn fault."

"What sign?" Ross said.

"The numbers," Wink replied, closing the coach door to show Ross. "Painted 'em on there myself."

Ross turned to see the bloodred numerals marring Cy's fine paint job.

"You the dumb-ass who wrote that?" Cy said from the driver's seat. "Hell, boy, don't you know you can't take away seven from three? That's less'n zero."

"Don't you call me boy," Wink said.

He angled his pistol toward Cy, and Ross lunged, punching Wink hard in the jaw. As he reached for his own revolver, he heard Cy shout at the team, saw Parkhill groping for a weapon. One of the Parkhill men fired, spooking the team and the saddle horses. The coach jerked forward.

"Ross!" Julia shouted. "Get in!"

Ross swung his Remington up as he heard a whip whistling. The leather cut Parkhill's horse behind the ears and the animal twisted in terror, wrenching the big man from the saddle. Ross jumped onto the iron step as the coach began to roll over the pass.

Cy screamed bloody murder and shook the reins. Splinters flew from new bullet holes. Ross fired at one of the gunmen as he passed, saw a shoulder take the impact. The whip cracked again and the coach rocked dizzily down the grade.

"Git 'em!" Parkhill yelled, springing from the ground as his horse bolted back toward Virginia City. "Mount up, Wink!" His voice grew weaker as the Last Chance Express rattled away.

Ross looked back and saw Parkhill pulling the wounded man from his saddle as Wink led a horse from the trees. "Stay low!" he said to Julia, and began scrambling to the driver's seat as the coach bucked over a rock. He heard Fay start to wail.

The team hit the bottom of the grade at a full gallop, slamming the coach down on its running gear as it started up the next slope.

"Why didn't you tell me about the numbers?" Ross shouted at Cy, clawing his way to the seat.

"Didn't know they meant nothin'." Cy cracked the whip at the team and looked over his shoulder.

"You want me to explain it to you now?"

"I saw the rope."

Ross looked up the road, trying to wish the coach faster. "What are the chances of us out-runnin' 'em?"

"Up this mountain? We better plan on out-shootin' 'em."
He whistled through his teeth. "That baby sure got some
good lungs."

Looking back, Ross saw the four riders coming. He had
four rounds left in his Remington, and no time to pack new
loads or fix percussion caps. His Henry rifle was in his office at the jailhouse. A lot of good it did there. Cy had six
loads in his revolver and two in the shotgun. That made
twelve rounds. Every third shot would have to count, and
from the top of a teetering stagecoach.

Ross waited for them to pull within range, but when
he raised his revolver, they split into pairs and took to
the trees. He could only catch glimpses of them between the
pines. "They're gonna try to get in front of us!" he yelled.

The coach lumbered out of the coulee and began to pick
up speed through a level park. The way was flat, but it
snaked around big trees, throwing the vehicle onto two
wheels as Cy lashed the team harder.

"They're gonna catch us!" Cy shouted. "Just don't let
'em get their hands on the team!"

Ross hunkered down on the seat, catching flashes of
horseflesh among the trees over his pistol sights. One of
Parkhill's gunmen made a dodge for the team, but swerved
back off the road when Ross fired. A blast from behind
glanced off an iron strap and sang over Cy's shoulder. Ross
wheeled and fired back, but Wink was already angling for
cover. Another man burst from the timber for the right side
of the coach. Ross missed with his first shot, saw the man's
hat fly away with the second, and watched him ride blindly
into a low tree limb.

Cy's revolver pealed, and Ross turned to see him fire a

second shot under his left arm, the puff of black smoke falling instantly behind.

"Save your loads!" Ross ordered, but he wasted his last in driving Wink away from the team.

As he reached for the shotgun, Ross felt a heavy thud against the coach and saw Parkhill's horse pass the team with an empty saddle.

"Ross!"

It was Julia's voice, a muffled scream from inside the coach. He looked over the right edge to see Parkhill riding the iron step, aiming a pistol into the coach.

"Give it up!" the big man ordered.

Ross saw the hammer drawn back on the Colt, like an ear of an angry outlaw horse, and knew he would risk his wife and child if he tried something. "Whoa, Cy!" he shouted. "They got us. Parkhill's got Julia!"

"Damn!" Cy said, his lips twisting in frustration, his eyes cutting desperately back and forth. Fay's voice fell off with the speed of the coach and faded as Cy drew rein on the team and stopped between two towering pines.

Parkhill's laughter roared. "It hit me about the time I hit the ground back there!" he shouted, looking up at the driver's seat as he jumped down from the step. "She called you Ross. You're Ross Caldwell, you son of a bitch!"

"So I am," Ross said. "What of it?" Nervously he watched Wink move in on the left side of the coach, the third gunman taking a position in front of the team.

"Wink, what we got here is a couple of Yankee-lovers."

"Two white niggers and a black one," Wink said, his eye flickering like a moth's wing.

Parkhill waved his Colt. "Get out, Mrs. Caldwell, or Mrs. Beauchamp, or whoever the hell you are."

Julia stepped to the door. "Don't you hurt my baby," she warned.

"Wait a minute, Parkhill," Ross said, climbing down from the seat. He hit the ground and raised his hands. "I'll make you a deal if you'll let everybody go but me."

Parkhill bellowed with laughter. "You ain't got much left to deal with!"

"Yes, I do," Ross said, glancing at Julia. "You let Cy drive Julia and the baby out of here alive, give 'em a good head start, and I'll tell you who the Hermit Bandit is."

Parkhill's tobacco-stained teeth disappeared as the smile changed to a frown. "You know?"

"Yes," Ross said. "And I'll tell you, if you'll let the coach go on to Last Chance. It'll never come back, and you can have your road to yourself again."

Parkhill chuckled. "Wink, get that niggra's guns and keep him guarded. Charlie, give me your rope and watch these two."

Ross put his arm around Julia and felt her trembling. "What about my deal?" he said.

Parkhill put his pistol in his holster, took the rope from Charlie, and looked up. He searched beyond the top of the coach, beyond Cy, and spotted a good tree limb over the stage, jutting from a huge trunk. "Caldwell, you sorry Yankee-lovin' Georgia cracker. You can take your deal and go to hell. When this coach pulls out from under that black buck and leaves him kickin', you'll tell me who the bandit is."

"Like hell I will," Ross said. "You hurt anybody here

and I won't tell you a damn thing." He had felt this way before. The day he was ordered to march into his first battle. The day he stepped into the prison yard at Camp Douglas. The day he saw Heck Beauchamp embrace Julia. But today it was worse. The rotten dread in his stomach just kept growing, pushing out all the hope he had taken north from Virginia City.

"You'll tell me anything I want to know," Parkhill said, stepping up on the wheel of the stage, the coiled rope in his hand. "I don't think you want to see me hang any white people."

FORTY-THREE

Heck saw the riderless horse trotting toward him and reined his mount back to a lope. The loose animal tried to get around him, but he cut in front of it and caught a rein.

"Somebody's madder'n hell at you," he said, habitually looking the animal over for evidence. It took him only seconds to find the streak of brown tobacco juice on the horse's right hip. "And his name is Parkhill." He pulled the new Winchester Yellow Boy rifle from the boot of the empty saddle. "Don't mind if I borrow this, do you?"

Ross Caldwell's wild claims came back to Heck as he spurred his horse to a full gallop northward. If Parkhill really was a vigilante bent on keeping control of this road, the Last Chance Express would be a tempting target, Cy Rose would be a likely victim, and Julia would be in the wrong place at the wrong time right about now.

In a strange way, he felt a small measure of relief. He had been wondering what he would do when he caught up with the stage. Would he shoot Caldwell for resisting arrest? Would Caldwell shoot him? Julia was likely to shoot him, for all he knew. But now he suddenly had a new viewpoint. He was coming to rescue Julia, instead of riding to catch her and her felonious husband.

When he came over Bear Pass, his horse almost jumped sideways out from under him before he saw the wounded man in the road.

"What happened?" he asked, but the poor bastard didn't have enough life in him to answer. The stream of blood running from the dying man's shoulder was only about four feet long, trickling steadily down the steep grade into the coulee. He had been shot just a few minutes ago.

Charging into the coulee, Heck checked the breech of the Winchester and found a live round ready. He hit the bottom of the grade, slacked his horsehair reins, and spurred his mount up the rough trace carved in the opposite bank. His horse was heaving when he came out of the coulee, traveling slow enough that Heck could read the tracks, the coach skidding with speed around a curve, reeling to the left, riding on two wheels.

He passed a horse standing in the road, saw a dead man lying nearby, shot in the head. Parkhill's men were taking the worst of it so far, Caldwell and Rose shooting to kill.

He came to a straight length of road in a level park and

spotted the bright red coach at the other end. "There she is," he said to himself, reining his horse back to a walk. His eyes found Julia first. Then they saw Ross beside her, both of them under guard of a gunman. A second gun barrel pointed up at the coach driver.

Heck reined his horse off the road and continued to approach at a walk along the tree line. His left hand gripped the reins with the forestock of the Winchester, his right filled the steel loop of the lever. Lifting, his eyes made out the chiseled frame of Parkhill standing on top of the coach. Then he saw the rope, hanging slack from a tree limb over the stage. The neck he saw in the noose was Cyrus Rose's, the stage driver's hands tied behind his back.

"Oh, my word," Heck mumbled to himself, turning his mount broadside, cocking the Winchester. He could hear Parkhill's booming voice:

"Come on, boy! Tell 'em to git up!" The big vigilante knocked Cyrus down on the seat with an overhand blow, lifted him back up with the rope. "Start them horses, or I will!"

Over the iron sights of the Winchester, Heck found the gunman guarding Julia and Ross. A long shot, offhand, on a heaving horse. He used a few seconds finding the rhythm of the horse's breathing, then began pulling the trigger as he watched the irons drift from the gunman's hat to his gun belt.

The shot made every man, woman, child, and animal on the road flinch, and spun to the ground the man guarding Ross and Julia. Fay burst out in a squall as the dead man hit the ground.

Through the blur of his own blood, Cy saw Parkhill

look south, and seized the moment. He threw himself down on the seat and kicked the big man in the midsection with both feet, bowling him off the stage. He felt the team start and rolled from the seat, groping for the reins with the hands tied behind his back. He felt the leather under one finger, but the rope tightened around his neck, pulled him away.

"Whoa," he started to say, but the noose choked it short. The coach drove under him as he stumbled over it, grasping for a way out. He felt the rear luggage rail under his heels, knew the next step would be on air. He leaned back on the rope, tried vainly to draw a breath. The last thing he saw before the whirling fogginess covered him was Heck Beauchamp charging down the road.

FORTY-FOUR

Ross had shoved Julia toward the trees and was about to make a dodge for the dead man's revolver when he saw Cyrus swing like a pendulum from the back of the moving coach. Wink was lifting Parkhill to his feet, firing wildly. A bullet cut through the fleshy part of Ross's thigh, feeling as though a fisherman had set a big hook there with a hard jerk. He hobbled, holding his breath for some reason, and braced himself to catch Cy.

He had to dodge the black man's flailing knees as he caught him around the thighs and lifted. It wasn't enough. He could hear Cy choking. Gunshots and hoofbeats were coming from down the road, and still Ross had not looked to see who the rescuer was. He hooked an arm under one of Cy's legs, lifted Cy to his shoulders. He made stirrups of his hands and felt Cy standing in them. He heard a gasp and knew the stage driver was getting air.

He looked for Julia, saw her shielding the baby behind a tree, Fay still screaming with terror. He watched the stagecoach roll down the road, Parkhill and Wink retreating behind it. For the first time, he felt the cross fire. The muzzle blasts appeared in front of him like raindrops splattering in dust. Directly behind him, he heard the rapid fire of a rifle, the growing rumble of hooves.

He felt a bullet slap the leather of Cy's boot top between his arm and Cy's leg. Dirt flew around him as the horse planted and slid. The animal came around, protecting him. He looked up and saw Heck Beauchamp holding the brass-bellied Winchester and the horsehair reins in his left hand. The right hand held a long, tarnished blade.

Heck drew the knife back for a swipe at the lynch rope, but a horrible flinch shook him and blood erupted from his vest. He dropped the rifle and reins, but as he fell, he made the swipe at the rope over Cy's head.

The three men fell in a pile, and Ross kicked his way out from under Cyrus and Heck. He grabbed each man by the collar as he stood, and dragged them toward the trees. Cy helped by pushing himself along with his legs, but Heck Beauchamp was limp.

"Oh, my God," Julia said, taking the blanket from Fay and pressing it against Heck's chest wound.

Ross drew the revolver from Beauchamp's holster,

pulled his legs in behind the tree, and looked up the road. He saw the Last Chance Express disappear around a bend, but caught no glimpse of Parkhill or Wink.

"You gonna make it, Cy?" he said, looking back at the stage driver.

"Yeah," Cy groaned, nodding, his back against the tree.

He looked at Julia and found her ear over Beauchamp's mouth, trying to listen over the baby's yelling.

"He says to hold out," Julia said. "Hold out because Fritz will be coming."

Ross looked at the revolver in his hand. "Julia, untie Cy's hands for him. Then watch the road south. Let me know when you see Fritz."

A bullet splintered tree bark, and Ross fired back at a puff of smoke across the road. He saw Wink dive behind a tree and wasted another round. He had four shots left in Heck's revolver, then he would have to use time reloading. He looked at the road to see the Winchester lying on the ground. No telling how many rounds it had, the way Beauchamp had been firing as he charged. The dead man in the road still held a pistol, but Ross didn't know how many live rounds it contained, either.

"Sheriff," Cy said hoarsely, rubbing his swollen neck. "If Fritz don't get here in time, I just want to thank you for keepin' me from hangin'."

"Don't mention it," Ross said, scooting to the other side of the tree to watch for an attack.

Cy started chuckling, his laughter coming out like a wheeze.

Ross looked back at the sorry-looking group he was protecting. Sorry-looking except for Fay and Julia. The two of them were beautiful, and Fay had stopped crying now that the gunfire had let up. He saw Beauchamp's eyes looking alertly from side to side. "Cy, what the hell is so damned funny?"

"The things that cross a man's mind," Cy whispered. "All the time I was hangin' there, sittin' on your shoulders, I just kept hopin' nobody was gonna shoot you in the head. Then I thought, it don't matter, 'cause if they do, I'll hang, anyway."

"That's interesting, Brother Cy, but shut up and keep your eyes open, will you?"

"Can't shut 'em," Cy said. "Thought they was gonna pop out of my head."

Ross heard Heck muttering.

"What's he sayin', Julia?"

"He said to stall them. Give Deputy Green more time to get here."

"How?"

"Talk to them."

"What am I supposed to say to 'em?"

"I don't know," Julia snapped. "Think of something."

Ross sighed. He heard someone scampering, caught a glimpse of Wink, and fired a wild shot. Three rounds left. Julia was right. He had to stall. "Parkhill!" he shouted.

Silence held the mountains except for the rattle of Heck Beauchamp's breathing.

"Parkhill, what about our deal?" Ross yelled. "I can still tell you who the bandit is." He looked back and saw Beauchamp smiling.

"Who?" Parkhill yelled from up the road.

Ross had them both located now. "You ain't gonna believe it when I tell you."

"You're probably right, Caldwell. Try me, anyway."

"It's your right-hand man."

Some aspen leaves rustled faintly on a breeze that came through the park.

"Wink?" Parkhill said.

"That's right," Ross answered.

Parkhill's laughter came bounding down the road like a boulder. "Wink, I'd kill a son of a bitch for talkin' about me like that!"

Ross saw Wink's shadow on the road alongside the shadow of a tree trunk.

"Ross," Julia whispered, "I see Fritz."

"Where?"

"Around the bend in the road. He's already off his horse and sneaking up through the trees."

Ross sensed Wink getting ready to cross the road. "Well, I can't stall any longer," he said. "They keep movin' in. I'm gonna try somethin' else." He held the hammer of Heck's Colt back and rotated the cylinder two chambers, to the last live cartridge, leaving the hammer cocked.

The moment he saw Wink spring out into the road, he leaped from cover and fired. He missed, as he had figured he would. He never had been much good with a handgun. Wink was firing back, but Ross stood his ground and pulled the trigger again and again, letting the firing pin fall on the spent rounds. He stood stupidly for a second, as if he couldn't figure out what had happened. Wink slid to a stop in the road. Ross made a dodge for the Winchester rifle, but the cross fire drove him back to cover.

Fay started crying again when Ross slid to safety.

"What are you doing?" Julia growled. "You almost got killed!"

Ross shushed her and glanced down the road. "Come on, Fritz," he muttered, spinning the cylinder to a live round.

"Park!" Wink's voice said. "I think they're out of shells!"

"Like hell we are," Ross shouted. "We've got plenty of damn shells."

The cruel laughter rolled down the stagecoach road again. "He's lyin'," Parkhill yelled. "Go ahead and move in, Wink. Take 'em alive."

Ross put the barrel of the revolver in his hand and held the butt toward Cyrus. "Brother Cy, how would you like to have the honor of blowin' Parkhill's head off?"

"I'm a little stiff in the neck," Cy said.

"You're still a better shot than I am."

Cy came alive like a miracle cure in a medicine show. He took the pistol, pulled his feet under him, and got ready to spring from his crouch.

"What are you going to do?" Julia asked. "Who's going to get the other one?"

"Fritz, I hope," Ross said. He cupped his hands around his mouth. "Parkhill!" he shouted. "I'm comin' out in the road. Don't shoot. I want to make a deal."

"What are you doing?" Julia hissed.

"Relax, honey," Ross said. "We've got 'em hoodwinked."

"Honey?" Cy said to himself. He hoped he would live to hear an explanation to all of this.

"All right, step out where we can see you," Parkhill said.

Ross looked at Cy. "Don't shoot until somebody else does."

Cy nodded.

"Ross," Julia whispered. She was bouncing Fay on her shoulder, crouching over Heck. "Be careful."

He saw the fear in her eyes and smiled. "Comin' out!" he shouted, raising his hands. He ambled toward the Winchester, looking both ways down the road. For a moment, he seemed to be alone. Then Wink stepped from cover, aiming a revolver at Ross from the hip. Ross looked the other way, saw Parkhill approaching along the tree line. When he glanced back at Wink, he caught a glimpse of Fritz taking position behind a fallen log.

"You don't have much to deal with," Parkhill said, grinning.

"We've still got our knives," Ross said, "and it'll get dark pretty quick. We'll fight to the last man unless you meet our conditions."

Parkhill laughed, and Wink echoed.

"Just out of curiosity, Caldwell, what conditions are you talkin' about?"

Damn it, Fritz, shoot, Ross thought. What are you waiting for? "Let the woman and baby go. Give 'em a horse and a good start north. Then the rest of us will surrender."

"So she can tell everybody what happened here?" Parkhill said. "I don't give a damn about the baby. I'll leave it in the coach. But that little Yankee-lovin' bitch is gonna disappear with the rest of you." Parkhill raised his pistol, looked over its sights. "I'm gonna enjoy the hell out of this."

Ross stuck his hands higher in the air. Fritz needed something. A signal. "For God's sake!" he yelled out of the side of his mouth, trying to make his voice carry in Fritz's direction. "Don't shoot me in cold blood! I'm unarmed!"

He heard the cadence of the slug slamming into Wink's back, followed by the powder blast that had sent it, followed by the first of a dying line of echoes. He was lunging toward the Winchester when Parkhill's shot shattered his shin, wrenching him to the ground. As he crawled on his stomach toward the rifle, he saw Cy jump from cover and fire, catching Parkhill high in the chest.

The big man dropped his pistol and staggered backward three steps before regaining his balance. "Goddamn you, boy," he said, pressing his palm over the wound. He walked deliberately to his Colt and stooped to pick it up.

"Don't, Parkhill," Ross said, levering a live round into the chamber of the Winchester. "You're whipped." He twisted his body a little getting the rifle to his shoulder, sending a streak of pain down his wounded leg.

"Kiss my ass," Parkhill said, rising to his full height, the Colt in his hand. "I've been shot worse than this." He cocked the pistol, angling it upward.

As Ross pulled the Winchester's trigger, he could see the pistol bucking in Cy's hand, and almost felt Fritz's bullet hurling over his shoulder. Parkhill fired a shot into the dirt as the triple load of lead picked him up and slammed him lifeless to the ground.

Julia released a belated scream and sprinted into the road with Fay to fall sobbing on Ross.

"I'm all right," Ross said. "Just a busted leg is all." He rolled over and embraced his wife, her tears joining Fay's in a cascade onto his chest. "Hush, Julia," he said, smearing a tear across her cheek. "You're upsetting my daughter." He looked beyond them to see Cy Rose and Fritz Green looking down on him.

"You gonna live?" Cy said.

"Yeah," Ross answered. "Drag me out of this road before somethin' runs me over. I want to see how Beauchamp is doin'."

Fritz took the Winchester and set it aside. The deputy and the stage driver pulled Ross behind the tree and lay him beside Beauchamp.

"You've got a lot of explainin' to do," Fritz said.

"I know, Fritz," Ross answered. He rolled to his side to look over Beauchamp's face. "I didn't want it to turn out like this, Beauchamp. I'll admit I didn't know how it was gonna turn out, but I never wanted this."

Heck nodded feebly and looked up at Fritz. "Deputy Green," he said, mustering all the strength he had to speak. The mountains were quiet now, except for the baby sobbing, and they could hear him. "Did you speak to Miss Sage?"

Fritz sighed. "Didn't get a chance to. She hung herself in Sheriff Colby's cabin."

Ross stared up at Fritz, then looked at Julia and Cy. When he turned his eyes back to Heck, he saw the deputy marshal give him a curious grin.

"But I found the disguise," Fritz continued. "I'm afraid I'm gonna have to put you under arrest for robbin' stage-coaches, R.W."

Heck laughed, bringing on a weak cough. "You already

killed the Hermit Bandit, Fritz. It was Wink. He was stealin' from his own boss. Ain't that a hoot?"

"How do you know?" Fritz said, stooping over the dying man.

"He was in it with Sage. It was Sage's job to keep Sheriff Colby busy so Wink could rob the stage. But she wanted all the gold herself, and double-crossed Wink. Tipped the sheriff off, and the sheriff got a glimpse of Wink on that last robbery. We searched Wink's place a couple of days ago. Found the disguise and the gold and hid the evidence in the sheriff's cabin."

"Why didn't you just arrest Wink?" Fritz said to Ross.

Ross stumbled for a moment. "You tell him, Heck."

"I talked Sheriff Colby—Caldwell, I mean—into waitin'. We both wanted to catch Parkhill in one of these vigilante raids, and figured he might not pull one if we distracted him by arrestin' Wink."

"Well, why was R.W. on the coach with your wife?" Fritz asked.

"That's another story," Heck said. "I'll let him explain that one to you."

"Fritz, I've left you in the dark a long time, but you've never let me down. If you and Cy will go find the stagecoach and drive it back here, I'll explain the whole thing to you on the way back to town."

Fritz sighed. "Well, I guess you're still the boss. Come on, Cy, let's catch the horses."

Heck had no strength left to open his eyes, but he could hear the two men shuffle away. "They gone?" he asked.

"Yeah," Ross replied.

"I've always been a hell of a good liar," Heck said.

"Used it to my advantage plenty of times. The mistake I made was I had you figured all wrong, Caldwell. Thought you was some no-'count backslider run out on a good woman. But them lies . . . They catch up to you. Lordy, they catch up in the damnedest way."

"Yeah," Ross repeated.

"I know you don't owe me nothin', but I'd like to ask you a favor."

"What?"

"I want to have a word with . . . your wife. I want to speak to Julia."

"She's right here," Ross said. "Go ahead."

Heck grunted. "Julia."

"Yes, Heck."

"You almost got widowed twice in one day."

Julia just looked at Ross, then out across the park, rocking Fay as she watched the shadows creep into the meadow.

"Come closer, Julia." His voice grew weaker with every word. "I want to whisper somethin' in your ear."

Julia looked at Ross. He nodded. She handed Fay to Ross and leaned over Heck's face, her hair brushing his closed eyelids. Ross let Fay stand on his stomach and held on to her hands. She smiled, her eyes sparkled, and she jumped with excitement, almost squeezing the breath out of her father's innards.

Julia was pulling away from Heck, relief and sorrow mingled on her face.

"What did he say?" Ross asked.

"He didn't say anything," she replied. "He just died."

FORTY-FIVE

Good morning, Sheriff Green," Mary Johnson said. She stepped up behind Fritz and hooked her arm around his.

"Morning, Mary," Fritz replied, lifting the hat from his head. "You come to see the Caldwells off?"

"Yes," Mary said. "Where are they?"

"Getting their pictures made in the photographic gallery." He heard the jingle of trace chains and looked down the street to see Cyrus Rose's bright red coach rounding the corner onto Wallace Street. "Here comes the Last Chance now."

Cy stood on the footboard for show, bracing his legs against the seat. "Whoa," he said, reining the team in at the Virginia City *Post*. "Right on time, Sheriff," he shouted. "Special charter to Idaho, Utah, and Salt Lake City!"

"Decent of you to make the special run," Fritz said. "Mrs. Caldwell wouldn't want to ride all that way with a bunch of stinkin' miners."

Cy bounded to the street, stepped up on the boardwalk, and greeted Mary Johnson with a bow. "I been needin' to make a run for supplies, anyway. You know how much them freighters charge for haulin' from Salt Lake?"

"High, ain't it?" Fritz said.

"Yes, sir." He turned to Mary Johnson. "Miss Mary, I heard you took over the relief fund."

"That's right," Mary said. "Do you wish to donate something?"

"Well, I'll make you a deal. Passenger service has sure picked up. I got a full coach almost every run. How 'bout if I donate every tenth fare to the fund?"

"That would be wonderful! I need every penny I can get. I don't know how Ross Caldwell did it. I haven't been able to collect half as much as he used to."

"I'll be glad to throw in my share," Cy said, "but you have to do somethin' for me in return."

"What is it?"

"Find a home for a mammy and her seven little young'ns."

"My word," Mary said. "Where are they?"

Cyrus reached for the door handle of the stagecoach. "Right here." He opened the door to reveal a languid cat nursing a row of tiny fur balls no bigger than their mothers' feet.

Mary Johnson gasped with delight and pushed Fritz aside to get at the kittens. "Fritz, go get a crate or something to put them in," she ordered.

"Put 'em in here," Fritz said, taking his hat off, "and we'll find a place for 'em together."

Cy was beaming. "She thought that would be a nice quiet place to have some babies," he said.

"She don't know the Last Chance Express," Fritz replied.

As Mary carefully lifted the mother cat from the coach, Ross stepped out of the photographic studio and, in spite of the cumbersome crutches under his arms, insisted on holding the door open for Julia and Fay.

Before the family could reach the coach, Johnson burst out of his newspaper office with his pad in his hand, a pencil behind his ear. "Any idea where you'll be going?" the editor asked.

Ross paused to grin into the hat full of kittens. "There's a vacant sheriff's job in Denver," he said to the editor, "and I thought I might . . ."

Julia hit him with her handbag. "We're going to find a town that needs a hardware store," she said.

"You'll write us, won't you?" Fritz asked. "Let us know where you've settled?"

"Sure," Ross said. "It'll be someplace on about a five percent grade."

A look of intrigue crossed Cy's face. "What do you mean by that, Brother Ross?"

"The doc says this wounded leg'll heal a half inch shorter than the other one, and by my calculations, it'll take a five percent grade to keep me from limpin'."

"Till you have to turn around and walk back," Cy said. "Then you're liable to fall all over yourself. You better find some level ground and just limp."

Ross chuckled. "They can have that flatland down below," he said. "I couldn't leave the mountains now. I'll just hitch one stirrup shorter than the other and make do."

The group stood in a circle for a few seconds. Then Mary hugged Julia, the cat in her arm tickling Fay, making her laugh. Ross shook hands all around, then slid his crutches into the coach. He helped Julia step in, hopped one-footed up on the step, and sat opposite his wife in the coach. Cy climbed up to his seat and filled his hands with the slick leather of his whip and reins.

"Good luck, R.W.," Fritz said, holding the hat full of kittens in one hand, shutting the door with the other.

"Same to you, Fritz." He was going to advise his former deputy to watch his back, or sleep with one eye open, or something like that, but decided it would only upset Mary.

The whip cracked and Cy's jubilant voice turned heads, up and down the street. The horses sprang against their collars and started the long pull. Up on the high seat—his feet braced against the footboard, reins between his fingers, momentum already gathering his coattails behind him—Cyrus Rose descended on a clot of miners blocking the street.

"Watch it, gentlemen!" he shouted. With a sure sweep of his arm, he flicked the whip over the team and split the thin mountain air. "Make room!" The vital roll of the coach under him was almost like that of a practiced woman, but longer-lasting and less dangerous. "Last Chance Express comin' through!"

The miners came back together in the dust after the coach had passed.

"That ain't the way to Last Chance," one of them said, watching the coach roll by the turn to Parkhill's former toll road.

Another pulled a fallen suspender over his shoulder. "Hell, they don't know where they're goin'."

But Cyrus Rose knew. Ross knew; and Julia. Even little Fay could sense it. It had no place name, no flat label on a map. It drifted unseen on thin mountain air, eluding every mortal sense. None of them could speak of it, but each felt the Last Chance Express carrying them ever closer.

"Mary and Fritz make a nice couple, don't they?" Julia said, waving to the vanishing group of well-wishers.

"I guess," Ross said. He took Fay from his wife. "They would have made good friends for us."

"Oh, hush. Don't start. That's not the kind of life I want for my family—wondering from day to day if you'll come home alive or in a pine box. We were perfectly happy with our hardware store in Athens, remember?"

Ross sighed. "Barely. Seems like a hundred years ago."

Julia watched the buildings pass outside, the faces of strangers staring up at her. She turned to look at Ross, his face lit handsomely by a slanting ray of sun. He didn't look like a hardware man anymore. Back then he went clean-shaven, his skin smooth and pale. He would never be that innocent again. She moved gracefully across the coach and sat beside him, putting her arm over his shoulders.

"Honey," he said, trying to keep Fay from crawling through the window, "I hope I never have to spend another day out of your sight. Trouble seems to cloud up and rain all over me when you're not around."

"Oh, you're just saying that now," she replied. "A week from today you'll be chewing your leash in two."

"You know I can't tell what I'll be thinkin' a week from now. I'm talkin' about this minute. But if I do go to chewin' at my leash next week, you just put a stouter one on me."

She smiled and stroked the hair at the back of his neck.

"You really think Mary and Fritz make a nice couple?" he said.

"Yes, don't you?"

He shrugged. "They've got nothin' on us. I'm just a freemillin' ore, Julia. I'm not worth a nickel on my own. But you get around me like quicksilver and draw pure gold."

She smiled and clutched a handful of hair on the back of his head. "Except for that silver tongue." She turned his face toward hers and risked a kiss, struggling to keep her lips on his as the Last Chance Express pitched wildly down the road.